The Forgotten Tribe

the forgotten tribe

a novel

MICHELLE MORACZEWSKI

Homestead Productions 2019

Designed by Carianne Lance

Illustrated by Michelle Moraczewski

ISBN 978-0986149603

Printed in the United States of America

For my Father, the storyteller in my life.

"The subtleties of the balanced world are like a dance. For man to live in harmony with the earth he must learn to dance with her."

PART ONE

The Ghost Dance

"The battle is in the mind of the thinkers. There are the thinkers and the thoughtless. The thoughtless are those who walk on autopilot— who follow."

CHAPTER 1 *The Meeting - March*

A dark gloom hung over the street as the Agnelli's trudged through the humidity towards the Coopers' huge brick home in an old Houston neighborhood. This was a sharp contrast to the blue skies of West Texaas and New Mexico. With a furtive glance at the sky, and back at her family, Mariah knew a shaky spring struggled to emerge after a bitter winter. Soon, the tornado season would begin again.

David and Mariah Agnelli, and their teens, Tristan and Isabella, gathered for a minute on the doorstep alcove, out of the misting, fog-like rain. Mariah raised her hand to knock, knowing full well by the sounds she could hear through the door, no one could hear her. David squared his shoulders, reached past her, and opened the door. The family strode into the Coopers living room and found it crowded. Good freinds, people from their meditation group, and aquaintances, were everywhere—scattered on couches, chairs and the floor. The smell of herbs and tea emanated from the small, overstuffed kitchen. Isabella grabbed the salad from her mom and stepped over and through the paisley mix. Mariah smiled her thanks at her willowy thirteen year old.

"Where have you guys been?" Jody Cooper handed David a sweating bottle of beer. Jody's big size was softened by his long sun-streaked-surfer locks. "Mariah, can I get you anything?"

"Thanks, but no." Mariah waved him off.

"We took a road trip out to West Texas and New Mexico." The fizz foamed to the top as David took his first sip of the proffered Dos Equis.

"Glad you could make it over tonight. We have been trying to reach you because it's all coming down now. We've called a short notice meeting of most of our close friends and members of our circle."

The Agnelli's had driven in late last night, exhausted from another long camping trip, to find the red light blinking on their answering machine. Mariah was surprised at the abrupt tone of Pats voice calling an urgent meeting of their meditation group. The family had visited the Apache reservation in Ruidoso, New Mexico. Although she wanted to see everyone, all day Mariah's thoughts had returned to the *why* of the meeting.

I love these guys. Mariah's heart filled with warmth for her dear friends. She glanced around the room at those she'd come to care for these past seven years.

Isabella bounced back in. "Mom, can I go find Julia? I have looked everywhere upstairs. She must be outside in our tree-fort."

Mariah nodded out the window at the gathering clouds. "The storms are headed this way." Thunder rolled loud punctuating her look.

"Mom, a little rain won't hurt me." Isabella's dimples showed when she grinned. "Of course I'll be careful." With that she was gone, out the back door before Mariah could stop her.

Mariah found Pat Cooper in the kitchen pouring a glass of red wine. She handed it to Mariah.

"Thanks, that's more my style." She took a sip. "Pat, Jody sounds sort of serious. What's up?"

"This time he's not exaggerating." Pat had an open face with small features. Her frank brown eyes betrayed nothing. She wore the pants around here. "I'll go over everything as soon as things settle down." Heat blasted the room as she pulled a tray full of baked sweet potato fries out of the oven. She swiped a brow beneath her artfully spiked cropped hair. "Tristan looks thoughtful."

"Something happened on our trip," Mariah said. That was an understatement. The something had been over seven years ago but this recent trip to New Mexico had brought it all back to the forefront. Arriving in time for the Feast of the Maidens, Mariah had sought advice from a wise Apache woman. She studied her thoughtfully as she spoke, trying to keep Tristan's description of the Indian brave he had met in her mind and compare it with the reality of the Mescalero

Apache woman. She told her stories of Geronimo and his long time hiding out to avoid capture in Arizona. The stories disturbed her. Real life was not as fantastic as the myths her imaginative children were concocting. Face it, she was into fantasy. Something must be wrong with her. It had all seemed so real.

As she sipped her wine, her eyes darted out the window. In the back yard, trees were waving like swing dancers in the wind. "I'll tell you all about it later."

A large clap of thunder startled both women. Mariah wiped up the drops of wine that spilled. Another clap sent her moving toward the back door, and she looked out just in time to see Isabella and Julia scramble out of the tree. Wind grabbed the door as Mariah opened it to let them in. A fat raindrop splatted on her head.

"Just in time," she breathed in relief as another downpour pelted the tin roof of the tree fort.

"Told ya," Isabella said, as she and Julia plopped on the floor to remove their sopped tennis shoes.

Mariah shuddered and turned back to Pat. "Kids are resilient. I have seen one too many storms in Houston." She took a careful sip of wine. "Oh, by the way, our friend Paul is coming. He's from my dark college days." She smiled. "Anyway, he's changed a lot since then—he used to live on The Farm--and he'll probably want to join our group."

Pat looked at her quizzically. "You don't seem to understand. This isn't a party." She softened her tone. "He used to live on a farm?"

"No. '*The*' Farm'. The one Steven Gaskin started in Tennessee. Paul's become quite the expert on communes... and *everything*." She rolled her eyes.

Jack Java entered the crowded kitchen with a Cheshire grin and cheerful humor in his blue eyes. He was a round man with longish brown hair below a bald crown. Mariah felt the buzz—the excitement— the dread or uncertainty—in the air. Jack greeted Pat with a cheek kiss. Pat's sister Stacie breezed in and plopped a platter of brownies on the counter. She winked as Pat grabbed her hand. It was a "who's that?" wink between sisters.

"Have you met Stacie? She's the re-birther I told you about." Pat made perfunctory introductions.

Jack beamed his good cheer at the quiet brunette, and then crossed the room to hug Mariah.

"How was your trip?" he asked. "It's amazing country out there."

"Yes it is," Mariah said, amused when she saw Jack fumbling to open Stacie's beer with a flirtatious look.

"Will you invite me next time?" Jack said over his shoulder.

"Actually, I think the more the merrier," Mariah yelled after him as he moved on.

She felt a cold chill when the door opened and slammed with more arrivals. Her hands shook as she helped Pat take the food to the dining room. Everyone milled around the table laden with salad, rice, beans, breads, and other vegetarian dishes. Soon, with plates piled high, everyone ate and talked at once. She observed their grim faces. Her mouth was dry as she tried to choke down more hummus.

The tinkling of a small bell sounded twice. Pat's voice bellowed above the murmurs. "Welcome friends and newcomers. Usually we start with an Aum, if you could just gather in a circle."

Mariah slipped back to the living room, where twenty people crowded around the walls into an egg shape. She glanced around at those she'd come to care for these past seven years. She scanned their faces—most of whom she knew—until she spotted David and Jack. Relieved, she slipped between them and took their hands. With eyes closed, beautiful smiles stole across faces, erasing years and stress at once. Even Paul, whom she hadn't seen in eons, resumed their friendship like a lost elder brother. Friend-family—extended-family—seemed just as close as blood family. In truth, their family adventures off to the edges of the wilderness had a significant draw back; she missed her friends. They found glorious vistas, invigorating hikes, nights filled with stars that stretched from the horizon to infinity. She'd often wanted to share all of this magnificence with her friends. One great big circle of fun, is how she thought of them all.

Pat started the Aum low in her chest. The sound filled the room, increasing in pitch and volume. The pitch climbed and harmonized in different lows and highs. David had a serene smile on his face. He squeezed her hand. As the sound continued, her mouth opened to find high G above the C's and A's of the group.

Pat had seemed an unlikely comrade at first as they were opposites. Pat's practical insights and brusque manor were a comfort to her. She had often rescued Mariah from a hair brained scheme. People like us, Mariah thought, as she noticed the small room off to the side crammed with paints and jewelry supplies. Kids' art decorated the walls, climbing up the stairwell like a wild vine.

Pat then got to business without additional preamble. "It has been quite a few years since Jupiter was hit by the asteroid. That marks the time when we began meeting. We have all been feeling the vibrations— in our personal lives..." she nodded to her blue eyed husband across the room. "I know Jody and I have."

"We have gathered now, in response to an intense weather forecast. All it takes is a few super-storms..."

"Storm surges and tectonic plate shifts," Jack said, "and voilà, Tennessee is ocean front property. It seems Houston and La La land are both in severe danger of ocean proximity floods."

"Tectonic what?" Melanie asked.

"You know, in the city of angels," Jack offered. "Los Angeles has a fault line running through..."

"Later." Pat waved him off. She wasn't one to be thrown off course. "Last year was one of the worst hurricane seasons in history. The year Katrina was followed by Rita, the city was a disaster. We thought we would lose everything. Houston was impacted both physically and fiscally, and still hasn't recovered. Now, there are already ten of us who are planning to disappear—go into hiding, if you will—for as long as it takes this to pass."

There was silence as people digested this.

"Wow," someone said.

Mariah was surprised. So this is what Jody and Pat had in mind? *Go for it. Just leave.* Mariah's thoughts raced, escaping her grasp like a bevy of helium balloons. She just didn't want to be here in the wet dismal floodwaters of Houston sewage. People died in this kind of storm. At sea level, intense rainfall quickly rose to dangerous flood levels. The storm sewers emptied into bayous, that once full, spilled their banks all over the streets, yards, and houses. Even in a minor flood, damaged houses were ruined, with black mold seeping into the sheetrock and wood floors. When they were kids, she remembered, they had once floated down the street in a rowboat rescuing animals. After Hurricane Rita hit Houston, anticipating hurricanes wasn't fun anymore.

"Of course, no one knows what is really going to happen, but we've been listening to the predictions for years." Pat was talking.

Mariah tuned back in to the grim reality they were now facing. She felt that buzz again. Her heart skipped. David and she had a game. If the dramatic picture of world collapse was really on the horizon and they had to leave, who would they want to be on that deserted island with? Their list of friends was growing. Jody knew all about the *true* history of North America and could regale you for days. Jack Java was enthralling with his endless stream of stories. Her new friend Hazel, was full of wisdom and insights. Robin had a unique view of the world. Yes, Mariah was prepared to leave the world as we know it, but it would be ideal, if her friends would join her. Have your cake and eat it too was her motto. After all, what was really more important; stuff or relationships?

Pat opened her mouth to speak, but instead they heard a male voice ring out from the other side of the room. "Perhaps since we're already surrounded by government corruption, the earth is simply fighting back."

Mariah turned to see her old friend, Paul, his long frame slouched against the doorjamb. Black curls outlined his rugged features.

Pat started at the presence of this stranger. Then she noted his astute observation. "We don't know how, or why, but the situation has become untenable. Most of you, I know, have developed your own income in jewelry, massage work, crafts, or healing arts, and are off the tax role. We are, after all, a small unit in a large universe. It may be easier than we think to disappear into the country."

Jody added, "Texas is one place that has vast amounts of unexplored territory. Much of New Mexico is reservation land. The question we put to you tonight is this: Are any of you prepared for this radical move? Are there any of you who care to join us?"

"I think," Paul added, "if things continue at this exponential rate of warming, we will all wind up living in caves below the earth's surface. And we will only visit the surface in space suits, as protection from the poisonous atmosphere we have created." An aquiline nose and dark brows put his intense gaze in shadow.

Pat's eyes flicked around the room as if to say, *who invited this guy?* "That's a very drastic picture of our future."

"Perhaps we should break up to discuss this. This will greatly impact all of our lives," Jody said.

The room was as silent as a tomb. No one had expected this, at least not so soon.

Mariah thought of their latest trip to New Mexico. Ever since Peter's death, they could no longer return to The Ranch. Instead, they took family camping trips all over the Southwest. They had first climbed the hill, then the stone steps to the door of the adobe, Mescalero Apache, Church. They could already hear the sounds coming from behind the massive wood doors. Music filled their ears as classical piano was played at full volume by a priest in a simple brown monk's robe. They tread softly in awe, as they studied the symbolism, both Christian and Apache, that filled the church. The altar held an icon of the Apache Christ, a handsome Indian brave in robes, covered in stars and crescent moons. Tristan could not take his eyes off him, or the portraits of famous Indians decorating the walls.

Then David had taken her hand in his, as he had always taken it, ever since their first meeting. Together they watched Isabella, turning and dancing solo down the aisle, as the piano chords filled the huge church. They looked at each other and their eyes locked in mutual love and understanding.

As long as their little family stayed together, she could handle whatever happened. She knew that is where their strength lay. Before God, they renewed their marriage vows at that altar. Their voices were covered by the trilling music, but the intention in their hearts shone clear.

That was three days ago. Now everything was to change. Their *life* shot like a canon infused with a new momentum, that continued even now that they had returned to Houston. Not for long, Mariah mused silently, comforted as always by the warmth of David's palm in hers.

"You've all been meeting for seven years," Paul said, "and in that time nothing substantial has improved. Forty years ago we could make fuel-efficient vehicles, use solar collectors, and we had the knowledge to make compost toilets and waste removal systems, that did not contaminate the water supply."

Jack piped in, "I have been studying the oceans and planetary geothermal shifts for thirty-five years, but nobody notices. Finally, the media today is giving a nod. We think change is about to come. But..."

Robin, a still-single friend of Pat's from college, tied off a necklace she was making. "...while they are giving the green light to all things green."

"We need massive change," Paul concluded. He was serious. He had lived in the biggest commune in America. He had no time to play with wannabe dreamers.

"Yes, but they are using technology and making discoveries at an alarming speed," Pat said.

"Logarithmic advances in technology, you might say." Paul stood still, his arms folded, but his hawk eyes took in everything.

"*They* are trying to control the weather," Jack said. "When Katrina hit New Orleans it was too perfect to be an accident."

Mariah always wondered who *they* were.

"Are you implying, using a storm to bomb a town? No retaliation necessary. Very clever," Stacie nodded.

"Then Rita hit Houston," Jack said.

"Perfect. Someone destroys all the oil reserves in New Orleans, and then hits the ship channel," Stacie said.

"This is the *New War*," Paul said.

Just then, the screen door slammed in a gust of wind. Folks jerked up and looked around.

"Exactly. Now it's spring," Pat said. "In May, the tornado season will begin. *Again.*"

Robin began undoing her braids as she scooted in around the circle. "You mean, when they say they are diverting America's economy for a war on terror effort, a bulk portion is going for the 'weather manipulation project?"

Mariah remembered David had a bookcase full of flood damaged art books from Grad school. He had done a whole series of flood paintings. The one with a man clutching the swaying palm tree curved in the wind, his body blown sideways, ferocious waves of Galveston in the background, was one of her favorites. Yet, she couldn't get thoughts of the blue sky out of her head. Texas... West Texas; 100 degree days of endless summer. That thought cheered her, as she tuned back in to the jumble of chaotic energy that trilled through the room.

"All construction price surges, and inflated oil prices, are based on the Wars on Terror," Jack was saying.

Robin rolled her baby blues. "Oooh, scare me some more. I am serious, if you wait and debate too long you'll be stuck in the traffic nightmare that happened in Hurricane Rita."

"Exactly," Pat said. "They haven't declared mandatory evacuation yet. We have little time left. We should just go."

Paul found his audience in Melody, and the two retired to a corner by the fireplace. He explained it all. "Everyone I know worries about impending disasters. Five level-five hurricanes swept thru in one season. On top of that, global warming makes catastrophic predictions for the future, a no-brainer."

Melody looked scared, her eyes open wide in disbelief and awe, but she just nodded.

"With comets falling from the sky, natural disasters and numerous wars tucked in around the globe, who can tell when or what the final blow will be?" Paul expounded. "Anyway, I don't plan to stick around and find out. Do you?"

Melody couldn't wait to go home and try to explain all of this to her musician husband. He had stayed home with the kids.

Amidst the flurry of talk, David and Mariah looked at each other. "We will have to take a group to The Ranch," Mariah said. "No one knows I'm connected to it. Most of Peter's friends are still in San Antonio. Houston people at The Ranch, that's perfect." Mariah liked these guys. David was a loner not a joiner, but a big move like this may be better as a group. Even he might agree.

CHAPTER 2 *The Plan*

Tristan had been quiet in his seat on the piano bench, staring at the black and white keys. He'd stopped playing, to tune-in to the talk around him. At sixteen, he had classic good looks, an oval face, inquisitive eyes and a sensitive, well-proportioned mouth. He grinned now, showing perfect even white teeth. At six feet, with the long, lean, swimmers build, Tristan was just like any American teen. He looked fine—with thick bronze hair, his ancestry the quintessential American hodgepodge—on the outside. His hazel eyes lit with green and yellow sparks as he contemplated his long held secret. This always held him apart.

Six years ago he had been too young to do anything about it. If his family returned to The Ranch, he would have his chance. He realized he didn't want to reveal his mysterious finding to anyone.

"Hey, Tristan, don't look so somber. What's up?" Jody broke his reverie.

"Hmm?" he smiled. There was that flash of white again. "Nothing, Mr. Cooper."

"Have a good trip?" Jody pressed.

"Yeah, it was great. Hiking, exploring." He let his voice trail off. "And you, sir?"

"Good, good." Jody patted him on the head as he went on. "Nice to have a young man around here. Especially when I'm surrounded by daughters."

Tristan nodded politely at Mr. Cooper. He had been avoiding them too.

He'd have to talk to his mom. If they were planning a party at The

Ranch, he was going to make sure she was aware of all the ramifications. He hoped she'd understand.

He glanced at his mom who sat on the sofa, cross-legged, her hands in a Buddha position, her dark hair smoothed back from her face. She was the only Catholic he knew that prayed like an Indian. Of course she'd understand.

* * *

David coughed, as he brought the room back to attention. He was charismatic when he was passionate about something. He smiled at Mariah as she looked up.

Mariah held his look. She could read a lot in those blue-grey eyes. It seemed like only yesterday when she had fallen backward into love with him, literally. She was freshly back from studying art in Paris at an atelier, and putting a résumé together for a hoped-for career in New York City—when they met. Mariah couldn't believe sixteen years had flown.

"I know you guys had a spot near Austin in mind. We haven't had time to find the ideal location for our little 'experiment'. But my wife, Mariah, and I, have a suggestion. We spent some time a few years ago at a mega-ranch in West Texas." David's eyes sparkled as he glanced around the room. "This vast land stands vacant and it may be the best option on such a short notice. This storm is actually the perfect cover for our departure. We will have to act quickly or—Robin's right—we'll be stuck in a traffic nightmare. I know we're not one hundred percent ready, but who is ever really ready? It's a radical move,"

There was a buzz and a few nods, while others just remained silent.

"We've dreamed of this," Pat said. "And we certainly talk about it enough. Now it's time to act."

"For all intents and purposes, this place has been abandoned. For all we know, the estate could be up in the air, or tied up in legal issues. In the meantime, we could have a trial run," David said.

Mariah's mouth dropped open. David had said it. The Ranch. "It's just an idea ..." Mariah added, trying to gauge the reactions of the others. To finally put their ideals to the test—for even the most gung-ho among them, this was a scary thought. As she glanced around the room, people were buying it. The age of action was about to replace decades of talk. Mariah watched Pat's eyes scan the room—after all, she had handpicked most of the people present—to see who was *all-talk*. Each family went back into a huddle. Even the rain had stopped, leaving the evening grey and still.

Isabella, who had been in the other room, came to stand by her mother. "What's happening? Is it the storm?" She tucked a thick strand of auburn hair behind her ear.

"Yes, we're thinking about going to The Ranch."

"Us or everyone?"

"Everyone who wants to." Mariah watched as her daughter's large brown eyes grew even bigger.

"For real?"

Mariah nodded. She flushed as she recalled the last scene, almost seven years ago, at The Ranch. Tristan's form, still and chilled, in the waning light.

Isabella's eyes searched the room until they landed on Tristan, at the piano. He knew. Their eyes met. The two smiled at each other as they considered the possibilities.

Mariah heard the murmurs grow louder and turned back to the others.

"Everyone has to be a pioneer in his own country," Jack spoke above the rumble of conversations. "Find their own land. Keep their own water clean, grow their own food." He shrugged. "No one is going to do it for us. It's the American way, after all. Our ancestors did it."

"Jack, it's time to take all your gardening knowledge and lead us to the desert," Mariah replied. "The storm is headed here in a couple of days, and I, for one, am not waiting. We have planned our exodus, so let's take it. Soon they will do mandatory evacuations and these pathetic freeways will be jammed completely."

"Oh, that is scary. Sitting there on frozen freeways because the transportation artery is plugged," Stacie quipped. "Then the storm hits and the whole damn city is captive in their SUVs."

"Can't you see it?" Robin's eyes were wide. "Maybe they haven't even perfected the weather war machine yet."

"And they're not all that accurate." Jody winked at her.

Jack leaned forward conspiratorially, "I had a dream. All the roads were lined with vehicles and the traffic was crawling. The storm was coming, the winds fierce. People ran out of gas—stalled, abandoned cars everywhere."

"Enough," Pat demanded. "Let's take a vote."

The room fell silent again. They'd spent years talking about it. Talked over cocktails. Talked over glasses of wine at local wine bars. Discussed it over cappuccinos with the morning crowd. Recounted nightmares and apocalyptic visions with therapists. But talk, no matter how passionate, or engaging, or intellectual, wouldn't make it happen. It was now or never. The bluff had been called. The cards were in, the die cast, and everyone had to play his hand.

Jack grinned. He was in his element. "One question. We have thirteen families here. How long will it take to be packed and on the road?"

"About four hours." Paul was hopeful.

"That's good." David flashed his mercurial smile, "Paul, you can help us pack."

Pat looked impatiently around the room. "All in favor?"

Everyone raised their hands. Then, oddly enough, each family began to gather their kids. It was as if they were on autopilot, for the moment unable to believe they were giving up life as they knew it for a move to the middle of the Texas wilderness.

Pat stood, her calm presence drew the attention of the others. "Should any of you decide to wait out the storm, don't leave until it's safe to travel, and then stagger your departures. We will be there."

The group filed out of the house. Only Mariah and David stayed behind with the Coopers.

It was late when they finally gathered Tristan and Isabella and headed home. Mariah felt a calm like a contained exuberance. The calm before the storm she realized. She knew they were on the edge of something momentous. She was also secretly glad they were whisking the thirteen-year-old Isabella off to the wilderness before she realized that boys were not just hanging out with her for her homework answers. They were looking at her as a young woman now, not just a brainy, if

21

intimidating, school whiz. And Tristan. What did this mean for him? As excited as he was, it might be hard for him to leave his high school and his friends.

Mariah pushed the thoughts from her head. It was just plain hard. You could kill any dream if you thought about it too long. She shuddered. Tristan's mysterious fall had been all it took to keep them from The Ranch the last seven years.

She wasn't the only one determined to forge ahead. After all, it wasn't as if the members hadn't planned for this; in fact, even before they met each other, they had been gradually simplifying their lives in preparation to get off the grid. Most were self- employed. They dealt in cash—never using credit cards–and owned everything out-right. Each family had transferred titles of cars and property to other family members. Mariah and David's went to her mother. Now all they had in their names were their drivers' licenses.

For Mariah, the only thing missing was her father. Steven French would be right there with them, had he not passed away from cancer the year before. An old soul, everyone called him. Yes, she could still picture him at The Ranch during those childhood trips; he had made everything magical. Whenever she caught herself feeling sad, she imagined him smiling and cheering her on in this big adventure. Now she would focus on her new extended family. Her spiritual family versus her blood family.

It was the last day of a rainy March. They hit the road at first light and by ten a.m. they were breakfasting in San Antonio. Everything was timed to depart San Antonio separately and take different routes to The Ranch. There was the fast way through Uvalde, and the scenic way through the hill country.

* * *

No one spoke much in the car, but there was an undeniable undercurrent of excitement. David's mind was on his role as head farmer. David and Jack had become fast friends when they first met at a permaculture workshop. David joked he was a painter -slash-farmer and had done a huge self-portrait in a corn field. He had merely pretended to be a city boy, yet lately he was *literally* putting the food on the table for his small family. He was proud of the fact that the family garden produced crops—spring, fall, and winter. That was the best system to work around Houston's unbeatable heat. Of course it took up the entire backyard. David was an advocate of biodynamic farming and studied the methods of Rudolph Steiner. That trumped permaculture in his mind, thus, he and Jack had hot debates over gardening strategies.

He still thought of it as *his garden,* no matter that until this point he had only worked in his own backyard. This was about to change.

Beneath his humble exterior, he believed himself quite capable of anything. Yet even he was concerned about how he would get plants to grow in the rocky, unyielding, Texas soil. He was prepared. For his first task; the soil, he had brought with him choice bags of his select compost. He had created his own amazing admixtures over the years. He took advantage of "zoo do." It included elephant dung, which had cooked, along with everything else, in his compost pile for the past few years. It would act as yeast, to jump-start the composting that would begin in earnest once they were at The Ranch. Once they were settled he planned to till the plant beds with this homegrown mix. He'd even asked Paul to bring ten more sacks of the stuff when he joined them. This was the "magic soil" he would infuse to begin the transformation of this forgotten land.

He smiled as they drove through Laketown. They wouldn't stop there, just as they hadn't stopped at any of the other small towns they passed. There was no need to attract busybodies who might take notice of the many Houston plates on the same day. Mud-splattered plates—a suggestion of Paul's—should do the trick.

* * *

Paul would come out with the second wave. Mariah looked forward to his arrival, for his prior experience at The Farm would be critical for their success. In the meantime, they had Jack Java, who despite lacking Paul's gravitas was no slouch when it came to knowledge of communal living.

Jack had lost his wife and son after his wife decided to opt-out and exchanged him for a wealthier specimen. Shortly after, he'd set up a tent in his father's yard and lived minimally for an entire summer. Some say he went crazy, but those close to him knew he had been disgusted by the growing materialism in America long before his wife's departure. The tent was just his way of putting his beliefs into action. If he published some of those wild stories he carried around in that worn blue spiral notebook of his, Mariah surmised, he could hit the big time. She was glad he'd chosen to be at The Ranch with them instead.

A yellow van transporting three families followed the Agnelli's as they turned off the main road and onto the obscure rutted path that would soon disappear into the undergrowth. "The world's longest driveway," Mariah always called it. It was another twenty-minute drive into the familiar stomping grounds. Two jackrabbits jumped out of the way of their approaching car, and wild turkeys scurried off into the woods.

"I guess we should drive our cars right in, as if we own the place," Mariah said. "Don't you think, honey?" Her voice was quiet, muffled by the drumming in her ears. The anticipation of years catching up to her as they neared the gate.

David squinted into the distance as if he would find the answer there. "Yup, that's the safest. We'll park them off the main road."

So they trespassed. Drove right on past all the 'Keep Out' signs, and came to a stop, one car at a time. Mariah looked around in wonder. The rain had stopped an hour or so ago, but steam was still rising from the meadow grasses that stretched out before them. They stood in the vast empty field and watched cars arrive one by one. The cars and vans pulled up in a circle. "Circle your wagons boys," she drawled in southern slow speak to no one in particular. She heard the opening and slamming of doors, and watched as the others untangled their bodies from their cars and looked around at the scrubby trees and live oaks. Some twisted around and rubbed each other's shoulders. A few did yoga stretches to loosen up.

She took David's hand. "David, it's like the old days. It's great to see all the cars pulled up in the meadow again."

"It looks rather bleak to me," Stacie said, as she twisted her torso from side to side.

"Well, it is. It's Texas, after all. At least it's wet now. In summer everything will be dry and dusty."

No more time for small talk. She didn't want to think that far ahead. For now they had to focus on the task at hand—setting up camp before nightfall.

"I feel safer in numbers," Mariah said as they worked. "I was so nervous last time we came, I nearly squeezed water out of my lapis lazuli sphere."

David looked surprised. "You seemed so calm. I had no idea."

"Mom," Tristan called out, "can Isabella and I explore a bit? Or hike?"

"Let's get everything set up first. There will be time afterward."

David and Tristan unloaded the essentials while Mariah and Isabella cleared rocks from the selected spot of meadow between small live oaks. Father and son had the tent ready to anchor in place by the time Mariah had the area clear and the rucksacks and the coolers out.

"You warm enough? Take a windbreaker or an extra sweater." Mariah called to the children. She could tell there wasn't a moment to be wasted if they were to be back before dark. "The temperature could drop."

"You sure it's okay to go?" Tristan squinted up at her.

"Sure, where are you headed?"

"Toward the Blue Spring."

"The Blue Spring? That's miles away." Mariah shook her head. "You won't have enough time to get there and back before nightfall."

She walked over and handed him a couple of apples. "Look, I know you're eager, but we are here now, and we plan to be here for quite a while. There's no rush. Why don't you and Isabella check out Jade Cove? That's not far away. Tomorrow you can have all day at the Blue Spring."

"Sure, Mom," they said, then headed off toward the Cove.

She stood there watching them, then sensed David beside her. They were on their own. They stood on the earth with everything that really mattered to them. They had their health, their spiritual wealth, their children, and each other. To top it off, now they were standing on their favorite spot on earth. Earth that could and had sustained generations for two millennium. Now *they* were prepared for the new millennium.

"Bring it on," Mariah said to no one in particular.

CHAPTER 3 *Setup Camp*

A strange colorful oasis sat in the somber muted landscape of Texas wilderness. An uncommon scene, once it was set. If a local rancher happened upon this group, they might just turn around and go back to where they came from. A campsite in the middle of this barren wilderness? Obviously it was a hallucination.

The camp was off the road, hidden in a clearing behind overgrown shrubs and scrubby live oaks. The members of this new community were no less colorful. Most of the men had beards, sandy hair, and blue eyes. The women were rosy cheeked and healthy. Most wore long cotton dresses in rich shades of reds and gold. Linen, flax, and paisley prints were everywhere. Some wore Guatemalan tapestry sack dresses. Most wore sandals of thick leather. They wore their hair natural, long, frizzy, straight, or braided with streaks of silver and grey.

Most of the community were forty-something's - a bit older than Mariah and David Agnelli – and well-educated. Some were still single; others had spouses or life partners who had practiced birth control until they decided it would be cool to have kids. The *cool* kids were smarter than they were obedient. It lent itself to lots of creativity, and in their situation, where they were all about to face the unknown, that was a good thing.

The smell of basil and mint hung in the air. Colorful blankets were strewn in front of the white muslin tents and baskets full of grains and fruit. They had each brought a month's worth of supplies with them. Homegrown herbs hung from tree branches, drying in clumps. Someone brought gourds; they were set about and used for supplies. Small and scrubby trees held blankets like lean-tos, casting shade on the hammocks set to swing from the branches. They had a variety of grains: wheat, spelt, couscous, quinoa, beans, and lentils. The camp buzzed with activity. Laughter and song rose from the meadow, as they worked. Enthusiasm left little room for fatigue.

Those early days were all about basic necessities: prepare and eat three meals; watch the children; clean up three meals; get organized; and try to stay clean. Everything took getting used to, and no one knew what to expect. Still, to them it was the Garden-of-Eden-Ranch.

Thanks to the women's group, they were well prepared with groceries. They had been baking bread during the winter, which they froze to extend its shelf life. Now they had straw baskets loaded with loaves. They used wooden bowls and pottery for most of their dishes. Breakfast consisted of thick pots of oatmeal sprinkled with honey, nuts, and raisins prepared at the breakfast tent. Cheese and avocado sandwiches on thick slices of seven-grain bread kept hunger at bay until dinner time.

It was Day Four at The Ranch. Mariah watched as some of the men gathered around on camp stools, drawn by the smells of dinner bubbling on the grate. With their long hair, beards and some of them with pipes, they looked like a colorful bunch of hippies. Was she really a hippie underneath it all? Mariah wondered. They wore thick cotton tee shirts and well-worn jeans adorned with belts, or oversized Guatemalan shirts. Definitely not your typical West Texas rancher. Mexican blankets served as seats when there weren't enough stumps or logs around. Mariah could tell by the sounds of happy chatter that everyone anticipated a good supper.   Appetites were sharpened out here. No matter how hot the day, the evenings were always pleasantly brisk—at least for now.

Robin touched Mariah's arm, then gestured for her to help with the salad. She wore her hair in long thick braids, long enough to sit on. Mariah guessed she had most likely never cut it. She prepared three large wooden bowls full of mixed greens, raw veggies, mushrooms, and almonds. She smacked Jack's hand as he tried to snatch a mushroom. Robin intervened and he went to help her. As Mariah worked she could see the kids. She marveled as she watched them.

There were eighteen kids in total; they came from nine families and ranged in age from one to sixteen. Many, like their parents, had blonde hair, long and messy. Precocious five-year-olds were looked after by the ten-to-twelve-year-old girls who were very bossy and responsible. There was constant music around camp, but not the folk tunes the older guys usually played. The teens with guitars, violins, recorders, and penny whistles were playing a familiar Irish tune. Thank God, since most of the kids had been home schooled, many had learned an instrument and played in local bands. Even the young twins, who studied Suzuki, knew their Irish tunes. Someone, Mariah noted with pleasure, had even brought wind chimes to string from the tent. She realized they resembled a bunch of gypsies.

Everything was reusable. No paper or plastic, no room for waste. Mariah had brought gallon glass jars for sun tea. Most of the tea she made was from her garden herbs. She had some lavender–mint brewing as an experiment.

Days and nights passed with the rhythm of the daily tasks. David planned to meet Paul and the new arrivals in Laketown to show them the way. Nothing new had happened, but Mariah missed David. Now she'd finally begun to realize the grandiosity of their undertaking.

Jody and Pat Cooper were the ones most prepared for community living-off-the-grid. In Houston they owned their own custom jewelry and clothing business. Pat was the practical one who made it all work. They were well prepared for this inevitable relocation. Together, they were skilled in the science of hygiene. Once they arrived, Pat and Jody took charge of latrine location and construction. They organized teams for the initial labor-intensive layout. They also created a dishwashing center. After that everyone pitched in to set it up at the central cooking tent.

After some debate they agreed on the ideal location for the latrine. It was situated off the path away from the water. They were located up from the rivers, in the general direction of Jade Cove. The "Potty Crew" had cleared an area between four pine trees. They strung ropes between the trees to create a place to hang sheets for privacy. They dug five, five-foot-long ditches that were each eight inches wide and one foot apart. This was the perfect "squat and eliminate" dimension. Some folks brought a portable toilet seat so they could place it strategically over the hole when in use. They kept a metal garbage can full of fireplace ash by the ditch. After each elimination, you just threw in a scoop of wood ash. This method had the least impact on the site. Once each ditch was filled, the potty crew covered it completely with dirt and packed it down. Later, bushes or trees could be planted. The process continued on the next row. Thus they could then dig new latrines once the first field was filled. This would give them time to construct a more *advanced* composting toilet complete with outhouse later. Pat considered bamboo to be a fine construction material in the future. So the garden crew planted some shoots they brought with them. Bamboo grows quickly when fertilized and watered.

Isabella beguiled her parents and Jack to execute her design for a stone and cob oven. So far she hadn't succeeded. She had seen one at the Kerrville folk festival and was convinced this was essential for quality of life. *'Quality of life'* was the big buzzword in their family. It was the reason they had long been growing most of their own food. It was why at home they spent money on quality foods and organic cheeses. It was why they didn't eat in chain restaurants or work at jobs they hated, for that matter. "Do what you love. Don't waste precious time on earth in mundane or unnecessary activities. We don't have a ton to eat but by God it's going to taste excellent when we prepare it properly." This had become their motto and mantra.

The community soon realized that certain tasks were crucial to survival and others could wait—or they could do without. Like the stone ovens. Isabella didn't like her pet project being vetoed. She resolved to regale able looking newcomers with her ideas.

David and Jack were focused on getting the gardens planted. They brought some fruit trees from home which they had to plant right away. Paul's experience at The Farm had been with the orchard. Consequently, the three men bonded as they made quick work of tree planting. They also staked out the garden areas. They prepared and readied the soil to plant in May and June. They had to plant all the grains right away.

Isabella finally recruited Paul and Uncle Rob in her oven

construction project. They decided that one oven would suffice. They could take turns using it. Isabella generously decided to locate it at the Coopers' site because their three daughters loved to bake. All of the baking could be done there. Rob soon enlisted the teens to collect rocks and bring them to the designated location.

Mariah's younger brother Rob and his wife Roxi had come with the second group. The moment Mariah told him about the plan to move to The Ranch, he endeavored to join. They were a young couple and hadn't started a family yet. He and Roxi still camped and fished all over Texas. Mariah was pleased to see Rob had grown into a tall outdoors man, having devoted much of his teen years to nature. He worked on a horse farm as manager of Arabian horses when he was barely twenty. He was now a self-proclaimed horse whisperer; he had such an ability with animals.

CHAPTER 4 *Tristan - April*

Tristan's mind was a million miles away, while his arms and hands went through the motions of helping his dad as a good, obedient son should. He was strong and enjoyed working. Like most sixteen-year-olds, his mind was often elsewhere. He had been nine when he quite literally fell into the Indians world. Now seven years later was he too old? He had never forgotten. Tristan knew he must go soon and alone. After what happened last time, his parents might even forbid it. His curiosity outshone any fear he imagined. He heard that fairies and elves may appear to some children while they were young, but as one got older such 'magical' friends disappeared forever, returning to the underworld from whence they came. The memory of the underworld Indians had seated itself in his mind and mixed with memories of fantastic dreams. He remembered the experience as though it were yesterday—the glorious blue-green of the water as the sun shimmered down from the top. He had swum through the tunnel under the rock threshold and presto, into a cave. He could breathe in there. His mind raced. How could he find them again? He was convinced the Indians he met were flesh and blood. No matter how luminous they seemed, they were real.

This evening was already too late. Days flew by. He would hike in the early morning. That would give the Indians all day to ascertain his presence and pull him in to their magic world like they did before. *If* they were still there, of course. His heart leapt in a panic at the thought. Nothing could have happened in these intervening years. They must be there.

In the end, it was another three days before he could get away. In the meantime, he made newcomers feel welcome. He helped his mom and Isabella introduce everyone to the delights of Jade Cove and the water wall of freshwater springs. He was proud of all The Ranch had to offer. A whole bunch of his friends drank their fill of the fresh water and filled jugs to take back. They explored the tributaries and small icy limestone pools of fresh water. Everything was unchanged from the last trip. The sun beat down and the water flowed to the sea in an undisturbed and unchanged continuum. While over the years he had changed and grown up and even moved. Here everything was timeless. The lake at Jade Cove remained still a cool deep green framed by low rock cliffs and opened up to a rocky beach that led to the headwaters. The springs still continued etching the water wall in a hundred tiny streams.

Surely the Blue Spring and the hidden cave would still be there. He debated whether to take Isabella with him but decided to go alone. The morning he set off burned like coal. The rain had left things sparkly clean. The sun beat bright and intense on his back. A welcome breeze rattled the pecan trees that grew along the stream edge, the branches a lime green fuzz of new growth.

The three mile hike to Blue Spring took longer than he remembered. He knew he wouldn't get lost because all he had to do was follow the tributary upstream from Indian Point until he found the Source. He checked his compass a few times along the way.

Tristan peeled his pack from his sticky back when he arrived. Bone white cliffs etched against a bold blue sky framed the deep pool. He plopped down on one of the huge boulders at the edge of the pristine water and swiped the sweat off his face with his tee shirt. It was just an ordinary day at The Ranch. White water churned up by the waterfall shone in the splice between the cliffs. An army of dragon flies circled his head. The place was loud with the pounding water. A hawk screamed overhead and he watched it circle above the pool. Small birds flew in its stream. All was still.

The untouched aspect of everything impressed upon him. He realized with a pang how far away he was. And really just at the precipice of endless acres that lay beyond this point. No roads. No people. Only the community back at camp. He had never seen anyone else here since they arrived. The water beckoned but he knew it would be like ice when he jumped in.

The unlikelihood of what he'd come here to find hit him smack in the middle of his pounding head. What was his plan? Just to jump in and see if he could find the cave? Well maybe it had all been a dream. Perhaps he had hit his head when he'd jumped and imagined the whole thing. After all it was only he who'd seen them. Those he'd told just believed him, rather humored him. They hadn't experienced it. As his thoughts tumbled for attention in his brain he gave up making sense of it.

He threw his shirt and shoes off and dove in. He swam strong sure strokes toward the waterfall. The cave was in the depths beneath the crevice. He kicked hard and pushed deeper. He had to fight the force of the water to get close enough and he had to go deep. He kicked down below the water's surface with strong legs. Nowhere near the bottom his lungs burned and he surfaced for air.

He filled his lungs and tried again. The numbness of his body made him weak as he battled the water and went deep again. He saw lime green fronds swaying in the depths. His lungs burned and his throat began to close so he swam up. He paddled around at the top as he assessed the cliffs and decided on a new approach. Last time he'd jumped from the cliff. That might give him the boost to get down deep enough. Then he'd be in the right position. *Now to get up there.*

In the old days a rope hung in the boulders. They could grab it and scale through the waterfall. His legs thrust against the current again. He struggled to find a finger hold on the rocks and pull himself up. He grabbed the edge of a sharp rock and swung to the edge. He avoided the slime of the center rocks and managed to scramble up. Panting hard he found his way to the top of the cliff.

He stood up, wet and warm from the exertion. Adrenaline pulsed through him as he observed his surroundings. Sun burned his back. Then a sudden gust of wind teased him as he took in the enormous vista. A palpable stillness surrounded him and he felt his aloneness. Not a soul was anywhere near here. No human sounds or voices. He scanned his surroundings to see if anyone could be hiding in the nearby woods. There were woods everywhere. He squinted at the green black darkness between the trees. Well, he could not see a thing past the edge. Who knows? He glanced down at his feet. He moved closer to the shear drop to the water below. His head swooned.

He looked out at the sky and horizon, shouted 'wahoo' and jumped up and out far. One big cannonball of a splash. He swam with all his might downwards towards the blue-black darkness.

And then it happened.

He felt the pull of pond fronds on his foot and he let his body follow. He swam with sunfish, trout, and gold-spotted snapper. He went through a narrow opening underneath a rock ledge. He focused on the light ahead as he pushed through the narrow part of the tunnel. Just as his lungs felt like fire he found he was in the cave and could breathe again. The Indian that pulled him in looked immediately familiar. He knew that this must be Joseph. Now a young man. No longer the teen he remembered.

"Look what I found." Joseph smiled and laughed as though he had just gone fishing. He was helping Tristan through the rock crevice and into the antechamber as he spoke. The room glowed with a mysterious blue light. Tristan still gasped for air as he swam into the room behind Joseph. It seemed smaller than he remembered but it was definitely the same room. Two shadowy figures were seated cross-legged in the low-ceilinged space.

Tristan looked around. What he had dared hope was happening. It was not a dream. This was the same room beneath the Waterfall. This was his Joseph, of long ago.

"Let me make the introductions," Joseph spoke, "My Uncle, Chief Nuage and my cousin Daniel."

Daniel was older than Joseph, wide shouldered with a strong firm build.

Tristan smiled as he watched the three study him. They looked pleased to see the young man he'd become. He noted the almost proud smile Joseph bestowed on him. He followed the three from the antechamber into a deeper cave. This cave opened to a sunny meadow he could just see beyond the exit. It seemed the pool was an entrance into the realm the Indian families called home. He didn't ask. He remembered the words of a wise friend. 'All will be revealed in time.'

The garments they wore were soft deerskin. The crude wood bowls full of fruit, apples, berries, and nuts were placed on a blanket woven with rich hues. The puff sound on the pipes they smoked comforted him in the quiet cave. All eyes were on the Chief. He took his time. Indian time, Tristan thought. It seemed they had a serious caution in there welcome. As he extended his hand in greeting, they ignored it and embraced him in turns. His entrance must change things—his very presence must be a harbinger of things to come. He belatedly wondered about the affect this might have on the secret lifestyle they had carved out for themselves.

The others present passed the pipe in silence. One by one they each took a turn. The mood was solemn and even Joseph stopped grinning. Then the Chief looked straight at him. His gaze was calm, focused on him alone. Tristan sat up straight. He prepared himself with full attention to face this humble but powerful presence.

Or was it the other way around Tristan wondered. Who was to be the more profoundly changed here?

* * *

The wisdom the Chief held, electrified the still silence between them. Tristan held his breath. Many thoughts rushed through his head as he waited in silence. He let out his breath and slowly inhaled as the chief spoke.

"The soul of Man and the earth are intimately connected. All life forms deserve respect. The honor and respect is born in the nature of Life. The balance is delicate and absolute. The subtleties of the balanced world are like a dance.

For man to live in harmony with the earth he must learn to dance with her.

Timing, rhythm, balance. Breathe in, breathe out."

The wisdom of the old Chief is transmitted in a simple way and Tristan got it.

"Indians have been waiting six generations since Geronimo, to trust a white man. The earth is in grave danger. There is a solution. The only solution is to share our wisdom with the white man because

the destruction white eyes is yielding on the earth—in the perpetual
ignorance—is so rapid it has a disastrous effect on all people, all races,
and The Earth. This must stop."

Silence. The Chief, Nuage, Joseph had called him, just continued
to puff on the pipe and stare straight at him, or through him. Tristan
waited, wondering if he would say more. But the Chief looked at
him with eyes of honey warmth, profound depth and understanding.
Tristan felt he was seen fully for perhaps the first time in his life.
He knew he need not speak or question. He knew he could live up
to the words, the invitation, and the challenge in them. As the chief
watched him and smoked, the aroma was sweet and reminiscent of his
grandfather's pipe. The puff on the pipe sound was one with the beat of
his heart and the muffled sound of water from far away.

On the walk back to camp Tristan's somber mood intensified as he contemplated all that had transpired. The information was clear. That he would take action was certain. Who could he go to with this burden? He slowed his pace, allowing the long walk to delay the inevitable. He thought the Indians he had just met seemed different from the reservation Indians he had met previously. These guys were health personified. They glowed with physical health. Strong, lean muscles with skin glowing a rich brown tone from the sun. Their hair was thick and blue-black shiny. Everything about their whole existence was purposeful. Their bodies were the honed tools of the warrior.

CHAPTER 5 *Jack and Mariah*

The morning glow sat on the horizon for a pregnant minute before the red ball of flame that was the sun began to rise. The sun's fire fingers illuminated tall grasses, boulders and quiet tent forms arranged in a circle. Normal campgrounds at parks are always in rows, with the chaotic jumble of stuff people bring ruining the harmony of the landscape. But this was easy. The big communal fireplace and cooking tent were in the center, and the couples had privacy in the back.

Tristan sat down with his guitar under a tree and broke the morning stillness with a serenade to the sun. Mariah put the pot on the fire for camp coffee. The coals had burned hot during the night, she had only to add a few sticks and blow softly to coax the flame.

The sun rose higher. Jack came out of his tent with his hands in his pockets and a plaid wool blanket around his shoulders. "I had an amazing dream last night—I was astral projected into an India of the future."

"Did you?" Mariah stirred the fire as Jack launched in. She smiled at Tristan under the tree. "Coffee?" she asked Jack.

"Sure."

Tristan was patient. He just wished this bit of solitude would last longer. He had to tell his mom what happened, but in private.

Mariah heated up a pitcher of milk and poured two cups of coffee. She used the large blue metal fish cups. "Honey?"

"Yes," Jack said. She passed it to him and was relieved when he fell silent; apparently he had forgotten about the dream. She sipped her hot coffee in silence. Her thoughts floated with the melancholy strains of the guitar.

She looked up as Jack and Rob stood warming themselves by the fire, a study in opposites. Jack's round thick body contrasted sharply with Rob's tall lean one. Jack looked up at Rob and with a big grin began telling him of the dream—in which he was astral projected to India in the future. Rob grunted and helped himself to coffee and found a log seat on the circle. Rob had grown up when she wasn't looking. Now he stood at least six foot three she estimated. Was he almost thirty? He wore his dark blonde hair long and straight down to his shoulders. His face was chiseled and handsome in the morning light. She noted he still looked groggy. He was silent with eyes half closed as he let the brew work its magic.

Mariah grabbed her sketch book, always nearby, and began a quick sketch of Jack while he told dream stories.

"When does David arrive?" Jack asked, interrupting his dream story and Mariah's reverie. David had to leave for supplies the moment he'd returned with the second group.

"Today, hopefully this afternoon. Word of mouth has spread and a third group is on the way from Houston."

"We will have to stop meeting like this."

Mariah rolled her eyes. She kept her attention on her pen and ink. She moistened her finger with a bit of water and rubbed the lines, achieving some blue tones.

Tristan could see he had completely lost his opportunity. He continued to play his melodic tunes.

"Rob, how is Roxi?" Mariah asked.

"Sleeping like a baby," he grinned.

"With all the political changes in the country, the reports have it that martial law may be declared," Jack launched in. "There has been an incredible change in government policy as regards personal privacy. This has enabled the government to monitor all personal data: driver's licenses, library cards, credit cards—and all the information is going into a huge database."

Rob perked up, he was in his element. "But as with all bureaucracies, there are cracks, and since all of us here are self-employed and don't own anything, it will be easier for us to slip through those cracks."

Jack turned to Mariah. "The others are going to be surprised when they see this place."

"Do you like it?" Mariah asked.

"Like it? It's amazing I don't want to leave. You don't?"

"Oh no, being here these weeks has let me settle in to the groove here. It speaks to me this place."

"Yes, it does."

"I take it for granted, I guess." Mariah's green eyes showed clear. "I've been coming here since I was sixteen. I keep coming back. I'm called to this place. When I leave, I can't wait to return." Mariah watched the flame. If they could believe the beginning of the story, perhaps they could accept where we are today. If not, then she wouldn't push it.

"I'd like to see this Blue Spring," Jack said.

"Oh, we'll go there all right, when David gets here. Perhaps tomorrow morning, sunrise, will work."

Jack smiled. "Then today I'll take the kids to Jade Cove."

"All the kids?"

"Oh yeah, they've been following me around every day now. They're playing Cowboy and Indians. It's a game they started."

Tristan jolted, momentarily worried his secret was out.

"I thought you were out hiking by yourself every day," Mariah said.

"I did too. But the kids are playing Indians. They love the fact that no one is restricting them. I'm the cowboy. They follow me in hiding. I didn't even realize it until yesterday. If I go to Jade Cove to fish. I guarantee you that's where every kid will be. They started the game and they haven't broken character yet. It's more fun than planned activities. They only pretend to be whiney hungry kids when they're back at camp with their parents. Glad I don't have any kids."

Tristan exhaled.

"Jack, you do have kids," Mariah said.

"Oh yeah, my ex-wife has them."

"Correct, because you kept forgetting you had them even when they were under foot and you were still married."

Jack grinned sheepishly.

"Tristan would you like some apples?" She reached in the straw picnic basket to get them, as she looked back up he was already beside

41

her, his hand reaching for the fruit. "Hey, that was fast."

"Thanks, I love apples," he grinned as he grabbed two large ones. "Isabella up yet?"

"I'm here." Isabella emerged from the tent pushing her black frames up her nose, and securing her blanket with the other. "Coffee?"

"Yes, honey, come sit by the fire. Honey?"

"Yes please."

Rob nudged Isabella, "Your brother knows his tunes."

Isabella tightened her blanket shawl and nudged back. She wasn't used to having an uncle.

* * *

For his part Rob thanked his stars he was living here. Rob had thrived in nature. At a difficult fourteen his Mom had sent him to live with his big sister and her husband in Austin. He'd been so lonely that first year when his older sister had divorced and left the two of them to fend for themselves. His mom never returned any of his letters, instead she just left him in the Austin trailer park thinking a Big Brother (Kristen's Husband) would be preferable to life as a latch-key kid in Houston.

At first the long trek he had walked to high school down rural roads and thru the woods was a hardship. Until he realized that was the best part of his day. When school was out he spent the long hours alone in the woods. Some days he never made it to school at all. Then he spent the entire summer in the woods, fishing in the creek and hunting before he made it back to Houston on a Greyhound bus. In the lonely quiet year he'd developed a deep communication with the wooded world. He was schooled in the interdependent layered hierarchy of nature. Yet he became sullen and closed off towards his parents and most adults. He could not really ever forgive his father for leaving his Mom with all the financial responsibility while he quit commercial clients to follow his dream as an art-photographer.

Rob could lose himself in nature. It was a language he understood. Ultimately his lack of education in the basics was embarrassing. He became an avid reader. He read nonfiction voraciously—history, philosophy, esoterica, divination, psychology. He combed used bookstores and the Goodwill and by twenty-seven he'd amassed a huge library.

Lately he lived back in town, with a job he'd resented because it took every hard won penny to survive. His life was crap. Of course when he'd been bonding with nature he should have finished high school. Instead he was destined to a life of manual menial tasks. No extras. No time. It was the time part he craved. He came alive when he led kids on trips—he volunteered at the local nature preserve—both adults and kids hung on his every word. He could talk about the natural habitat for days. The understanding came so natural to him.

He'd finally snapped on the realization that his sad upbringing had opened up a unique vision of the natural world to him. When Mariah called inviting him to join the *experiment in the wilds*-trip he felt like he'd won the lottery! He had just listened while she begged and cajoled. He would have paid to join the group had there been a fee.

* * *

"Care for a stroll?" Jack asked Mariah. The two rose and followed the worn deer path.

"I have been trying to figure out what to do," Mariah confided, "but I think I know now."

"Lost me. Do about what?"

"I mean, here we are, out in the middle of nowhere. All of you guys came out here without knowing what it would be like. And yet Tristan and Isabella, David and I, we always knew what we were coming to."

"One day at a time. Don't over think it. You are here with your family, your friends."

"What if the others don't like it?"

"That's what you're worried about? Everyone else? Relax. Give it a rest." Jack laughed and patted her arm. "I think we can let The Ranch decide. I think she chooses us, calls to us." Jack spoke with the quiet confidence of a sage. "Perhaps she already has."

Mariah glanced up quickly at Jack, her sharp green eyes penetrating the side of his face as he stared at his feet while he walked. She glanced up at the sky, blue and crystal clear again. Seven days of crystal blue, the dry grass crisp under foot.

"This place looks much the same," she said, "It doesn't change. Slow growing live oak trees, growing older and more gnarled. But not up. There are folks here from all over. They might not even like it. Somehow all this dry dust and dirt has grown on me." She was taking it all too personally, like it was her place. Her slice of heaven and she so wanted others to know it as she had. "I love it here," she blurted. "I love these craggy rocks and crystal blue water. The gnarled live oak and sycamore trees in the creek beds. I even love the old goat smells. I don't know how others feel about it."

"I know," Jack grinned, panting slightly at the incline.

They had climbed to the top of the rise. The endless horizon at the top shoved all doubts from Mariah's head. She was staring out at an endless flat sea of atmosphere. When she squinted, she could envision the sea that had been here thousands of years ago, the sea that had carved the Edwards Plateau. The world below–the community teeming with cares of survival—was forgotten.

Jack plopped on a flat rock mesmerized by the panorama. She enjoyed his wonderment at the view. From here they could see far.

* * *

Mariah's head was buzzing with Tristan's story. He had been patient since breakfast. She knew it was hard at Camp Central, which was always swarming with people and their questions. The rest of the afternoon had been all Jack. The last story—or was it a dream—Jack told Mariah was about aliens and cow experiments. By late afternoon, Mariah felt like Jack had talked her ear off for days. Eventually she came up with the bogus idea to ask his help inspecting the latrines. He declined. She tagged Tristan. When they were tucked off in the woods, he'd taken the lead through a small deer path through the brush. He told her he found the Indians. He had jumped into the Blue Spring like he had done many years before. She masked her shock.

"You went alone? You should have told me. I would have come, stood watch, something." She had believed him when he told his story back then, and now she felt the warmth of a mother's pride, as well as confirmation of his story. She felt relief, solid and sure. He had survived.

A broad smile lit Mariah's face as she finally heard the sound of the Volvo in the distance. Jack and Mariah sat in the shade sipping sun tea when David pulled up, his car loaded with supplies packed in around him.

He staggered out of the car, a big grin on his face. "We made it."

Mariah danced to his side and gave him a big hug and messy kisses. Jack greeted him with a sweaty bear hug.

"I'm stiff from driving." David twisted around, stretching his back. "I forded all the streams. I counted five, although I'm glad the water is down." He patted the trusty Volvo wagon. "She made it."

Mariah looked in a box. "Yay, you brought fresh peaches."

"I passed a few orchards on the way. They are early, though, they may not be quite ripe yet."

Mariah eyed this guy she'd been hanging with for the past seventeen or so years "I missed you," she said, "Glad you made it safely."

He sat her down on his lap. She took his hand. It was soft and strong at the same time.

"Hmm, you need a minute?" Jack cleared his throat.

"No," they said in unison.

"The Coopers are doing dinner tonight," Mariah told David, "and it will be ready at about seven or eight. You have time for a quick dip in the stream—unless you feel like a proper swim. No one is at the lake this time of day."

"You know? I'd love to swim, but only if you join me. Are you up for a run to Jade Cove real quick?"

"Sure, give me a sec while I change," she said.

"Jack, my man, what's up?" David asked.

"Oh, it's been some day." Jack looked ready to launch in. "Tomorrow you and I are going to trek with Tristan to the Blue Spring Site."

David nodded, he looked over Jack's head at the cliffs beyond. What a view they had from this perch.

Mariah emerged in a wraparound skirt and tank top over her suit. A shy smile peeked from behind her messy dark hair.

45

"You joining us?" David looked at Jack.

"I'm bushed, you two go on ahead."

They heard the bustle of activity from the camp below at Big Meadow. It was fun to steal off together.

"What's the town like?" she asked.

"More like a ghost town. That's why I had to go all the way back to San Antonio. We are really in a lost place. Far from everything. Where's Isabella?"

"She went with Tristan this afternoon. Now that you mention it, it's been quite a while. Something serious is going on."

"Do you want to tell me about it? I thought you just wanted me, but you have an agenda."

"I always have an agenda."

David led the way along the narrow trail on the edge of the hill until they got down beside the water and the path widened.

"I do want you," Mariah said. She followed him on the path aware of the river that rushed along just below. They were headed to the deep wide lake dubbed Jade Cove. "Tristan met the Indians. He met Joseph and was in the cave again and he met the Chief, Nuage, I think he said his name was."

David stopped dead in his tracks. "Woh, start at the beginning."

She went on to retell what Tristan had told her. "Chief Nuage said, *'We have been waiting six generations, since Geronimo, to trust a white man. The earth is in grave danger, and the only solution is to share our wisdom with the white man because the destruction white eyes is yielding on the earth—in the perpetual ignorance—is so rapid it has a disastrous effect on all people and all races. This must stop.'* " Mariah sighed. "That is pretty much a quote. I think Tristan memorized it so he could tell me." She stated it all rather matter-of-factly, as they jogged along the pine needle path. "He has taken Isabella into his confidence now," she concluded. "I'm glad you are up for a swim. It's been crowded down here all day."

"That is extraordinary. It seems they are willing to sacrifice their peace and seclusion and share their knowledge with Tristan." David and she walked in silence. "I assume so he can tell others? Us? Did Tristan explain our presence here?"

"I don't think so. He was too surprised to say much. That would be our—my, job rather. Don't you think?"

"If they will appear to us as well. Perhaps they only want to communicate with Tristan? Only let him in their peace circle."

Mariah had never seen David unsure of himself.

"I'm glad to have the lake to ourselves this evening, too," David said. "You do realize it was your idea to share this bit of paradise with everyone?"

"It is paradise, that's true. But not ours. It's Peter's place. He always shared this place with everyone."

"I wonder if Peter knew about the Indians. Well, all the same, if it was up to me, I would be happy to settle out here with just our family. If you get disturbed by the noise and the bustle. Don't look at me."

"You... well....yes. What can I say? You are right. But it's better this way. Isn't it? I mean wouldn't you be a bit lonely—feel a bit isolated, if it were just us?"

"You would. But not me. I am fine with just us." David pinched her backside.

The deep green water that gave Jade Cove its name was still, smooth like green velvet. David slipped out of his shorts, then shattered the surface as he jumped in. Mariah took her time. She folded her clothes and piled them on the bank. The day's sweat was still clinging to her body. She watched David swim out in long graceful strokes. His strong arms pulled his tapered white form through the green expanse. The thick water swallowed him and became calm once more. His body seemed small once he was far out in the lake.

The water invited her in to shatter its mysteries. She watched for stones as she put one bare foot at a time in the cold mud incline of the bank. With one smooth move she slipped into the water without a splash. While David swam, she floated on her back, suspended, and gazed at the cloudless blue of the sky. Memories flashed of the peaceful teenage summers she'd spent in this magic place. Time stood still out here and awaited her return. Was this her final return?

"Race you," David called.

"You have energy."

They swam to the distant shore, Mariah tried to catch up. Then

47

breathless, she climbed out onto the beach piled high with small bleached stones and rested.

"These hot rocks feel so good. Tomorrow we can hike. Now it's great to relax, take it all in." Mariah lay back, she enjoyed the hot stone massage. Chills ran up her body after the cool water. She glanced up at the cliffs that surrounded them, and then back at the dark caves hidden behind the scruffy trees. "Do you think anyone's up there? Watching us?"

"Maybe there are Indians. Let's give them something worth watching." David rolled over and stole a wet kiss. "It's hard to tell from down here."

Mariah smelled his musky mix of soap and body heat as he wrapped her in a strong bear hug. She rolled on top of him, her hair like wet seaweed on his chest. "You do believe me—us—about the Indians?" She arched her head back as she spoke.

"I do believe you. It is fantastic." He stared at her white round breasts, then looked back up into her eyes. "I don't know what to think *or do* about it. I do think we should avoid showing folks the Blue Spring."

"So do I." Mariah broke away from David's embrace reluctantly. "Another thing he said was *the balanced world is like a dance.* I like that."

"You would, you love to dance."

"I'm serious. This is what the Chief said, 'For man to live in harmony with the earth he must learn to dance with her. Timing, rhythm, balance. Breathe in, breathe out.' Does that mean I can dance and save the earth at the same time?"

"You will have to learn *the* Dance." David smiled. "It's later than I thought." The two dove back in the water and began the long swim back to the bank where their clothes were.

"Tomorrow we're going to check out Jade Springs."

"In the meantime..." David playfully grabbed for Mariah while she attempted to swim. They swam side by side until they made it back.

The evening rested calm upon the green velvet smoothness of Jade Cove. Once they were out they dried each other off. Then with clothes and shoes back on, the water lay perfectly still once again, hiding all her secrets beneath the surface. From her perch, Mariah looked long at the flat mirrored plane, wondering if her sheer wanting of the truth would entice The Ranch to divulge her secrets. Her mind could hear the past laughter of innocent children swinging on the rope swing that stretched the length of water. Now, that and the glass-bottom boat, both gone. In its place was a pregnant stillness. She shivered and looked up to see David watching her.

"Penny for your thoughts?" He put a warm arm around her shoulders. In silence they held hands as they tread the path back to base camp.

* * *

When David saw how much had been accomplished in the first weeks, he was amazed. Mariah showed him the minimal attempts at civilized living. Things they never concerned themselves with when there was just the four of them.

They had organized a new way to shower. Cold water was good in the summer, but there was nothing like a hot shower after an intense day of gardening, or stone building, or whatever work someone thought of next. Again ropes and blankets were the most minimal attempts at privacy. Isabella and her cousin, twelve-year-old Anya, thought they could improve on this by making a panel of reeds like bamboo harvested and woven together with twine. These panels could be lashed to the rope enclosure.

Anya, Mariah's niece, was her sister Maxine's youngest daughter. She, like Isabella, enjoyed creative problem solving, especially when it involved crafting solutions. Anya was small and practical with renaissance long, curly-on–the–verge-of-frizzy brown hair, framing an oval face with small facial features. She was more classic than pixie. She was creative as well as exceptionally smart with an imagination that complimented Isabella's. They spent hours together.

For the solar shower, the Coopers suggested a system of shower bags. They filled about twenty shower bags with water. They hung one at a time from the slender branches of a tall pine. These were heated by direct solar gain. When you showered, you would stand beneath and pull a rope and the sun-warmed water would shower upon you. After someone finished his bathing ritual, he removed the empty bag and hoisted up a new one in its place. Later, while at the river, each person could fill an empty shower bag and put it back at the end of the line upon return. This gave the sun time to heat the water before the next use.

The shower contraption was near the water. There had to be enough distance for the run-off to sink back into the land with no direct contamination of the water. There was a stock tank big enough for bathing and soaking sore muscles. The hose siphoned the water from the river and filled the tub. All was done by gravity flow. The shower crew anchored the tub in amongst the rocks. They placed Dr. Bronner's soap conveniently for hair washing and bathing.

Theirs was a smart group, and they had planned for most of their needs here. They found endless uses for rope and duct tape. Muslin cloth and sheets came in handy. Still, there was the odd thing they could absolutely not live without, along with the stuff they ran out of at a rapid rate. As a result, there was a long list for each bi-monthly trip to town. Other things would require more thought—like refrigeration once their ice supply ran out.

CHAPTER 6 *Tristan and the Indians*

Of all the many chores that were part of the daily routine of their new lifestyle, Tristan liked chopping wood. His arms and chest glowed with the effort. As he sliced each piece smoothly with the sharpened axe, his face flushed and his body slick with sweat, he thought of Joseph. He was eager to get back.

A few feet away, David paused in his chopping and looked at his son.

"Okay, son, I see that glint in your eye. What's up?"

Tristan put down his axe. "Dad, I've been back to the place behind the Blue Spring."

David waited for Tristan to continue.

"I managed to find Joseph again."

"Whoa I need to play catch up here. Your Mom mentioned you had already established contact with the Indians."

"I did. They're not aliens." Tristan put down the axe and wiped a hand across his brow. "I went right away. Mom must have told you. Joseph and I are becoming best friends. I don't hang out much with the other kids anymore."

"Are you sure that's a good idea?" David was thrilled that his son was bonding with the Indians, but not at the expense of other relationships. After all, that's what their community was about.

"I don't want to blow Joseph's cover. I can't risk exposing the Indians' presence, and besides, I have to be around them if I want to learn their ways. Ask Mom, she knows. She told me to ask you."

"Wow, that's a first."

"I knew you would understand."

"What exactly?"

"I need to live with them."

"Okay...but Tristan, you're only sixteen, are you ready for this?"

"C'mon, Dad, Indian boys my age do all kinds of dangerous stuff. I'm way behind. I understand I was brought up differently but I am eager to catch-up."

"Tell me about Joseph." David leaned on his axe, prepared for a story.

Tristan smiled. "He's great. He's twenty. He knows everything and he can do so much." The two set loads of brush down on the pile.

"They invited me to join them. Only for a couple of weeks to assimilate the Native American ways."

"Do you plan to abandon us?" David smiled, but he was only half-kidding.

"Don't put it that way. It's for the good. I've got to meet them this morning to let them know you gave me your permission. They'll let me know when it's time. Soon I hope. To tell you the truth, I can't wait."

"They wanted you to get permission? That's hopeful."

"Respect of one's elders and the Chief is one of the most important things in their culture."

David leaned on the axe with a faraway look in his blue eyes as he contemplated his son. "I know it's an honor to be invited to join them. They obviously appreciate you."

Tristan flashed him a grin. "I think they were impressed when I told them I wanted to be immersed in their culture."

"I'm impressed that you know what immersion is," David said, laughing. "I sure as hell didn't when I was your age. Anyway, it's the best way to learn a culture." He picked up his axe again. "All the same though, I think it's better if you stay with us a little longer and continue on as you are doing, sharing your time with us and them."

If Tristan was disappointed with his father's decision he gave no indication. "Well, either way, I said I would meet up with them this morning and let them know your decision."

They chopped in silence for a little bit longer, then David set down his axe again. "I think we've caught up on this wood pile for a while."

"Sounds good." Tristan placed his tools by the tree and tightened his bandanna. "Well I'm off."

"Tristan," David called after him, "will we get to meet them sometime? Your Mom and I?"

His heart hurt a little. His Dad looked disappointed he was leaving with more work yet to do. Yet when he turned back, he saw something else in his father's expression—he *wanted* Tristan to go, to have this new venture into the unknown.

He grinned. "Sure, Dad, that would be a good idea."

With that Tristan turned and jogged off on the trail through the trees.

* * *

"Hey, Tristan wait up."

The sound of his mother's voice in the quiet woods startled him. Tristan turned and saw Mariah running to catch up.

"What's up Mom?" He had only left his father a few minutes before but Mariah had been nowhere around.

"I ran into your father," Mariah panted a little. "He told me you're off to meet Joseph. I should go with you. Explain our situation."

Tristan gave a relieved sigh, "You will? That's great. I really didn't know how to bring it up."

"You shouldn't have to. Dad and I brought everyone here. We should be the ones to deal, with it."

The two walked through the wet spring forest in silence, each lost in thought. Then they angled up a small deer path over rocks and boulders. When they neared the top of a cliff just past Jade Cove, Tristan motioned for her to slide past him. There was a dark crevice slotted vertically in the rock. Mariah hadn't noticed it before. She looked questioningly at her son and at his encouraging nod squeezed into the narrow space. The space widened and opened into a small cave. She paused to give her eyes a chance to adjust to the darkness then started when she saw a dark silhouette leaning against the wall.

"I am Jet." The dark shape had a voice. His was a deep baritone that resonated in the small chamber.

She was not prepared. The resonance of his baritone voice surprised her. He was so male. His sweat pungent. The taught skin of his muscles glistened even in the shadow. His very foreignness slammed the reality of what might have been half playful fantasy. His darkness fascinated her on a primal level.

"Hello, I am Mariah." She stuck out her hand. Her tan hand paled in his dark one. She knew her voice sounded over-bright and too friendly. As her eyes grew accustomed to the darkness of the cave, her breath caught at the flash of white as a grin split his face.

"I remember your last visit well. Good to see you are in health." His thick black hair swung heavy as he moved toward her from his lazy stance against the wall. "Tristan will join our tribe and live with us for a week or so. Later, he will do a Vision Quest. Our Chief wishes it."

"Your English is remarkable." Mariah was taken aback by his presumption.

"Just because we live in the wilderness doesn't make us ignorant of your ways. Not knowing your language is how our people got in trouble in the first place."

"Yes, of course," Mariah said, her tone now somber. "I came to meet you and to discuss another matter. As you probably know, we have brought a bunch of folks with us. To live off of the land, off of the grid. We don't intend to trespass on your territory."

Jet, crossed his arms as he relaxed back against the cave wall. "Here, let's sit together." He motioned to the dirt at their feet. She glanced outside and he shook his head. "We are too close to your camp for that."

Tristan stepped forward to join them and the three situated themselves on the ground.

"What do you have in mind?" Jet said, his voice stern. "How do you intend to survive out here in this vast Texas wilderness?"

"Well, I don't know exactly. It was all kind of a big idea. A dream of mine—of all of ours. I just knew when the storm broke that we had to go. Just go for it. I thought it was a sort of sign."

"Yes." He paused and waited.

"Well I figured there is plenty of fresh water and..."

Jet cut her off. "The earth is hard. The summers are over one hundred degrees. The winters are bitter cold, with the wind sweeping through these creek draws. Summer alone will kill you, way too hot for your white skin."

"It's not that white," Mariah said flippantly, then sobered again when she realized Jet didn't get the joke. "I thought there would be a way. Settlers homesteaded out here in the 1800s."

"Yes, and they left. That is how we were able to have this land for one hundred and thirty years." He rose and paced the cave. He said nothing while he paced softly in his moccasined feet. "No one else wanted this land."

Mariah's mouth hung open in surprise. "You've managed to stay hidden out here for one hundred and thirty years? Living off the land?"

"Six generations. Our tribe has been here and grown and lived off this land. Unknown. Hidden."

Mariah wailed, "Oh, I feel terrible. I just brought many families—urban hippie wannabees—out to this place. Too close for comfort. Will our presence here jeopardize your lifestyle?"

"You say you are not on vacation this time? You plan to stay?" Jet melted back down to the floor.

"Yes, we plan to stay."

As the three sat in silence they heard the waterfalls from down in the canyon below. The air in the cave felt cool. The dirt floor soft.

"Do not worry," Jet said finally. "We have a great leader, a Chief. He will advise us, as he advises us on all things. Tristan will go on the Vision Quest with us."

Mariah shook her head. "No, I'm afraid that won't be possible." Next to her, she felt Tristan's body tense.

"You surprise me," Jet said calmly. "You say you do not know how to survive, and we invite your son. This is the way he will learn. We seek vision in these times of change. That is how we learn how to proceed. That is our way. You do want to know our way?"

Mariah held her lips pressed tight as he studied her firm expression.

"Tristan will be ready to lead his people one day," he laughed when he saw her startled expression. "One step at a time. After Tristan comes back then I will take you personally to meet our wise one. Together we will make a plan. In the meantime, you are welcome here amongst us. You have much to learn but I will be proud to be your guide."

Mariah could stay silent no longer. "I appreciate your hospitality, but you seem to forget that I'm his mother. You assume Tristan can just go off with you and join your Vision Quest, but I say no. Please don't misunderstand me. I'm glad you have invited him, and wish to take him in. But, first let him visit by day and come to us in the evenings as he does now."

"Ah, yes. You are reluctant to let him go, but you must realize that to our people he's not a boy, but a man, and he is eager for our ways. He has a destiny. Please. Do not stand in his way." He walked back toward the mouth of the cave, clearly, the meeting was over.

Mariah glanced at her son and could indeed see the eagerness on his face. "I promise to consider your offer, and I'm deeply honored for him." She did not move or add any more explanation, she had decided 'no' and that was final. "Do I need a Vision Quest as well?"

Jet turned to look at her, a slow smile spreading across his face. "Don't you remember your time long ago, little one? In the teepee?"

Mariah was struck speechless for a moment. How could he know? "Yes, yes I do. There was a wise woman who came to me in a dream."

He smiled again. "I was there with Sun-on-Water, who watched over you while you slept. Protection from wild creatures and unhappy dreams. One hundred and thirty years we have hidden. It is a long time. I'm glad that you have come. As for the other, we will meet again soon."

Mariah raised a hand to her eyes, which had filled with tears. When she went to thank Jet again, he was gone. She looked at Tristan, but he just shrugged.

"I'm used to it."

He was quiet as they walked back, but his disappointment showed in the way his toe kicked at the dirt. Finally, he reached over and squeezed her hand. He was smiling.

Mariah sighed with relief. She had passed the test.

CHAPTER 7 *Welcome*

Friday night everyone gathered together at Indian Point, full and mellow after a few weeks of camping and fresh, delicious food. The chilled night air was a stark contrast to the intense heat of the afternoon, and the fires crackled bright. Children on blankets near their parents, rubbed their eyes after a day of swimming and careening around. Most nights, they would have been asleep in their tents by now, but tonight was special. Pat had announced that they would celebrate the newest arrivals to The Ranch.

Jody played a simple melody on the guitar while, Stacy and Pat sang bluegrass harmony. Jack tried but he kept slipping off-key. Paul joined in with a deep baritone.

"You hungry?" Mariah nudged Tristan.

"No, I'm fine. I ate with them," he said quietly.

Mariah stared at her son thoughtfully. He was taking meals with the Indians now. It wasn't all that surprising, not really; he had been allowed *in* long ago. She had expected some rebellion about her not giving her blessing to move right in with the Indians. Maybe he was grateful for the ability to walk between his two lives.

David cleared his throat and half-stood up to get everyone's attention. The music stopped, and the others, their faces aglow in the firelight, turned to him.

"I want to welcome ya'll," he said, his voice loud and clear. He didn't smile though, a sign to Mariah that he was still adjusting to his new leadership role. "Especially those who have just joined us."

Several people murmured solemn thank you's, some even smiled. All had that same nervous–excited expression Mariah had felt when she first arrived.

"We have each come here for our own reasons, united by a common purpose. I'm sure there are others with the same idea all over the country—probably, like us—who join forces and work together to find unique ways to solve the problems of survival in their own creative way. In my heart, I know nature is abundant. The Ranch has chosen us. We must remember that while this land is vast, it's not ours. We're only guests here.

"That said, please invite others you feel may be a good fit. Most of you know of, and share, my conviction that this world is on the brink of collapse, and we all want our loved ones to be safe. Their experience and knowledge could bring a diversity that may be essential to our continued success. Be open. Invite friends and neighbors, cousins or beggars. However, it's imperative that we keep our presence here quiet." He paused as if waiting for questions, but the only sounds were crickets, the crackle of the fire and the lone hoot of an owl.

"Which brings me to my final point," David continued, "some of you may find that the challenges of life here are too much. Of course you may leave, but we ask that you be discreet." His eyes scanned the crowd for emphasis. "Also, once you make a decision to leave, it's final."

Mariah watched the fire glow through her fingers, as she considered her husband's words. Was *she* sure she was ready to leave the *real world*—with all its artificial sameness and predictability—behind? Most of the time, she thought she was. They had been camped out for weeks now, and she had already gotten used to stretching out after a long day on her down filled sleeping bag and staring up at the brilliant star-filled night before rolling over and drifting to slumber. There was peace and simplicity. The earth felt firm under her. Yet that old, fear-based doubt tugged at her —was this dream-life really sustainable or just wishful thinking? Her thoughts continued to race as David answered questions around the circle.

Robin sat cross-legged on a mat, across the fire from her. She had unwound her braids, her long brown hair framed her delicate features in a sort of frizzy cloud. Robin had recently moved back to Texas after six years in the Midwest. She lived in one of the thousands of small, utterly forgettable towns dotting the U.S.. Yet, it was still a life full of modern conveniences. In their many conversations together, Mariah had never sensed an ounce of conflict in Robin about walking away, and found she envied this single-mindedness more than she could any material object.

Mariah listened quietly to the conversation, most of which consisted of logistical questions about what life would look like on The Ranch. How would they survive? Some wondered aloud, without all the things they were used to?

Get up in the morning, your feet land on warm cozy carpet (plastic) and walk into the linoleum kitchen for coffee. A glass of contaminated water comes out of the tap. It tastes weird and smells like chlorine. A pile of the empty plastic water bottles fills the recycling bin. You scoop up your baby, who you barely see, along with the diaper bag and formula in its plastic bottle and then it's into the garage. Drive the car, down the driveway, onto the highway, to the city, to the day-care to drop her off, and then to the office. From the parking garage up the elevator to the fifteenth floor of the carpeted and ceilinged steel and glass office tower. You find your plastic laminated desk in your plastic-coated cubicle and drink some contaminated coffee grown with pesticides out of a Styrofoam cup. This is where you spend eight hours a day, five days a week, fifty-two weeks of the year.

Oh my God, no operable windows, sick building syndrome mistaken for flu. Gotta get my flu shot! Mandatory now to control the productivity of the middle class work force and to maintain the efficient profits that our country is built on.

The bones of a dead construct.

The loud snap of a twig on the fire pulled Mariah from her mental rant. She raised her hand to signal she had something to say.

"I've been thinking a lot about my daily life back in *civilization*. It looked great on paper—great home, car, and computer—but was that living, or dependence? I needed that car just to survive. I haven't driven a car in two weeks now, and I feel freer than ever. Back there I took many things for granted; here everything is a blessing or a huge accomplishment. There, it seemed I *had it all*, yet I was really just standing on top of a graveyard—a pile of bones with a manicured lawn on top. This *illusion* is maintained at a huge cost. What is the real

59

cost of a barrel of oil? Is this a subsidized price? Or a real one? And the cost of doing business with the Saudis? The real cost of the war?" She looked around the group and knew they understood. "The cost of the lives lost in the war effort? The total American casualties...the total Mid East casualties?" She had stood and as she looked up, she noticed the moon was already out in the indigo sky. She answered her rhetorical question. "The war is about oil. Blood for oil." She breathed in the indigo blue, and answered the real question she had been asking herself for as far back as she could remember. Whose blood? What is the value of each human life? "Can we build a whole civilization on a dead construct? Should we?" She looked around. "And if not.... What? What then?"

"It's true," Pat said. "And for what? So we could have all those so-called comforts that remove us from nature?"

"Back home, a person could go days without touching the earth," Jody agreed.

"Speak for yourself," Jack laughed as he extended a bare, very dirty foot.

"After three generations of this, people believe the world is not clean unless it's encased in plastic," Pat said with a grim smile. "From doctors with rubber gloves and boyfriends with condoms to watching the world on TV from the safety of the vinyl recliner."

Jack chuckled. "As the saying goes, 'Cleanliness is next to Godliness.' Religion and our first world culture go hand in hand. Even God approves of the plastics industry."

"We're laughing," Rob said, "but it's not funny. Look at the 'Green' Movement. They push plastic products, saying they're low maintenance, will not rot, and will save a tree and therefore the earth. Don't touch a "real" tree you will destroy the earth. They are also selling acres of thick foam insulation so you can seal your dwelling from outside temperature. God forbid if air leaks into your home. Now people can sleep comfortably entombed in their plastic-coated houses. What most of them don't realize is that this is not a Green movement, but a plastics movement. The real problem is that people no longer think for themselves; they just take whatever the media or the internet says as gospel."

Mariah's mind wandered again in her dilemma. Despite all the discussions, she could not deny that she had left a great life behind in Houston. It seemed unfathomable that one could get in a car and in ten hours go from modern suburbia to an austere world the likes of which their ancestors had struggled against...yet that's what they had done. Mariah could already imagine the shock on her sister Kristin's face when she described the situation. It would sound unsustainable and even dangerous.

I have lived fourteen days with cotton and down, the earth under my feet and the sky above my head. I have not driven at all and I have walked everywhere. Or swam. My legs take me everywhere I want to go. The only plastics I have on are my chako's and the cell phone (out of service).

In thirty days they would be low on supplies. They would have to change how they eat or *starve.* No stores, she thought and felt the return of her panic, no rows and rows of food waiting to be purchased with a little plastic card.

Just then she felt David's arm go around her. "You okay?' he asked.

She turned to him, trying to assess whether he shared her fear. All she saw was a sort of peaceful confidence. Then again, David always had that way about him.

"Yes," she smiled, pushing her worries to the back of her mind.

Just breathe, Mariah, she told herself, *and take it one day at a time.*

CHAPTER 8 *Fireside Discussions*

Mariah spoke her thoughts aloud, "We live in a world built on the graveyard of the earth. An artificial construct coated in plastic and good taste."

"The reason the battle cry has become extremely loud," Jack said, fired up and slightly drunk, "is that at one time there were a handful of *first world countries*—in the Americas and Europe—and plenty of well-populated, poor *third world countries*." He untangled his arm from around Robin's shoulder and picked up his drink. "An economy based on the consumer needs more consumers. Therefore, those in the third world—basic, down-to-earth, you know, strolling barefoot on dirt roads with donkeys or rickshaws—are now being lifted up, educated, and cultivated towards consumption. Yes, '*welcome to our plastic store with plastic arches and have an imitation burger wrapped in plastic with plastic fries and wash it down with a non-dairy vanilla milkshake*—and we now take plastic. Hence the third world can consume themselves into debt, just like we in the first world have become so adept at. And we can encase the whole world in plastic." He slammed the beer bottle down to emphasize the point and succeeded in knocking over several empties.

Mariah noticed Robin smiling at him in a certain way. *What happened to Stacy?*

"Clearly, many yearn to return to the old ways," Mariah said, "even in this country. What about all those Civil War re-enactors? For nine months out of the year they meet each weekend and leave the modern world behind. And it's not just about the battles. They sleep in real canvas tents on the hard earth and use simple tools. They weave and spin real wool. They make hats and scarves and forge iron. They construct leather boots and make soap. Why do they do this? Because it feels good."

She heard the sounds of agreement from around the campfire, saw from the corner of her eye Jack's arm snake back around Robin.

"And what about the thousands of children who play violin each weekend at Suzuki gatherings? Just a 16th century wood instrument with a horsehair bow. It had a loud and real sound without electricity. Such young musicians grow up without any time for TV watching because they are practicing and doing homework."

"All the Baptists boycott television. Whole segments of society are trying to keep Christ in Christmas, avoiding the distraction of the tensile covered shopping frenzy," someone added.

Even as she listened to the words, the internal battle raged on in her head. *I could decide to just sit here under the stars like Buddha under a tree and refuse to drive back the eight hours into the repeat of the sameness of the world until it collapses.* It would be like living in a dream world, a house of cards.

But she also couldn't ignore the reality that was about to hit. She had been a leader, inspiring everyone to come out here. And with leadership came decisions. Like what they would do when the food ran out. Yes, they had placed seeds in the ground but they had yet to emerge. What if they never did? She was really an urban person. Who's to say those stony bits of brown seed could transform magically to green shoots and eventually plants, and presumably food? Did anyone really know if anything could actually grow here? As far as she could tell the trees hadn't grown much since her last visit. She was surrounded by optimists. That was it. Not a realist among them.

Yet, a few hours' hike away were lean brown smiling Indians, still living in the abundance they had enjoyed for the last thousand years. Sure there had been struggles, yet they had not only survived, they'd prospered, in their dance with nature.

Unlike the whites of America, who had cut themselves off from their roots, in embracing their new nation. Their individual stories, heritage, folklore, and folk medicine were lost. The Irish had the Celtic and druidic traditions in Ireland; Norwegians had their stories and customs delightfully retold and celebrated in the Tolkien trilogy. Those who had come to the New World had lost their sense of how they connected to the earth. The Industrial Revolution, with it factories, had further homogenized the people, as had the public education system. Russian, Swede, Polish, Irish, English, and French, all sacrificed to the *American mold*. Mariah thought of her Polish heritage; she'd missed out on the traditional three-day weddings and three-day funerals. She suspected the brainwashing began in earnest in the fifties, when the desired lifestyle was conveniently proffered on television. Men do this, woman do that; every living room has a bar cart; sophisticated people smoke; white bread is cleaner than wheat. And, all housewives obediently dumped Ajax all over their bathrooms to keep them clean, only to find out decades later how toxic such cleaners were.

Now where was I, Mariah thought, as she stared into the blanket of night. The pop from the fire brought her eyes into focus. She looked around at the friends she had come to know and love. Each lost in their own thoughts. She noticed Jack had both Robin and Stacy, one on each side.

"We are giving up life as we know it..." she said slowly, as if still figuring it out herself, "but we will be gaining life as we have never known it." Her voice sounded strong and calm with a surety she hadn't felt before. "The earth will most assuredly slough us off sooner rather than later, but today we have been given a choice. We can choose to stay here. Then what? Slow death? Somehow I don't think so."

There was silence for a space, then Paul laughed. "You think too much."

"It sounds strange," Hazel said, "I already feel more alive than at any other time in my life."

"Our pleasures have such a high price," someone said. It was Stacy, her face aglow from fire light.

"We have been selling the earth from the inside out," Mariah said, "pulling out valuable rich oil, a complex molecular structure from the center of the earth, and burning it. In the process the atmosphere, the ozone, is destroyed and our water is polluted." Suddenly she was keenly aware of the soapbox she was standing on. She hadn't intended to be, especially since she was preaching to the choir. It was to convince herself, she realized; voicing what they all knew to be true would harden her resolve. There was a silence in the darkness as no one could begin to justify the leap from the simple to the complex world our society had made. The stars sparkled brighter in the sky, Mariah noted, as if they had been listening to the conversation from their perch and heartily agreed.

"We have created inorganic substances, which are used until our landfills are overloaded with non-decomposing waste. We wrap baby poop in plastic, then not even human manure can biodegrade. Even the impoverished mothers of babies have forgotten how to use real diapers. Welfare children are given free diapers as a service. Poor folk used to be the healthiest because they lived on simple grains, rice, potatoes. Now the poor are fat and suffering from malnutrition because sugar is cheap and tastes good, but has no food value." Mariah was on a roll.

"That's true I read it somewhere," Pat interjected. "Some bleeding hearts were trying to get government funding for some very fat poor folks in Mississippi, yet they were having a difficult time proving they were starving to death, due to their obesity from over sugar consumption."

"It's my guess that the oil was not meant to be pumped out of the center of the earth and released on the surface. The oil must have another purpose. God created all of this. He created us with brains so we could comprehend how best to use it," Paul said.

"We have simply learned how to destroy our planet and ourselves with all these resources," Jack affirmed.

"The Hay field battle in Montana was a battle about the prairie. The sustainable growth of the prairie. The balance of which was destroyed by the farming and mega-agriculture that was soon to come. The Indians couldn't speak English, yet they knew it was urgent. They couldn't express the complexity of the delicate balance. Who knows if they "understood," they knew they lived that way, and it worked. It had sustained their way of life for thousands of years." Paul knew his history.

"Imperialism is always based on the upper class gathering riches at the expense and suffering of those at the bottom. Today those at the bottom live on welfare and Medicaid, paid for by the wealthy or the middle class. The middle class are the ones that work in a mindless frenzy and bear the bulk of the burden. The wealthy gain profits only by consumption, with welfare paid by the government with taxes from the middle. That way the poor can consume as well. Again profiting the big guys." David's tone was professorial as he summed up.

"Anesthetized society. No psychic can keep his or her intuition intact without contact with the earth. It's called grounding. Psychics know this. They stay grounded in the earth. The Medicine men and Healers are grounded. Yet the ordinary mortal is lost. At sea in sameness and anti-anxiety pills," Mariah said.

"Housewives in Suburbia survive on Xanax. While the kids with A.D.D. get legal drugs to calm down," Hazel pointed out.

"Today we have a choice," David added, a distinct note of optimism in his voice. "There are thousands of alternative communities, just like this one, and we *can* save the earth. Avert disaster. Lead a grass-roots revolution, one month at a time." He reached over and squeezed Mariah's hand. People turned to one another in the dim glow of the ebbing fire light, then suddenly Jody picked up the guitar and with a tune, broke the silence and changed the somber mood. The group burst out in laughter, and Mariah shook her legs and stretched. They had a lot to think about. Everyone began gathering their things. She would think about this tomorrow.

Isabella was curled up and quiet beside her. Mariah brushed her long brown hair from her daughter's forehead, then helped her to her feet. Isabella wrapped her blanket tighter over her shoulders like an Indian sage. She walked with her parents and brother through the meadow toward their tents. The moon was bright enough to see by.

"I got carried away," Mariah said, smiling up at David.

David squeezed her to his side. "I like it when you get carried away," he whispered.

CHAPTER 9 *Lifestyle and Farming*

Mariah found Hazel at the Painted Meadow-Yellow's group camp. Hazel was originally from the West Coast and had intended to go back there after graduating from Rice. Now, years later, she had found herself married with kids and still in Houston. When she saw Mariah, she flashed a big smile of straight white teeth.

"Hello, Mariah, what's up?"

"I was curious about your choice to come out here," Mariah asked. "Your children are still so young. What are they, eight? Seven?"

"Oh, Rosie just turned eight and Josh is six." Hazel ran a hand absentmindedly through her thick auburn hair. "But the children *are* the reason. It's all about them for me. I know I don't have much hope for the world we will leave them if we don't make the change ourselves. And that means *us*. Now. And well, me. I must do it. Not tomorrow, now."

Mariah nodded. Hazel had met and married Fred, an oboe player with the Houston Symphony. Now Hazel and Fred headed up the Painted Meadow-Yellow's, a relatively small group made up of two other couples whose children had attended the same Montessori school as Fred and Hazel's. The *Mellow-Yellows* Mariah dubbed them. They kept to themselves and visiting was the best way to keep track of everyone.

"I have some friends, several friends, actually, that never had kids. Will never have kids. Their line, their mantra is: 'It's not responsible to bring kids into a world with no future.' In fact, I was just talking to one, Sally, before we came out here. She was going on and on about how terrible everything was. She's a bleeding liberal, you know. And the *toxic this* and the *government that* and the mountain top removal. Her Land Rover is covered with bumper stickers. You know the type. She and Jerry are musicians, no he's a musician. Travels with a band. She does photography. No kids. Actually I hadn't seen her much now that I have two. She's older than us. She chose that life, and that's fine. But you know, in ten years, I could just be her. Complaining, smoking weed, and complaining some more.

"And I just said no to all that. I—we—Fred and I made a decision to have kids. Now I must do something. Do my part about the world I'm bringing them into."

"We may not even have ten years..."

Mariah and Hazel turned in the direction of the sweet, childlike voice. It was Melody, a young, freckle-faced woman sitting nearby; she held her five-year-old towhead in her lap. Like Hazel, Melody had also married a musician, albeit of a very different sort. George, her singer-songwriter husband, had played several Houston venues and over the years had cultivated a small but loyal following; even Mariah had seen him a few times back in her old life. Hazel and Melody had met through their daughters, Katherine and Rosie, who were in the same Suzuki violin class.

"...If people like us don't just carve out new solutions." Her honey voice cooed as she rocked back and forth and patted Graham's head. Then she was quiet. Her face serene, her mouth in a soft smile under her freckled nose.

Hazel looked at her a moment, then her face split into a grin. "You may be right. But right now we are here."

Mariah smiled too. They were here, and they would make the most of whatever time they had. "Yeah for us."

The three women turned on their seats and patted one another on the back.

* * *

The weather in April was perfect for the gardening venture, however, time marched fast towards May and by June the heat would be intense. They planned to keep the garden as natural as possible and the impact on the land minimal. The permaculture gardening method

Jack preached, advocated companion planting. This was the chance to test concepts they had discussed at length in theory. This way they could intensify the use of small garden areas. Berries and grapevines were placed next to trees so they could climb up the trunks. Lettuces and greens were planted in the shade. The tomatoes and melons could handle full sun.

Now they had to find areas for planting that could fit into the open meadows hidden by groves of trees and forest edges. Tree lines bisected fields, following natural waterways and tributaries. They mapped out growing areas a short walk from the main meadow. They wanted to work with the natural landscape, the rise of land, and the flow of water. The fruit trees wouldn't mature for a couple of years, but fruit would be a welcome sight by then. The garden areas were not large, but close enough to existing waterways they could redirect for irrigation.

The garden group planted greens, potatoes, carrots, celery, turnips, and grains. Soon they would plant the warmer weather crops like tomatoes, peppers, herbs, summer and winter squashes, melons, and cucumbers. These crops needed a lot of water.

Early the next day, Mariah went on a hike to find David. Her mind raced with new concerns. *The vacation is officially over. We must organize ourselves. We must plan how to proceed. How are we going to make it?* The heat was getting more intense with each passing day. It made the kids gripe, which brought to mind another concern. Children needed to be included in the structure too. A school of sorts? Mariah wasn't sure. She added *brainstorming* with the other women to her long to-do list. She pounded her forehead. Oh, she didn't need to be alone with her thoughts.

At the sound of voices, all these concerns that rattled around in her mind were put on the back burner. A moment later Mariah found David and Jack hidden behind a grove of trees that opened to a meadow, she stood and watched them work for a moment, enjoying the feel of the warm sun on her face.

Jack and David, having analyzed the water flow with the fall of the land, were trying to find a place to build a ram pump. This way they could gather water from the existing supply. They had already tried other methods of water conservation, including a cairn that involved rock piles, but Jack, experienced with ram pumps, said it was a sure thing. Mariah hoped he was right. It would almost be like having plumbing. Even more important, they'd be prepared for the inevitable periods of drought. The list of supplies to build a ram pump was fairly minimal. Next on the list was to improve the shower situation.

David saw her standing close by and waved. As she walked over, Mariah regretted interrupting them. She certainly didn't want to be drafted. She was glad to observe however, that solutions to important concerns like food and water were being handled.

She lifted a hand to her eyes to shield them. "Wait a minute; you don't have any trips planned?"

"Not tomorrow," David said, "we can have a great day together tomorrow, but yes, I promised some folks I would meet them on Thursday."

"Is there a way to get around that? You get a lot done when you're here. Everyone looks to you for guidance. Plus I think too much when you're gone."

"It will be a very short trip this time, I promise. Besides, absence makes the heart grow fonder."

"Yes, but presence makes the heart grow stronger." She smiled at her little witticism.

He looked at her funny.

"Don't you worry, I will think of a solution. Just leave it to me." She left them to their garden escapade as a whole cluster of eager wanna-be gardeners strolled up to join in the fun.

Mariah tried to focus on what she was grateful for, like her siblings being there. Even Josie, their youngest sister, had joined them after two weeks and quickly began working with the teens. She was also pregnant when she arrived, but thankfully, Becky, one of the original members, was a midwife and knew exactly what to do. Josie's son Mason was the first child born into their new life, and Mariah was indebted to Becky for safely bringing the healthy, nine-pound boy, into the world. Becky, a small woman with cropped dark hair had moved to Texas from California several years earlier, bringing her midwifery practice with her. Perhaps health practitioners, herbalists and midwives would sustain them without the need for traditional medicine.

Max's kids were proud of their accomplishments. Isabella's cousin Nikki was petite with black hair, thick and curly down her back. Her square, sculpted face had a pure, perfect olive complexion. She and Isabella were only a few months apart in age and shared the large almond- shaped eyes they had inherited from their mothers. Steven French's genes were strong. Anya was a few years younger than her sister. The family resemblance extended to the cousins making them appear more like sisters at first glance. Isabella, although with the strong features and the large eyes and mouth, by comparison had fair skin, and sun-lightened hair.

The teens formed a comfortable synergy amongst themselves born of working and living together in such close proximity. They took initiative, starting large weaving projects for winter blankets and wall hangings. Mariah was elated about how synergistic everything was. They spent mornings gathering plants and berries and boiling them down to make dyes. They experimented on the jute, hemp, and grain sacks they had with them. Recycling took on a whole new meaning. *Reuse* was the operative word.

Back in the solace of her tent, Mariah decided she would solve this planning issue. With so many people here, it would be quite possible to share the work load without everything falling on the few group leaders. Then David and she would both have more time. She didn't want the experts like the Coopers or Jack Java burning out, while newbies turned into helpless freeloaders. After grappling with times and tasks and abilities, writing and rewriting, walking around in circles with her hands clasped behind her aching neck, before she tore all of her hair out, she was able to organize a schedule of sorts. The end result was a chart with the number of tasks, the number of hours, and the number of people.

Humming with exhaustion and excitement, Mariah half-walked half-ran to Painted Meadow with the plan. There she found Pat, Robin, Melody, Hazel, and Becky hanging out in the shade. *Not for long,* Mariah allowed herself a small smile.

Becky was great friends with Melody. Mariah had danced often at the various venues Melody's husband George played for. Mariah sat cross-legged among them and waited for a natural break in the conversation. Then she launched into her tentative plan. Her enthusiasm was contagious, and the women spent the rest of the afternoon in discussion. They began with those structures and tasks critical to their immediate survival: the Garden, Fire/Water and Sanitation. Becky was most adamant about sanitation; many illnesses could be avoided by attending to it from the beginning of things. Remember the plagues of the Middle Ages, she reminded them?

For the garden, they created two- two-hour time slots, seven days a week. That accounted for forty-two work slots a week with three persons per each task.

The Fire and Water crew had two separate tasks, both of which had to be done on a daily basis. The first was gathering dead wood and fallen trees to be cut into logs, and gathering drinking water. The second task involved taking a boat across Jade Lake to the freshwater springs and loading jugs. The women figured that, with a team of two or three people, each task would take about an hour. They also decided on a schedule that would rotate each week. Assigning a three-person team to the sanitation task was a way to share the latrine digging and filling duties. They eventually decided that the Coopers, who had spent years planning and were well prepared for sanitation concerns, and had created the initial design, should train each team in the procedure. Digging would occur at the beginning of the week, then, after the trenches were filled, the garden crews would plant some native plants in their place. Voila! Sanitation.

It took several painstaking hours, but in the end they honed out the schedule. The women had compiled seventy-seven job slots to be divided among thirty-two adults. Each person would have three tasks a week, with each task taking an average of two hours. The chart they created was simple enough, yet to them, it was like a work of art.

CHAPTER 10 *Get Organized*

Each of the women took the plan back to her own camps, most of which were located in the *'Painted Meadow,'* so dubbed by Pat Cooper because of the red and gold wildflowers that ran riot throughout. Pat hiked back to Painted Meadow- Orange, which she headed up with her husband Jody. Hazel returned to Painted Meadow- Yellow, which would begin with the water tasks. Robin and Becky headed off to Painted Meadow–Blues. This group, composed of single adults, would take leadership responsibility over the tasks. Mariah shared it all with David and their family at Indian Point.

Impressed with the women's plan, the groups eagerly signed on. It took about a week for everyone to be on task and in the groove with the system. In the beginning there were only three mandatory tasks. Every adult did all the required tasks, with a teens help until they got the picture. Later they added Group meals to the Task List, which brought the list to five required tasks, five times a week. The result: each person worked five times in a seven-day week—once at each task per week. This arrangement would be crucial down the road when more people arrived. Everyone would be able to show new folks the ropes.

At first only lunches were organized, served at Painted Meadow near the dish washing center— People were on their own for breakfasts and dinners. Toward the end of the summer, after everyone had helped create an abundant harvest, the dish washing center doubled as the food distribution area. It reminded many of the farmers market they bought their veggies at when they lived in the city.

Gardening was done in two, two-hour slots, early each morning and late each evening; they had enough volunteers to get the planting beds in and new plants started. They began with a three-person crew plus a leader, but as the community grew and more garden areas were started, the crews grew, and soon six people were working twice a day. David was in charge of assigning the crews to their various tasks and plots of land. He wouldn't admit it, but Mariah knew he loved this system; it was certainly an improvement over the disorganization of the early days. Back then he was recruiting one or two helpers, and then wearing them out with four straight hours of gardening. The Intensive Gardening method had provided bountiful produce for him before. The beds were dense and crowded into high productivity with no room for weeds. The plants grew on their own. David hoped all would participate at harvest time. Many hands were a welcome sight after years as a solo farmer. Yes, this communal chore thing certainly had its perks.

The weekdays were structured so that all activities were completed by six or so; by seven, most were gathered at their home camps for dinner. Each group gave their dishes a cursory rinsing at their own camps, then brought them to the dish washing station every few days to be sanitized with boiled river water.

The young kids followed along to see how it was done. But everyone, age twelve on up was expected to hold their own. Meals were flexible in the beginning. Mariah's camp usually had dinner at home four times a week, and would be invited somewhere else at least three nights a week. They were still operating on the stores each family had brought with them; along with a huge dose of faith that all would work out. "*Everything's going to be alright*," became a sort of mantra. Some of the teens even began putting the words; "*Everything's going to be alright*," on some tie–dye tee shirts they were making to trade with newcomers. The teens embraced the Trade and Barter method of finance. With the thirty-two people in this initial group, plus some young kids, it added up to seventy seven task slots to fill per week. Each person did three tasks a week, designating approximately two hours per task depending on the team working. All in all, it was a big change from a forty-hour work week. This left plenty of time for folks to develop creative personal projects.

The Initiators were those who thought up these new projects; of course, they needed the manpower to carry them out. *Doers* were those that jumped right in to these and other huge tasks, often attempting to go it alone. Everyone else learned to join forces where they saw fit. Everything was happening at once. Those who didn't get a job they wanted found themselves fair game on an Initiator's project. Yet somehow, all that dreaded work was getting done. There was still time to play music, learn new songs from one another, or try something new.

In the beginning it was like a great creative stew—a gradual, organic progression with everyone trying to feel his own way within the whole. Eventually, each person began to see his or her part in the larger scheme of things and how their natural exuberance affected the others, a kind of self-perpetuating energy.

Of course there were enormous challenges, the largest being the gardening. David had been a successful painter in his previous life in the city, but it was time to take his gardening experiments to a whole new level, a whole *new* alchemy. Painting is like alchemy—you take some pigments, oil, and brushes and create an illusion. Where once there was nothing, a 3-D image appears. Gardening was alchemical too. A bit of dust and seeds, just add water—some sun rays of course, and presto, green shoots in abundance.

Gardening slots filled up first. This was a good thing, for the dusty, hard earth was going to need a lot of coaxing before it bore fruit. Secretly, people realized this might be the breaking point of their venture. If they could meet the challenge of this dusty dried up place and produce food, it would supplement the native wild edibles they hoped to gather *-or rather scrounge* -from the earth. Fish, wild turkey, and deer were abundant. But most of the group were vegetarian and ate little meat.

Decisions were easy because getting along was crucial to their eminent survival. The bottom line was: people wanted this to work. Everyone was well aware that while this system may not be perfect, other systems outside this domain—especially the *'American system'*— were broken.

As Hazel stated with that humorous note in her voice, "We are all adults and we're pretty smart at that. Pulling together is working." She flexed a bicep. "I'm getting more muscles from hauling water than I ever did at the gym. And I'm having such fun with my kids."

If someone offered a new idea, the group motto was, "Just try it." Give it the benefit of the doubt. If it works, fantastic; if it doesn't, no sweat. What's there to lose?

"Friendship," Jody said. "That's what we have to loose. Friendship and relationships are what we are really creating out here. If we have that, we can survive. I'm convinced of that."

* * *

Stone gathering was the first step in building anything, so it kept them busy in those early days. The tillers guided the young ones to remove the stones from the future garden plots. One day, as the "guys" were off stone building and the young ones were either helping or exploring, Hazel sat enjoying the peace and quiet of her camp. Moments of solitude were all too rare, and she was not about to waste it sitting idly. It was the perfect opportunity, she realized, to start that pottery project she had always meant to do but never had the time.

After a quick dip in the spring stream to cool off, she gathered some of the other mothers and they were off to hunt for good clay. They followed the meandering path of a tributary brook keeping cool as they went. They found a shady inlet near a grove of willow and maple trees. After filling the buckets, they collected as much of the clay as they could in their bare arms. It was enough for several quiet afternoons, experimenting under the shade of the trees with hand-rolled and flat clay forms.

"I have a new appreciation for the Etruscans," Melody said as her third try began to wilt. "How did they figure all of that stuff out?"

"Maybe we should keep hunting for different types of clay and soil mixtures to see which holds up best through the process?" Hazel looked down at the lumpy form in her hands. "This is all so trial and error."

"How come I can do so much creative work on my computer at home," Stacy said, "and with hands-on stuff I feel so klutzy?"

"Because back home we got out of the habit of using our hands, or our bodies," Hazel mused. Her eyes widened. "Wait. That gives me an idea. Once we have some small successes, and have passed our learning curve, we should get our kids back here. We don't want them to grow up without hand-sense."

"You're right." The other mothers agreed, and doubled their efforts, spending hours gathering clay, making admixtures, including river sand and sticks and then drying to see which vessels held up the best. They also developed some handmade tools to use. The work was steady and patient.

"I *am* an artist," Hazel said one afternoon.

Mariah looked up from her clay bowl. "I thought you were an attorney..."

"In my past, sweetie, my long forgotten past. As I was saying, this is all part of the process, you know. I really do appreciate some of our early successes...but when you think about it, it's all been quite accidental."

"You know it's cool that we have the time to do this. Discover and create with enough time to explore the medium," Melody said. "There are no real deadlines or any 'clients' breathing down our necks."

"No deadlines, no bosses." Pat chimed in, "And no *husbands*. Where are they, by the way?"

"Well, between the gardening and the stone oven projects they are being extremely productive," Becky smirked, "it's awesome."

"My kids are tickled to have time with their father," Hazel said.

"I heard the kids are being helpful." Pat wiped a hand across her sweaty forehead. "There's all the mud slopping part. You know, they layer the mud and straw over the stone form to keep the heat in. Kind of like a cob oven but it has a stone base layer." She smiled. "Then of course they all have to jump in the river to get clean. At that rate we're lucky if they ever come back."

"Ah, but they do get hungry," Hazel said.

"That is a guarantee," Melody agreed.

* * *

While Pat and the other mothers continued with their pottery project, her husband Jody focused on a more practical challenge: keeping things cool.

"We have to find a way to chill more than a bottle of white wine." Jody put his hands on his hips looking like a mother hen.

His wife looked at him and chuckled. Jody was still wearing the apron from a bread-making workshop earlier in the day.

"Haven't you ever heard of a spring house?"

Jody raised an eyebrow at her.

"You forget I'm from the South," she said, then corrected herself. "I mean the Deep South. The early pioneers would build a stone house right at the mouth of a freshwater spring, and that's where they kept their milk and butter. You dig it into the land by a spring about three feet deep. Then frame the base out of stone, and go up another three or four feet. It only needs to be about six or seven feet square."

"Of course!" Jody enthused. "We should make one near the dish washing station. We should find a tributary near the river."

"We could use some of the clay admixtures to fill the cracks in the rock. That would seal it up a bit," Pat suggested.

And just like that, they had a cooling system. Thus, the group carved their way into the long endless summer days.

* * *

Tristan had a lot on his mind. His walk between two worlds, he realized, had been as transformational as a Vision Quest. It was gradual, but he could detect the changes within him. The Indians way of life had seemed so natural, and now he had a new family. They had welcomed him completely.

The walk felt like time travel. The way the Indians live seemed old, timeless, but advanced at the same time. The world he knew as modern was antiquated and stilted. The world of the Indian was beyond anything he had known before. It made the *European*—'White Man's' world, seem heavy-handed and overdone in comparison. So much in life was unnecessary. Actions that distracted one from the main purpose and essence of what life was. As if there was a cosmic trick designed to waste precious time with meaningless toil. In the process Man's true purpose and destiny on earth was disguised, hidden, and finally forgotten altogether.

As he grew closer to his own camp, his thoughts naturally turned to his family. He couldn't wait to share his new found insights with them, especially Mariah. Tristan knew his mother was dying to drop everything and just move in with the Indians. He knew it wasn't going to be that simple. He hoped to explain it all to her. But still, he argued with himself. He wanted it to all work out, just as much or more than she did. Yet, just as he knew that he loved people, especially these friends that had come out, he never quite fit in. He participated in all the fun and work in a friendly way, just as much as the next guy. Yet, he held back. Always with the reserve of the observer. It was almost as if a second sense watched him as he intermingled with others; inside himself, and outside himself, at the same time. This coupled with the sense that he often had a feeling of what was about to happen before it happened—like he was somehow privy to some cosmic secret. It had always been there, but had grown more acute since visiting with the Indians.

Isabella shared his "sixth sense," though in all other respects they were different as night and day. He liked sunshine. He was full of fun and pranks and made many friends in the process. Actually not so much these days, he realized. He had changed. He might be too serious himself. He would have to give some thought to that. Isabella had always been shy around people. Like she lived mostly in her head. She told him once that she had thoughts about her thoughts while she was thinking.

He could make his decision. He was certain Mom and Dad would make theirs. Then there was the *big* decision, and that's what burdened him in the first place. He flashed upon the time when they had watched the Indian Joseph catch the fish. Maybe it had started way back then.

Those were the happy years, before the brutal murder of Peter. The years when as children they camped here every summer. He and Isabella had been allowed complete freedom as their parents de-stressed and reveled in the pure joy of being together. The two of them could climb the cliffs and explore the caves for hours, while his mom and dad swam.

He had lost the point here. He glanced up and realized his feet had taken him faithfully towards home camp, even as his mind wandered. The sounds of laughter and shouts in the distance warned him he was near. He could hear the bang of pots and knew dinner was underway.

The rhythm of the day was familiar. Back to happier thoughts. His old friend Andre ran out of the woods, a Frisbee in his hand.

"Play with us, Tristan!"

Tristan grabbed the Frisbee and tossed it in the direction of John Java. John jumped up and grabbed it. John was the only son of Jack Java, and at sixteen years old, the same age as Tristan. The two had never met until this ranch trip, as John lived in Chattanooga. John had large green eyes framed by long dark lashes that would make any girl jealous. He wore his hair thick, shaggy, with bangs in his eyes. He swept them back in the sweaty heat enough times to make an endearing habit of it. Sometimes Anya and Julia would do an exaggerated gesture to mock him. He was way too cool. He had been a skateboarder at home, and as he jumped for the Frisbee, his super baggy clothes threatened to be left behind.

Soon there were ten of them in the clearing, far enough away from tents to avoid a crash into busy mothers. They laughed and chased one another in circles, then Josh, Hazel and Fred's oldest, threw another Frisbee into the mix. Little Matthew was always running in anticipation but falling down before he made contact. He was an overachieving blonde toddler, part of Becky's clan. She had adopted him and he was a lot younger than her other two. Another fun evening at camp had begun.

"What's for dinner?" Tristan glanced at Mariah, then back down at Matthew, who he had picked up after another fall.

"You're back. Dad's here too. He returned safely from his supply run."

"Good, good. What's it this time?"

"Ram–pump, the parts are an odd assortment of pipes he can find at any hardware store. The Coopers are cooking tonight so I get a break. Everyone will gather at their camp in the meadow." His mother smiled. "I like this communal living."

"Did any more cousins decide to join us? What about Liz and Denis?"

"Yes to your first question," she glanced towards the woods, "but Liz hasn't come yet. She and Denis are planning to get married. I hope they have the ceremony out here."

"They're not even here yet, so don't get your hopes up."

"Well I know Denis will love it if Liz ever brings him."

"Is that Jonathan?" Tristan gawked at a tall young man with black curly hair as he emerged from the shadows. "Hey cuz, long time no see." The two long lost cousins embraced. Jonathan now nineteen, knew how to travel apparently, even though the families had become estranged. "Hey Mom, look who I found. Can he come eat with us at the Coopers?"

"Of course," Mariah shook her head, her heart full at the realization that her family was coming together at long last. She had been shocked when Jonathan arrived earlier in his beat up Malibu. It was clear that her and Kate's estrangement wasn't going to stop the cousins from being friends after all. He would join their camp at Indian Point naturally.

Her sister Kate and she had lost touch. Kate's kids, Tristan and Isabella's cousins, were older and could think for themselves obviously. Kate was long gone, to virtually another world, in her career as a New York super-model. She and Kate didn't see eye to eye as far as the fate of the earth was concerned.

But maybe one day....

CHAPTER 11 *Tristan and Mariah*

"Mom, I will not take anyone to Blue Spring, that's our secret," Tristan said. "I think everyone's having a blast here at camp. There is plenty to explore, at Jade Cove. There are many springs and caves there. But I've got to go now. Before it's too late again."

"You're right." She lifted her hair from the back of her neck and fanned herself. "Boy, it's hot today. I thought that rain when we first got here was a sign of a wet spring." She waved him off. "Go on, have fun."

Mariah surveyed their tent tucked into the trees. They were organized campers and there wasn't a lot left to do. She watched as Tristan's figure disappeared into the distance. Her breath caught as she studied his escaping form.

"Tristan! Tristan." Mariah called as she ran to catch up to him. "Can I come? I'm finished for now, and everyone's busy." She waited a beat, her smile eager. "Well? Do you mind if I join you?"

Tristan hesitated. She should go and see the Indians' home cave for herself despite the long walk. So far, her time had been consumed with all the newbies. "That's a good idea. It's about time actually. But you have to keep up."

Mariah ignored that slight. Mother and son walked in silence for a time. The path stretched out over the hot open plain. Heat pounded into Mariah's brain in a way that seemed to say *hide, hide, hide*. She didn't know what to say so she said nothing.

Tristan was preparing himself. The anticipation made his heart beat fast as they moved through the grove of maples and over the icy stream. He'd been tied up at camp for a week. There had been many new arrivals, with their number now swelling to fifty. This was what his father wanted—an open door policy—but it meant a lot more work for him and Mariah. So far it had been members' family and friends, staggering in from all parts of the country. This included Mariah's siblings and their children. Uncle Rob had joined in right away; then his Aunt Max had sent her two kids with Rob although she hadn't visited herself. Despite past circumstances, he still held out hope that his Mom's other sister, Aunt Kate, might come with the two younger cousins. He found their growing community exhilarating, yet he was glad to get away. There was a kind of urgency out there. Maybe others felt as his parents had about the stability of the world. He worried that with so many people the Indians might retreat deeper in to the forest.

* * *

The drums' beat was quiet and incessant - a low thudding echo in the deepness of the unexplored territory of the forest. The message was not a warning but a gathering call. The Indians stopped what they'd been doing, and via secret routes began to move silently through the trees to the gathering spot.

* * *

Tristan and Mariah intuitively moved in their swift silent way. Tristan veered off the familiar path and took a new route to the Blue Spring. By the time the two climbed up the side of the hill and up over the waterfall to get to the place above the spring, Tristan was ahead of Mariah, disappearing into the trees. He had explained to his mother that the Indians had shown him a new way in. By climbing above the spring and leaping over the crevice, you could avoid jumping into the blue water below.

* * *

Mariah was glad for once she wouldn't have to get wet; besides, she had anticipated this meeting long enough. A few minutes later Mariah came to a place where she would have to leap over the space and continue on the trek up the cliff. After a momentary pause, she reached for a tree branch, confident that she could use it for support. At the moment she jumped a strong arm grabbed her about the waist. She knew it wasn't Tristan, he had disappeared. She was about to cry out but stopped herself as a gentle hand touched her mouth. She closed her eyes and experienced a drop in altitude. In her heart she smiled because she knew she was being admitted, like long before, her son, Tristan had been. For a while she couldn't see and all was darkness.

"Relax, relax." He spoke to her in English.
The dim form before her became clear.
"Where am I?"
The Indian who brought her sat before her, legs crossed, watching her with wide expectant eyes. He wasn't young. He wasn't the Joseph that Tristan had described. The world seemed crooked and she realized she was on her side. She rose up on her knees in one smooth motion and saw they were on a ledge open to the dim sky.
"It's late," she said, half statement, half question.
"Yes, you have slept. You fainted when I brought you over. Most likely due to a combination of exhaustion and anticipation. You must have been tired. I was afraid you would never wake up." His voice was melodious and held a trace of an accent, but she couldn't place it.
  His hair seemed silver or white, his skin bronzed. His eyes a soft grey color. He reached out to touch her hand. Mariah jumped, as was her custom when being touched or approached by men. He reached up and brushed her hair from her face.
"Who are you?" she asked.
"I am Sunowa," he replied, like that explained everything. "You desired to come here, did you not? You asked to come. I heard you. I've been walking with you since you and Tristan left the camp. I have waited a long time."
Mariah smiled, "You look all silvery. Can I call you Silver-One?" She cast her eyes down and thought of her days as a young maiden. When she slept in a teepee, hoping to wake up and understand all. But she only got glimpses. Her whole life had been peppered with glimpses. A glimmer here and a hope there. Always another signpost leading her a little deeper in. But she never quite got there. Now all of a sudden, after a nice stroll at the end of a long hot day, everything happened at once. She tried hard to take it in; follow what he was revealing to her.

She felt sixteen.

"I watched you sleep in the Teepee, many moons ago. Years, in fact. I gave you a gift, a dream."

She started as she realized he'd heard her thoughts. As if to test this theory, she glanced at the purple amethyst ring on her finger, and he reached out and touched her hand. This time he picked up her hand and turned it over to study her palm. He placed a seashell upon it.

Mariah placed the shell to her ear to listen to the sounds of the ocean. When she raised her eyes, her face beamed, and she studied her new friend. He was watching her intensely. She heard something in those ancient ocean sounds. She listened. She wasn't sure but her mind raced as fast as her heart. She sat here in a strange place with a strange man. Her mind should be buzzing with questions, but she just sat, feeling oddly content and normal as she listened to the ancient ocean sounds. Some sort of hypnotism, she thought. Her new friend was friendly and funny. Gladness filled her with a feeling of kinship. Boundaries are different with him, she'd decided. We're not speaking, yet he is in my space with his whole attitude. It's as though he's listening with the pores of his skin to the pulsing in the air. His eyes, as well as his ears are tuned-in to all. She held her breathe at this thought. She tried to focus as a sea of colors, images, and impressions floated all around her like a mist. It was a mist mystery.

"I feel like time stands still, yet I am knowing you for a long time." Her eyes flew open as she realized she'd spoken aloud.

"I am not an Indian as you think. I am a man. I am cousin to Joseph, who is now with your Tristan."

She translated his meaning: *I am a human being, like you. Not separate.*

"Tristan likes Joseph," she said. "He has spoken of him often."

Mariah was aware that the mist forms had become figures, moving in the distant reaches of the cave.

The Indian didn't seem to notice. "My friends call me 'Sun-on-Water.'"

She laughed and he looked hurt for a moment. Then he smiled. "You know how brilliant the sun is on the water? Like diamonds. But when you try to reach out to touch it, it eludes you. I am so. Very bright and elusive."

When he finally smiled, she breathed with relief, letting air out in one long sigh. "I used to have a nickname in college," she said, "Sunshine. I know, it's kind of boring. Not thrilling like Moon Shadow or Spirit Dancer."

He had been thoughtful and serious throughout the encounter and she hadn't realized his humorous side. The sun broke through the clouds and shot a ray of sunlight into the interior. The last ray before the sun set shined deep into the cave, illuminating them. The cave was a slice in the cliff. Mariah noticed for the first time what lay beyond the entry. There seemed to be several figures and vessels of various shapes and sizes. Some colorful rugs were scattered about.

"It's late and it's true," Sunowa, or Sun-on-Water said. Mariah wasn't yet sure what she should call him.

"You and your people are living here at The Ranch, in the caves. Tristan and I came back here to warn you, we have brought many families with us from the city." Not knowing what else to say, she shrugged. "We wanted to explain our presence." She rushed her long thought out speech.

He laughed. "Fifty people now? Many car loads. Men, women, and children. You come like a herd of elephants." He looked very serious. "This is no secret."

Mariah looked wistful, "No, you're right, I suppose. But we have come, actually, to live here. And to learn your ways of survival on the land. We hoped you would teach us, show us. The white man's world– the world we have left–is crumbling. We hoped to embrace a new way. Out here...start over. A kind of second chance for those of us that know better." Her words rushed past each other in her effort to get them out. She took a breath. "This is your home. I'm here to ask permission and assistance."

He reached out a hand and silenced her lips. "Come. You have had a long journey and a shock." He rose, she followed. "Are you steady?" His eyes took everything in as he deliberately studied her.

She brushed her jean shorts and smoothed the bit of sand from her legs. Her fingers pulled through her tangled hair.

"You must meet the others."

It was then that she saw the two women waiting.

"Here," he said, "prepare her to meet the elders. I'll give the call." He bowed, turned, and left.

The women gave her friendly smiles but did not speak, just motioned her to a bowl of water. She washed her hands and face, drying them on a soft towel. Then they bade her sit on a rock like a stool. They combed her hair, and sprinkled sweet smelling water on it. She relaxed, breathing easier as they massaged her shoulders. Several delicious moments later, they handed her a shell filled with a special ointment that smelled of lavender and myrrh. One of the women rubbed it into her hands and arms, while the other offered her a different ointment for her face. Mariah obediently smoothed a small amount of the strange ointment on her dry cheekbones and forehead. They then stepped back and nodded their heads in unison and smiled. One handed her a shawl made of very light spun wool. The shawl smelled of cedar and stars as she wrapped it around her shoulders, grateful for the warmth in the cool of evening.

Mariah was glad she had briefed David on what may occur on The Ranch once they arrived. She knew she would have to work at the pace of the Indians. They had waited all these years to reveal themselves, and now was the moment she had been waiting for. She smiled at the two ageless women with long glossy black hair that hung heavy down there backs like a veil. They beckoned and she followed.

After a long walk in a territory that seemed at once new and familiar, they arrived in a clearing bustling with activity. There was a fire with men and women gathered around it. The space, surrounded by trees, with soft moss for a carpet, felt like a large outdoor room.

Under a midnight blue sky, she saw him standing tall and erect in a position of command. He emanated calm as everyone moved about their tasks. His hawk eyes met hers. His eyes were deep-set and fierce in the shadow of his brow. She stepped gracefully toward him, her long white shawl flowed from her shoulders to her ankles. Her legs glistened as she stepped forward. He must be the Chief, she thought. He was truly splendid in his dress. Strong muscles rippled in his arms and lean tan abdomen. She walked elegantly with her two escorts, conscious of his eyes on her. Nine Indians were gathered in a circle. Sunowa introduced her to everyone. With a sigh of relief, she saw Tristan there too; he was talking with someone. She approached them.

"Is this Joseph?" she asked.

"Oh, Mom, I barely recognized you!" Tristan threw his arms around her. "I'm glad you are alright." He pulled back and looked at her, his eyes shining. "Here, let me introduce you. Joseph, my Mom, Mariah."

They greeted each other, then Joseph grabbed and hugged her spontaneously. "I feel as though I already know you."

As they took their places, a hush fell over the gathering, then Joseph began to speak.

"Mariah and Tristan, we welcome you into our small gathering. We know Peter would have wished it so. Tristan has asked many questions. I am sure you are both full of wonder. We have requested our Chief, Nuage to address you tonight briefly with our story. Also, we can be of service to you, and you likewise to us. This meeting has been ordained. With much anticipation we bring you here tonight. First, our Shaman, 'Sun-on-Water', will lead us in a prayer to bless this night."

Small drums appeared and a light tapping on the drums began while the Shaman sang, at first low and mournful, then a strong, vibrant yet haunting melody. Mariah squeezed her son's hand, her heart nearly bursting with awe and gratitude.

Chief Nuage looked around at all who had gathered, then he spoke directly to Mariah and Tristan.

"We are THE LOST TRIBE. To you, we are APACHE. We have come here with Geronimo many moons ago. He brought us here to preserve the Apache Nation. Some of our members are very old and they remember the years of the great battle. Geronimo, along with Chief Naiches, led us here. In order to protect us, Geronimo then went far away as a decoy. He let himself be captured so that we could make this great land our home. We have kept our old ways alive. We live with the land, as reapers and gatherers. We have kept the old law and the stories alive. For over one hundred years we have lived safely in secret. The white man, Peter, who lived here before was our friend and his great-grandmother before him. Those are the two who knew our secret. The rest of his family has no love for this land, and as Peter had no wife and children, he leaves no heirs. His love for the land is what unites us. We hear news. The Apache on the reservation carry the name but not the way. It's as Geronimo said, they do not live Apache. Their soul is dying. Much has been taken. The land they live on is a mere fraction of what was theirs. Peter told us many stories of the white man's world. Peter's lament about the world kept him here and kept us Brothers. Before his death, many moons before, the changes were coming to this land, our home. He had all the legal means of ownership of his mother's land to keep this land whole, holy and preserved. Big powers were moving in. We had many prayers and many pow-wows to help him win the battles. He has gone to a higher plane ,but we have not lost hope.

"The earth is in danger. Our miles of wilderness are but a microcosm. This land that has been home to us for one hundred and thirty years is changing. This land too is affected by all the changes around the earth and her atmosphere. Our ways tie us directly to our Earth Mother. We nurse at her breasts our old and our young. Water from the spring sustains us. Animals are born and live and die here. The Deer, Rabbit, Turkey, Birds of the air, and the Goats are plentiful, as are the Fish in the river. All the native plants grow in abundance. This place sustains us. The caves shelter us. We have caves and homes far away, hidden where no white eyes ever go. We have raised six generations of our people on this land. Our numbers are huge. We are a much larger tribe than those on the reservation. Their numbers diminish from loneliness. They are lost and confused without *the way*.

"Geronimo has truly saved his people. He is still here with us. His spirit comes on the wind and guides our Chiefs and elders. Not even Peter had an idea of how great our numbers are."

Mesmerized, Mariah studied the serene face of the man before her, and it was only after he stopped talking that she noticed the cacophony of night noises all around them. He watched as understanding dawned on her. She began a slow smile which spread across her countenance, smoothing the furrow from her brow. He broke into a grin that lit up his whole face.

"Enough. You came to us for our help. Now how can we help you?"

Mariah found her tongue, "Yes. The earth is in great danger, also, her people. All our governments are corrupt. Yet now the noose has tightened, so to speak. I mean, it's arguable. All our degrees of freedom in the past were a bit of an illusion. Some would say we were always slave to the dollar. But now there is so little wiggle room we can barely maintain the illusion of freedom any more. It's like a game, and no one knows how tight the noose is until they try to move."

"This is no game." The Chief was serious.

"Our cities are not sustainable, at least, not in the way you describe this place. For example, if the population is locked into the city, the lifeline of electricity could be turned off. Everyone could die." She looked into his deep eyes that had never left hers. She felt his compassion.

"The groups of folks—friends of ours from the city—foresee this destructive path we're on. They all wanted to disappear. Leave the multitudes of tax-paying citizens behind and carve a new life in the wilderness, a sort of alternative community. This is the only place we knew remote enough. It's filled with freshwater springs and game. We have come as you already know, and camped by the two rivers in the open field. Our numbers have grown and we are forty-five or fifty, and growing. We have brought supplies and camping gear.

"I realize this is your home. I only suspected you all were here, but I had no idea. Now that we meet, I honestly don't know what to do. I would like your permission to continue with our plan, but I in no way want to disrupt this beautiful life you have, or your people. There is so much to learn, and I cannot guarantee all these folks will be able to hack it." She stopped at once, and searched his face. "I seek your wisdom and advice." By now she was almost pleading, asking forgiveness and permission at the same time. Bowing her head, Mariah sat back in her place on the circle and waited.

"Ah Mariah, *Wind Angel,* I am glad you have come." After he spoke there was silence. She felt a calm surround the circle. A night bird called and the wind rose in a wail. Then a lone Indian chanter began his song, his lone call in the night, both sorrowful and comforting. For a long while Mariah remained with her head bowed and let the sounds envelope her body. The Indians began to disassemble. In silence they moved away to melt back into the night. A hand lay on her shoulder,

90

and when she turned her head Sunowa, Sun-on-Water, was beside her. He peered into her eyes for a long moment.

"You must rest. *Sleep on it*, as they say in your world. I will escort you back to your camp. Do not cause your friends worry."

She acquiesced and glanced around for Tristan. "But what is the plan? What did he decide?"

"It is already done, you all are welcome. Wait little one, you will see. Tristan has already gone with Joseph."

She placed her small hand in his large one in a trusting gesture. He glanced at her feet.

"Here, try these." He handed her some moccasins. "Now run with me as an Indian brave would, and we will be there in a flash."

She agreed and watched his back as he led her at a slow trot through the woods. Soon the path was beside the stream, the moon glistening on the water. They trotted beside and over the stream along the grassy path and then saw the open field before them. The strains of music and voices of the campers floated in the night breeze. Sun-on-Water stopped and turned to her. She panted to a stop beside him, as he grasped both her hands in his. He searched her face. "It is difficult for me to let you go back to them. You are one of us."

Her heart filled as she grasped his meaning. "How can I find you?" she asked, "And when?" She hoped he would say tomorrow.

"Come to this spot in three suns' time. I will find you."

"In the morning?"

"Yes, you shall be my guest for breakfast...Wind Angel." He chuckled.

"Oh, thank you." Relieved, she wanted to hug him in gratitude, but stopped herself. He looked straight, erect and untouchable again. She bowed her head.

"Until then." He nodded, then watched as she made her way back to the camp.

CHAPTER 12 *Delegate – May*

The sounds of merriment grew louder and flames were all Mariah saw through the darkness as she neared camp. When she reached Painted Meadow she saw the usual group of singers and guitarists gathered around a roaring fire. Fire and song, Mariah thought, as she slipped in on a crusty log seat beside David. On his other side, Isabella had fallen asleep on his shoulder.

"Come here you," she said, and scooted Isabella closer in, forming a pillow on her shoulder with her new shawl.

David put his drawing pad down and put his arm around both of them. "Long time no see?" It was a question.

"Was I missed?"

"I told the others you weren't feeling well and retired early. I watched from a distance when you joined Tristan this morning."

"Thanks for being so understanding. I had no idea *what* would happen, *how long*, *if* or *when* it would." Mariah was glad she'd prepared for the inevitable meeting.

"He beat you back, by the way. I was a little concerned. He said everything went great."

"That's an understatement. He's a master. It's our secret. I have a lot to think about. For now it's nice to be back with you and listen to the music. My legs are tired. I didn't know I was so out of shape. Play, David. Play that song, you know I can't remember the name."

Someone handed David a guitar and he played rock-a–belly, with everyone joining in on the chorus. Mariah listened for a while. Her sleeping daughter nestled comfortably, but her mind was whirling with thoughts of the Indian Chief. It was unsettling that they knew her and called her Wind Angel, and she was just now getting a glimpse of who they were. Even as she half-carried, half-walked Isabella into the tent and, after folding her new shawl with great care, lay down beside her daughter, his words replayed in her head. She made the shawl a pillow and eventually drifted off to the guitar strains in the distance.

She awoke to the sounds of clamoring outside the tent.

"Mom?" It was Tristan.

"Tristan, I hear you, I'm coming. I have to grab my shawl."

She came out with the white shawl draped over her faded rose sundress, surprised to see it was still dark.

"Tristan, are you okay? What time is it?"

"We can't keep living like this, Mom. We'll have to learn from the Indians."

"I had so many dreams last night. What do you suppose we were smoking with that Chief anyway?"

Tristan laughed. "Who knows? You dream a lot anyway, Mom. Seriously, we'll have to learn from the Indians. Mom, aren't you paying attention? You heard them yourself. They have been here since 1880. What is that? Five or six generations? We must give up our ways and merge into their ways. Otherwise we won't make it."

"Yes, I heard you the first time." She adjusted the gauze light shawl more closely to ward off the morning chill. "But how? That's the question, isn't it?"

"Mom, no one else knows the Indians are here, just us."

"Yes, we will have to reveal their presence at the right time. After we see which folks have the stamina to stick it out. We have our schedule, we're figuring out our survival tactics."

Tristan rolled his eyes in exasperation.

"Tristan, I heard ten new arrivals came in yesterday—that means we're close to sixty now. Up to this point newcomers have acclimated well, but we're still in unchartered territory here." The camps were discretely arranged along the edges of the meadow amongst the trees. She suspected there were more people here than it looked at first glance.

Mariah chose her words carefully. "We—you, Jack, Rob and your dad—know more than most about survival and farming, but... we're so, so *white*. We still have our white western ways embedded in us, just like the pioneers who came out here two-hundred years ago. I don't want to repeat that. All of that struggle. I truly believe there is a new way. And the Indians have figured that out. Are living it, in fact. They have been here a hundred and thirty years, and there were tribes running around the Americas for over a thousand years before that. None of them destroyed the land. There is a way to live on the earth —a peaceful, gentle and harmonious way —and they know what it is."

"Mom, that's why we came out here in the first place!"

"Yes, but it's been like a vacation so far. We're still getting a feel for what it would be like to really *live* here."

"Agreed. Now you must agree that I need that Vision Quest."

"Wow. That was quick. Vision Quest?" Really? What next she thought. Not answering him directly. "They have revealed their presence to you, Isabella, and me. All of us have respected their secret. Look at all these people."

"How many supplies do we have left?" Tristan asked.

"It's hard to tell. New folks bring more supplies with them, and so far everyone has been eager to join forces offering goods and skills for all to share. Quite amazing, actually."

"Mom, this is about more than just survival skills. The Indian way is a way of *being*. I love the peace and presence I feel when I'm with them. It's difficult to explain, but I don't have to, because you've seen it for yourself. It's something intangible, and the more I'm with them, the more I feel something growing inside of me. It's almost like magnetism, the pull I feel. I keep going back." Tristan was on a roll. "We'll have to learn skills from them. We must also learn how to develop a deeper connection to all living beings." He paced in his enthusiasm. "Perhaps we could learn to track and observe animals in their natural habitat. And share knowledge. Adapt their ability to cultivate the soil and bring abundance from the Mother Earth. Most important are the native wild edibles that we can learn to recognize and use." Tristan's voice was urgent, "We'll have to learn fast. Our survival depends upon it."

Mariah was deep in thought, her head heavy in her hands. "I believe you, Tristan, I just hate to reveal the Indians' presence to people we cannot personally vouch for. What do I do? Invite the Chief to be a dinner speaker?"

"No," he ignored her sarcasm. "I have some ideas. I have given this a lot of thought, so hear me out."

"I'm all ears." She smiled and breathed.

He sat down in front of her, brushing his long bangs out of his eyes as he spoke. "It's like a metamorphosis. We must change and adapt to the new situation."

"I agree wholeheartedly, but how?"

"Let's begin with who we can trust *now*."

"Well, I see where you're headed, Jack and Rob for sure, and maybe Paul. They would starve before giving up." She paused for a moment noting the determination on his face. "You are right, we can't reveal any serious information to anyone unless they are completely committed. There are, however, those who are here for the long haul. We should name those the 'inner circle' or something, and call a meeting to reveal the existence of the Hidden Tribe."

"I agree. Let's have a meeting, a private one away from camp. With all of us."

Mariah looked at the meadow below. Dawn had arrived casting an icy glow on the dew drenched grasses. People were emerging from tents and tending to their small campfires.

"Up there, that cliff top." Tristan pointed to the bluff.

Mariah arched her neck back to see beyond the trees. "Up there?"

"If we get Jack and Rob and head up now, we can have a private talk."

"If you think you can get those two to wake up, be my guest. Just like that? Just 'oh by the way.' "

"Yes, just like that, blunt. It's a fact, drop it on them. Now, this is urgent. I'll grab Paul."

Just then, David stumbled out of the tent. "Good morning, everyone." He glanced around for coffee. "What's urgent?"

After Mariah clued David in on the plan, the seven made their way up the narrow stone strewn path.

Once on top of the cliff, David peered around at the huge view. "Texas is a big place."

"Whew," Jack panted, as he brought in the rear. "I bet we can see for miles up here."

"Yes, and we are truly in the middle of nowhere." Mariah was stunned at the reality of how isolated they were.

"Just endless sky," Isabella added, "Kind of mind-boggling."

"Look how small all the people are." Rob looked down. "Seriously, you got me up and out without coffee but this is truly worth it."

Everyone was silent as they watched the sunrise turn the valley below amber. Isabella hugged her Mom's shoulders as they took in the sobering view. "We had a beautiful meeting last night," Mariah told her quietly.

David smiled as he moved away to address his friends. "We came up here to share a secret with you. Before we came we told you The Ranch is a secret. Isolated and abandoned. Forgotten after the death of Peter. We have since found out that Peter had an even greater secret. One we were not aware of. Peter's dedication was to more than the land and the animals. We've decided to share this secret with you now, before we tell the group as a whole."

"Actually we're not ready to tell them yet," Mariah said. "You are our chosen few."

Rob looked worried, "Stop it this minute and tell us! I'm all ears."

"There is a lost tribe, living in the wilderness here." David paused, "Apache Indians that hid out during the time of Geronimo."

"Are you kidding me?" Jack looked around.

"It's true," Tristan stated flatly. "That's where Isabella and I spend a lot of our time of late. With them. They're teaching us."

"Have you met them?" Paul looked at Mariah and David.

"I have," Mariah said. "I've only spoken with them twice. But it was a transformative experience. Last night was only the second time. Tristan and I were invited to a Pow-wow to meet the Chief."

"Let me get this straight," Rob interrupted, "you met with the *chief*? Did he have a peace-pipe as well?"

"Yes, how did you know?" Mariah said.

"We are very serious," Tristan said. "We tell you this in strictest confidence. I feel they have entrusted me with their presence. We're in this situation because Mom and I believe we need their help."

"Let me explain," David said, trying to bridge the gap between Tristan's impatience and Rob and Jack's wonderment. "Right now it's summer, we still have lots of supplies. Everyone has been amazingly well prepared and new people bring a lot with them. It's all fun and easy in the summer. Sleeping outside, swimming, and bathing in the waterfall. But Mariah and our family intend to learn how to truly survive out here in the wilderness. Really live off of the land."

"There is a lot we need to know in order to be successful," Mariah added, "and this tribe has been out here for one hundred and thirty years."

"And no one knows the secret. No one knows of their existence," Isabella said.

"You see," Tristan said, "they believe, like we do, that the earth is out of balance. However, they know how to live on Mother Earth, *in balance*. They have been doing just that, and they have offered to teach us their ways. Instruct us in all manner of skills. Survival skills way beyond what you would imagine."

Rob was curious, "Like what?"

"Well, survival for starters. Change. How to be invisible, how to stalk, what to eat to thrive all winter," Tristan said.

"Hum, I see," he said. But of course he didn't, not really. All of this was hard to imagine, take in all at once. Mariah and David had time to get used to the idea, and even they couldn't believe it sometimes.

"The thing is, they want to teach us. They want us to know their ways. We are bringing you guys into this conversation because we want everyone to know eventually. However, we don't want word of their presence falling into the wrong hands. You know, someone comes out to play wannabe nature lover out here and when they go back, they blab to everyone *out there* what we're up to."

David nodded. "Our open door policy will be in effect for the next few months, anyone who can't hack it is welcome to leave. That means if the secret were to get out, beyond the few of us, the tribes autonomy will be compromised. Then God only knows what would happen."

"That's why we need your help," Mariah said. "We thought if we could have an 'Inner Circle' of eight or nine of us that could train with the Indians, you know, in secret sessions; the nine leaders could in turn train everyone else. No one would be the wiser about where the information was coming from."

David nodded in agreement. "For instance, Rob, we could say you specialize in tracking game, so you would train a bunch of us in that. Tristan would train a group in fishing. Jack, you could work with wild edibles."

Mariah continued, "It's more than just hunting and gathering we need, it's weaving," she fingered her shawl, "using all the parts of the plant, or making goats milk. You know we are pacifists, we have no guns."

"It's also about being physically fit and strong. Able to run for hours, climb cliffs and trees, swim at length underwater," Tristan said. "These are skills they do have. It's why they've been able to stay hidden. No one has spotted them. They are probably listening to us right now."

Isabella smiled. "Of course, few people ever come out here in the first place. When we do we make so much noise."

Jack laughed, "You got that right."

David asked, "So, are you guys up for this?"

Paul and Rob glanced at each other, then agreed with heartfelt handshakes.

Jack said, "I'm a little—no completely in shock, but I'm totally relieved. I love you guys, but I have been hungry a lot lately from trying to ration our supplies."

"You're in shock? You are the one with all the tall tales. I thought this was a plan made in heaven just for you." Mariah smiled. "These guys live abundantly. They glow with health. They don't need doctors, they have medicine men. Isabella, they have special creams and ointments, like spa treatments. They literally glimmer."

"I know Mom. I've been out there with them remember?" Isabella said. "Yet no one knows the secret of their existence."

"Seriously, we're only seven here. Do you have any ideas who else can join us?" Rob asked.

"What do you think of Jody and Pat Cooper? That would make nine. That's a good number."

"Five men, two women and two teens," Mariah said, "Sounds balanced to me."

"I'm sure all these guys are as committed to seeing this thing through as we are."

"That's the key, isn't it? You have to be truly committed to put in the effort."

"Some people act like they are on an extended vacation. When it gets difficult, or they get too hungry, they may just bail."

"Okay. It's a deal then. We will have our training sessions with our Native American brothers and sisters, and then we can disseminate the information."

"The goal is to have a metamorphosis," Mariah said. "Once all of us, or whoever remains, are adequately trained, we will disappear into the interior. We will then live amongst the lost tribe. Our knowledge will grow exponentially.

"This way, we will survive our first winter. In fact, survival depends upon a true transformation. We will let go of old superstitions and beliefs and be transformed. This will enable us to co-exist with all species on the planet and become one with the land."

"The land that trusts us, that hosts us to live here, and dine, and be held in the breast of Mother Nature," David continued for her. "At that time, whatever happens in the rest of the world; disaster, earthquake, financial ruin... it will not ruin us. We will have gone beyond that. We're orchestrating our own transcendence. Or shift to put it simply."

"I get it, like the earth shift. I get it. Whew, this is big. When will we move into the interior?" Rob asked.

"When Joseph and the rest of our Indian brothers say we are ready," Tristan said.

"Let's get on with it. It seems we have a lot to do," Paul said.

"If we're committed now as we organize and train, I'm convinced our transformation will be swift," David said in that almost hypnotic way he had when he was passionate about something.

Mariah gripped David's hand, her relief was palpable, "I feel much better. Let's tell Pat and Jody right away. We'll have our first training with Joseph together. Tristan, do you need to let him know?"

"I'm on it." Tristan beamed and took off.

The sun had climbed in the sky during their talk and began baking the land. The group barely noticed as they skipped down the trail back to camp, each lost in his or her thoughts.

The tent was cool inside as the cedar trees blocked the direct sun. Mariah folded her white shawl, fondling the fine thread and careful workmanship, as she placed it on her bedroll in the corner. She knew it was hand-spun, possibly of goat hair. It would be wonderful to learn how to make such a fine garment. She shivered, but this time it was with anticipation. She couldn't wait to meet Sunowa again.

CHAPTER 13 *Breakfast with Sunowa*

On the anticipated third morning Mariah awoke with a mixture of exhilaration and fear. Sunowa had said he would find her; still, she figured the smartest thing would be to hike in the direction of the Blue Spring. Mariah endeavored to be discreet as she packed a few supplies in a small pack. She must look guilty, she thought, everyone had wanted something.

First she stopped to check on the weavers as she'd promised Isabella. They were doing new experiments with color. It turned out that wild onions, when boiled with vinegar, had a wonderful hue. She stopped also because Jack wanted to discuss some wild edibles. "I think I know where to find some watercress," she'd told him, "but it's a ways so I'll head out now."

She took off in a light jog through the woods along an old road that paralleled the creek. She'd dressed in what had come to be her uniform now, black bike shorts and a tank top. Her thoughts were on the new task the "Inner Circle" had just worked out—training.

They planned to train with the Indians. They only hoped the Indians were on board. Her friends trusted her instincts thus far. She'd set up the first meeting, and pair up the leaders with teachers. Who should be in charge of all this? Too many questions.

She came out of her daze in the woods, the light and shadow of the trees stripped her path. She stopped abruptly. She strained her eyes in the bright light and dark shadows. She didn't see anything. What she sensed had made her stop. She moved carefully, it was a smell. She looked closely at the grove of tall pines in the woods. There standing stone still in the shadows, against the tree was Sunowa. She put her hand to her throat as she gasped. He had blended in well. It was the eyes bright and humorous that didn't fit in.

"Ooh, you startled me!"

He strained to hide his smile. "I said I would find you and you found me."

She looked around and realized the tall trees formed a circle. "We're near the same spot from the other night, aren't we?"

"Yes, but I'm afraid you missed breakfast."

"Sorry, I had fifteen tasks as I was escaping from camp."

He grinned. "Never mind. Here I brought you some flat bread, fresh baked this morning."

She smiled and reached for it. "I brought you something as well." She reached into her pack and pulled out a large peach.

"Thank you," he said, with a juicy mouthful. He gestured for her to sit down on the pine needle floor of the forest. "Today I will give you a small training. I must get to know you, then we will work. Eat." He wiped the juice with the back of his hand.

Mariah ate a few bites of the wheat bread. "It's good."

She carefully wrapped the rest and placed it in her pack. "I'm eager to begin. I will finish later."

He threw the peach stone over his shoulder, then stood up. "Good, follow me."

He strode ahead with a loose swing of his long arms and shoulders.

As they walked through the woods, he spoke softly to her. In a few words she got the idea. She followed him through the woods, matching his pace and step. With no idea where they were going, she fell into his rhythm.

She followed him up a cliff to a new place she had never been before. She stood transfixed by all that lay before her. The river snaked silver below into a hazy distance. The heat waves seemed as tangible as water. She believed this place had once been an ancient sea.

He was quiet while she took in the majesty of their surroundings. "I like privacy," he offered as he opened his arms wide and shouted. It was a strange long call into the wild. A bird was floating on airwaves high above them. "That is an eagle," he announced, his chest a little fuller as he spoke. "He lives here."

"I see that," she whispered.

"Tell me your plan." Suddenly he was all business.

"Well, we have decided on the nine of us we trust to train. I hoped some of you would train us and then we would share all we learned with the others."

"Joseph and Tristan have spoken." He watched her face. "I have decided to introduce you to Running Wind. He will work with you personally. There is a group of eight of our family that will begin to instruct you. The first goal is survival. This means you must learn hunting skills, foraging for food, and weaving blankets and clothing for winter. You bring your family and we will lay out the plan to everyone. I will continue to teach our customs and beliefs to all of you, every new moon. Heed this, you must always honor our Mother with the dance on the full moon. That is a ritual you can enjoy with your whole community. Everyone knows how to dance and to sing out from the heart the song of joy for Our Mother to hear. This is important, my dear one. Remember your survival is *always* at her mercy. You suck from the Bosom of the Mother. This is how she nurtures and sustains you. Man has always done so. It is time that you are aware of her infinite goodness."

He rose and stood tall on the cliff. Then to Mariah's surprise, entered into a lone mini-dance. He stomped his foot rhythmically and spread his arms like the eagle. He went around in a circle, his movements smooth and deliberate. She watched his ritual dance. His feet softly thud thudding in the downy carpet of grass on the plain. She had a weird feeling of déjà vu. She looked around sharply, confirming that she had indeed never been here before. She wasn't even sure where she was.

Then all of a sudden he lay on his back and laughed long. Finally he propped up on one elbow. "You see, your first dance lesson," he exclaimed. "Come on, dear one." He grabbed her hand and pulled her up.

"I remember once when Kristen and I climbed to the top of the cliff above the Petroglyph. Where you there then? Before? Had you been up on top like we are now, then as well? Am I right?"

Sunowa watched her, a big grin on his face, hands on hips.

103

She looked down at the flat, dry, rock strewn dust. "You know I felt someone else was out here back then. That was a long time ago. Wow." Twenty years she speculated. "I wonder what Kristen is up to now? Our lives took separate paths."

He was mercurial. He could go from so animated to stillness. Yet she sensed it was an active stillness. He nodded, his eyes bright, perhaps from the earlier laughter. With one more look at the fantastic vista, Mariah followed him down the cliff.

* * *

Today the Inner Circle would meet with the Indian teachers for the first time. Mariah decided the cave Tristan had shown her earlier in the week was the perfect meeting place. As she walked, she took slow deep breaths to calm her excited heart. As Tristan led Rob, Jack Java, Isabella, and Paul up the cliff face, she stared proudly at the straight back of her son. Tristan had grown up before her eyes since he'd spent much time with the tribe after his initial initiation. When they reached the chamber not far from Jade Cove, she and Isabella waited at the entrance until David and the Coopers were in, and then followed them into the darkness. Hit by the smell of musky cave air mixed with incense, they took their places on the dirt floor. The speaker, Sunowa, addressed them without preamble.

"Human evolution has climbed through four different brains. The first brain is reptilian: survival, War, Defense. The second brain - Mammalian: reproduction and family The third brain - Creative: Co-creation with God and with one another. The fourth brain - Oneness: harmony. Is being 'at one' with everyone and everything. It's also called the "Apothic Brain" in this phase; we are all One and Competition is no longer necessary." Sunowa sat erect, his silver hair shone like an aura, framing his serious visage.

"As you know, there are wars and all that accompany them still going on in our day. Mass destruction, genocide, and crimes against the species are commonplace." He paused and looked around at the shocked faces. This was a hard list. "All in a quest for power. Yet evolution has been continuing. Some tribes, or individuals that wish to evolve, simply agree to disagree with the mass consciousness and move apart and therefore do develop. Evolve; ascend gradually to a new level. There are many tribes like this I assume. We came as a group long ago when the Native American culture was being annihilated. Thus we made the decision to vanish and became a *hidden tribe*. It was how we could preserve our beliefs and continue to ascend.

"Since these are the ideals of our culture, it affects how we relate to the Earth. Why we tread lightly upon the planet. We have always held hands with Mother Nature. It is our way. Our Ancestors came here from Atlantis, they lived through the great destruction and promised our Creator God that we would stay on the earth and bring healing to her and her people. We have always held hands with Mother Nature, respecting her power and partaking of her bounty.

"As your community adopts the stamina and courage to live with the Earth, your mental attitudes will also open up to the fourth brain. The desire for atonement and harmony will permeate your being. The result is the joy of society with fellow humans just for the sake of it."

"Oh, I see, I see. I do see," Mariah whispered. Chills ran up her arms as she tried to grasp the implications of the highly evolved teaching coming from the articulate man before her. "It will be a sort of Apotheosis." Her eyes focused on the warmth emanating from the deep pools of copper-brown of his eyes in the tanned serious visage before her. "And I see that many on our planet are still at war. War is like a language that permeates our world culture, maybe the whole planet. Yet those are the guys that are in control right now, still after all these years. All these years since Egypt or Atlantis, we still haven't learned what the Ancients knew. The guys that are in control and govern are interested in a 'New World Order'. Not a 'New World Mass Consciousness Raising.'"

"Yes. And you left for something else," Sunowa said.

"Yes. We are close to this ideal, I can feel it. Our members are in the creative brain. The third one as you call it. We feel a great creative energy here. I see new ideas blossoming in our groups all the time. It is such a positive and empowering place to be."

"All the adaptations will affect the mind and heart as well," Sunowa said.

"How will you know when we are ready?" Mariah asked.

He gazed at her thoughtfully without speaking. Her own words hung in the air, dancing in her head with the desperate pleading, hollow ring. She gazed back into his eyes, warm like brown pools of honey, that made him look soft, accepting.

"We are honored to work with the nine of you. You have chosen well. Those that are here today are in a perfect state. We will give each a different teaching. In our way; in our time. You can in turn teach one another. Otherwise you will not have enough skills or knowledge to survive over the next four months, let alone the years you will need for the transformation. Through this method you will monitor the changes in your community as they evolve. If it's too much for some, they will leave of their own accord. New people will show up. You will not have to ask anyone to leave. Just leave each to his own decision. I predict in six months you will have a core group, solid and ready for the next step."

Mariah's eyebrows raised in question.

"We will join together; you will come into the interior. All together we will make the change." He looked around the room at the open expectant faces. "I can see it." He smiled and grew in stature as he imagined the possibility. "It will be seamless like a wonderful weaving of fine gold thread. By an extremely skilled weaver," he added. He looked back down to earth and glanced around at his audience as if surprised to find them still sitting there.

"*The Dance.* You will hold the dances, every full moon. We will dance at our home, you will dance at yours. You must know that for every footfall and drum beat pounding on the earth, your dance and our dance will be together—only separated by space. The space between us will grow smaller, in time.

"As each moon comes and each dance occurs, we will move into greater harmony and rhythm until finally, on the sixth moon, the October moon we will be dancing together. With each dance we will pound our intention into the earth. Our prayer will rise up to the heavens with the smoke from the fire. All the wood will not die in vain. The sparks will be our messengers. The smoke of both our fires will find each other in the night sky—smoke woven with dreams unique as each dancer dreams. By these fires and rhythmic drumming we will hear the harmony of your tribe. We will dance until all dissonance disappears. All sour notes have vanished. And all that is left is complete atonement."

"Yes, I can see that. I can get that. The nine chosen leaders are here: Tristan, Isabella, David, Jack, Paul, Rob, Jody, and Pat." She looked around at her colleagues, hoping they were all as eager as she to begin. "And me? Am I to train as well?"

"You can come with each group as you choose. You will get an overview of everything. Like a rover."

Was she not even needed? Was he humoring her? Her doubts raced in her mind.

He coughed at the look of utter dejection on her face. "Keep the world view. Let the others have the detailed specific training. You need to keep your mind open. Your vision like the broad expanse of prairie to which you were born. I know you understand a part of what I say, but just a glimpse. More like a shadow, enough so you can trust me. The truth is, all will gain clarity *only* through action. You must *live* the WAY."

She laughed. Of course, he had read her mind. "Hey, I've come a long way and I am enjoying the journey."

"That is the spirit," he replied.

"Aho," Tristan said.

"Aho."

Mariah thought she could detect a smile behind Sunowa's stern, stone-like bearing.

CHAPTER 14 *Tree of Life*

Jack waded up huffing, out of breath from the uphill climb.

"How was your day?" Mariah greeted him with open arms.

"I'm too hot and sweaty," he waved her away. "Good, good. It's exhausting. I have a new circuit routine to lead my group on tomorrow. Two-hour hike, run, and swim ten laps. And Little Bear had me do it three times. He said he used to look like a bear that's how he got his nickname. This will cure me, he said. I have to have it memorized. I'll take folks on it tomorrow." He wiped the sweat from his face with the proffered towel.

Mariah was speechless, with her hands on hips she took in Jack Java. "Well we were hoping you wouldn't want to eat tonight. We were planning an all-adult fast. Just feed the kids." She arranged two platters of fried potatoes and buns on the table. "They're the growing members of our community. We get to abstain. It will be a twenty-four hour fast if we go from breakfast today until breakfast tomorrow."

He was reaching for a skillet-fried potato, but stopped, his hand in mid-air. "Cruel, cruel. You guys are cruel."

"It was just a suggestion. No one makes anyone do anything around here. Think of all the calories you just burned and how much effort that was. Shame to put them all back in. Just for a few moments of culinary pleasure."

"What else do I get to miss?" Jack's face fell.

"Veggie burgers and fries. Kid food."

"I'm a kid," he pouted.

"You've a point there."

"How will I ever make it tomorrow?" He groaned in pain as his stomach growled.

"You can have a fresh blackberry shake and granola tomorrow for breakfast?"

"Oh, I guess you're right. I'm too tired to chew anyway. I'll just hit the sack early."

"Whoa, wait up. Your group is on clean-up tonight," Tristan interjected.

"That is not fair. Who is in charge here anyway?"

"Hi-five." Tristan put his hand out. "If I can do it you can. I usually eat every three hours."

Tristan was an amazing leader, Mariah thought. In a mere two weeks' time this was evident. Within a week they had the teams and systems down. They continued to get up with the sun. People were in groups training before breakfast when the air was still cool. They switched leaders every two hours until six p.m., when it was time for dinner. After dinner it was finally free time. Everyone was relieved to do absolutely nothing as it grew dark but sit around the campfire and tell stories. Thank God no one had time to speculate or worry about the future.

Jack and Rob took on the task of assimilating new people. Jack, usually a social butterfly, could talk for hours. But not tonight she mused. He got to know people well enough to ease them into work that suited them. They guided each new arrival into the right group for their interest and skill level. This way, presto, everyone acclimated.

There were plenty of jobs to choose from. Gathering herbs and wild edibles on walks was a daily practice. The teens were eager to share their new found knowledge, pointing out the virtuous plants from the poisonous ones.

The garden was another labor intensive place, but thankfully one newcomers gravitated to. The garden meant food, which was high on everyone's list. No more doubts about should I grow lettuce or buy it from the store? No more store. What will I ever do with all these tomatoes? Well there were plenty of mouths eager for fresh vegetable stew, or grilled tomatoes with goat cheese and basil. It didn't hurt that several chefs had defected to their small band of survivalists.

David insisted on using all the soil-science he knew about food and soil cultivation. He was an advocate of biodynamics. He had the skills and the science to produce abundant food—all naturally, of course. He brought the necessary biodynamic preps and now grew valerian, chamomile, yarrow, and stinging nettle along with everything else. A private person, he secretly planned to bury horn manure in the fall. Just a bit of magic he'd picked up. After infusing manure with the preps, the mixture was stuffed into a cow horn and buried for nine months. He planned to uncover it next spring. Some things he learned from Rudolph Steiner he kept to himself.

Other than that, gardening was practical work a lot of folks could join. David did rotational planting. New plants went into the ground while new planting beds were dug and seeds germinated for future use in makeshift green houses. Harvesting of baby greens, lettuce, spinach, and kale happened daily. The plants could keep producing until it got too hot. Then the garden group would harvest the lot. The cooks combined wild edibles with salads that were raw and high in protein.

David came out from around the lower camp, he brought some fresh picked nasturtium for the salad. "Hey guys, what's for dinner?"

"It's kid night." They all three said in unison.

His expectant smile vanished. "Adult twenty-four-hour fast. Okay. It's okay. I can live with that. I love watching people eat."

* * *

The next afternoon, after her time with the weavers working on a new blanket, Mariah was still on cloud nine. In her peaceful reverie she stopped by camp to get some cool water from the huge stoneware jug they kept near the picnic table in the shade. Rob joined his sister, he could tell by her dreamy look she was in a good mood.

"Hate to interrupt but there is something else I want to discuss with you."

"Yeah?"

"You are a bit of a taskmaster."

"Me? What do you mean?"

"Look around you."

She looked around at the same trees and dusty patch of earth. "So?"

110

"Not that many people around."

"What are you getting at? Spit it out." She was dumbfounded.

"Tons of people are at the springs soaking their bodies, tending sore muscles, and they're all limping around. They're burned from the sun and can hardly walk. Tomorrow is Wednesday and you're gonna show up all chipper with the climbing crew. No one wants to give up or throw in the towel, but today is Tuesday and my group is just three weeks in. The swimming part was the only part they could handle— staying in the water, underwater. Most people are pretty white and they're burned and blistered, sore, achy, overweight, and out of shape. This is the second week of training and the romance has worn off. It all feels like work."

"Why does that make me the task master?"

"You're the one who said mandatory work outs six days a week."

"I thought they would get used to it. You know we all have to make that trek to the interior and we need dedication."

"You know, I bet they are detoxing too. Look, they have a whole new diet. We eat tons of veggies and barely any meat," Rob said.

"It hurts now, but it's bound to be transformative. I hope. I mean I know I'm getting faster and more fit. I can actually swim underwater now for 72 seconds."

"You are kidding! I thought you were a floater," Rob said.

"I'm learning to go deeper."

"I bet everyone will turn in early out of sheer exhaustion after a good soak. I'll see you tomorrow morning. Just look around and pay attention. You might have to administer to the sick."

As she tucked Isabella in that night, Mariah asked about the cream experiment. "We may have some need for the aloe cream you've been working on. I might invite a lot of the runners to the herb study meeting after breakfast. We can spend time caring for some sunburns and finding a remedy."

In the morning, Rob and Mariah kept the groups close to home and did a gentler workout. They had relay races in the meadow with teams and winners. They ended a little early so everyone could eat a hearty breakfast.

"After breakfast, all of you come to Isabella's herb study class. We are going to take turns massaging one another and putting special crèmes on. We will make a large supply so everyone can take some with them. I should have realized earlier. I'm burning too despite my olive complexion. The sun's not what it used to be," Mariah apologized. "Rob is the only exception, he never burns."

* * *

Mariah sat in her cross-legged position, while beside her a small cluster of the Tribe conversed. They spoke in hushed tones. She wasn't meant to hear and didn't know their language anyway. Both Mariah and Tristan coveted the daily time spent with the Indians. The two tribes were feeling each other out.

The lilting tones of their back and forth had a musical quality that drifted into her consciousness like a soft lullaby. Indians left the cave gradually until only a few were left. Mariah glanced at Tristan, who sat alone nearby as Joseph had left and Sunowa, Jet, and the Chief remained.

"Come here, my sister and my son." Sunowa cleared his throat. "Come closer, my young ones." Mariah and Tristan came to the tapestry rug that lay before them. Sunowa bade them sit, Mariah kneeled and Tristan sat cross-legged.

"We have a secret to share with you. It would be a way, in good faith, we can help you greatly succeed in your mission to join us."

Mariah's green eyes opened in anticipation. She wondered what other secrets these people kept. The truth about their presence here was mind boggling enough. The Chief, saying little, smiled, as he proffered a large basket for her to peer into. The firelight glinted in his shiny dark eyes. "One thousand seeds."

"One thousand seeds?" Mariah peered into the straw basket.

He put his hand over his mouth as if he was barely able to contain himself.

"For you. Our gift for you."

Jet put his hand in the basket and let the round golden seeds no bigger than pebbles slip through his fingertips. They watched and listened to the quiet shhh sound of the seeds sifting through.

"The Tree of Life," he said, "Our secret is the Tree of Life."

Jet then moved a two-foot plant that was sitting in another basket. He moved it in front of his Chief. "This small plant grows tall and becomes a tree. The leaves, the seed, the flower, the stalk." His large hands caressed the parts of the plant as he spoke. It had a thin stalk with many slender, pale green leaves with serrated edges. He gestured to the flower, which resembled a lotus blossom gone in a crazy frenzy.

"I could give you this plant. From this one plant you could do much. From this plant you can make cloth from the fiber. You can make medicine from the flower, you can take nourishment from the seed. The seed can be ground to make flour for bread. This is the bread we have just eaten. The nuts can be ground to a fine powder, and with water added you have a type of milk. With a fermentation process this milk can become cheese."

"Oh, like they do with soybeans to make tofu," Tristan said. This made sense, a plant that could be used as a staple. "That's good if you don't want to keep animals around for milk and cheese. Whole oriental cultures have the soybean as a staple. Perhaps this is from the bean family. Or maybe it's something native to this area..." His voice trailed off.

Mariah watched the old Chief, his hair silver-grey and thinning, his headband a colorful weave, his shirt an intense purple-pink. The bright colors suited him as he was always smiling.

He pushed the basket towards her. "Not to eat," he said. "To grow. You need this plant in the moist soil of Mother Earth. You grow many trees with this seed. You plant in the new moon. You water much for three weeks." He dusted his hands, "Leave it. It will grow. This one moon." He pointed to the tender plant beside him. You grow big in three moons. Then cut it down! Collect the flowers, collect the seeds, cut the leaves, and let them dry. We will show you. Now you take your plant."

Mariah was wearing the white shawl the women had given her at the first meeting. She wore it every time they came. She slept with it as well. It was made of a miraculous fiber. It kept her warm in the

113

chill nights and felt comforting to put on after an evening swim. It was surprisingly absorbent despite the thin weave.

He smiled. "Yes. That cloth comes from fibers woven from this plant. The *Tree of Life*, I tell you." He smiled and rocked back and forth like he had some private joke.

Mariah was used to such treatment. She was gullible. "I thought it was alpaca or cashmere at the very least."

Jet looked at her and shook his head. "No. We eat plants and we weave plant fibers. We are isolated here, we have no llama."

The Chief offered his arm to her. She reached out to touch the colorful fabric. It was soft and fine like silk. It seemed unlikely but she smiled and nodded.

"There are many things we can teach you. But first take this gift and plant it."

Mariah looked at Tristan. "He is giving us another gift, a highly prized possession, what do we give in return right now?"

The Chief conferred with Jet and Sunowa. The Chief was pointing at Tristan, holding up his fingers.

"He wants Tristan to come live with us and take a Vision Quest for two weeks. Also, he wants a tree that you grow to be given to him at the time of the Harvest. In three months you give him three trees from your harvest. Then we will show you what must be done," Jet translated.

Tristan nodded, "Of course I will attend the Vision Quest. It will be my honor."

Mariah smiled her ascent.

The Chief, nodded, he did not smile but Mariah felt his pleasure. Then he lit the pipe. The small circle sat in silence as they passed the sacred pipe. Mariah guessed this is how we seal the agreement. Jet secured the lid in place on the basket of seeds. Mariah realized the basket had a long strap attached making it easy to carry if she slung it over her shoulder.

Mother and son walked back to camp as in a fog. Mariah felt dreamy, as if her head were floating in the sky like a balloon. She glanced up at the night stars studded across the sky like a cosmic wonder right above their heads. When you studied the sky in the daytime it felt far away and removed; at night, though, planets seemed so close to the earth. Her head arched back and her neck ached as she studied the sky while they walked, one foot in front of the other. Her body was the string delicately balanced on the earth like a tendril. They knew the way, they didn't need lights. The shimmer of the stars, the intense brilliance was mesmerizing. She broke the silence with a question. "What do you suppose is in that peace pipe they pass?"

"I'm not sure, but it's nothing you or I have ever had before."

"I'm sure you're right. It's not tobacco. If it's the 'sacred herb', it must be the purest version, or their own blend." Mariah wrapped her shawl tight around her in the cool air. Life went on and she would learn to roll with it.

CHAPTER 15 *Painter/Farmer*

"David, what does every farmer need to excel at his profession?"

Mariah looked over David's shoulder at the new watercolor sketch he was doing. It was rare he had a moment between work and too dark to see, so she hated to interrupt.

"Hmm? Soil?"

"You are listening. Nice sketch. Well yes, but guess. Something else."

"I don't know, I give up."

Mariah didn't speak.

"Aren't you going to tell me?"

Mariah threw up her hands. "SEEDS. I have brought you seeds from the Chief."

"Wonderful. Corn? Potatoes? Something we can eat I hope?"

Mariah thought that would have been helpful. "Well, not exactly. The 'Tree of Life.'"

"Come again? Have you gone biblical on me?"

"Yes, exactly. Just like in the Bible, 'The Tree of Life.' Here just take a look. One thousand seeds. We must plant them in the new moon."

"Great, perfect timing. That's tomorrow. One thousand seeds tomorrow." He threw the pad down. "How are we going to do that?"

"With help. We have new recruits. More people to feed and more food to feed them, perfect timing. I was laughing because I was thinking this is a real exercise in patience. We are planting seeds and waiting for trees to grow. That will take a while. I guess they are expecting us to be here for a good long time. Then he says we can harvest them in three months. Some tree. You can harvest them for all these cool properties in just three months; like cloth or cheese and medicine too." She then recited Jet's detailed list.

"Okay," David said. "What did you trade for the honor?"

"Our first born son. We just have to give the Chief our first born son for a couple of weeks."

"What if he marries him off to his daughter?"

"You have a sense of humor today."

"I like getting gifts, especially seeds. This makes me happy. I'm a farmer after all."

"You used to be an artist."

"I am an artist. I have been concocting the perfect admixtures for our soil here. Did they tell you anything about planting all of this?"

"We have to do it. It's a must. The most important gift they can give us. It's a first and it is essential. We plant them and water very well for three weeks. Then we let nature do what she does deep in the darkness of the soil. And presto, little trees."

"I still can't believe it. You just traded our first born son for a basket full of seeds."

"It's just for two weeks." Mariah paced, stirring up dust. "Anyway he's already sixteen. It's an immeasurable benefit for him. We won't be living in the dark here forever. My baby is growing up. That is a sobering thought. C'mon. They have been patient. They've been asking since we first got here. Now they are negotiating. They must think our son has a great destiny."

"So, what did you say?"

"Hell yes. I said yes. I know them all much better now." Mariah went on to explain. "You see, Tristan has decided to scout out the interior of The Ranch in order to locate a suitable location for winter. While away, he'll be absorbing everything from the Indians, but when he returns, he can tell everyone that he located the perfect wintering spot."

"What are you...oh, that's right. You and I know where he's going, but two weeks is a long while. He must have an alibi."

"When he returns he'll say he found an abandoned settlement," Mariah said.

"Or not. Who knows what it will be like?" David said.

"The Anointing Oil is prepared. It's made with flowers from the Tree of Life, olive oil, cinnamon and special herbs."

"Regardless, he will be leaving in the next day or two."

Having arranged Tristan's long awaited Vision Quest, Mariah pondered her next task.

"Isabella, I have a bit of a problem. Kind of a fun one. We must have an Indian Pow-wow. We can do it on our own. You know, with our own take on all the main points. Keep it fun and casual. Our Indian friends will have their own dance at their site. I suggest a Five Rhythms dance. I'm not sure how to make it legit."

"What's the occasion for their dance?"

"They have one every month on each full moon. I'm not sure how it's supposed to be set up. The dance is a Sacred Ceremony, you know, to honor Mother Earth. I don't know all the rules. I had hoped the right intentions would make it work."

As they spoke, mother and daughter paced around the fire circle at Indian Point to see if it would be big enough.

"I know quite a bit about it," Isabella said. "I googled it when we still lived back home. We should make a circle out of stones and honor the six directions: North, East, South, West, and Grandmother Earth and Grandfather Sky. It's actually called a medicine wheel."

"Then we dance... no first we have drums. Drums, shakers, and flutes." Mariah said. "I could mix in a little Capoeira. Let the spirit lead us."

"Yes, and like the Five Rhythms it will be cathartic."

The two high-fived each other, they had this one.

"What's all the commotion, big sister?" Rob asked as he moved over to eat his desert of fresh peaches drizzled with lavender, honey, and walnuts, beside Mariah.

The dinner conversation between David and Mariah was loud. Was the perfect couple getting a little testy? Mariah hadn't intended it to be. She was letting off steam after planning their first dance. Designing the medicine wheel, had invigorated her.

"I was just suggesting to David that we grow some grapevines."

"I think we should stick to local foods," David replied, "and besides, whoever heard of grapes in west Texas?"

"I understand a vineyard is very labor intensive." Mariah smiled as she tried to soften her approach.

"I haven't seen you working in the garden lately," David observed. "So you shouldn't really have a say in what's grown."

"It's not that I don't appreciate the harvest we are producing," she said, and she meant it. The trees and vines were in place for an abundant crop of peaches and blueberries the following year. "What I'm saying came out all wrong."

Jack spoke up. "I'm very much on the garden crew. I'm intrigued, what do you know about grapevines?"

"Nothing, except for what Mariah just said, they are very labor intensive and you have to find the right varietal. Tell me," David said, leaning forward, "have you ever heard of Texas wine?"

"Yes, actually. In fact, Texas is one of the top five wine producers in the nation, and I would sure like to have some of it." He smiled and turned to Mariah. "What's your impulse for this latest inspiration?"

"Well, there are places in Italy this hot and dry and they are big wine producers. France is the same latitude as Texas, and they practically invented wine."

"Next you'll say *your* ancestor invented it. Now you want to make wine. Aren't you ever satisfied?" David asked.

"Yes. No. I mean yes wine would be good and no I'm always striving, pushing for more. What's wrong with that anyway?"

"It's exhausting. Your desire for change is exhausting." To emphasize the point, David wiped a hand across his sweaty brow.

"I'm an idea person. Ideas just pop in my head and I don't ask why, I say why not?"

"Ideas just pop in your little head – pop, pop, pop – and I have to explain why not. I repeat, it's exhausting. Why don't you just pop over there and get me a beer?"

Mariah rolled her eyes. She knew he knew they didn't have beer.

"Okay, okay," Rob joined the conversation, his hands held up like a referee. "So far we have Italy is hot and dry. Is that all?"

"Well nothing has ever grown here, right? I mean, that's why all the dirt farmers gave up and moved to town. But look at all the stuff we are growing successfully. We have cantaloupes and watermelons on the

120

way, as well as beans, wheat, corn, and potatoes. If those other farmers had been this successful ...," Mariah said.

"Oh I get it, if everything else has been a first, then why not expand and do a vineyard?" Rob asked.

"Not a whole vineyard, just some grape vines," Mariah said. "Do you know any wine makers?"

Rob smiled. "Now we are getting somewhere."

"But it's labor intensive, all the bugs, mildew issues, and pruning that must go on," David frowned.

"But we have labor," Mariah said. "That's my point. If it was just the two of us and our two kids, it would not be possible. But I heard the garden crews were reaching record numbers. Kids can join in with their parents." Mariah swiped her own hot face. "Mildew? Texas is dry heat."

"It's true," Rob said, "many families came here because their homes were foreclosed on and they were broke. The idea of creating fresh food appeals to those who have been starving a bit or living on cans of chili-beans poured over popcorn. I don't know why we have lots of garden labor. Perhaps because something's take more skill, like pottery and weaving? Food is an immediate survival need. Everyone benefits from the garden." Rob looked at David. "What do you think? It's your call."

"I'll look into what varietals will grow in this type of climate."

"Thanks," Mariah shrugged. "It would be great if we could learn to make wine."

When everyone had gone back to their private conversations, David said, "I know we have help now. But do you really believe all these people are going to stick it out? It's summer. Most of them are on vacation. When summer's over, who will want to hack this lifestyle?"

"We'll see. We will see." Mariah's eyes traveled to the fire then back to David. "Don't forget we have our first dance tomorrow night. Perhaps we can dance about it? You know the grapevine issue?" She felt a chill and leaned her body toward the warm blaze. "David, the chill night air is another thing that's good for wine."

"When did you become such a sommelier? And the French didn't *invent* wine by the way," David wined, then changed his tune. "Come here, I'll keep you warm."

Mariah felt a bit apologetic as she snuggled in for warmth. "Tristan will dance with us. It will be the perfect send-off before his trip."

"That it will." David mused.

CHAPTER 16 *The First Dance*

Tristan joined the other teens, Jonathan, Ian, and John to gather stones for a proper medicine wheel. Jack and Paul got there in time to direct all the momentum. They helped cut logs and gathered brush. Rob stacked the logs like a log cabin. Everyone got into the festivities. Jody baked corn bread, and Sean made some Indian flat-bread in the stone ovens. The girls hummed as they waved the smoking clumps of herbs and sage tied with string over each person before they joined the circle. Rob waved a hawk wing fan to direct the smoke.

By the time the sun set, the smell of sage wafted strong around the gathering at Indian Point. Rob did the honors and set a match to the dry wood that burst into a fine blaze. Ian led the musicians, beginning with a steady drum beat. His dark curly head nodded to the rhythm as he played. The chanting continued as the crowd honored all six directions. The cedar aroma brought them all back to memories of years spent around a warm blaze. Mariah remembered her father's stories. Isabella smiled at her mom as she thought about her own childhood.

Childhoods spent finding stories in the burning flames, as one finds shapes in the clouds, was a family tradition.

Suddenly, everyone broke loose. The musicians jammed and the crowd began to dance freestyle. At first four or five broke from the regular steady footfalls. Soon it caught on and everyone joined in. Musicians and drummers traded out to keep the continuous flow of music and drumming going. Mariah danced or played the flute in turns. Adrenaline ran high.

After what seemed like hours, the couples, exhausted from dancing, gathered back at the bonfire. The timing for the Dance had been perfect. A new bunch of ten, who had intended to start their own commune, arrived from Alabama. They decided instead to try their luck at the Ranch.

"Do you guys have this much fun all the time?" One of them asked Mariah.

"No. This is our first official dance/pow-wow. We don't really know what we're doing. We just play by ear."

Small groups formed as people, flushed and sweaty from the dance, strolled back to the home base-camp at Lower Meadow, leaving the teens to make music at the fire circle.

The newcomers were eager to hear how the community began.

Jack and Stacy walked up, swinging clasped hands, it made them seem younger than their forty-plus years. "We are so happy to be here. We wanted to let you know," Stacy said.

"I spent ten years, disappearing, getting off the grid, cutting credit cards, becoming self-employed," Jack said.

"Becoming self-sufficient and self-reliant," the Coopers finished for him as they came up right behind them.

Pat Cooper explained the name Painted Meadow was due to the reds and gold's of wild flowers mixed in with grasses.

"This is America. Let freedom reign," Stacy shouted out to the darkness. "Lots of us have studied Indian and early pioneer ways."

"That was our whole intention in the first place," Paul said. "It's the American way. The early pioneers fled the corrupt governments for good reason. There seemed to be nowhere to go. I never thought I'd be grateful for identity theft but I think it's actually helped." He smiled, adding, "Some folks want it. So be it."

"Independence is the prime motivator." Mariah's brow furrowed as she tried to share.

"All the early pioneers really wanted was their own humble spot of land," David said, "to sustain themselves, and their independence. Freedom, that's what my ancestors wanted two-hundred years ago. They ended up on Cherokee land."

"Somehow it's all become twisted in the struggle for wealth, power, and ownership," Mariah said.

"That must change. The Earth cannot sustain herself in this pattern of things. And if she cannot sustain herself, then where are we?" Jack asked.

"So the power structure as we know it today won't always be that way?" Mariah asked.

"We have got to go back to the garden. It's a new Millennium. We have to get back in," David replied.

"Is this the Garden?" Mariah wondered aloud.

David looked at her. "What do you think?"

"You know what I think."

"It's true." Pat Cooper joined in.

"I'm suddenly afraid," Hazel said.

"They want you to be afraid. That's the big power they have over us," Pat said. "FEAR. Fear that there is not enough. Not enough food, shelter, energy."

David continued the theme. "Fear of the darkness. Supply us with electricity forever to get rid of the Dark."

"It's a myth," Jody responded. "The myth we have all bought in the past two hundred plus years."

"I've seen it, Mom," Isabella said, "a haze of pollution so thick that the sun is nearly gone by day. Streetlights are needed by day and electric lights are on all the time."

"Oh my God," Jack wailed, "solar collectors won't be able to work at that rate."

"And people sleep like sardines on the concrete balconies of tall multi-story tenement structures that stretch acre after acre," Mariah offered. "I've seen it in my dreams."

Jack said, "I've seen it too. Ocean water so full of oil, junk, refuse from boats, submarines, and scum. A junk ocean with barnacles attached to every metal surface. Water, a shiny, steely grey oil slick under a sunless sky."

Jody added, "You've convinced me."

People gathered at a leisurely pace, coming from the darkness into the light of the fire pit at Painted Meadow.

"That's why we came here," Paul said. "We wanted to make a quiet effort, a unified front of non-participation in the economics of the world structure as we know it today. I thought that if we could come out and live in some forgotten unspoiled piece of nature, far from every city or town or people, we could pay homage to *Life for life's sake*. Do you know what I mean?"

"We could live to thrive in nature's natural abundance," Hazel said, as she opened her arms to their surroundings.

Jack watched her in amazement. Dancing all night had really opened her up. She spun around in a circle, her arms wide. He'd never seen her express herself without words.

Mariah, who had been studying the dirt, looked up. "Beauty beating like a pulse." Her eyes shone as she smiled. Her look was part winsome and part mischievous.

David smiled proudly at his wife. "That's why they called you Sunshine in college."

"You may be surprised," Rob added, "that some folks were on the brink of losing their homes. They had already lost their jobs. It has been tough to make it out there for some. This place is a lifesaver for them. Otherwise they would just be homeless. Working hard here is their last hope for any kind of life."

"I hadn't thought of that," Mariah said, and from the other's expressions she saw that they hadn't either. It was a sobering thought.

"You haven't met a lot of the new people like I have. Word has gotten out in the Intentional Community network. Coupled with family and friends of friends, people are talking. I make it my business to make sure everyone feels welcome."

Mariah smiled at him; he was such a good soul. "Some of that is inherent here. Shared food, shared dinners, shared tasks...the sense of gratitude. It's the fabric of the community. All the new growth has increased our skill base as well as lightened our individual workloads."

The others agreed, then the group fell silent. The only sound now was an occasional sigh of contentment mixed in with the sputtering fire as those last thoughts of camaraderie settled in upon the night. Mariah enjoyed the peace by the fire before she gathered her crew and headed back up to her tent on Indian Point.

* * *

"Get up," Tristan commanded. "Come with me."

"You sure are bossy today, who raised you anyway?" Mariah was exhausted. Last night after the Dance, everyone had a spontaneous burst of energy and they had hung out, talking long into the night. It was part getting to know the new group along with the excitement of having survived for two months. They were established diehards now.

Tristan looked up with a serious expression. "I missed that, come again?"

"Sure," she smiled up at him. He sounded so sure of himself.

They walked in silence along the familiar trail through the wooded live oak. They took the high road for speed. She kept his fast pace, listening intently. This was a part of her new technique. She followed him up a rock-strewn cliff side, her head so full she barely noticed where they were going. "We're going somewhere special?"

"Just come on. Hurry!"

She was hurrying. Her mood lightened with the effort as she stretched her legs in the warm sunshine. As she climbed, she focused. Careful with each footstep, as the smaller stones were loose on the rocky path. She heard the scream and noticed a hawk circling above them in the deep blue of the sky. All trace of that angry cloud gone.

"We're here." They had reached the mouth of a cave. Mariah followed Tristan inside.

"This place is huge. Absolutely amazing." Her voice echoed and bounced within. "It would be great to have our meetings in here."

"I think it's great for emergencies, but do you think we could drag everyone up here?"

"The Bluff is covered. We could meet there just fine."

"Go on in, let your eyes get accustomed and look at the walls."

Mariah looked. Crystals grew everywhere.

"Well do you like it?" he asked.

"It's a great room. I love it. How did you find it?"

"I just came across it, magically. I thought you'd like it."

"I feel privileged being in here with all these crystals. There is a palpable, almost physical presence. I don't know, I've never experienced this feeling before. It's energy isn't it? Pure clean energy." He lit a match. The room took on a warm glow. "This place is private too, Mom. You don't have to share everything with everyone."

"Thank you, Tristan." She breathed, relaxing into the crystal glowing light. In the stillness she heard distant chants and drum beats. They were so distant they seemed-to-dwell in another time. Maybe the memory retained in the crystal room had reflected this year back, to her ears. "I think this cave would be absolutely perfect for our meetings— you know when the Elders want to address us," Mariah said.

"Perhaps. I agree we should have another meeting soon, but let's keep it at the Bluff for now. I thought this may be a good place for you to come and meditate. A place to be alone and work on some of the exercises." Tristan paused, "I use it. I will be gone..."

"Tristan, you have something to tell me."

"Yes. Mom I do. It's my time now. Time for me to join the Indians for the two-week quest."

"Yes," she sighed. She hugged him. "I will miss you." She gestured around the cave "You're right. And thoughtful. I'm better with crowds once I take the time to be centered and focused. Thanks again." She breathed in the musky scents that rose off the cool stone.

Mariah hadn't spent much time in caves. She was amazed at the sense of peace in the place that enclosed her. It was perfect for her daily meditation and yoga practice. Sunowa encouraged her to strengthen her communication with the Divine, to balance the outward flow of energy that teaching involved. He praised her as a natural teacher, her enthusiasm contagious. But she did not want to appear scattered or flamboyant.

She embraced Tristan again and looked into his eyes. "I know you will return, but this will alter you."

Tristan smiled half way. He looked puzzled. "Hey, it's just two weeks. Cheer up, I'll be back. I have waited long, but, you're right, I don't know what's in store. That is for sure."

"I'm saying goodbye to 'my' Tristan. But I will embrace the new you when you return.

CHAPTER 17 *Vision Quest*

Tristan had that feeling again—anxious excitement that something major was about to happen. It happened a lot these days, but now, as he left his mother in the Crystal Cave and walked away, it hummed under his skin. With this chill of foreknowledge, he knew his first long anticipated vision quest, would be life changing. After months of an unrelenting *no*, the journey was finally upon him.

As he headed toward the Tribes Camp, he didn't think; his feet knew the way. As far as everyone was concerned, he was off scouting and would return in a couple of weeks. In the meantime, Paul would take over his training sessions.

* * *

Tristan focused his mind as he approached the camp. He climbed the rock wall and jumped the cliff break, landing like a cat. When he looked up, Joseph's wide grin greeted him.

"Welcome." Joseph ran up and hugged him. "It's time. Chief Nuage is ready. Are you?"

Tristan's slow smile spread across his face. "Awesome! I've got a full two-weeks."

Joseph led the way to Chief Nuage's dwelling made of a thick, colorfully woven material, unlike any teepee Tristan had ever seen. These Indians had a small encampment, away from their permanent home, much like a summer campsite. The people went about their daily tasks, and unlike the people back at Indian Point and Painted Meadow, they had a seamless flow. It was the way their people had lived for millennia, it was in their DNA.

An air of ease surrounded the place. Tristan inhaled the scent of garlic and spices, listened to the faint sound of distant drumming, the low babbling of a baby, and the subdued morning sounds of people preparing for the day. He breathed in peace and contentment. As Joseph and Tristan approached the Chief's dwelling, Chief Nuage looked up. "Tristan, it's very good to see you. Did your dance go well last night?"

"Yes. Everyone has put their own spin on the proceedings. Isabella and the teens did a fantastic job. I had a great time."

"Good. Sit, sit. You have a long journey ahead of you. You are ready."

"What kind of journey?" Tristan sat down cross-legged on the woven rug the chief supplied for visitors. "Am I really going to hike further into The Ranch?" His voice sounded kid-like and over eager to his ears.

"Yes, most definitely yes. It will be unlike anything you've ever experienced." He waved his large hand. "First, the cleansing. In these last few weeks, you have shown great mastery of your physical body. Running and swimming—both are exercises that prepare your body, but they also prepare your spirit. Today you will run with Joseph for the entire day.

"At dusk, you will swim in the Blue Spring and scrub your body with a smooth stone. Scrub hard, from your feet to your head, for you must shed your old skin. Tonight, you will don a new one. From the baptism in water, you will receive the baptism of fire: the sacred and holy anointing ceremony that will bring you face to face with all of your demons." Chief Nuage studied Tristan, gazing directly into his eyes as he spoke.

Tristan clung to one word, *demons*. His tongue stuck to his dry mouth and he couldn't speak.

"This, most sacred ceremony, has allowed our people to flourish in peace these last one hundred and thirty years..."

"What do you mean by demons?" Tristan asked. He'd thought he was prepared. Surely they knew he was one of the good ones?

Instead of answering, Chief Nuage asked, "Have you ever killed another human being, Tristan?"

"It is well to be the master of your body before you can take on Nature. As you push your physical body your heart will actually grow to greater capacity for love and humility."

Tristan's face grew pale. The chief waited for an answer.

Tristan choked on the words, "N...Never," he cleared his throat, "Never." He'd been raised to seek non-violent resolutions to everything. Wars were an abominable reality of their world. David and Mariah would never even allow him to consider joining the military, or play football, for that matter. Surely, the Indians knew that?

"Good, then you will live." He was deadly serious here, Tristan could see. "The rest you can handle." A serene calm settled over Chief Nuage's face.

"Can you explain?" Tristan asked.

"No. You will learn. Go with Joseph. Run. Swim. Shed the old Tristan and be ready to embrace the real Tristan, tonight."

Tristan knew he was dismissed. He contemplated what Chief Nuage had said. *Shed the old me.* He was a bit miffed. He was well-liked; in fact, he'd thought he'd been chosen because of his character and integrity. He'd felt like a Chosen One. He had been conceived at The Ranch on his parents' honeymoon during a solar eclipse, and he assumed the chief knew of these auspicious beginnings. And those who followed the stars would know the significance of that. He pushed the thoughts away and continued his mission with Joseph, replacing them with a big grin. He was on a vision quest!

They ran everywhere. They jumped crevices, sprinted through wooded trails, launched themselves over fallen trees, and ran some more. His body felt awesome and light. He was made for this. Like a horse, born to run wild and free. They took short breaks, but they drank little and ate nothing.

"It's best on an empty stomach," was all Joseph would tell him.

Tristan could tell that Joseph had survived his *baptism by fire*, as Chief Nuage called it, but he wouldn't say one word about it.

An hour before dusk, Joseph left him alone at Blue Spring to prepare. After he stripped down, he saw a smooth stone lying on the shore. He placed it by the pile of his clothes. He jumped into the ice cold spring and gasped as the icy water swallowed him. He swam hard to keep his blood flowing. When he got out, refreshed, he picked up the stone and scrubbed his entire body. It stung from cold water and exertion but still he dragged the stone hard across his flesh. He scrubbed as if trying to shed his old skin. Soon his body was tingling and pink from head to toe. It was time. He pulled his clothes back on, then sprinted back along the wooded path toward camp.

The sun was crossing the horizon when the woods opened up to the clearing. He was shocked. The entire tribe stood in a large circle in the middle of the camp. The crowd broke in front of him, leaving a path to the center, where Chief Nuage waited. He was flanked on either side by three men in ceremonial attire. The old chief stood on his right and someone new was on his left. He reminded Tristan of Geronimo.

"Come forward, Tristan," Chief Nuage, said. "It is time."

Tristan looked around at the faces he'd come to love, as he stepped forward. There was an air of expectancy. They had come to witness his baptism by fire. A cold shudder ran through him. His sense of inner knowing grew stronger. With careful, bold steps he moved into the center of the circle.

Tristan felt Chief Nuage's warm breath in his face and counted the pores on his skin. Three women accompanied the chiefs. The central figure was Swan Cloud, Chief Nuage's wife. She looked regal, her jet black hair like silk, long down her erect back. Nana Lola, the weaver, and Lily, Joseph's younger sister were silent beside the chief. To Lily's right, stood the Shaman, - Sun-on-Water, with a two-foot-tall clay pitcher on the ground next to him. Tristan nodded to Swan Cloud in greeting before locking eyes once again with Chief Nuage. Geronimo, silver and glistening like a mirage, stepped back from the circle, leaving the other six standing like sentinels. Tristan realized they surrounded him, like the spokes of a wheel. The smell of sage burned his nose as smoke billowed from a seashell that held the burning herb.

Chief Nuage gazed out over the whole tribe. "We've gathered here today to bear witness to Tristan Agnelli's baptism by fire. Tristan, you are safe here. All gathered will witness and protect. It is time to remove your clothes."

Tristan's face reddened at the thought of being nude. Even so he stripped quickly, as the cool evening breeze stung his raw pink flesh. He laid his clothes in a pile.

* * *

The Anointing

Chief Nuage raised his hands and lifted his head to the darkening sky. "Grandfathers, Grandmothers, Great Spirit, in the weaving of Thy Creation, Thou has set before us an ever present table of life. Our thanks to Thee for Thy bounty. May your guidance be upon Tristan this night."

As he finished, Sunowa stepped forward with the pitcher and whispered, "As I tip the vessel over your head, rub the stream of oil into your hair, face, and all down your body—even upon your feet. Completely anoint yourself."

Sunowa then raised the heavy pitcher and poured the thick, sweet-smelling, blood-red oil from the spout. It ran over Tristan's hair, down his back, across his forehead, and into his eyes. He closed them, but too late. He vigorously smeared the oil through his hair, down his face, arms, and chest. He smoothed the oil into his tender skin. The sweetly strong scent of cinnamon burned his nostrils.

He felt the effects of the oil at once as his scalp and face burned intensely. No longer chilled from the night air, his entire body radiated warmth. As he bent over to smear his feet, Sunowa poured the last of the oil down his back. Tristan twitched as chills erupted along his spine. Sunowa then stepped back in the circle, setting down the clay pitcher.

Tristan heard a thud as the heavy pitcher hit the ground. He blinked the stinging oil from his eyes as he straightened up. The Chief began to orate in a loud, commanding voice.

In his core, Tristan knew what was about to occur, and as Chief Nuage opened his mouth, Tristan heard himself joining him with the same words.

"Since the beginning of time..."

As he uttered these words with the Chief, Tristan grabbed his chest and felt an enormous expansion of energy inside him.

"OH. MY. G O D." He pronounced each word deliberately.

Chief Nuage nodded his head, and Tristan grabbed his chest, his entire body aflame with heat. Tristan spoke aloud, "And this is the point..."

"Yes," the Chief said, and raised his finger level with Tristan's heart, pointing with clear precision. "And this is the point..."

In unison they said, "And this is the point you DIE."

Tristan heard the echo from the lips of all those six who encircled him. "You die, die, die..."

Time froze. Tristan stood at the edge of the circle, with his own eyes; he watched his body, still standing in the center, his hand clutched to his heart. Standing as his spirit self, his consciousness could see everything. Six old—no, ancient—Indians stood by his side, at the edge of the circle. Their faces like the skins of turtles were ageless as the mountains and stars. Ancient forces of the universe coalesced in this one point in time.

His gaze rested on them. They said, "Grandson, you see what is happening here? You see this? You're being cleansed by your friends of all your cheating, lying, dark thoughts, and gluttonous ways. This is where you die to the ignorance and insanity that you have harbored. For you have been brought up in a tribe steeped in madness, with all manner of depravity. No one wakes from this dream of destruction until they have slept long, and gorged on the darkness of these depths, until they finally comprehend that there is something more."

Tristan felt cosmic shame for many things known and unknown. His whole life passed before him, and he remembered and saw all the things he had done. Things he had known were wrong in his heart. And things, which his society had said were right, that he'd done without giving a second thought. He was ashamed, and the Grandfathers saw this.

"It's all right. Don't be afraid. This is how the process works. This is how you learn."

A sense of cosmic embarrassment washed through him. He saw now, with clear eyes, that GOD was his mother, his father, his sister, his brother, and every person he had ever bumped into at the store. They are nothing short of the spirit spark of Divinity ready to awaken, just as he was awakening now. Tristan felt a calm assurance from the Grandfathers.

"Death is what ignorance deserves, but this is just the beginning of YOUR story. We will give you the seed of understanding. We will put it inside your heart. If you let it grow, if you nourish it, then you can share it with everyone. You can bring the people from the black road of death, back to the red road of life."

In those words, they said more than he could understand—yet, at the same time he was also able to grasp more than they said. When they finished, they pointed their fingers to his body, and he saw six arrows fly from the four directions, and from the Earth and the Sky. They slammed into his heart.

He gasped. He knew he was back in his body, but all was black. His body was on fire from the inside out. His nostrils burned with the smell of the sweet fragrance. His eyes blinked, and he saw colors swirling. He tried to focus. All was color. Swirling, vibrating, colors of light encompassed him. Embraced by the very Beauty of Life, vibrancy wrapped him in brilliant hues of cobalt, aquamarine, gold, lemon yellows, cadmium orange, and ruby reds. All the pulsating, living, vibrating, atoms of the Universe swirled in tornado formations around him. He relaxed every fiber of his being. He became One. Then he heard a voice:

"There is a God. I AM all around you."

His body filled with an electric current that coursed through his being. It brought him to his knees and then onto his back. He felt the energy of *Life*. He was alive and he was falling. As he lay sprawled on the ground, his face turned up toward the night sky, he knew he was, for the first time in his life, truly *alive*.

A vision formed before his eyes. There were two versions of himself, both grown men, standing in a meadow. In front of them was a banquet table filled with all manner of foods. One half of the table was colorful and succulent, covered with pears, mango, pomegranates, papaya, avocado, tomatoes, kale, and other vegetables, grains, nuts, and fragrant herbs and spices. On the other half was an assortment of prepared meats, cooked and seasoned to perfection. One version of him reached for a large slice of mango. As he ate, his body glowed with the same vitality that radiated from the fruit. The other version of himself stepped to the other side of the table and reached for a large turkey leg. As he ate, his body began to grow dull, lifeless.

Both versions of himself, continued to dine on the bountiful array. One ate from the half vibrant with life, the other from the dead. As the man ate the meat dishes, his body began to grow heavy, his back bent, his limbs failed, and he grew old. He slumped, with swollen belly, arms, and legs, pulling his weight to the next piece of meat, barely out of his reach. As the man ate the fruit, his body grew strong, firm, flexible, and he reached forward across the table with ease to sample a pomegranate. When he was satisfied, he sat with abundant food still before him. The other man also stopped, stomach bulging, finally sated, but unable to stand upright.

As one sat erect at the table, the other, who had slumped and fallen to the ground, began to change. He was like any dead animal, with flies, maggots, and worms competing for the flesh. Decomposition, the recycling force of the universe, took death back into its bosom of the soil.

The other man, still seated at the table, glanced down, and in the twinkling of an eye, the worms were gone. The meadow itself, pure and clean, stretched out before him. Death was gone and standing in its place, all living creatures were running, flying, frolicking forth in this timeless, beautiful place.

Tristan opened his eyes. Dawn light clothed him and illumined the tips of the meadow grasses. He turned onto his side and realized that someone had wrapped him in white linen as he slept. He could still smell the faint aroma of the oil, and a slight heat radiated from his body. He knew without a doubt that the chief had spoken the truth. His skin was as new as a newborn babe's. He had been given a gift by the Grandfathers that would forever continue to grow in his heart. Through his vision, he knew he had a choice. He had free will.

Tristan sat, naked on the grass plain, with only the cloth over his shoulders. He could see far. He watched the sun, fierce in its redness, rise, bringing forth a new day. He had no idea that tears streaked trails down his face.

He whispered, "I choose Life."

CHAPTER 18 *Lifestyle – June*

Back at camp, new arrivals dribbled in, in twos and threes. There were couples and families, virtual strangers who just hiked in as if they had found a kind of haven or paradise. Mariah would need a new plan soon to deal with the growth. All of the original families had been planning for years. They had been here for David's Welcome speech and knew the drill. But these new people? Surely they were briefed by the family and friends that invited them? She trusted Pat, Robin, and Stacy. She trusted in general. If we really believe the world is in danger, it only made sense to invite friends and loved ones. Regardless, now she must organize it all.

* * *

They hadn't planted a moment too early. As the vegetables came in there were plenty of folks to help out. Weeding, watering, and harvesting took many hands. Most people overestimated what to bring on a trip. Of course, with more folks, came more supplies. So far, everyone was grateful to be here and glad to share.

Integrating the Indian teaching soon become a natural flow. The Inner Circle met separately with their personal Indian guide. These meetings occurred about once a week. The new information was assimilated into the pertinent class and passed on to the community. The maintenance of camp was running efficiently. Now Mariah added the activities everyone was eager to learn to the schedule. She incorporated the questions newbies asked when they first arrived: How do we survive? What plants are safe to eat? How can we tread lightly on the earth with a natural way of doing things?

The day was divided into five, two hour sessions, six days a week. Each class met three times a week. Sessions were held Monday, Wednesday, Friday or Tuesday, Thursday, Saturday. This way nine topics were covered a week with Gardening daily. Every evening concluded with a big dinner—which of course evolved into nights around the campfire full of music and drumming.

The herb group began an apothecary. They studied herbs, focusing on the most useful, and how to extract the oils, dry them, and make teas or tinctures. Garlic, a natural antibiotic, had to be planted, harvested, and braided. It was taken as a medicine to cure colds and sore throats. Each person attended a meal crew three times a week, cooking one dinner or lunch, and working on the cleanup crew for one meal. In short, that task would interrupt a different class every week. Some chose to attend three classes a day and spend more time in a given area. For instance after lunch the building group met. Most folks stayed there the rest of the afternoon until six p.m. when they joined the afternoon swim or meditation. The pottery group met at four p.m. three times a week.

The running and climbing group met at six a.m. while it was still cool. Animal tracking was held at the same time, three times a week. Morning was a good time to observe animals in their natural habitat. Tasks like water hauling, or wood gathering, were squeezed in around their respective classes. Thus the days went in a flow of routine. It was easy for a core member to disappear for the Indian trainings. Mariah noticed the Indians taught them as needed. Current skills were assimilated before new techniques could be introduced.

In the magic hours of dawn, during the workshop on wildlife observation, Rob demonstrated how to track animals, know their sounds, and read body language. With the Indian guides' help he incorporated many species. It was similar to the work with horses he'd done back home. The basic body movement has a clear meaning. Herbivores and carnivores shared a common language within their respective species, a language Rob could understand better than English.

Back in the woods, Jack led the wild edibles workshop. They identified and gathered food supplies—mushrooms, leaves, barks—

and brought the plants back for the day's lunch. They left a small portion of each patch so it could re-establish itself. They also harvested wild mint, blackberries, raspberries, sage, wild onion tops, and watercress, careful to note the differences between poisonous and edible plants. Jack used broad and narrow leaf plantain for salad greens as well as its medicinal properties. Isabella used it in the face creams she prepared. Queen Anne's Lace seed was used as a salt substitute. Cattail tubers, reeds, watercress, and edible Texas wild flowers were used in salads. They gathered grasses for grains as well as edible barks, like sassafras and oak, for teas and relaxants. Oak bark was an ingredient in the biodynamic preps they used.

Isabella learned and taught the weaving workshop simultaneously. The best weaver in the Tribe, Nana Lola, a white-haired grandmother, taught her how to gather, dry, and weave grass stocks, reeds, and small limbs for large screens. They used these for privacy, as there were no walls anywhere. The smaller projects on the Navajo looms were her favorite. Her group made shawls and scarves that could wrap around as skirts. The teens made skinny colorful ties and bartered for favors with the guys.

John, for example, had a natural aptitude with animals and he hung on every word Rob uttered. Upon finding the wild goat herd, John, worked patiently to befriend a young nanny who turned out to be pregnant. He had a secret crush on Isabella and when he had successfully tamed both the nanny and the babies, he sheared many of the herds' goats. He proudly presented his cache' to Isabella's weaving group. Of course, having the goats available for milk and cheese was the real benefit to the community. Isabella made John a rainbow colored cap from the goat's hair. He wore that hat.

David learned new concepts from the Indians to include in his gardening and soil cultivation workshops. The Indians were able to show him fantastic techniques for success in the West Texas region such as bio-intensive planting. He organized the daily gardening crews that tended the scattered garden patches. He taught companion planting, forest gardening, bio-intensive plant spacing, and of course, biodynamic preps.

As Mariah finished up at the herb group and headed to the weaving group, she spotted Max. She grabbed her sister's shoulders and embraced her. "Max, what are you doing here? When did you come?"

Max was Mariah's little sister. Maxine, was the oldest of the little kids—the middle kid exactly. She was just as bossy as Mariah, because there were five kids younger than she. She had shortened her name from Maxine ever since high school. She just couldn't grasp the whole femme fatale thing. Mariah thought Max suited her down-to-earth pragmatic nature.

"I have been looking for you, sister."

Pat and Mariah had been fine-tuning some of the essential oil extraction processes.

"Pat, this is my sister Max from Houston. She's Anya and Nikki's mom."

"Ah yes, two talented artists in our group. I have heard a lot about you." Pat welcomed her with a hug.

Max looked pleased. "Nice to meet you, Pat."

"OK, big sister," Max began as Mariah put supplies away. She turned and looked at her, hands on hips. "Just what are you playing at? I thought you were came out here like some sort of avenging angel?"

"What's up?" Mariah was mystified. "It's true I have had my hands full setting things up, ensuring everyone's settled. As a matter of fact I have been dying to tell you all about it. Hey come with me, I'm on my way to the weaving group. Hurry. Pat will finish up here." She dusted her hands. "Anya and Nikki are doing great, have you seen them?"

"No."

"They will be at weaving too."

"What's going on?" Max demanded.

"We have adapted the schedule, I have a whole chart I can show you later if you want to see it." Mariah laughed as she briefly outlined the system and routine. "The Classes and teachers are David- Garden, I lead –Herb study, Rob and Paul-- animal tracking, Jack and Jody – Wild edibles, Tristan – Running/Climbing, Rob – Swimming/ Diving." Mariah was moving at a slow jog on narrow paths, "Come on, hurry. We can visit when we get there." She glanced over her shoulder as she spoke, her long pony tail bounced on her back. "You will be amazed at what Anya is working on. I'm weaving a blanket for winter."

"Mariah, hold on. I need to talk with you." Max tried to catch up.

"Hazel and Pat—Pottery. Isabella and Pat, Weaving. Paul- Building/ Archery," Mariah continued to elaborate. "There is an opportunity for nine classes six days a week. Each person only cooks once a week and the other duties are at different times of the week so you only miss a class once. Each person can take three classes a day and use the other two time slots to spend more time in their chosen task, which could be building projects, pottery, weaving, running or herb study. This way folks can advance in their favorite activities. They can finish projects they start in a class, and can begin to teach the newbies."

"Mariah..." Max sprinted up and grabbed her arm. Mariah danced backwards and waved her off.

"Shoot, but let me finish," she slowed to a walk and grabbed her sister's hand, "It's so wonderful, I can hardly contain myself. You see there is much to learn, and we have worked it out like this." She waved her hands in the air. "The Exercise group is mandatory. Everyone participates two hours six days a week. That is an absolute minimum; there is absolutely no way to get in to the physical shape we need otherwise."

Max tried to interrupt, but Mariah was so proud she wouldn't be deterred. "Over time as people join us, the classes will serve to integrate new people. Of course newbies are encouraged to share their expertise with us. With so many classes and groups being flexible, new people showing up....I'm crazy busy, everyone is learning so much." Finally, Mariah took a breath as she tucked in on a stool at a large Navajo loom braced against a tree. She adjusted herself so the sun fell across the nubby rich tones of her thick wool weaving on its frame. "How long are you here?"

"Glad you asked. It all depends on answers to some questions."

"Are you upset? For heaven's sake. Okay. I'm listening." Mariah stopped everything she was doing and stared at her sister.

"I will get straight to the point. I was asking around about Peter St. George. You know, after I let the kids go off earlier this summer? In order to get the particulars of his death, I decided to ask around about our dear friend Peter. Did you know he was brutally murdered?" Max didn't wait for a response as she rushed on.

"Right out here. At his home in this secluded private place. I am just killing myself. I was so busy on that case with the big law firm last spring, I barely looked up. I was glad the girls had a place to go for the summer. But Murder? I know you said Peter died but I had no idea about the brutality of it. Needless to say I was extremely concerned. I did a bit of research on my own last week. I trusted you! I shouldn't have let the girls come. I only blame myself for being lax."

Max had seated herself and caught her breath; she was calmer now. She leaned back against the tree while Mariah, lips pursed, swiftly threw the shuttle back and forth through the warp.

In a quieter tone she continued, "I wanted to talk to you directly first, before I got all alarmed. I tried to phone, but...." she shrugged as she looked around at the primitive life they lived. "I see why I couldn't get through. Of course I want to see the kids but I want to speak with you first. I did more research on the internet to check out the story."

"I know I told you about what happened, back then, but you were younger. I'm sure I spared you the gory details."

Max interrupted, "Well, I know now. Peter was brutally murdered by three teens who showed up on his property to sell him some guns." Her voice mirrored her outrage. "They just shot him in the face."

Mariah was dead silent.

"For no reason. No provocation."

Mariah let that sink in. "I myself was completely devastated at the time, but you must know I do not believe this story."

"The teens confessed. They were arrested and incarcerated. Problem solved. Except for one thing. The fact that there could be loony's wandering around these parts that could just shoot anyone for no reason. I don't like the vulnerability. The danger my girls might be in."

"I understand you are worried for your girls. But we are not all that isolated now. Peter lived here alone. But I don't believe for a minute that's how it went down. First of all, his body was found twenty-four hours after his death, and he was alone out here. How does anyone know what really happened? Without an objective witness, who's to know what actually transpired?"

"The confession to murder, for one. I'm a lawyer. Confession trumps everything."

"I don't want to dwell on the fact of his murder because, for a long time I was, like you, too spooked to even step foot on this land. Now everyone's here. The land has been lying vacant since his death. We're transforming tragedy with life. Look around. Everyone's learning exponentially, creating...living out here."

Max opened her eyes and truly looked around. "I'm amazed. The size. Who are all these people? Were all of these people in your Houston meditation circle?"

"We began that way, but now a bunch of new people joined us. Everyone invited friends and family."

"The energy is like a beehive."

Mariah leaned back, taking a break from her work. She was proud as she looked around. She hummed softly as she resumed her flow.

Max watched her work. "It seems you've forgotten something in all this burst of productivity."

Mariah's hands stopped mid-throw of the shuttle. "You mean Peter? I haven't forgotten him."

"Does anyone know? Aren't you the least bit concerned? I come out here full of urgency and I find you out here la-la-ing around. Peace, Love, and harmony. All this shaman talk while everyone in the meadow is out practicing Tai-chi."

"Hey, I'm getting in shape. See?" She flexed a muscle.

"That's not the point and you know it. Nice abs, by the way. What if the murderer is lurking in your midst here? Mixed in with all you peace-love types. Are you practicing non-violent communication techniques too? Do you really know all these people?"

"We don't have any screening, or exclusivity, or joining fees like you do at the Houstonian Club back in Houston."

"Don't get in a huff, this is still the real world last I checked. Before you left Houston, you told me you wanted to solve Peter's murder. Those were your words. Right back atcha." Max continued, "I know what it's like to be busy, I let my two kids ride out with Rob, but I had no idea what you guys had undertaken. Don't you find it a bit odd? What if your suspicions are true?"

145

"You mean about the teen murder scenario not being the truth? That someone else was responsible for his death?" Mariah slumped. "Well you know, you're absolutely right. I tried to forget about it. I have been caught up. It's been like a whirlwind." Mariah looked deflated. She knew she shouldn't let others' perceptions affect her mood. But she had slipped into it again. Her sister was right. This was Peter's land, well protected and cared for in its pristine state by his personal commitment and inheritance. She needed to face that brutal reality. But the work they had undertaken brought such happiness, not just to herself, but to all that had joined them. They had opened up what Peter had preserved. Many lives were being transformed before her eyes. Even Max's daughters had blossomed into responsible young women, no longer the bored teens they had been in Houston. Did she really have to worry about avenging Peter's death now?

"Go ahead, tell me more about your program and then I might have a plan up my sleeve. Deal?"

"Deal," Mariah shrugged and looked at her sister. "I already told you the gist of it. Go on."

Max continued. "I couldn't find out enough info on the web so..."

Mariah glanced around to see if anyone was listening. All of the others were off in the circle close together weaving, as they chatted. No one seemed to notice them. "Go on."

"I stopped by the courthouse in San Antonio on my way here. I just wanted to see what I could dig up. You know, I couldn't reach you. Quite by chance I ran into a friend who was clerking there. He turned me on to a position in a San Antonio firm for the summer. It's a huge firm. If I take it, I could be based in San Antonio, and visit you guys on the weekends. Isn't that great? I can work and still be close by."

"It's interesting. You went there for one reason and ended up with a job opportunity. I think you should take it. Your proximity might work out as a benefit to us. You need to work, and now you could be in the closest city to us."

Max watched her sisters steady rhythm in the slow back and forth process of warp and woof. Mentally she shifted gears. "Mariah, I'm proud of you. It looks like you're doing what you have talked about for years. Can I come join in and work with you guys?"

Mariah looked thoughtful, being here had a healing effect on people. "I can give you a copy of the schedule to take with you. You can start today if you want. Now, if you're so inclined."

"Thanks, I'll just watch you, you're good at this. I'll hang out and visit the camps today. It's fun to have a day off."

"Anya should be around here somewhere." Mariah twisted around and spotted her with a bunch of teens.

"Wow, she's so brown I hardly recognized her." Max kissed her cheek as she dashed off to greet her daughters.

Mariah was torn. She loved weaving. This one she planned to use as a blanket, although it looked more like a tapestry. She could lose herself in the rhythm of the warp and woof. She truly looked forward to this meditative part of her day. The weaving grew steadily beneath her fingers. In an hour or so she planned to lead some folks down to swim at Jade Cove, as they avoided the afternoon intense heat of the one hundred degree days. She glanced over at Max and saw her amazement at her two daughters' creations and smiled. Perhaps Max wasn't too mad after all. Mad Max—that was an image for you. Something Max said nagged her. *Peter had made all of this possible.*

Max, Anya, and Nikki came back to Mariah. "They will give me a personal tour of the campsites," Max said, walking backwards as her daughters pulled her, eager to share the place. "See you at the lake later."

"Ciao, Max."

"Ciao Bella. Just like home away from home."

Six p.m. was set aside for meditation. It was the lull at the end of the day, before the meal. Walking, resting, meditating or swimming was done in silence. The camps had a hush this time of day and the only noisy areas were the centers where the cooks prepared the evening meal.

The cooking crew arranged everything in bowls and placed them on three picnic tables to serve family style. The bowl collection grew as the pottery group successfully turned out more wares. At first they made bowls and pitchers, and then mugs. When all the paper plates were gone they made plates too.

All were equal at meal times, as they sat down together to share in the feast. After dinner, which was easily a couple of hours, the cleaning crew cleaned the area and took all the dishes to the dish washing stations. Each person scraped and placed their own plate and silverware in soaking tubs. Ages four on up were capable of this simple task. They had five recycling bins for scraps that could be fed to animals and used for compost. Also, there was always plastic and paper trash brought by the newbie's coming in with things from the outside. Most things such as glass bottles that could be reused would be. The trash was taken back to the city when someone made a run to town.

"No one's a guest here," Mariah explained when Max joined them for dinner. "Everyone's family. Some who join us stay for a week. Some never leave, obviously. After dinner, all visitors are welcome to join in clean-up."

After clearing the table, they loaded the dirty dishes in a large box to carry to the dish washing center. "After cleanup you should join us at the fire circle for music. There are some great players here, and David's got some new licks on the harmonica."

Mariah jumped up as a couple tentatively approached the group in the dim light. "You must be Meghan," Mariah embraced the newcomer.

"Jeff," David greeted his friend with a hug. So glad you decided to join us. We just finished eating, but grab a plate. There's plenty."

"No, sit back down. We're fine. We stopped and ate already."

"OK then. How was your trip? It's a long way. I'm glad you found us."

Max shook her head as Mariah was absorbed in the new arrivals.

CHAPTER 19 *The Good Life*

The sun beat down hot on the tiny seedlings that poked their green heads up from the freshly dug beds. The intense heat continued for five days in a row without a hint of clouds. On David's last trip to town he'd purchased piping, which they installed to water this new, very special crop. Sufficient water for three straight weeks would give it a solid beginning. He could then move the piping to the second field. They had already dug the beds and used soil preps. They used the compost they had made here, even though it hadn't completely matured. David trusted that the land had much to offer in terms of mineral content, as it hadn't been tilled in over a hundred years. It had required a monumental effort to turn over the parched soil and remove the rocks.

Jonathan, Melody, and Roxi had devoted a couple of hours each day to gardening, and by June, David thought the plants were large enough. He had his team spread them the recommended eight feet apart, and give them some space.

* * *

Jack, Ian, and John helped Meghan, a newcomer; unload her gear from the faded red hatchback she and Jeff had driven in.

"Where's Jeff?" Jack asked.

"He's visiting with David. Thanks for helping. I didn't realize we'd crammed so much stuff in here," Meg said.

They helped unload crate after crate and cardboard boxes bulging at the sides. Flies, bees, and butterflies darted around in the June heat, attracted by the contents. "We live on a farm," she explained, "in Tennessee. Just the two of us. We have beehives, grapevines, and a huge vegetable garden with squash, melons, greens, and beans. We have devoted years of our lives to tending the land. Put down roots so to speak. But now both of our kids have grown up and moved on. It's just the two of us. It was pure, and satisfying, and a lot of damn hard work. Mega- work when I have less energy."

Ian noted her strong, tan, freckled, arms and shoulders. Muscular legs in baggy army green shorts with sturdy brown boots laced up tall.

"What part of Tennessee?" he asked. He had family there.

"Middle Tennessee, near Nashville. Anyway, a friend of a friend told a friend, and someone told us about this place. And I thought to myself, it's the same life. The same good food, the same hard chores, but in a community of others it sounded sane to me. So we packed it up and drove straight on through till morning. Walla we are here! I brought our entire harvest to share. I'm sure there are plenty of mouths to feed here. How many are there, anyway?"

John lugged the last crate out and carried it to the growing stack by the picnic table. "I'm not being flippant when I say I honestly have no idea. I know we came out with thirty or so. But more and more people come in every week. This has been going on since April."

Meghan sat in the shade to catch her breath. She watched, laughing as the others crowded around and opened boxes, their faces lit up like it was Christmas morning.

* * *

And so it went Mariah noticed. Each new person, couple or family, had their own story. Their own dreams, hopes, and vision of what life could be like. To share that quest with like-minded people made it more real. The more people who shared this vision, the bigger it became. It spoke of a desire for community and deeper understanding. *We are not alone. We are all in this together.* Sharing meals and ideals. Each person was unique. And they came together from all over the country.

Mariah had quickly adapted to the new training regime. This morning she was headed to meet Running Wind for their scheduled training session. This week they were running and cliff climbing. Last week they had run and climbed cliffs till she no longer complained.

150

She recalled their first meeting as a group. The nine of them had met back behind the cliff beyond the springs. As promised, Tristan had already arranged everything with Joseph. Eight members of the tribe were there to teach the first level of skills. "These skills are basic," Joseph explained, "Doing these will prepare your minds and hearts to receive advanced skills later, the skills that Tristan is learning from me now. If learned well, you will survive the first winter, and then on to bigger things." Joseph smiled. "Besides, learning them is necessary if you ever want to get to the fun stuff."

Jet, an older, clearly seasoned teacher, took over from there. He paced back and forth using big hand gestures to back up his few, well-chosen words. So different, Mariah thought, from Joseph's lyrical, sing-songy way. Jet had paired each one quickly: Jack with Little Bear, Pat and Isabella with Nana Lola and her granddaughter Lily. Running Wind would work with Mariah, and Daniel with Rob. Jet worked with David.

"You must be the master of your body before you can take on Nature. As you push your physical body past its limits, your heart will actually grow to greater capacity for love and humility. You must push your physical body to reach its potential. You come from a culture that worships the mind and wants to fill your brains with information, like a bunch of regurgitating guinea pigs. That is not what the mind is for. The brain may be a computer, but not the mind. The mind has so much to offer you. Your culture is still in baby school. Here you will learn that your mind's first task is to control the self. Some of you are at the mercy of the whims and whines of your body. In truth, to survive, it must be the other way. Your mind is the boss of the self. That means that your mind must decide first and your body must transcend weakness and perform. It's not only possible, but challenging and fun once you get the hang of it."

At her breakfast meeting with Sunowa over a month ago, he had set up the introduction to Running Wind. Like his name suggested, he was both strong and so very fast. He was the challenge she had longed for. Why did she always get what she wished for? She loved working with Sunowa because she felt like the acolyte at the foot of the guru. She could hang on every word and admire his wisdom. With

Running Wind it was purely physical. One long push until the brink of exhaustion. She and Tristan were grateful Joseph, Jet, and Running Wind took charge.

Still pacing, Jet continued. "Your movements must be deliberate and careful. You must be slow to speak. Use your mind first and your tongue second. Read all parts of each other as you relearn how to communicate. Look at the face, the eyes, and the body. A whole story is told there, learn to read it. If you are always speaking, how do you ever hear anything?"

Mariah smiled. How perfect that she had been chosen to work with Running Wind, who was all action and spoke little.

Thus went the first few weeks of group training.

They met four or five hours a day at different locations all over The Ranch. Caves, cliff tops, the bluff, the Petroglyph ledge and on one particularly hot day, at the springs. Mariah noted Joseph was present every day teaching, even though Tristan had gone on his Vision Quest.

She and the others soon realized that the tribal delegates were teaching them how to teach, as well as specific survival skills. "You must trust and respect each other," Jet told them. "Remember, a good teacher listens as much as he speaks. Be watchful, for one of your students might teach you a few lessons."

Nana Lola, the white-haired wise woman and her granddaughter Lily were the weaving crew. Lily, who was Isabella's age, was already incredibly skilled. Nana Lola, was a true master of the craft and had trained every weaver in the tribe. Although weaving was the primary subject, those who learned from her came back knowledgeable on many esoteric subjects. It was part of the nature of the weaving rhythm. Secrets, meditations, and intentions were woven into the garments and blankets.

Soon they were all learning a lot about wild edibles, which was Jack's specialty. Rob and Paul focused on hunting. The weeks of running and mind over body control were actually a prerequisite for hunting. The hunter can become the hunted if not careful, Jet had explained.

Rob got special underwater training from Daniel, Joseph's older brother. There were caves down below the surface, and a whole magical underworld Rob had just begun to discover. The Blue Spring was sixty feet deep and Jade Cove, much larger, was very deep in a few spots.

Mariah kept a rhythmic pace as she ran to the meeting place. When Running Wind joined her she imitated his technique, whether they ran side-by-side, or she followed him. She learned best by osmosis and imitation. He taught her to leap fences like a deer, a skill she greatly enjoyed. It felt like dancing. At the end of every session they swam. She learned to use her body in the water in a new way. Almost like a mermaid or a dolphin, she held her legs together and undulated in the water. Her lungs increased in capacity, allowing her to dive deep under the water, although she still couldn't go as deep as Rob and Tristan.

As she learned by observation, they worked mostly in companionable silence. Running Wind always asked her to visualize the outcome before she was allowed to move. Once he threw a rock up to a hard-to-reach place half way up the cliff. "You are that rock," he said, and suddenly it seemed easy and light. She somehow found herself halfway up the cliff, not sure how the mechanics of getting there worked.

Mariah considered the miraculous, exquisite design of the human body. She was in awe of the human form. Most healthy people start out as equals, with legs, arms, feet, and fingers. As far as she knew, little about human anatomy had changed in the past two millennia. Yet, other than dancers and athletes, few people explored their full potential for movement. Few appreciated this amazing gift.

With cars, they no longer needed to walk very far, let alone run. With guns, they could stand still and hunt from a distance. With computers, they no longer had to use their brains to add, subtract, multiply, or divide. With radios they no longer needed to make music. With television, they no longer needed to tell stories. With telephones, they no longer needed to communicate telepathically. Now, living without all of these conveniences, all that untapped potential changed to pure kinetic, focused energy.

"We keep second-guessing what in our hearts we know to be true." Once Jet put it into words, they all readily agreed. It was as if someone had taken the lid off, exposing new abilities, ready to be mastered.

CHAPTER 20 *Rob and Chloe*

Rob sat by himself playing guitar. Chloe saw him and slipped down on a nearby log to listen to his melancholic melody. Chloe was a small, wispy-haired blonde, big-eyed and diminutive, but a pistol. As she watched Rob focus on the guitar, she saw him in a new light. She could see he was tall and tan with rugged good looks, but with a guitar in his hand, instead of a drink, he was unguarded. She suspected he was unaware of what he betrayed.

"Hey Rob, do you know "Stairway to Heaven"?"

"Sure. I might be rusty, but I used to play it way back when."

Rob began to strum a rough version and after some finger fumbling eased into a version of the song. "Hey, there it is," he said, a little embarrassed. "Where's Roxi?"

"Oh. She went with the others who are scouting out a new route. "Stairway to Heaven," what a title."

"Yeah," said Rob.

"Have you got a Jay?"

He looked up surprised. "Well, how did you know that?"

"Wild guess," Chloe drawled with a slow smile.

Rob put down the guitar just long enough to dig a reefer out of his blue jeans, then he continued to finger pick the song as she lit up. "How'd you get on this expedition anyway?"

"Oh, I'm a friend of Robin's, Pat and Jody's neighbor. My husband and I had just gotten a divorce... Headed our separate ways." She took a long drag on the joint, sucking in. "I thought, 'Perfect, he's an attorney, we don't have kids. He'd probably get everything anyway.' What I wanted was out. This was 'out' with a big O." She shuddered as if shaking off a bad memory. "Perfect for me to start over. Start fresh. Anyway, it was my fault."

"What did you do?" Rob's forest green eyes studied the petite woman and realized she was older and tougher than she seemed at first glance. "Cheat on him?"

"No. Should have. It would have given me something to do. I was bored." She gave a half- laugh, and stretched in place while Rob continued to play.

"I know what you mean about stuff," Rob offered. "I've been downsizing all my life. Last year I went on a vision quest in Wisconsin. One week with nothing. It grows on you."

"Mariah said you ran naked in the snow?"

"That about sums it up."

"You know Mariah?"

"She's my sister."

"She seems like a neat person. I'm surprised at how the community's grown."

"I know, friends told friends who told friends. Only a few people from our family came here. My sister Josie and Max's two daughters. Then of course, Mariah and her family, and Roxi and me."

"It's like one big extended family."

"It works better somehow. We had a close family, but then we are all so different, and finally we just didn't get along anymore. One half turned on the other and sisters quit speaking to each other. But here, people who don't know each other well, or at all, are united by this common thread."

"That's what I was gonna say. A common vision uniting everyone. We've become closer than family."

Rob looked across the horizon of field grass to the cliffs beyond. Chloe studied his face quietly from the close proximity of sharing the joint. She looked up at him in that adoring way young women have when they want something.

He glanced down into her brown eyes. Shocked at her closeness, he laughed a little uncomfortably. "What?" He drawled in that Texas slow speak.

"Your eyes remind me of the woods."

"Do you have plans this afternoon?" Rob asked innocently.

"I do now. I'll go get my bathing suit."

Rob picked up the guitar while Chloe stumbled off to her tent. Soon the two of them were engrossed in conversation as they trudged down the stony path, both in leather sandals.

"You know I tried that too, the vision quest thing. I went out with some Indians in Santa Fe."

He looked down at her. Her serious demeanor in the cute face was growing on him. "No kidding?"

"I don't even know why I married Mark. That was a mistake. It seems after college I was just bumming around without direction. Dad said in a couple of months I should have a job or something and my allowance would stop. Then in Santa Fe with the Indians, things took on a new meaning. I ran into Mark out there and he swept me off my feet. He was on vacation at the time, fun loving, adventurous. But once he got back to work... it was all work. Ten years flew by before I knew it. Then I said, 'Stop. I have to get off.'"

Rob had been listening intently. "God, I know what you mean. I've been shifting around since high school. I read a lot, though. Have you ever heard of Hank Wesselman? He wrote 'The Return of the Bird Tribes.' "

"Well, no. But I'd like to read it. Do you have a copy?"

The two found a wide deep pool in the river a distance from the camp. "Here is the cold plunge!" Rob threw off his shirt and waded out to Big Rock where the water was deepest. Chloe pulled her sundress over her head and stood in very white skin in a bikini. She stepped tenderly across the clear, ice-cold rock-bottomed stream. He watched her float like a reed as she made her way out through some tall grasses and plunged in. She squealed at the sudden chill of icy water on hot skin. Rob disappeared underwater. He grabbed her from below and pulled her under. Laughing, Chloe raced off in the other direction. The two shared an invigorating playful swim, becoming fast friends underwater. Rob helped her to shore. The two were a study in contrasts, he so brown and she so white with thin fragile arms wisping by her sides.

"You have got to watch that skin out here in West Texas."

"That's why I'm always in the shade and I usually swim later in the day. Sunscreen is a way of life for me."

"What did you study in college?"

"Philosophy and psychology."

"So what do you think of Plato?"

She laughed a bell laugh; Rob thought the sound was nice.

"Ted used to grumble that I didn't know anything useful."

"What did he study?"

"Business and law. You know, *useful* pursuits. Why Plato?"

"That's where I first learned about Atlantis."

"Atlantis?"

"The lost land. The island that fell into the ocean. I've spent a lot of my life searching for it."

"You're a real dreamer." She took another long look at him. The two walked back through the tall grasses toward the camp.

"I'm cooking tonight at our camp. Care to join us?"

"Is that all right?"

"Sure."

* * *

Mariah straightened when she saw David's figure in the distance. "You're back! I'm glad that was a short trip. Is Maxi back too? I didn't see her."

David trudged up the hill. "She's visiting the Painted Meadow camp." Max had acclimated to the routine since her first visit.

"I'm glad to see you." She rubbed his shoulders as he plopped down on the chair in front of her. "Anya and Nikki are eager to show Max their latest discoveries with color."

"Speaking of color, have you seen my sketch pad?"

Mariah bent over and kissed him as she handed him the pad, buried under his khaki shirt just where he'd left it. "Be back soon." She called as she headed down to the other camp. Max was standing there in her Jesus sandals, her baggy shorts rolled up. Her hair was pulled up in a messy bun on top of her head.

"You look hot."

"Thanks, I'll take that as a compliment."

"That's not what I meant, but..." She gave her the once-over.

Max gave her sister a hug. Mariah looked into her eyes, trying to read the results of her brief excursion. "Were you spotted?"

"Me? I'm stealth. David explained how to come and go from here with out detection. I know you guys are squatting." The two sisters walked arm-in-arm to the stream, shimmering silver in the late afternoon sun. Mariah hiked up her skirt and tucked it in her waistband. They splashed around, washing hands and faces. Max splashed Mariah in fun.

Mariah had been pleased when Max let her daughters come for the summer; it foretold, at some point, Max herself would visit. She was a bit of a workaholic, a necessary trait for a law firm. At least it was in San Antonio, relatively close by. Mariah wanted her to become their outside contact for supplies and new members. Max was entirely urban and athletic and hadn't really developed her artistic side. Yet, it seemed, both of her daughters were extremely gifted.

"I want to join you guys out here permanently. I admire what you're doing."

Even as she said it, Mariah knew she didn't mean it. Max liked her career too much to give it up.

"Your kids are younger than mine. And I'm sure you don't want to stay a single mom the rest of your life. How will you meet a cool guy if you join all of us diehards?"

Max glanced around. She watched the tanned muscles bulge against white T-shirts of two shaggy haired guys as they lugged a picnic table under the shade of a tree. Nice build, she thought, as she all but stared.

"I dunno," she said finally.

Mariah waded out to a rather large boulder in the middle of the stream and pulled herself up on it. "Look, I have something serious to say. I may just blurt it out. I'm warning you, it may come out all wrong,"

"Shoot, now you've got my curiosity up." Max pulled herself up.

"After you brought up Peter's murder on your last trip, I couldn't get it out of my mind. I just know I'll never feel settled until we solve the mystery. All we are working for will be lost. I mean when we're here, it's easy to forget, to think this is all there is."

158

"You are right, of course. Have you got any ideas? I was fired up when I visited you last. Then when I saw what you and the girls were up to, I was enthused by all you had created, and how happy the girls were."

"Me too. Survival and creative-problem solving were the first things on my mind. And yet I was full of good intentions when we first came here. I came full of respect for Peter and what this land meant to him. I want to live that life. Pick up where he left off and finish what he started. But I don't want to ignore the fact that he died an untimely, unjust death. He was murdered in cold blood. Its unforgiveable."

"Don't whine about it. It's a sore subject."

"I'm not whining," Mariah said, hurt. "I'm discussing it with you to arrive at a solution, or a plan, or... I just don't know who to talk to." *I'll have to discuss it with 'Running Wind next time I see him,* she thought, but she doubted it would happen. Whenever she was with him she became caught up in the moment and all other thoughts disappeared. It was all so *'be here, now'* and old problems were seldom on her mind.

"Peter has a best friend," she continued, "He doesn't know we are out here—at least I don't think he does—and I don't know what he'll think if he finds out. But if all else fails, I may have to find him."

Max put her hands on her hips. Her glance took in the flat silver river, the pewter rocks, and the wheat waving grasses. The sun was just lowering, silhouetting a sugar maple. The amber leaves glowed hovering just above the water.

"Let's face it, this is paradise out here."

"I know." Mariah smiled with a bright faraway look in her eye. "And David's back safe and I am happy. Thanks to you volunteering to be our link with the world, he'll be able to stick around here for a while." The two waded through the water in silence.

"You do want me to poke around until I discover something, anything? Is that why you brought it up?"

"Yes. No. I was just remembering Peter out here, so quiet and unassuming, even though he owned all this amazing land. And he welcomed our dad way back then. There were so many of us. Eight kids, all coming out here to play in the rivers. We were sun worshippers. We ran around like we owned the place."

159

"Look at you, you're still doing that."

Mariah laughed. "I know, and I feel guilty about that sometimes. I'm wondering, would he want us to do something?"

"I don't know what he would want, but it's negligent not to." Max shrugged. "I could follow a few leads, starting with Peter's family..." Her voice trailed off as she looked at Mariah. "...if you want me too."

"I'll have to think about it. I don't want to jeopardize our presence by digging too hard."

"You must. I must. Maybe the stranger amongst you is really a killer?"

"That's an awful thing to say."

"You really don't know do you? You don't know half of the people."

They wandered over to Jade Cove. Mariah watched as David swam the breaststroke, his strong arms slicing through the water. He pulled himself up the stone bank and out with a swift practiced motion. She strolled to great him with an appreciative smile.

"Hey girl." She leaned in, he moved her dark hair from her face and gave her a wet kiss. He noted her somber expression. "Don't worry. We're home. I made it back quiet as a mouse. There's nothing near us for fifty miles in any direction."

"It's not that." Mariah's green eyes shone in the late afternoon sun.

"Come on in." David dove back in the cool water.

"Think about it, Mariah. You don't have a choice. Too much at stake," Max whispered.

"I was hoping to watch one of your swan dives from the cliff," Mariah shouted out to David.

"You're getting quite a tan." He knew it was an understatement. Mariah glanced down at her brown legs and arms self-consciously.

"I'd better find the girls," Max said, "I'll be swimming early tomorrow with them I'm sure." The sisters embraced.

"Tomorrow then," Mariah waved at Max. She removed her skirt and prepared to dive in to the cool calm lake. She enjoyed being alone with David.

David swam fast. By the time she reached the middle of the lake he had climbed the cliff and was preparing for a dive. Mariah floated on her back, as she watched him. This was the most satisfying thing she did. She watched his perfect form as he sprung up into the air, then turned his graceful arch into a perfect swan dive. His form was silhouetted against the sun, a star of light, shone around him like an aura.

"I love our swims," Mariah said when he swam near.

He smiled. Then he pulled her under for a race to the bottom. He always won.

After the swim, on the bank drip-drying, Mariah turned to her husband. "David, you know I didn't tell Hunter much when I saw him last year, but I got the impression that none of the old crowd ever comes here anymore. Do you ever see him when you go to San Antonio?"

David shook his head. "No."

"I wish I had told him," Mariah sighed. "We were such good friends. But he's a Texas lawyer. Who knows who his friends are now?"

She took her skirt from the rock and wrapped it around her suit. She felt David's arms go around her waist and spun around to face him. He held her close as she prolonged the kiss. They touched fingertips, then turned and strolled on the dirt path by the creek.

"You're worried and thinking about Peter again, aren't you?"

"Guess so." Mariah squeezed his hand. "Changing the subject, Chloe and Rob are spending a lot of time together these days. She's friends with Robin, and a good five years older than Rob. He likes that. He digs the attention."

After dinner, the group gathered around the campfire. No one said much, everyone was exhausted after a particularly hard day of training.

Roxanne's harsh voice broke the stillness. "Rob, got any cigarettes?"

"No. I quit." His words hung in the darkness.

Mariah glanced up in surprise, but didn't say anything. Rob was showing Jessie how to tie lures, and he looked different, she realized, without the odd cigarette hanging from his mouth. He smiled with satisfaction as he successfully tied a lure off. He had nice hands, bronzed with long fingers. *They're Dad's hands.* God, she wished her Dad were here with them now. Chloe wasn't far off either. She was always hanging around their campsite. Roxanne, oblivious, was knocking things over as she rummaged through a rucksack, looking for a light.

CHAPTER 21 *Blissful Ignorance*

"Why can't you be happy with how things are?" David found Mariah hard to please. Mariah was sketching with a vengeance while she waited to have this 'talk'.

She looked at her husband, trying unsuccessfully to keep the demanding tone from her voice. "It's time now. Everyone is glad to be busy and focused on a goal. We have time to investigate." She was sketching the Indian flute Jet had given her, but it was more of a scribble in her frustration.

"Why do you alone fret over the past? It happened. He was our friend. There is nothing we can do now. I just don't understand your concern." David was placating her. He did that when she got intense.

"It's like evil in paradise, you know?" The black ink made a dark tear in the paper as she stabbed it with her pen. Giving up, she arose and began rubbing David's shoulders where he always held tension. "Ignorance is bliss. I know that. If evil penetrated this land before and ended a human life—an innocent life—who's to say we are immune?"

"Owe."

"Sorry. We don't even know who the real enemy is. Yet forewarned is forearmed. If Peter had a clue this never would have happened to him. I mean, if we don't know who murdered Peter or why, the person could be among us and we wouldn't even know." Mariah stopped what she was doing and spoke in a firm voice. "My original intent when we came out here was to find a way to solve Peter's murder."

David replied, "'Uh-huh."

"Well it was! That was the point of the original trip. The whole teen thrill killing scenario always struck me as wrong. It was a guise, a sleight of hand. Now here we are. And I promised him I would avenge his death."

"You need to let it go," David said, "You can't bring him back. We've discovered his work, his life's work. That is way more important. Take care of the living. You know?"

"Yes, yes I know," Mariah said.

David glanced at her sketch where she'd dropped it. "You draw quite well when you're mad. I like the intensity." He was eager to get out and leave her to her musings. Peter was a subject he would rather forget about.

"Well, have fun," Mariah said. "See you later." She was speaking to the trees, she realized, he had disappeared so fast.

Max came up panting. She bent over her knees as she caught her breath from her run. "What's up?"

"Solving the crime. No one cares." Mariah threw up her hands in an overdramatic fashion. "They are here. Happy, happy. No one wants to stir up the past. Hornets' nest. Unpleasant. But we could all be in danger from the dark mystery man who wanted Peter gone if we don't know who and why. Solving the murder is important."

Max began stretching. Mariah joined her out of habit. "Tell me more about it, you know I'm committed." She listened to the story more closely as Mariah recounted the details.

"You know, I could be a sort of spy. I've learned a lot of techniques in locating folks over the years. It's a smart move. Like I mentioned earlier, I can be a go-between, give you guys news of the outside while I research the news about his death. I see you're concerned—finally. Hell, I'm concerned. I want to do it. He was a friend to all of us. I need contact names from you. A place to start."

"Well, you could start with his family and business associates."

"Tell me everything you know." She finally stopped doing push-ups and grabbed a towel to put around her neck. This time she gave Mariah her full attention. "You're doing the right thing. It's not smart to be completely blind to the outside world. I can continue to bring in the provisions. I know it's harder on you when David's gone."

"Wow," Mariah said "Are you for real? David's heart now is in getting a second planting in the ground, and the gardens take a lot of time and coordination. Plus it would be great to have some news of the outside world. Sometimes being out here is like being in a room without windows. Someone could drop a nuclear bomb and we wouldn't even know about it."

"Well, you worry a lot. That was the 80's. The Cold War is over," Max said.

"You know, terrorist threats and all that." Mariah rolled her eyes, Max thought she was the only one with sense.

"Very funny. These days, listening to the news is all about earthquakes, tornadoes, and forest fires. Natural disasters. It's tragic. Now, back to our plan. I'll do some digging. If I find something, I'll tell you. If I don't, well, then there's nothing to find. I know you don't want to accept that it was shear randomness, but if it is, then at least you can put that worry to bed."

"Good. As long as its the truth. I promised him I'd find out the truth."

"How can you promise a person who's gone?"

"Gone, but not *gone*, gone. He's in the spirit realm. I'm sure he contacted me anyway, to let me know, to be on guard. Prepare me for his death in some way. I feel his presence here. He's helping us. Or he's inspiring the..." She was about to say "inspiring the Indians to help us," but caught herself. She avoided Max's curious stare. "Or something. You know at first I was concerned with the new lifestyle and setting things up. But now I can't get Peter off of my mind."

"I get it. You see why it had better be me doing the research, rather than you?"

Mariah rolled her eyes. "I don't talk like that around strangers. Just family."

"I bet," Max said.

CHAPTER 22 *The Second Dance – June*

Mariah spotted John foraging for a snack. "Do you know where everyone is?" she asked.

It was time to organize their second dance, and she hoped to have some help. The first dance in May had relied on everyone's enthusiasm and energy and wasn't an authentic Indian pow-wow. As Americans they had an independent take on everything. This time she wanted to create a more authentic, sacred feel. This was a sacred ritual after all, was it not?

"Try the stream on the South Meadow, it's the closest favorite these days. Or they could be at Big Rock. Or they could be rehearsing in that cave they found last week. It has awesome acoustics."

"Thanks. I guess it makes more sense to just await their return."

She settled outside her tent to work on some macramé bracelets. Soon she heard the strains of guitar music in the distance. Mariah wondered if it was Isabella, she'd been writing some pretty good songs lately. It started with the teen girls' poetry reading group. Mariah often spotted Anya or Nikki perched alone on a rock, observing the subtle dance of nature that would serve as their inspiration. Sometimes the poetry would evolve into more epic dramas and the girls would take turns with a dramatic reading that would entertain the whole community. Isabella was writing some pretty good songs on her guitar as a result of the literary pursuits of the group.

Instead of needing to be entertained, Sean and Jonathan learned how to entertain with their popular juggling routine. Julia and Olivia had filled a different need, inventing solutions with the materials at hand instead of running to the store for the latest gadget. Necessity is truly the mother of invention. Most of the folks had found a niche of activity between survival and training that brought a kind of tranquil calm that permeated the place. Those who hadn't gotten *it,* had opted to leave. There was no room for hangers-on or wannabe's.

Isabella and Anya had started a game of sorts. As time went by there would be items they needed but couldn't run to the store for. So they would "ask the Universe." And then when new people joined the community they would interrogate the newbies for the item. It was a kind of wishful scavenger hunt. Each of the teens would have a different item in mind, usually something useful like wire-hangers, thread or pens. The winner was the one who succeeded in getting most of their wishes granted. It always worked. Besides finding needed items, it was a great icebreaker when meeting new people.

Most of the vehicles had now been given back to the outside world. There were enough poor families in the small towns surrounding The Ranch that a car left on the highway with no plates and the keys inside could easily be put to use. To say nothing of Mexicans crossing the border. To find a random car would be a pleasant surprise. It was no surprise that all the cars they'd left so far had disappeared. They had kept one of Peter's old three-wheelers at the house, just like the old days.

"Hey, Mom," Isabella called, pulling Mariah from her musings.

"Oh, great. You're back. Did you have a fun day?"

"It was wild," she said, swinging her guitar into position. "You want to hear my new song?"

"Yes, but first I have a big favor to ask of you."

"Sure, what's up?"

"Would you want to organize the dance this month?"

"Me? Wow. I don't know. I'll think about it."

"Okay, but I know you'd be great. Do the research and make it authentic. Now let's hear that song of yours." Mariah stretched her feet out as she relaxed into the melodic three verse ballad. How could this girl find these melodies?

Barely had the song ended when Isabella was up again, pulling her by the hand. "I have a surprise, come see." She carried her guitar aloft as the two walked down to the lower meadow.

"Surprise," she announced, her face aglow with the pride of her gift. The fire circle had been laid out. The new medicine wheel with stones was much larger than the first one. There were log benches neatly arranged around the circle. "I thought this area of the meadow could be our official dance place. We can leave it here for our monthly gatherings. John and Ian helped the most. We enlarged it so everyone could fit around the circle. Our numbers have grown."

Mariah opened her arms wide and held her daughter close. "I'm stunned. Here I was just too tired to come find you and you caught me resting." She smiled as she turned her daughter to face the meadow. "This is awesome. How did you know I dreamed of this? A permanent location. It's perfect, and just in time for the full moon. It's beautiful. It must have taken you guys all day."

"Everything has been laid out exactly on the north axis. It's one of the things I learned from the Indians, Mom. It's easy when you have a system, and help," Isabella said. "When is the next full moon dance scheduled?"

"It's two nights away, I think. We'll have to plan food for the feast this time too."

"Do you have any ideas?"

"I think that depends on the latest harvest. From my last look at the garden stores we'll be feasting on fresh salad greens, wild onions, and a large vegetable stew of the first tomatoes and peppers. Soon we'll have cucumbers. The Wild Bunch might have enough wild summer savory and the wild grains that Jack's group found and harvested. We could have the bakers prepare wild grain sweet rolls with honey. We have a lot of honey with us from Meghan and Jeff's bees."

"Yummy. I'm glad our food is not only based upon what we can gather," Isabella said, "but what we worked so hard for these first lean months."

"And catch. We can still catch fish. There's an endless supply of fish it seems."

"Do you think Uncle Rob can organize fishing teams?"

"Great idea. We can let him plan the menu. I think the teens will be glad to assist him in the prep. He's been a big help these days."

"I'll be glad to work with him on that. We have our teams."

"Oh, who will work with you two?"

"Josie wants to. She's like a big kid, Mom. I am glad your sister decided to join us."

"I am too. It'd been years since I'd seen her. She married at such a young age." She turned back to the dance area. "Do you have any ideas about lighting?"

"Isn't the fire supposed to be the light?"

"You're right. But I thought as there are many new people coming in this month, we could make it festive. Celebrations have a social role for us, as well as the impact on a global scale."

"You mean like torches or candle lanterns? Custom designed lighting hung from the branches? How many people are here now anyway?" Isabella brainstormed.

"About sixty. That's just an estimate, though; some left last week but a new group showed up last night. Lanterns from the branches? I can see that, it would be pretty if we're careful I mean." She glanced at her daughter. "Are you making new friends, honey?"

"Yeah. I think partly because it's summer vacation. Families are traveling together. Luckily they have kids my age. They find out about what we're doing and drop by to check us out."

"That explains a lot. It's only June, we may grow a lot by August. By your theory it may taper off in September."

"Maybe." A shadow of concern crossed Isabella's face. "It's not a problem, is it? All these new people?"

"Actually, I think that's how it's meant to be. Now play your new song again. I'd like to hear it at least twice."

Isabella smiled and picked up the guitar again just as her cousin Nikki walked over. The two sat on the flat white rock that jutted out prominently near the fire circle, then Isabella played while Nikki sang harmony. Mariah loved the spontaneous surprises that rounded out each day. One day at a time, they were moving through the summer and making progress in their mission.

CHAPTER 23 *Max Visits*

"The last time I was here we discussed my moving in as soon as I finished my 'investigation'. Well, that time has come. All leads are dead. Stuff that used to be on the internet is gone. Completely wiped. No records or data on Peter's murder at all. Are you listening to me?"

Mariah looked at her sister, who had driven out straight from her office. Standing there in her suit she looked like she was a visitor from another planet.

"There is absolutely *no record*. Even that's highly suspicious."

"How is that possible?" Mariah asked.

"Anything's possible if you're willing to pay for it. But it takes a powerful person to be able to kill all stories, especially about such a gory crime. Local people don't easily forget tragedies of that magnitude. I can't find any traces of the newspapers that covered it back in the 90's."

The two women looked at each, nonplussed. "But let me tell you about what I did learn," Max continued, "You know how you search the internet for one thing and end up sidetracked. What's weird is, either no one knows, or no one cares. This never made national news or anything."

"Go on, I'm listening."

"You wouldn't believe what they're up to with corn. This is why I'm eager to join you guys in your boycotting of all things American. It's such a simple thing. Corn—which just happens to be the staple of all US Indian reservations—is a huge industry for the big GMO producer, Taglot Industries."

The two continued the conversation as they prepared supper. Mariah listened intently to what her sister was telling her. This was a safe topic of discussion that the others would benefit from. Underlying this was disappointment that there were no new clues about Peter. "Taglot Industries is a chemical fertilizer company." Mariah was confused. "Why corn?"

"Well, it's time for a fireside chat about that. Let your little sister enlighten you." Max took a sip of the mint brew Mariah had poured her, then offered some to Isabella, who had come over to help.

"You mean to say there are no national news channels that proclaim 'the major agri-giant Taglot Industries is poisoning the food supply in America by covering our waving fields of grain with contaminated product?'"

They turned to find Rob, who had walked over in time to hear the latest. Next to him stood Chloe, wearing a silly grin. The two were rarely apart these days.

"Actually they have self-promotional adds boasting about their scientifically advanced methods to solve global food shortages and 'feed the world'. They plan to *feed the world* with contaminated corn. The presence of this corn in one farmer's field can cross pollinate with the pure corn plant and ruin it as well," Max said.

"I know this seems to be burgeoning out of all control," Max continued, "but folks are not as gullible as they used to be. This is proven by the success of organic grocery stores, giving us Whole Foods and Trader Joe's in major cities. Also veggie co-ops, CSA's, and even 'healthy meat' co-ops have waiting lists in most urban areas. Since the FDA doesn't require food to be labeled GMO—corn, or wheat or soybeans—buying organic is the only safe alternative."

"Or growing it yourself," said Jack.

"What does GMO mean again?" Isabella asked.

"Sorry, genetically modified organism," Max explained. "Anyway, everyone has to buy organic to ensure it's not a mass monopoly 'GMO' provided substance. If it is GMO is it even a vegetable anymore? They actually infuse animal cells into the plant cell membrane as part of the genetic modification. No one wants to ingest a mysterious substance when they are just trying to eat their veggies."

"You've got that right," Rob said.

"Oh gross," Isabella made a face.

"Look at religion. The old guard is still practicing traditional religion. But there is a mass movement out. Independent and nondenominational churches are thriving in small towns across America," Rob said.

Mariah smiled. Rob had moved the discussion on to his favorite subject.

"Like the UU is the fastest growing church."

"What's UU?" Stacy asked.

"Universal Universalist. I thought you went there?" Rob said.

"Not me. I'm Buddhist." Stacy smiled.

"There is also a resurgence of spirit-filled, Pentecostal churches. People are getting in touch with instinct and intuition. Opening to the Holy Spirit to guide them and inspire their actions. Many are listening to the small still voice inside, rather than taking orders from pastors, priests, and presidents," Rob said.

"That has a great ring to it. Pastors, priests, and presidents, or political leaders or policy. Shall we write a song?" Mariah said.

"Back to the food issue... sorry, I'm obsessed." Max was washing the tender fresh picked lettuce leaves as she spoke. "The weird thing is that all these third world countries—Mexico, South America, and Indonesia—are sending grains from America back. Got that? Free food is rejected because they don't like the source. They don't want to let the contaminated stuff reach their soil."

"You know, we sensed the rotten core when we made our move out. And now what we thought were mere ripples are more like eruptions all over the globe." Mariah hated that she was right about this.

"It would be great if there were small groups all over America, under the radar, meeting like this. You know, finding a lost farm or a hidden valley and planning their own survival," Paul said, startling the others. They hadn't even noticed his approach.

"Starting from scratch like we are, and eking out a new way," Rob said, nodding. "There is definitely more like us out there. Doing their own thing, living simply, with the earth, off the grid."

Mariah had a thought. "Perhaps that's why it's crumbling out there so fast. Business forecasters project record numbers of consumers in America, and then people abruptly stop consuming because of massive credit card debt, and then all of the projections are off. First it's off by two percent, then ten. That makes a dig into all the profit projections put forth by banks."

"Because all the major banks have credit cards, and that affects the bottom-line. And worse, the product companies are left holding all of the stuff," Jack added.

"And nobody is buying it anymore," Paul said.

"Right."

"All those goods, mass produced for pennies in third world countries. Cheap stuff," Jack said.

"What if no one wanted it anymore? They want Patagonia, or organic or handmade. All the goods would be left in storehouses without a market," Max said.

"That's funny, when you think about it," Rob laughed. "All the consumers are educated in consumption. Very efficient system. They can spend money at a faster rate."

"In the mad attempt to create markets, they go into Europe and Asia, then they find out those guys are not as gullible as the American consumers had been. They have high standards and won't *buy* American made."

As everyone carried on in animated conversation, Mariah realized she wasn't seeing an end to this *recession* as everyone was calling it now. More like the beginning rumbles of a huge collapse. "What should we do?"

"I guess we keep on doing what we're doing," Paul said.

"We're figuring it out." She laughed. "No more junk food, but we have a place to live and we're learning."

"Not like the first few months. I was ready to hike out of here a couple of times, and hitchhike to the nearest cheeseburger." Jack patted his belly, which had significantly shrunk since his arrival.

"I'm telling you we will get better at this. We are on a learning curve, on the way up," Mariah said.

"Don't forget we will be harvesting even more of our own produce soon," Jack chimed in. "If all goes well."

After dinner, Mariah and Max strolled back to the tent site.

"Thanks for the update," Mariah said. "The longer I'm here the less I care. I knew our society was rotten. I just thought it would last. That eventually someone would come along and put a Band-Aid on all the problems, everyone would wear blinders and business as usual would ensue. The trouble is, they always say the average American has a third grade education."

"But I know some pretty smart kindergartners," Max replied.

Mariah smiled. "I was operating on my own moral obligation to act upon what was in my heart, to follow my own spirit guides, no matter what everyone else was doing. As if I could make a choice—persist in the lifestyle that had been chugging along since the fifties—or go suffer in the desert like a martyr. Yet, when you come here and outline the speedy collapse out there, I just can't help but think, of the families with children and no homes. Soon there will be more foreclosures. Folks without jobs, accustomed to a certain lifestyle, watching as their nest-eggs disappear at the rate of two-thousand dollars a month without any funds coming in. No help, no relief from the government. Let's see, they could lose money at the rate of twenty-four thousand a year. And that's just for the basics. Look at each of the families here. We live simply. But we are alive. Two-thousand bucks could last a long time out here. We are learning. Our kids are growing and still squabbling or showing off. We're all thinner, but the kids are healthier, rosy-cheeked —blossoming."

"You're right, two thousand dollars a month is just an average house payment, plus utilities, food, bills, and insurance. Can't forget the insurance: car, house, and health. No extras. Look at me, I'm alone with a small generic apartment and I spend over one thousand dollars a month," Max said.

"And you eat here. Here we have extras. Can you just imagine the fear? The fear of some families with nowhere to go? Kids still in school like nothing is wrong. Friends dry up quickly. The fear for no reason. It could be palpable," Mariah said. "We live on an abundant earth, yet few know how to tap her riches. I know it's weird but there was a whole movement in the 1860's in England. They called it *Back to Nature*. They still had nature back then. It was when the Industrial Revolution threatened to block out the sky with smog. I wonder how much of the earth's surface we have covered with buildings since then. It's like man is in a mad race to obliterate nature."

Mariah's mind went into hyper-drive as she imagined this cool green earth, peaceful, bucolic ball of blue-green colors, and then someone pouring concrete all over it, smothering the very life or sense out of it. "People chose to live like this back then. Step out of the rat race and grow wine in the countryside. But progress marched on and didn't bother them because they had their peace. I thought we would be like that. Start our little commune with nature; grow veggies, live off the grid in a forgotten territory. Time stands still out here."

"And here I show up and burst your bubble," Max said.

"Too much reality for my tender ears."

"Get with it guys." Max's tone was all business. "You have got to step up the learning curve here. When the season changes you have got to be ready for winter. Soon I will not be making trips out for supplies anymore. The lifeline will be cut off. I will join you. This is the way of survival. This may soon be 'The civilization'. *Freedom* means one is not in servitude or starvation mode. Freedom and free choice may not always be an option out there. Out there everyone is on the censor. Everyone is named, numbered and pegged."

"Wow, they have it backwards." Mariah spun in circles as she slammed her fist into her hand. "God, I see how they think. Instead of seeing Mother Earth as a benevolent source of abundance, they look to other humans. Humans as a disposable resource for their lifestyle. Like they have to exploit humans for gain. It's never win-win. It's always us or them. Never coexistence or harmony. It's always a *lack* mentality. *Fear* mentality. As if all humans are not created equal. There's the richer-is-better-than-everyone-else attitude. The poor were created so kings would have footstools. They think that is what survival of the fittest means." Then she stopped talking, let her voice die out into the black night.

"That *is* what it means," Max said.

Mariah didn't want to end on a bad note. She put her arm around her little sister's shoulders. "It's a beautiful night tonight." She stared up at the star-filled sky. "Glad you could visit us." The two sat in comfortable silence by the fire.

CHAPTER 24 *Uvalde*

The courthouse stood watch over the square, its ornate, 19th century elegance a symbol of truth and justice. Stone columns framed the entrance with a dome-like cupola on top, similar to most small downtowns across America where these elegant structures crown the central square. Max wandered past the buildings that surrounded the square and read the names of law firms.

When she heard the courthouse bells ring, Max realized it was already four p.m. She had been misled by the bright summer sun. She retraced the events of the day she'd spent in this quaint Texas town.

Max had decided to go in person to the courthouse in Uvalde where the case against the boys had been tried. It was weird that all mention of the hate crime had been erased from the internet. All three boys had been found guilty of second degree murder and sentenced to five years in prison. One did his time in juvenile detention, as he was only seventeen when the crime occurred. The other two served time here and in the prison facility in Midland. They had both been released early on good behavior. They were long gone now; the crime, now ten years old, forgotten. It had not been considered a hate crime, but rather a random teen *thrill kill*.

All the families around here were poor, mostly old folks, as the young ones had all run to the nearest metropolis to make their fame and fortune. The bad boys had come from another county, so no one here knew much about them. Max wandered around the square of this ghost town, finally stopping at a drugstore counter to get a sandwich. She devoured a Reuben without thinking while she watched the locals. Damn, if they had been curious seven years ago, there would still be gossip. The crime was long gone. The teens had been eighteen then, now they would be twenty-eight. Free. Out in the world somewhere leading some kind of life.

It just didn't seem fair that they could go on while the dead were still dead. Peter's life was over. His life was stolen, with little repercussion on the lives of the guilty. Proven guilty. What could the connection be? Someone who is wealthy is naturally a target. They would attract enemies and rivals. If someone is killed it should be for a reason. Such a random act of deliberate violence seemed odd. Mariah was sure it had been a well-planned hit, with someone else the mastermind. Someone with influence. Who had the power to erase all trace of the crime from the modern research tools?

Who had defended the murderers anyway? She headed back into the courthouse to look that up. Hopefully she could find the defense attorneys' names. She wandered back in. The clerk sighed and grudgingly looked up the case. She had assured her it would be an assigned solicitor of the court. But no, it was a private attorney.

What happened at the trial? They pleaded guilty cutting the trial short. Everyone was spared the gory details, including the bloody pictures of the murder scene. One of the boys had confessed right away. He had gone home, thrown up and told his mom. What was her name? Mildred Tompkins. She had lived in town for years. She used to work at the drugstore. Max went back to the drugstore, sat at the counter, and ordered a Coke float. This time it was with a new sense of purpose.

"An aunt of mine used to work here," she began as the waitress prepared the drink. "Don't know if you knew her? You probably didn't. She goes way back. I don't know when she quit."

"Well try me. I've worked here twenny years." She spoke from a face as worn and faded as the apron pressed and snug around her well-padded middle.

"Okay. It was Aunt Millie, can't remember her married name. She was my mom's sister-in-law and they lost touch." Max spoke convincingly as she searched her memory and hoped a white lie was a small price for some answers she desperately wanted.

"Mildred Tompkins. Oh that's a bad memory for sure. Gives me cold shudders just to think about it."

"Oh, so you knew her?"

"Yeah I knew her. She's gone now."

"Oh too bad, what happened?"

"Well there was this murder in the next county. It was a long time ago. Everyone's forgotten by now. Her boy Kenny witnessed it. It was awful. She said he came home and just threw up all over the place. Scrawny boy he was, wasn't into sports or anything. Got in a bad crowd. I guess he hung with some bullies and they bossed him around. He was the only one with a car. Anyway story was, he went with them on some escapade or other way off in the country near some small town. Said they were gonna make some fast cash with some stolen guns. Then they just blasted the shotgun into this poor man when he came to the door. Mildred said he had nightmares for years.

"Come to think of it, I saw that boy who pulled the trigger once. He came in with Kenny. I could smell the trailer park on him. But his manners stood out. He could look at you with those pale blue eyes and tell you just what you wanted to hear. He 'yes mammed' and 'yes sired' me to death. I could kinda see how he had the edge with Kenny. Kenny was mild and apologetic. He was handsome and all but lacked confidence. The other boy had a swagger. Yes, Jared was a charmer. Ugh, I just said that about a cold blooded killer.

She placed the coke float in front of Max. "Anyway, Kenny went to juvenile detention after that. And that place is a good hour away from here. He straightened up, put on weight with all that prison food, worked out, learned a trade."

"So where is Mildred now?"

"Oh, she moved on after he left home. We stayed in touch for a year or two. Don't know now. She didn't want to stay in a town that reminded her of that day, or had such lost youth. I don't know what happened to them after that."

"You mentioned earlier, quick cash. Did they get any?"

"I don't know why I'm dredging all this sordid stuff up. Speaks poorly of the town folk roun' here. Cash? I don't know. With all that blood, who remembers details?"

Max placed a few bills on the counter and thanked her as she left, the door banging with a hollow clunk as she went back to the street.

177

The ice-cream melted and the fizz dripped with a red tinge on the side of the glass.

This meant she would have to tap her last lead, Mariah's friend Hunter. She would have to meet him after all. He was the only person that might have a clue. He knew Peter. He was also the family lawyer and knew about their business dealings. Much as she didn't want to involve someone else, she would do anything she could to understand how an ordinary business like a mill, a flour mill established in the 1800's could inspire murder.

CHAPTER 25 *Geronimo*

Ever since her first solo breakfast meeting when 'Sun-on-Water,' had introduced her to Running Wind back in April, Mariah had learned to anticipate her rendezvous with him. So she wasn't surprised this early July to find herself once again in the company of Running Wind.

"Run with me again. Just follow."

"Sure." They ran through the woods and came out by the creek draw. They ran alongside the water under the canopy of sycamores. She was moving fast, her mind relaxed in the steady rhythm of her effort. The trees suddenly opened to a clearing. A slender maple tree arched gracefully framing a lone Indian as he sat in profile, cross-legged in the grass. He was dressed in full leather shirt and breeches. He had a single feather hanging from the leather band that encircled his thick black hair.

Mariah, breathless, came to a halt. Unsure of herself, she bowed. Her racing heart slowed as she digested the stillness and utter calm of his presence. He looked at her with eyes so wide and dark she fell into them as though into dark water at midnight.

"Peter was an amazing person." The lone figure broke the spell when he spoke.

Running Wind interrupted to make the introductions. "Our High Chief."

Mariah nodded and said, "A martyr." She kept her head bowed, "I am honored, I don't know what to say, pleased, to meet you."

"Peter's family had this land generation after generation. Always family, prominence, and bloodlines. But he did not stay with his family. He lived out here and opened the land to friends; carefully selected friends." He stared intently at her as he spoke, "Think of his friends, architects, lawyers, artists, builders, children, old folk's, farmers, ranchers, laborers, teachers, painters, and musicians." She waited while his words sunk in. "All those who have come here these last thirty years have one thing in common—Love and respect for this land: her water, her game, her beauty."

Mariah straightened as she looked around, seeing the meadow glow.

"The world out there is truly crumbling and you need to invite those people, Peters' friends. You know many of them. Hunter, Matt Weston, their wives, their children."

"Yes, of course, I would like to do that." Her thoughts raced. This wise man knew much already. Would he perhaps also know about how Peter had died? She took the plunge. "I'm concerned that this place may not be safe. Already many from all over have joined us in our quest. I have come to believe that the man who murdered Peter is extremely powerful. He wants this land. He killed for it."

"Perhaps, ten years ago. And the land still sits quiet and forgotten."

Mariah's head jerked up, "Forgotten?"

The chief ignored her implied question as he continued, "You say powerful? What are you saying? Who do you worship? We have our ways, many prayers and many dances. We have placed our protections upon this land. It's a place of safety." His tone softened as he continued. "So far he has been distracted, chasing other fruit. He thinks this one is a ripe peach he can pluck when he's ready. The election year has kept his finances and attention in Washington. You have arrived here safe, unnoticed."

Mariah looked doubtful and an angst she could not hide marred her usually positive demeanor. How does he know this? "Jesus, when he came to the Indians..." Mariah blurted.

"Jesus?" The chief looked baffled. "Oh you mean the Great Creator."

Mariah looked at him closely.

"We have our own name for him, but Jesus, the Messiah, ephemeral. He did come to us. He still comes in visions. He spoke with us. He told us stories. Our culture is based on stories, his stories too. We have no

180

written language. Do you write?"

"Yes."

"See? The Great Creator brought you to us. To share our story." He dropped his hands and began to pace as he spoke. "Our story of hope, patience, and permanence. Man doesn't exist for twelve thousand years on the earth without gaining some wisdom. But teachers. We have had our teachers along the way. A people cannot live without her teachers." He smiled and he seemed less stern.

Mariah listened as the voice of the wind in the trees melded with the harmonious resonance of the chief's words. She knew if she were still, the hidden meaning of his talk would find her heart and calm her. She could not see Running Wind, but she knew they were not alone. She no longer felt alone in nature since she had been working with the Indians. The abandonment and disillusionment she had felt after Peter's death had been dispelled by the fullness of the presence of all things alive. The life forces were so strong now. In a world where there was no place to hide from Nature, you soon learned to live with Her voice. Her thoughts were interrupted as the High Chief's strong voice continued in warm tones.

"I get sidetracked, excuse me. Your culture of the white race is about to self-destruct. Because they are *not* all powerful. God alone is All-Powerful. Where is your faith?" His voice gradually increased in volume and precision as he spoke.

"Someone rich and powerful murdered Peter for a reason," Mariah pointed out. "I need to know why. I promised I would avenge his death." Mariah realized her voice had reached a fever pitch. "Perhaps they want this land."

"An evil power moved their hand to murder Peter. This power waved the greed flag in Gilbert's face, and he, who would do anything for money, murdered Peter. Gilbert is just a pawn in a bad game. Gilbert does not know all—about us, or you, or your family's presence here. But the evil one does. He manipulates and maneuvers. Do your hands feel tied? Feel helpless? Immobile? Faith moves mountains. We need your faith now."

"You need me?" She was sure they had the wrong person.

"Yes we do. We will chant and dance for four days straight. We do it at this time of year to tie in with our Apache brothers' and sisters' festival in New Mexico. All the energy of both tribes shall be sent up to the heavens. We will pray, and our prayers will be answered. The prophecy will be made manifest. Indeed, daughter, it is already unfolding as we speak. Again our presence remains a mystery."

"May I dance with you?" This she knew she could do.

"You must gather your people in song around your own campfire. And dance you must. Dance like you loved to do in your girlhood. But dance with a prayer in your heart like you've never prayed before."

His faith emboldened her.

* * *

Mariah was breathless when she finally found David at the latest planting field. She grabbed his arm and tried to look casual as she pulled him away.

"I know you're busy and exhausted, David, but I must talk to you. Can we go somewhere private?"

Concern flitted across his face as he led her to a secluded shade grove of weeping willows near the stream. Mariah glanced around. It was such a lovely spot, with sun shimmering like diamonds on the water. Lime-colored ferns framed the edge.

"David," she said, half-shouting to be heard over the water sounds. "I found some information on Peter's murder. The chief, Geronimo..."

"Geronimo?" David interrupted.

"He didn't say so, but I think he is Geronimo. Don't ask me why. Indians live in a different time. Age is affected. Geronimo wants us to summon all the friends."

"What do you mean? We already have tons of new people here."

"We do. But he was insistent that we contact Peter's friends. They love the land as we do."

"Actually, when you think about it, the intense training routine is a natural weeding out process. Because we have lost some folks that can't hack it, it's a good idea to invite specific friends of Peter's who may not have heard about us."

"Good David. I knew you would see the merit." Mariah was eager to satisfy the Indians. She desired the faith required of her. She thought her suspicions unfounded, but the High Chief seemed to be very aware of the spiritual high-wire act of the battle they faced. Light and dark forces were at war here. Every individual had to choose sides.

"David, Peters murder wasn't a random thrill kill. We have found Peter's secret. We are also sure the brother-in-law doesn't know anything about all this."

David raised an eyebrow at her. "Mariah, please be clear, what do you mean, 'All this?'"

"The Indians. He didn't know about them. His brother-in-law wanted the land for oil, and Peter didn't let him have it. Not for greed or because he wanted it..."

"...But to protect the land for all who dwelled on it," David finished for her.

They watched the pristine water magnify the glistening mica infused rock. "And you have no proof it's Gilbert?" David asked, but it sounded more like a statement.

"I know I'm grasping at thin straws, but whoever killed him, Peter died a martyr's death. And to honor him..."

"We pick up the work where he left off!" David said. "Mariah, don't you realize you are being distracted? You are getting all caught up in death instead of celebrating life!"

"Precisely," Mariah concurred, "and now we have brought all these people here."

They stopped talking as two figures approached from the dark of the cedar undergrowth. Jack and Rob were on the way back from an intense hike. Their loud voices preceded them. "Wait just a minute you're losing me. We are in Texas what has New Mexico got to do with it?"

Mariah smiled at the interruption. The two men continued their debate at full volume.

"I'm not sure. But our friends here are Apache."

"Don't forget the octopus reach of the new world order and the big business behind everything the government's been up to the last thirty years," Jack retorted.

"Do you think it's about oil?"

As they reached the stream, they both turned to look at Mariah and David.

What in the world are they talking about? Mariah wondered at the snatches she had heard.

"Yes, human beings like us think The Ranch is valuable because of the life sustaining abundance of pure clean water," Rob said. "However, the power-brokers think there is only a gold mine in oil."

"The New World Order is undoubtedly the last hurrah for the energy machine which is still oil ruled," Jack said.

"What we are saying, Mariah, is that Peter was murdered by a force as much as a person," Rob said. "Those forces are one formidable enemy. And they still want this land."

"How did you know I was concerned about that?"

"We know. You've been ranting and preoccupied for days. We have been discussing it and I..." Rob said.

"I suspect they are in, or are part of our government. In that case, they are rich. Formidable. And untouchable," Jack surmised.

"What makes you assume *they* have such power?" Mariah asked. "Frank Gilbert is based in Washington, that's true."

"Who is he anyway?" Jack asked.

"He's Peter's brother-in-law."

"And you say he's in Washington? Rob asked. "That is too much to be a coincidence."

"I don't want to join you conspiracy geeks but if they are in the government, then this place could be very hot," Mariah agreed.

"Now we have jumped from Peter's family ties to oil magnates. It's all speculation until we find out something concrete. It's difficult to even contemplate while sitting in such a peaceful paradisiacal place." David sounded disheartened.

The silver stream glistened as it flowed over bronze speckled stones. Gentle ferns fanned in the breeze and a royal blue dragonfly landed on Mariah's knee. A chill went through her as a rare cloud blocked the sun. All she could do now was pray that Max found something more, something resembling an answer to the why of Peter's murder.

Rob and Jack continued on.

Mariah turned to David. "Well, the High Chief wants to make sure Peter's friends are given a chance to join us here. You know, we should invite Hunter and the others."

He could see she was right. "In that case, that's easy, we can call it a camp reunion."

"We'll have to go to San Antonio to find them, I guess." She grabbed his arm and headed down the path away from camp to continue their conversation. "David, remember all the people who knew about UFO's because they were on a government project? They all mysteriously died, either by suicide or they were lost forever in mental institutions."

"You amaze me. Where is all the paranoia coming from? You think that if the government finds out about what you know you will be mysteriously killed? We made a decision. Now you are acting paranoid. Faith, remember? What gave us the courage to come this far into the unknown? Now we're here. You have to stop this talk. We are not in government. We are a bunch of artists and hippie types. We are self-sufficient. We don't burden the Medicaid system. We don't ask for food stamps. They can ignore us because we ignore them." He smiled to reassure her. "And you are wrong, we don't have to go back to San Antonio. All we have to do is give your sister Max the task next time we see her."

"Good idea." She looked up at him and squeezed his hand. His blue eyes gleamed. "At least someone around here is brave. Thanks."

"I'm off to play with the actors. See you at dinner?"

"Of course. I can take it from here."

As he took off, she headed back. This was the time in the afternoon she had to herself. Once at camp, she picked up her pen and began to write. The Chief, Geronimo, she decided she would think of him as Geronimo anyway, said he wanted a story to be told. And this she could begin right now.

CHAPTER 26 *Paul's Peoples Revolution*

Paul's lanky frame darkened the door of Mariah's tent. He ducked his head before entering. "Sorry for the interruption," he handed her a sheaf of papers. "At last I find you still."

"You've discovered my secret," she laughed, then glanced at the papers. "You've been busy."

"I realize I'm preaching to the choir around here. I thought it would be a good idea to publish some of the current climatic data on the web."

Mariah felt the weight of the stack of notebook paper she held in her hand. She glanced down at the neat script and thumbed the pages, thinking her own writing was sparse by comparison. But she wrote poetry, mostly. His tight scrawl covered the pages from edge to edge.

"I had hoped that the next time you saw your sister..." Paul said. They both looked up as Max breezed in.

"Hey sister, whoa! I hope I am not interrupting anything?" Max said, and stopped in her tracks.

"Speaking of the devil, you are exactly the one we both wanted to see," Mariah said.

Max glanced from the thick pile of pages to Mariah's crinkled brow. "I'm a whiz at typing. What's the plan?"

"Paul and I were discussing the possibility of posting all of these articles on the web."

"I have done much research over the years on climate change," he said, "and now that I'm living here, quit my day job, as they say, I finally had time to compile my research into nine articles. I have documented the facts and outlined conclusions and predictions."

"He thinks we will all be living in caves soon," Mariah interjected.

"Oh?" Max said.

"You know, to escape from the unbearable temperatures caused by global warming. I feel we need... No. I *know* we need a revolution," Paul said. "Since we have a lot of time for our fireside chats in the evenings, we've had many discussions about the latest changes on the planet. I realize our friends here are well informed. We have stepped out of the rat race. I have taken the liberty of writing a series of articles based on our fireside chats. To fuel the revolution, these must be made public."

Max was all ears as she followed Paul out of Mariah's tent. Mariah resumed her posture, pen poised above her journal. So far she'd written Geronimo...

* * *

"Could we come up with a website that you could use to post all of these articles? I mean when you are back in town?" Paul asked.

"Sure, I can do that, as I'm back and forth weekends," Max said. "What do you think we should call it? Fireside chats?"

"Maybe, Fireside Peace Talks?"

"I thought you said you wanted revolution? Never mind. Can you give me a brief synopsis of the topics discussed here?"

"Certainly, I'd be glad to. Got a minute?"

"Sure." The two sat cross-legged on a woven blanket spread beside a live oak.

"I believe climatic changes are increasing at an exponential rate. One instance is the record heat of last summer that led to crop failures. Well, expect it to be worse. This will be surpassed by next summer. You know that means the price of food will escalate as well."

Max looked blank.

"Do you understand what is causing global warming in the first place?"

"Sure, I've heard of global warming but no, not technically," Max conceded.

"It's also called the greenhouse effect. The sunlight that hits the earth remains trapped in our atmosphere. It turns to heat. Heat and light are not the same thing. The trapped heat affects two main avenues of oxygen and carbon dioxide transfer.

"The phytoplankton in the ocean function to remove excess carbon dioxide from the planet. At one time, even twenty or thirty years ago, phytoplankton was in huge supply. Due to the warm ocean temperatures they can no longer survive and are dying. It's decreasing exponentially. The trees in the rainforest function the same way. They transfer carbon dioxide, which is what we expire, and they create oxygen. We're losing trees at a massive rate. The rainforests have been cut down by man. The droughts brought on by global warming cause a loss of trees. Forest fires also destroy vast amounts of trees. Extreme heat is also a breeding ground for fungi or insects—thus the microcosm is affected. This leads, of course, to higher greenhouse gasses, which trap the sunlight, creating more heat, which in time, melts the polar ice-caps.

"The brilliant white light of the frozen ice-caps reflects light back to outer space. Melted ice-caps lead to black water, and more land mass, both of which attract and absorb sun, thus creating heat. Along with the trapped methane which is then released into the atmosphere, we also have methane pockets which are disturbed in the excavation of fossil fuels on the earth.

"We breathe in oxygen and exhale carbon dioxide. So we are polluting our planet." He chuckled, "That's a joke."

Max held her poker face.

He went on, "The trees and the phytoplankton serve as natural filters and air cleaners. Fewer trees, less phytoplankton, fewer solar ice caps, all these huge land masses of earth, although they are unpopulated are necessary for the survival of what we know as our home, our planet earth."

"OK," Max nodded. "Thanks for sharing. So, what about 'Paul's People's Revolution'? 'Paul's Ideal Idea Revolution'? That's better we could call it Pi Rev. for short."

"Idea revolution is the viral madness I hope to inspire. This can be made possible with Facebook or by tweeting twitters?"

"Or the web ranting blogging bloggers," Max finished for him.

* * *

Paul's carefully penned, and laboriously wordy articles, hit the net when Max, in a late night frenzy back at her apartment, began typing at full speed. Her fingers flew, and for once all her skills developed over years of typing lawyer mumbo-jumbo took off like fire. She hit post and the first nine articles hit the web. By the next weekend she was back with piles of paper.

"These are the responses accumulated within one week." She dropped the pile in Paul's lap right after dinner.

"You would have thought he was a kid at Christmas, the look on his face," Max told Mariah later after Paul had disappeared back to his tent with a flashlight.

Paul then buried himself in a secluded cave for days to digest the massive response. All at once, a flash went off in his head. He would enlist help from David, Jack, and Rob. This was beyond him. He could pass these out to volunteers. Anyone who is up to it could pen the responses. Ignorance and confusion reigned; there was so much misinformation out there, no one knew what to believe. Many still denied that global warming existed at all. This became the pattern. Max collected the responses and fueled the blog with what was now a dialogue.

* * *

"Isabella, its time for a special Indian ceremony at our dance this month. Our Indian friends will have one at their site," Mariah explained. "We must create a similar ceremony."

"What is the occasion for their dance?" Isabella asked.

"This differs from the one they have every month. In July, they celebrate a special festival for the maidens at age thirteen. You know, a coming of age ceremony."

"That sounds wonderful. I'm almost fourteen. I'd better do it quick."

"Well, I think it's kind of like a Bat Mitzvah," Mariah said. "A coming out party for the young women to celebrate the transition from girlhood to womanhood."

"I wouldn't want to miss that. It's interesting the Apache's have a similar celebration to the Jews. Do they get to wear a special costume on that day?"

"I bet they do. All humans have a lot more in common with one another than one would think. We can certainly find out more about it."

"I'm sure the medicine wheel we have in the Lower Meadow would work. We need to know about any special rituals to include. We could give all the young women a special dance? Everyone loves to dress up. Braids and beads, ribbons and feathers are festive." Isabella was thinking out loud as she warmed up to the subject. "We can make more lanterns to hang from the trees. Like before, we will let the spirit lead us."

And so they did. After Ian, Jonathan and John cut a good supply of wood, everyone stacked the logs like a log cabin. The girls had clumps of herbs and sage as before, tied with string to smudge each person. John used the hawk's wing to fan the smoke. The teen girls discarded their blue jeans for long skirts, scarves and beads. They braided feathers into each other's hair. All the women caught on and let their hair down, putting on beet powder lipstick and rouge. Everyone enjoyed exploring their inner feminine.

Robin and her clan joined Jody in the baking, and they soon had honey-wheat bread and blackberry muffins. Sean had three apprentices helping with his Indian flat bread. By the time the sun was setting they were gathered at Indian Point with enough food to feed the masses when the dancing was over. From this high point they surveyed Lower Meadow and the Medicine Wheel with the stacked wood at the center. Rob, as the official master of ceremonies, once again lit the match. He soon fanned the small flame and it grew to a fine blaze. Mariah watched the snake like procession as all paraded down the trail to the meadow, shaking rattles and drumming as they made a pilgrimage to the fire. As they were already smudged, they encircled the Medicine Wheel and held hands. Some held candles and the line of seventy or so was a heartwarming site. Once everyone had a spot in the circle, the honoring of the six directions began. Rob called out to the North, South, East, and West; Grandmother Earth and Grandfather Sky. The rattles and the drums grew stronger with each cry.

The crowd hushed as Rob gave thanks and called for a moment of silence so each could speak his own heart. One lone drum set the pulse. Then the drumming began again led by Ian. Rob called for the teen girls. Nine maidens processed out in a dancing line between the fire and the circle of drummers led by Isabella. They floated in grapevine steps, their skirts, beads, and scarves flowing and swaying in the graceful dance. It had become a ritual. Isabella, normally quiet and content to stay in the background, led with feet that seemed to have a life all their own. She wove the group around the circle to the rhythm of the drums.

A lyrical flute sounded, rising with the flame and smoke up to the heavens. Isabella, lost in the dance, wove the girls in and through the circled crowd. Others clasped hands and joined the chain. Finally she joined hands with the tail and they were one big circle again. Everyone was dancing or moving out of the way. The grapevine steps twisted back and forth. The rhythm changed and the dance was faster. The drums beat in a frenzied tempo, inspiring a new burst of ecstatic dance as everyone let go and broke into spontaneous movement. Fiddle and flute players improvised in the darkness and the party was on. The girls merged into the crowd and a free-for-all took over. John grabbed Isabella's hands and the two spun around together. Swirls of smoke and swirling dancers floated in a misty haze up to the heavens like a prayer.

CHAPTER 27 *Max and Hunter*

"Okay, so far, I know you suspect Frank Gilbert, Peter's brother-in-law. It's perhaps because of some mysterious deaths. I must find something conclusive." Max explained this to Mariah after her trip to Uvalde, which had only confirmed their original suspicions. Max had to admit that Peter, being shot in cold blood, could be random, but the fact that his sister died on Thanksgiving from food poisoning less than two years later might be more than coincidental. That only left the third sibling, Ruth, who was married to Frank Gilbert. The Gilberts lived in Washington and supposedly had no connection with The Ranch.

"From what I gather, he's a very political guy, this Frank. In short, thanks to Ruth, Peter had a very high powered brother-in-law."

Max found that Frank Gilbert held a law degree but he was, in his own words, a 'bin-is-man' as southerners said. He was an extremely ambitious businessman and had fled Texas to cut his teeth on the East Coast. Coincidentally, his family had a huge Texas ranch as well. Lately the oily brother-in-law had been back. Doing lots of 'binis' in the bustling metropolis of Austin.

As a result of her demands, Mariah had given Max some information on the habits of Hunter Jones, the attorney who was a longtime friend of Peter's. Hunter Jones was the only way they could possibly get to untouchables like Frank. Hunter should be more accessible. On this they both agreed.

This led to Max's new brainstorm as amateur sleuth. Now, back in San Antonio, Max had taken a break from work to check out some local hangouts near the courthouse. This is more fun than the law, she decided. There were plenty of drinking establishments downtown. The first two she tried were a little too clean and had a stiff shirt, uptight crowd. They were pretty packed and it was 6:00 before she'd decided she was in the wrong place after all.

She decided to explore on foot. The evening was breezy and she welcomed the fresh air as she took a stroll around the block. She heard laughter coming from a shadowed alley and poked her head in. The place was dark with a comforting scent of cherry tobacco in the air. Country music was playing on the jute box. She bellied up to the worn wood bar, pleased to see that the bar had a variety of brews on tap. She ordered a dark one and retreated to a small table by the window, trying to be inconspicuous. She spotted the fair lanky man with the wire frame glasses as soon as she'd settled in. She recognized him from the faded photo Mariah had given her.

"Please be careful, Hunter can probably put two and two together and his loyalties are going to lie with Peter's family," Mariah had cautioned, worried as always about blowing their ranch invasion. Ranch *invasion*. Max smiled; Mariah always did have an interesting way of putting things.

Hunter was young to be so successful. He'd be in his early 40's, she surmised. Having Peter's family as clients was a big deal. She watched him carousing with a cheery, over-loud gang at the bar tables to the left of the bar. These guys were shouting at the bartenders and the waitresses were ignoring them. Clearly regulars, she thought. The waitresses were a sleek bunch, invisible in black skin-tight uniforms. Their dress contrasted with the rustic, casually worn, old world atmosphere of the place. She liked it here. Her beer was tasty and that was a plus. She slipped out as soon as she finished her beer. She felt she was noticed because she still had on her white silk shirt and black skirt, office attire in which she fairly glowed.

Three nights later she was back at the Pig and Whistle. When she didn't spot him, she thought, perhaps it was a fluke and he was not a big partyer. On second thought, tonight was Friday and everyone on earth had an after-work cocktail on Friday. She kicked herself mentally for not speaking up the first time. Time wasn't a luxury she could afford at this point. It was mid-July and she'd been getting nowhere for a month. She'd taken care to wear her softest silk with a good perfume and black pearls, but it was a uniform all the same. She hoped he'd be here tonight, as at this rate she was becoming a regular. Happy hour is just a quick drink before people went on to wherever people disappear to that have a social life or a family. She headed, business-like, straight to the bar and Hunter spotted her as soon as she stepped up.

"Hey, you look familiar."

Max looked up and raised her eyebrows. Somehow she had missed seeing him in the dim light.

"Hey Hunter, she's heard that line before," a friendly voice commented.

"No really, this sounds rude, you look a lot like someone I used to know. I'm Hunter Jones by the way." He stuck out his hand in greeting. "Do you know a Mariah French by any chance? No. Of course not, it must have been a trick of the light."

"Yes, as a matter of fact, I do." Max noted that his unruly strawberry blonde hair gave a jaunty look to otherwise plain features. "You took me by surprise, I don't usually get that question anymore unless I am in Houston." She studied his face. "She's my big sister."

"I thought there was a resemblance. Let me buy you a beer." She noticed in his relaxed state of after-work camaraderie his spotless white shirt had come untucked and his brown tie already loosened at his neck.

"Too late." She raised her mug. "Lots of work waiting for me. Next time." She smiled and managed to look quizzical and bored at the same time.

"Wait, next time I will buy you a real beer, a local one. You can't find it anywhere else." She retreated to a smaller table in the back room. Her foot tapped the barstool and her beer spilled a little. He was attractive in a bookish way. She thought, this could be interesting but suspected she was in way over her head. Well they had met. Now what? He's a gentleman. He'll make the first move.

CHAPTER 28 *Farming and Dancing Visions*

"You see," David explained to Mariah when she'd found him in a hidden meadow off the beaten path, "there's much from the Europeans that is worthwhile to be combined with the survival skills our native friends already have." His foot rested on a shovel as he gazed at the far distance with that dreamy look in his blue eyes she had come to love. "Therefore, when we have all merged and become one community, I hope to share the fruits of our summer labors."

"You're right," Mariah smiled. "That's what I came by to tell you. Like in the Findhorne Garden in Scotland, they spoke about the elemental spirits and fairies that guard each plant. That's similar to the practice the Indians taught us when we gather from the forest. We thank the earth and we give something back. I mean it's a physical gift, like tobacco or corn, not just words. It never dawned on me before but it's so important to acknowledge the fairies as real beings. The infinite respect we show to all of Nature is quite similar. In Findhorn they communicate directly with the Nature spirits in order to help the plants grow and thrive."

"You came all the way out here to tell me that?" He grinned. "And of course I'm using these ideas on our special secret-tree they have entrusted us to plant. The results are astonishing, I might add."

"Good, and true to my word, I brought a flute."

"Huh?"

"I promised I would help your garden, remember? I'm going to make music for all the seedlings and for the new trees we planted when we got here." Before he could respond to that, she began to play. He shrugged and went on with his digging. She took a breath, "Where are all of your helpers? I expected to see at least ten farmhands out here?"

"Over there in that field." He pointed beyond a grove of cedar trees.

"I guess you are a loner after all."

They had designed the gardens to be as natural as possible, situating the garden plots in sunny meadows. Sometimes they planted in concentric circles or spiral forms. She suspected that he rather savored his time alone as much as she did.

"Do you mind if I play a bit more?" she asked.

"Of course not. Do you mind if I hoe?" He selected a hoe from his assortment of tools.

"Do you need my help now that your crew has deserted you?"

"I like the music, go ahead, play. But don't be surprised if I sing along."

Mariah danced and sang around the garden amongst the grapevines and the blueberry bushes. She wove among the baby trees as she played. Others saw the swirls of colorful movement through the trees, the plaintive melody carried on the wind. Soon others joined in with penny whistles and tambourines. They made it a follow-the-leader game, winding around the trees and swirling around the garden beds in a single file train of dancers. They were dancing, singing, and clapping their hands as they wound around holding on to those in front of them.

David looked up and soon realized he was the only one working. "Why is no one helping?"

"It's Sunday," someone shouted, "take a break and dance with us."

Tristan laughed, and handed him his guitar. David leaned against a tree, and began to play.

Spontaneous random acts of dancing - that's what Mariah loved. She was in her element. More people equal more pleasure, more friends, more fun. From a distance it was a joyful, shimmering sight. Children, parents, and grandparents in colorful scarves, spun, dancing and laughing to the lilting bits of Irish melody that carried on the wind. Birds had always sung the plants into being, but Mariah hadn't thought about it that way before. Now they were flying in the graceful swirls of pollen dust that seemed to fill the heat hazy air. Birds and dust spiraled upward on the wind.

Mariah grabbed hold of the last person in the line and a new person took the lead. She was laughing so hard she couldn't play. Jack was panting as he stopped the dance and everyone fell over themselves laughing.

Later that afternoon when she headed back to camp, she realized she had blown the sacred schedule. Everyone had tunnel vision for the past few weeks of production and training. Now everyone appreciated the break. She could tell by the animated conversations all around her, folks were closer. What had gotten into her? She had suddenly lost her head and felt like dancing. It had occurred quite naturally. And, yes it was Sunday. What a wonderful, joyful way to celebrate the day. It took absolutely no effort and no planning. It seemed higher forms of wisdom had penetrated her brain after all.

Lilting voices rose and fell in chatter on the way back. People paired up with new acquaintances. Isabella asked if she could go with Julia for dinner at the Holts' campsite.

"Sure, of course."

"Tristan is invited too."

"That's great. You guys have fun."

"Wait for me," David caught up to her. She slowed her pace and the two strolled together back to camp. "Where is everyone?"

"Looks like we have the place to ourselves tonight."

"That's a first."

Then they had a romantic dinner for two. Mariah set up a small round table with a red and white checkered tablecloth one of the newbies had brought. She found candles and some handmade clay candlesticks. Tonight's dinner was grilled vegetables topped with fresh goat cheese and basil accompanied by a mixed wild green salad with walnuts.

"Can it still be romantic without wine?" Mariah asked.

"Next year we will have wine, our own vintage. I will learn to make that too. In the meantime your company is all I need my dear."

"Ah, spontaneous acts of romance?"

They sorely needed this slice of alone time. She smiled across the table at him. David's white teeth shone against his bronzed face when he smiled back. They clinked their glasses of the freshest spring water anywhere around. "Seize the moment, if not the whole day," she said.

"I think you got the better part of the day already," he winked at her. Her breath caught when he did that. She smiled, feeling warmth and contentment. He had such a cute wink.

CHAPTER 29 *Max and Hunter*

Over the next couple of weeks, Max saw Hunter at various places around town while she was lunching at a local deli or a favorite Tex-Mex place. During this time she had managed to figure out the difference between the local haunts and the newbie places and found that, thankfully, her tastes ran with the locals. There seemed to be a vibe around the seasoned born and bred lawyers. They were different from the transplants.

Another Friday had come around and although they had exchanged a few pleasantries she still hadn't figured out how to get to know him, or even have a real conversation, for God's sake. She was an ace at research—there was nothing she could not accomplish with a computer and a cell phone—but small talk in a bar? That was something else altogether. Max had never had the sort of glue some women had when it came to men. She had never minded this before; in fact, she had seen it as an invisible barrier, protecting her from unwanted male attention. Or had it? At thirty-two and chronically single, she had begun to see it from a new perspective. Attracting men was a new skill she would have to learn... but not tonight. It was Friday, for God's sake, and she was just going to sit at the bar and enjoy her drink. She'd figure out how to talk to Hunter some other time. But, she sat at the bar nursing her beer when Hunter came up behind her.

"Okay, got ya," Hunter said. "Try this pint." He placed a mug at her elbow. "It's my favorite, a local brew. Guess what it's called?"

Max glanced up from her I-phone in surprise, "You again, I'm Max by the way. I have no idea." It was as if she had conjured him with her thoughts. "Surprise me."

It was the messy reddish hair, she thought, that endeared him to her somehow.

"Calfskill Creek. Named for the creek they get the water from. So how's Mariah these days?"

Max sputtered on the beer as she digested the name. And then took a second sip. "Mm mm, this is very nice. Hope no calves were killed in the process."

"Yeah, sister of Mariah, I'm Hunter, Hunter Jones. It's weird this family resemblance thing. You definitely have your own look, don't get me wrong. But it's just kind of ethnic."

"Eastern European," Max said. "Or Mediterranean, we're not sure exactly."

"Okay, I will take your word for it. You are all very beautiful. I'm sure I met at least five sisters back in the day."

"There are seven of us."

"Wow." He took that bit of information in. "How's your dad?"

Her face fell a little. "Not so good. He passed away last year—cancer."

"I'm sorry, I didn't know."

Max was quiet a moment. "Yeah, we were close."

"All of you were close, as I remember. A tight family."

"Yes, you could say that." Her lips formed a smile to lighten the moment, "but to catch you up on Mariah, she got married and moved to Idaho. I don't see her too much. She has two kids...." Her voice trailed off.

"Happily married?"

"Happily married."

"Yeah, I figured as much. Good for her. I met the couple long ago, out at The Ranch. We were friends' way back." He slid onto the barstool next to Max. "So I've seen you around quite a bit lately. You work nearby?"

"Downtown."

"And?" he looked at her expectantly.

"With the Thorn Agency. It's a multinational conglomerate."

He took a sip of beer. "I know the Thorn Agency. What department are you in?"

200

"Research. I just transferred from Houston about a month ago."

He smiled. "Tell me, how do you like our little town?"

"Are you a native?"

"Born and bred. My father before me and his father before him. I'm actually Hunter Jones the third. Oldest son, family business, yada-yada."

"Oh, Randall, Jones, and Jones," Max said, trying unsuccessfully to keep the surprise from her voice, "You're *that* Jones?"

Even as she asked the question, Max had a vague recollection of Mariah dating another "third," Richard King III. How did Mariah make friends like this and why hadn't she told her? Better question: why had she married an artist/farmer if she had friends like this? Mariah had always said she'd married for love, and apparently she had. It made sense—why else should you marry some guy and live with him forever? Then again, there was one cool reason sitting right next to her--to be the wife of a prominent partner in a law firm. That sounded like fun. *Concentrate, Max, he is talking.*

"So you like our little town?" Hunter was asking again.

"Oh, I do, I do. The Alamo."

He grinned. "I was going to offer to show you the sites."

"That sounds fun, but I'm not here on vacation."

There was a silence, during which Max reminded herself of the new skill she was supposed to be learning.

"Well how about dinner then?"

"Aren't you the assertive one?"

"You don't like lawyers."

"Oh, I'm fine with a beer."

"I'll move on then, see you around."

He slid off the bar, leaving Max to wonder what the hell was wrong with her. And just like that, Hunter was back at her side. "Hey look, I know you don't know me from Adam, but your sister and I go way back. We met when she was just seventeen years old. I'm practically family. Your dad and I go way back too. I would love to buy you a proper dinner and talk about old times. You have to eat eventually."

"Okay, food sounds good actually. To tell you the truth, I have been doing a lot of late nights with peanut butter sandwiches."

"You let me know when you are ready, I know just the place."

"I bet you do." She smiled, giving him a knowing look. She thought for a Southern gentleman born and bred he sure was pleased with himself. Now that was all. She just had to be friendly and have dinner a couple of times. In the process when he said something, she would be around to listen. What was she so worried about anyway? Everything was going to be just fine. The ball was in her court. She would give him a call one of these nights.

CHAPTER 30 *As Above so Below*

The more Mariah thought about it, the more the Indians' story about their origins made sense. Geronimo had led his band of Apaches into the wilderness so they wouldn't have to live on a reservation with the other tribes. He then led the soldiers on a wild goose chase to divert attention from the tribe. With Geronimo's knowledge of shape-shifting, coupled with his shamanic gifts, he was able to elude the captors another twenty years. The white men trailed him out of Texas and into Arizona. The history books say that a white haired Geronimo had turned himself in. In reality it was another Apache that did the honors. After that Geronimo went back to Texas to lead his band. He lived to be one hundred years old.

At this point the story got complicated. Apparently, shortly after he died, he *consciously* reincarnated into a family. The willing couple were prepared to raise him to be High Chief of the tribe. Now in his third incarnation, he was, according to Jet, still leading their tribe.

Contrary to popular belief, Geronimo had not always been chief. During his first incarnation, he was the shamanic medicine man, and Cochise was chief. It was Geronimo's warrior capabilities that made many assume he was the leader.

Desperate to protect the Apaches and their way of life, Geronimo realized they would have to live in the wild, out of the white man's reach. The more he learned and followed his shamanic guides, the more his wisdom grew, and thus the training of his people increased.

He also learned that they were not the only tribes in hiding, and soon invited others to join the band of Apaches. As their numbers swelled with Zuni, Hopi, Choctaw, Iroquois, and Navajo, the tribe's strengths, skills, and wisdom expanded exponentially. With this wilderness available to them they were able to preserve the old ways and evolve in the ways of nature. Listening, dancing, meditating and staying close to the earth, they were able to put their old warrior culture away. As no one knew where they were, they had no enemies. They had no need to attack the white man anymore, they could live off the land in peace. For the past six generations—one hundred and thirty years—they had been doing exactly that. Living without technology.

Mariah viewed it like a fork in the path. The rest of the world is evolving with technology, while the Apache had chosen a different route. They didn't have technology but were still evolving as human beings on the earth. In the rest of the world, man-made technology is *evolving. Machines are growing at a rapid rate.* But mankind is not. As far as war and wisdom are concerned, we are the same warrior culture with new toys to play with. The Apache, under the leadership of Geronimo and his progeny, Sunowa, Jet, and Joseph, had continued to grow as God intended—in wisdom, in psychic and spiritual depth, and understanding. They also appreciated the diversity so many tribes brought to the mix. Geronimo was the High Chief and Sunowa, Jet, and Joseph were the sons and grandsons. They are all a part of his line.

Mariah, once again, walked on the muddy path through the grass fields, her mind lost in anticipation as she watched the steam rise from the pools of water trapped in the rough grass. She usually walked alone to her meeting with the Indian elders. She looked forward to her private instruction with Running Wind. He was named appropriately. So far they had spent time climbing and running, repelling and running, swimming and running. Besides, as much as she enjoyed the community of the camp, she craved some time alone.

Her thoughts ran to the dance they had earlier that week. She'd never danced into the earth with such intensity. She had felt the pulse beneath her feet and it moved her. She knew the Native Americans had been nearby watching. Just a few scouts, probably, but she could feel their energy moving the whole bunch forward, onward, deep into a trance-like state, with each footfall. On the surface it had seemed like a party, a celebration. Everyone loved the idea. They would celebrate their success month by month with a feast and a dance. These rituals had taken on new importance now that the act of survival was a daily task. One day at a time toward a thirty-day milestone. Thirty days of success. Time had flown, now they'd had their third dance, and a surety was the result. All had stayed for the last two months. There were about ninety people now. No one else had given up the rigorous training.

Her feet found their way up the rock face and she hopped over the crevice. She glanced down to take in the glorious view of the deep sapphire pool below her. Then she glanced out to the endless horizon of hills beyond. She tiptoed along the narrow deer path through a few sticky live oaks and low hanging cedars to the small clearing strewn with white limestone rocks. She was pumped, rested, and focused for the new task.

Running Wind sat cross-legged on the grass beside a large flat rock. She slowed and watched him in a yoga position, legs crossed, arms draped on his knees, palms up. The sun glinted on the black braid down his back. As she moved closer she noticed his mouth moving in a kind of low pitched chant. His face was serious. She stealthily joined him, mirroring his position and followed suite. In minutes she was in her own meditation. As she sat, he began to speak.

"Be ye perfect even as your Father in Heaven is perfect."

His eyes remained closed, so she waited, obedient, silent. "We are what we think. All that we are arises from our thoughts.

"Mariah, we have run and swam. Your mind has changed with the discipline and obedience." He opened his eyes. "Look at you. Your legs are strong. Your head is held high. Your brow is clear and free from stress. It is unwise for me or my family to say anything to your group until the body's attunement allows the mental clarity to receive the wisdom. *As above, so below. As in heaven so on earth.* You claim you do not know Heaven as you have not seen it with your own eyes. And yet you have been there. I know this, for I have seen you there."

The warmth of the sun on her face felt good. She smiled at his words.

"Is not the reverse true?" he continued, "You see the world around you. That is heaven. This earth is made by the Great Father. This earth is His world and all the creatures and souls who dwell upon it call it home. As you think, you who are His, make this heaven what it is.

What you see. As each of us are His, we think with Him, or He thinks through us, and makes manifest His power surging through our limbs and heart and desires.

"You see..." He looked at her, then took her face with such care, she barely felt his fingers on her cheeks. She felt the knowledge pouring from him to her as he found the words to pull his knowing into her being. Allowing her *to know* with the same surety he had. This confidence emanated from every core of his being.

"We are His. He made us. He lives in us. We make," he opened his humble large hands with reverence. "We make it with Him as we manifest our desires or our plans."

"If He is in you and He is in me?"

"Do you see how we are in at-one-ment? Do you see how simple it is to know no separation?"

The butterfly on his knee, opened and closed its wings like a prayer. A hawk called nearby. Mariah knew if she looked hard she would see the many creatures nearby in the shadows. But Mariah couldn't take her eyes from him. Is this animal magnetism, she thought. She knew not to speak. Yet thoughts of the chaotic world she had left raced in her mind; the war world. The tech world. The screaming—homeless, foreclosed-on, energy-crisis, freezing-people-in-the-streets—world. This was earth too.

"Ah," he answered her thoughts, to quiet her mind. "Those are someone's thoughts made manifest on the earth. The thoughts of vengeance, anger, power, and control are thoughts too. Thoughts and fears and dreads; poverty, hunger, cold, and lack. All thoughts come first before they are made manifest. Just two years ago there was a construction boom and everyone felt prosperous. Then someone spreads thoughts of fear and lack. People believe it, and then they worry. No one need spend energy on fear because we have a choice.

"The battle is in the mind of the thinkers. There are the thinkers and the thoughtless. The thoughtless are those who walk on autopilot; who follow."

Mariah interrupted, "Who believe everything they see on TV. The thinkers are the ones who put it on TV in the first place. You can manipulate a whole culture with a television. Most of the folks with us don't watch TV."

"The 'Thoughtless' are those who live on autopilot who act aimlessly and without direction. Those who let things happen, who are the done-to, not the doers. There are plenty of humans on the planet in this state. Therefore those who plan and think have little opposition. As each shaman thinks, so shall it be."

"Why would someone want poverty and hunger?" she asked.

"No. Those in control, send the message of fear into the populace to keep control."

"Like the Mafia strategy, when the big brother mafia in Chicago keeps the neighborhood clean for a fee," Mariah said.

"The person who pays the fee has the fear of *what if?* Every penny paid out reaffirms the belief in the fear." Running wind smiled.

"That reminds me. Four students were murdered by the Ohio National Guard in the Kent State peace movement sit-in in 1970," Mariah said. "Many others were shot and wounded. These students were unarmed passive resistors. This happened in America, our 'free' country. After this one clear and pointed message students don't revolt or sit-in for what is right anymore."

"Why? Because they are afraid to," Running Wind agreed. "Those in power don't need to waste ammunition. Real fear controls our future activists."

The air grew cold as the sun hid behind a cloud. The butterfly left. Running Wind sat still and yet there was no silence. Mariah's mind still buzzed with the chaos of the world she had called to mind and thus surrounded herself with in this peaceful garden. She concentrated on the sight before her until the sweet smells brought a smile to her face and voice. She joined in the chant Running Wind was now humming, quiet as a dove's wing. She let her thoughts dwell on the harmony and luminosity and Godlike qualities of each one of her children, her brothers and sisters, and her friends. She let each face into her imagination and into her heart. As she thought and loved each piece of humanity that she had come to know and care about, new faces popped spontaneously into her mind and heart. Her eyes closed in concentration and the sun warmed her safe spot on the earth.

When she felt a chill, her eyes opened. It was the shadow of the hill. The slow creep of darkness as the sun began its slide beyond the horizon. Her eyes blinked as she became aware. He was still there, guarding her meditation. He spiraled up silently, as his legs unfolded to a standing position. He reached for her hand. She rose. He turned without a word and she followed as he led her back to the threshold, the crevice above the Blue Spring. He hopped over and she glided over in acquiescence. Then as suddenly, he was gone. She smiled as she started to say goodbye, she was used to it by now. She, full of an unnamed joy and a sudden burst of vitality, ran the three miles all the way through the grassy meadow back to her home camp.

Tristan glanced up from his work washing and slicing potatoes as she greeted him with "hello," overly loud, with a smile on her face she couldn't wipe off. He placed one potato on the cutting board and expertly splintered it into French fry-shaped pieces.

"Now you know how I feel, been feeling."

She grinned at his knowing smile. "I feel as though I'm walking on clouds. I don't even remember walking back. Suddenly I'm back."

"You didn't walk, you ran."

"I'm not even winded."

"Isn't it great?" He studied the afterglow of joy on his mom's face. "You're getting it now. The mind–body coordination connection. Where our bodies begin to respond to our thoughts as though gravity doesn't weigh us down anymore."

"You're right. I couldn't quite put my finger on it. Good." Mariah patted her son on the back.

"Life is like a labyrinth, Mom," Isabella began.

Mariah looked up. "That sounds like an interesting premise. I always thought of them as a meditation tool."

"Well, we start at the beginning or entry point, then follow the path around and around. We keep coming closer to the center. We can see the goal every now and then. We get a mere glimpse, and then we're pulled away. Moving away again. It's rather like understanding these concepts. Always circling the issue. Just a glimpse, each time we move closer in understanding. We always circle the issue trying to find the source. Yet the beautiful journey is part of the experience. I mean I'm glad I am here. Glad I'm searching for answers or connection." Isabella shared her philosophical insights with her mom on occasion. Mariah had learned not to be surprised anymore.

"I think we should have a labyrinth here. Near our fire circle," Isabella said. "It could be a gradual thing. We can add to it over time."

"Isabella, that's a wonderful idea. You're full of surprises these days." The two put their heads together to design it.

Later people were seen walking the Labyrinth. It was always done in solitude. But even at odd times of day or night barefoot figures were seen stepping slowly, as if in a trance, along the path.

CHAPTER 31 *Max*

The two sisters, Mariah and Max, walked arm in arm to the stream shimmering silver in the late afternoon sun. Mariah hiked up her skirt and tucked it in her waistband. They splashed around washing hands and faces. Max splashed Mariah in fun.

"You're in a good mood. Spill it," Mariah said.

"It's Hunter. You know, Peter's best friend..."

"Yes, and..."

"And I like him. I've run into him a few times, at this bar after work. We've had a blast. The only thing is I'm so awkward around him. He keeps asking me out for dinner."

"You will need to get to know him a little better if you're going to find out anything. It's nothing he can reveal, so much as the people he knows. The crowds he hangs with."

"He's not your typical corporate guy. I was dying to tell him that we are all communing at the ranch. I didn't."

"He was married, I thought. Two kids?"

"Divorced."

"Too bad."

"Yeah, for her." Max had a mischievous grin.

"You didn't."

"No, but I know how to fantasize."

"You mean you want to get to know him better?"

"Precisely. I'm so nervous and overworked. I can't relax. It comes off as rudeness, though."

"Well, you could try being friendly. Try to get names of Peter's other friends from him. We want to invite them to join us. Those who love The Ranch as we do."

"Novel idea, is that what you do? Act friendly and get lots of dates?"

"Did." Mariah flicked water at Max. "But come to think of it, I was all thumbs around David. He's normally very shy, but he was the debonair ladies' man with me. Perhaps because I was tongue-tied."

"You, tongue-tied?"

"Well, you have to try to be friendly or he won't even know you like him. As a person, I mean."

"I think he's very attractive." Max nearly slipped on a polished rock.

Mariah caught her arm. "Really? You two should have a lot in common." Mariah studied her sister thoughtfully. Max was extremely bright, and an older man was probably a better intellectual equal for her. "Do you date? Often, I mean?" It seemed Max had always been working.

"Not much, actually. I guess I'm a bit of a workaholic. I like my work, I'm good at it."

The two walked back to camp in silence, the water of the stream still beading up on their skin.

* * *

The dinner table at Painted Meadow Blue looked wonderful. The wood picnic tables were set with colorful Raku bowls full of enticing concoctions, lit up by a row of newly made beeswax candles. Everything was glowing with the fruit of their labor, and Mariah marveled at the sight.

She was amazed at the things people brought with them. One of the new couples, Jeff and Meghan, had brought their beehives. Bees take a while to establish and this was already helping the garden, to say nothing of the beeswax they had made candles with and honey for their teas and tinctures. She shouldn't be surprised, after all, her David had brought bags of compost with them. What would the next group drag in she wondered? She couldn't imagine. She said, "Pass the potatoes please."

"Sweet ones or the Yukon gold?" Isabella asked.

"Both."

Tonight's meal was sweet potatoes with honey walnut topping, green beans, and steamed potatoes seasoned with basil and lemon. followed by a huge mixed green salad with goat cheese. All this was topped off with a colorful platter of melon and blackberries with a touch of honey and hemp seeds sprinkled on top.

That evening around the campfire, Anya and Nikki were glad to see their mother back for a visit. After hugs all around, everyone exchanged news.

"I have had it! I am back to stay," Max said. "I've done enough research. Perhaps finding nothing means there is nothing to find after all. You wouldn't believe what's going on in the 'real world' now."

"Tell us."

"The meat industry has gone crazy. The largest meat packing plant in the country, the one that produces the bulk of America's meat, deals in huge volumes. You know, they make those perfect round frozen hamburgers. Well, their hamburger is ground from a huge supply of meat from a diverse array of sources, everywhere from Bolivia to Texas. That means if the E. coli bacteria are in an Argentine cow, you can't track the cow and pull it. It could potentially contaminate the whole batch. The production is mass-produced at a huge scale, so all of the raw meat must be centrally located for cutting and packaging.

"Anyway, in order to prevent the one diseased cow from contaminating the company's entire meat production, the CEO decided to cleanse all the machines with ammonia, which is guaranteed to kill everything. Can you guess what happened next? The stuff is packaged and frozen with the ammonia residue and shipped all over America. The downside is, of course, too much ammonia is fatal to humans. It can cause diseases in children. Of course an eight-year-old did contract a very harmful disease with horrific side effects. That's what led to the investigation in the first place."

"That's awful," Jack said. "Who buys all that meat?"

"Schools, restaurant chains, and grocery store chains. They have contracts with McDonald's, among others. McDonald's sells so many burgers the suppliers had to create new sources to meet the demand."

"I heard that's why they are cutting down the rainforests in South America," Rob said. "To create grassland for cattle, specifically for

McDonald's burgers."

"So, in other words, to avoid eating this brand of meat you cannot eat at fast food restaurants, or purchase prepackaged burgers from Walmart," Isabella said.

"In other words, if you didn't raise and butcher the beef yourself, you don't know where it comes from. At this scale of production, E. coli would be inevitable because one contamination in one obscure location contaminates the whole lot. But it's impossible to trace. Using ammonia is the safest bet for this company to assure a safe product. I think the logic is ammonia contamination isn't as bad as E. coli," Max said.

"I think I would prefer neither," Anya said.

"My point exactly." Max was on a roll. "Look at how they are raised. In feed lots, fattened with corn in a density like two cows per square meter. I know the solution to these issues is, we just can't live this way."

"Okay, become a vegetarian," Isabella offered.

"I know." She took a breath from her rant. "Wait, you can't be serious. I need my protein. Meat is the best source, everyone knows that. Besides I want to be fit and strong, not flabby and passive."

"Well in that case," Mariah said, "if everyone quit buying the frozen burgers, they would stop making them. Everyone votes by their purchases in a consumer society. We all have more power to create change than we think."

"Create a new world, one thought at a time," Rob said.

"Or one purchase at a time," Isabella said. "I like that idea."

"I'm glad you do, honey. We don't have much choice now that we're here."

"We have already made our choice," Nikki pointed out.

"Then of course there are all the GMO issues. Corn, soy, wheat, all of these have to be purchased from reputable, organically grown sources," Max continued.

"We haven't had to think about that out here," Anya said.

"Do you know all the things they make with GMO corn?" Max asked. "Once they were able to produce massive quantities of cheap corn, they began to experiment with all the uses. The result is a ton of corn-based products. Such as, corn oil, feed corn, and hi-fructose corn syrup. This is the high-calorie stuff that is now in every commercially sweetened product from Coke to ketchup. Now there's biodiesel from corn, which means the oil from corn can replace all of the oil currently in plastic production. But that is where it should be. Not ingested into the human body."

"I get it," Mariah interjected. "We can quit wasting petroleum to create plastics and use this other product. But what about needing land to produce real food? We can't eat plastic."

"Bio-engineering is the wave of the future for scientists. Scientists can now fix the food shortage. We don't need farmers anymore." Max was practical.

"That sounds like advanced math to me. You can stop ranting now." Mariah gave Max a hug. "You have just cured my longing for a good old American burger."

"I'm not ranting," Max waited. "Am I?"

"Have some sun tea?" Mariah said, sidestepping the question. Max moved to sit by the smoldering fire, while the cousins cleared the table. "I brewed it myself." Mariah poured two glasses full of the amber liquid from a jar in the cooler, and joined her.

"Wow, this is refreshing. You're right, I was ranting."

"The sun makes the tea, and then we put the jars in the icy water to cool. Voilà, cold sun tea."

Mariah gestured around her. "That's why we came out here. Can't fight 'em, leave 'em."

"Do I taste mint?"

"Wild mint." Mariah curtsied. "We are roughing it, but...we have been harvesting it. It's mixed with a few other wild edibles like dried lemon grass and blackberry."

"Yeah. Mmm, good. Anyway, the corn GMO process is so gross. They take larvae and modify the genes of the corn in the lab."

Mariah sipped her tea as she listened to the outlandish practices of the world she had once thought she would miss. "Is it really corn anymore? Does it become a new species?"

"That's not all, they add an insecticide called Round-up—it's one of their own products—into the gene mix so the new GMO corn plant is immune to Round-up. This results in an easy farming method of mass spraying the whole valley, thus killing everything in sight except the corn plant. Then the new strong corn plant can begin to take over the world like kudzu did in the south."

"You're kidding!"

"No. And then it starts hopping. It ultimately shows up in other legitimate farmer's fields of normal corn. Which is a problem because then it contaminates the normal plants and suddenly the good farmers have GMO-contaminated corn, unbeknownst to them."

"That's almost diabolical."

"Agreed. Apparently it's a lawsuit. Taglot Industries police showed up at the screen door of one farmer's well maintained 1800's homestead and demanded payment for the "stolen" GMO corn, which is apparently owned by Taglot Industries. They have a patent on it."

"Definitely diabolical," Rob confirmed.

"You know? You just made my life seem like paradise out here. If I go to bed hungry a few nights at least I know this new harvest we are awaiting is honest real and pure corn, very far from the contamination nation," Jack said.

"These lawsuits are real. These hardworking farmers have to invest every hard won penny to fight this absurdity."

Mariah smiled at her sister, "If you're finished, help me get dessert on the table." She glanced over at the girls, laughing as they cleared. "Thanks," she said.

* * *

The next day, the two sisters went hiking. Mariah wanted to acquaint Max with her new world. Mariah started out at a slow trot, then picked up speed and ran full out. She jumped and scaled the nearby cliff, and within minutes she was up at the top, looking down at Max, waving.

"The views great up here," Mariah shouted, then cooled her jets and waited patiently while Max cursed and swore her way to the top.

"I see what I'm missing," she panted. "That's it. I'm coming in."

Mariah glowed. "It's fun to be fit. To be strong, to develop the God-given gifts we were born with."

"You've only been here four months."

"Yes. Focus. The training is focused mind-body coordination. You need both. The smarter, no, the more in sync you are, the quicker you get it. Max, you must know our work here has a larger purpose, right?"

"That, my friend, is a sobering diatribe."

The two women basked in the view over all the valleys and into a flat distant haze. Atmosphere of thick hot dust sat like a long lost sea upon the horizon.

"For now, I want to enjoy this open space up here. Do you see why I have decided to come back in? I can't take any more news."

"You've certainly cured me of any nostalgia for the old days."

Max nodded. "Right. It's easy to forget about the real world when I'm here."

"What if this is the real world?" Mariah posed the question. "Try this concept on. What if..." She tried to find the right words. "We are what we think. All that we are, arises from our thoughts. And furthermore, have you heard the concept, 'As above, so below?' Like, 'As in heaven so on earth?'"

"Not exactly. Go on," Max waited.

"This is a spiritual concept about bringing God into our life in an active sense on a daily basis. I mean to say, we are His. He made us. He lives in us. We make our world with Him. We manifest our desires or our plans. This place is to be a living example of that."

CHAPTER 32 *Paul and Hazel*

Hazel knocked on Paul's flap. "Paul, I hope you're decent because I'm barging in."

Hazel had become the self-appointed non-school teacher. She had explained to all the parents, "We must have home school once in a while so we can teach the youth history. Not just the partial truths and myths we were told. They must become well-informed adults. We can no longer perpetuate a myth-based society."

Everyone having unanimously agreed, the typical non-school class went something like this: the *teacher* would pose a list of questions that few knew the real answer to. Some typical sample questions were:

When did the first Europeans come to the Americas?

Was George W. Bush elected president?

Why are the pyramids in Peru and Egypt similar?

Where was Atlantis?

What is the Trilateral Commission?

How old is the oldest human skeleton and where was it found?

What are the similarities in math and music?

What is global warming and what is the real cause?

What is the relationship between the sun and climate change?

Why are we in a war?

How many countries are we at war with?

Should global climate change be a political issue?

What are the names of the constellations visible in the Texas sky?

Why do we perpetuate the war?

These were a few facts we should have learned in school but hadn't. The students would answer as many of the questions they chose in essay format. Sometimes the questions became interview opportunities for the young ones to ask various adult members. This was a stimulating way for folks to get to know one another. The class would then meet up later to share their findings. Each would share his essay in lecture format with the class. When they made the report, it became a rather dynamic dialogue. You know--stimulating conversations replaced polite conversations. Religion and politics were no longer taboo.

There were no absolutely right or wrong answers. It was a learning quest for all. This method allowed the teacher to become the student and vice versa. The supposition was that human beings just might be born knowing much and then loose valuable inner knowledge as society misled, misinformed or some would say *brainwashed* everyone into the accepted party line. In other words, as one ages one is educated *out* of true knowledge. People begin to doubt their inner guides as they grow up in a world with a different agenda. Thus, *non-school* became the antidote. Hazel and a team of parents took turns inventing a weekly list of questions.

"What's up?" Paul asked, prepared for anything at this point.

"I have a new assignment in mind for the ten and eleven-year-olds. Give me some of your favorite letters and we will let them pen the answers. Teaching the facts about climate change is the best way to learn them yourself. Let me see your latest pile."

Paul, relived with this new form of help, handed her a stack. Amused, he smirked, without missing a beat, and kept working as Hazel moved back to the sunlight so she could see better. She pulled her glasses from the top of her head, as she began to read the titles.

"'Phytoplankton'; 'Black ice'; 'The Carbon Footprint'; 'Revolution'; 'Issue of the Car in Third World Countries.'" She walked back into the tent to find Paul writing furiously. "Ahem."

"Yep."

"Paul, you have so many books in here. Would you consider letting us put a library in the schoolhouse?"

The schoolhouse was sometimes used for its original purpose. But it was far from the camp, closer to Peter's main house. They actually held some *non-school* classes there on those afternoons when it was

218

sweltering outside.

"Some of these terms may be way over the kid's heads, but with these books they could research them."

Paul looked up and adjusted his glasses. "What are you saying?"

"I believe kids have a fresh and innocent way of looking at the world. If they were to understand some of this, I'm convinced some of these young minds would invariably think of some imaginative solutions. You did say 'Idea Revolution,' right? That is what you ultimately want out of all this blogging, tweeting, and Face-shifting dialogue. Well, if our pre-teens can grasp these concepts, and write effectively about climate change, it may bring about a viral reaction in their age group."

Hazel sighed, and put her hands on her hips. "We are accustomed to viewing the world the way it was, in our day. We may miss something that could be obvious to one of our extremely enlightened youth. It's just a thought." She paced about in front of the piles of books on shelves or stacked askew. "But I see you have the resources. They must do research to be equipped to converse on these subjects."

"Man, I'm glad you said that. I've been working around the clock in here after all my outdoor classes are finished for the day. It was my big idea, so I feel obligated to take on some of the challenging questions."

"Let me elaborate this concept for you." Hazel pushed her glasses up as she warmed up to her subject. "I would like each student to study one of these concepts for a good week, then report on it to everyone else. In the process, someone is bound to stumble onto ideas we haven't thought of. Young minds are full of potential. I believe they're often lying there dormant until tapped. Here we have few rules. We are making it up as we go."

"It's worth a try. More than that, I do believe you have something there. I know I need the help." He looked around at his books, sticky notes, and scraps of paper sticking out everywhere.

"Did you bring all of those with you?"

"Not exactly, I have ordered quite few through Max. She has been a Godsend for me."

"I see." Hazel mopped her brow as she inspected the stash. "There's a lot of knowledge out there on climate change."

"So far it remains academic. The knowledge base hasn't filtered into action or policy change."

Hazel randomly picked up books as he spoke, reading the spines and the covers. "Why do you suppose that is?"

"Time for some fresh air." Paul picked up his tea mug and Hazel followed him outside. "Economics."

"Economics?"

"We have to throw out the current economic power base."

"I see. So do you have plans for that as well?" Hazel asked with a straight face.

"No." He had thought himself a radical thinker, but around here anything seemed possible. "Yes. This is what we are doing." He pulled both hands through the thick curls tangled on his high brow. "Moving the knowledge base from ten percent of the population to eighty percent. When eighty percent of the population discovers what's going on, they won't stand for it. 'I AM NOT GONNA TAKE IT ANYMORE'. You know like the guy on "Network"? Screaming out the window. No one will put up with the current way the world is run by two percent of the population at the top. They will no longer be able to get away with it.

"Knowledge is power. Ignorance is just plain ignorance. No excuse. This is the information age. Information can be an epidemic. The power will be back in the hands of the masses, as it should be."

"No wonder our numbers are increasing."

"They are?"

"Damn right they are. You've had your head in the clouds."

"Maybe so." Paul shrugged. "Glad I'm playing a part in things, though."

"Good." Hazel added, "by the way, I overheard Sean and Julia arguing about the climate. It's so hot out here and we are in a drought, so you can't blame them. Sean said, 'What about the sun? Why does everyone talk about all these other reasons for global warming when there is this great big hot ball of fire in the sky?' He has a point, we balance our whole day around it, you know. We are up with the sun. We step back into the shade during the high heat of the day. We watch the stars come out in the cool twilight evenings and finally in pitch blackness we close our eyes to sleep. Of course, then the whole cycle starts back up again."

"Wow," Paul said. "That's right. Sometimes the answers are simple."

"Julia agreed, of course. But she said, 'What if when we show the earth we love and respect her she can respond to that. You know how a nice wind comes from nowhere and cools us off? Or a billowy cloud blocks the sun, causing a bit of relief from the heat for a bit.' That's why I thought if they post some of their opinions it might shake things up a bit. New insights, you know?"

Paul nodded, then put his pen behind his ear. "Now let's employ some goats and sheep and move these books to the schoolhouse."

* * *

Max had to work twice as hard after her four-day weekend. Mariah was loosing it now: *The Ranch is the real world*? *This* was the real world, all right. Real deadlines, real bosses. She kept her head down. She had been slipping lately—even before her magic-world-Ranch trip. Her work was tedious but her fingers flew on the keyboard as she played catch-up on the transcripts that had been piling up in her in-box. As long as she caught up, her boss would be none the wiser.

By noon, Max was famished. She ran out to a small café tucked in between retail stores for a quick muffalata. Run down as the place was, it had probably been there for ages. She liked the old New Orleans feel to it, and so did everyone else in town. She had to squeeze through the crowd on the way to the counter. She had just placed her order and grabbed the last table when she heard a familiar voice.

"Hey, mind if I join you?"

"Hey, Hunter, it's great to see you. Sure sit down. There's not a lot of tables. We're practically old friends by now anyway." They had begun their communication on a pleasant note.

He placed a tray with his sandwich, chips, and iced tea on the table. "You look good in the daytime."

Max felt the heat rising to her face. "I'm exhausted by the end of the eighty-hour-week. You're seeing me after only four."

"Hey, that came out wrong, I didn't mean you didn't look good last time."

She waved the explanation away. "How are you?"

"Well there is so much work in my office I get out so it doesn't bury me alive."

"Cheers." She toasted him with her ice water just as the clerk shouted out her order. She squeezed thru the crowd and retrieved it. As they ate, Hunter cajoled her with lawyer jokes and anecdotes from his office. Max found herself relaxing with his jovial nature as she took a bite of the juicy salami and provolone that oozed out of her muffalata. She'd given up trying to be dainty long ago.

"Hey, Max," he said in between sips of tea, "There's a dinner in honor of the mayor coming up. A fund-raiser thing. Will you join me?"

"I don't know if I'll be in town," she demurred.

"This weekend. It's this weekend coming up."

"Okay, sure. It will be fun."

"Correction, it won't be fun. I'll be indebted to you."

"In that case, I'll do it on one condition."

"What's that?"

"I'll think about it and surprise you."

"Okay," he smiled. She has some real mood swings but he was fine for the ride.

Max noticed three suits chatting rather loudly at a nearby table. The short stocky one spotted Hunter on his way back from the restroom.

"Hey Jones, thought that was you. Come say hi to the guys."

Hunter glanced up, and half-rose from his chair, "Hey, Sharky, long time. What's up?"

Sharky extended a well-tanned arm to shake Hunter's hand. The gleam from his gold Rolex caught Max's eye. Hunter turned from where he sat and saluted the other guys. Sharky made small talk peppered with lewd jokes while Hunter nodded and smiled. They were totally ignoring her presence so Max ignored them back. When Hunter tried to introduce her, Sharky stared at her as if she was a species of bug. "Nice to meet you," Max mumbled, to a pair of blue eyes that were the coldest blue she had ever seen. She turned back to her sandwich, grateful for the inattention.

"Gilbert and Walters are in from Washington. You know, the mayor's dinner?"

"Wouldn't miss it."

"I'll be saying a few words. Just a few. Not to bore anyone with long winded speeches, eeh, eeh?" He boxed Hunters shoulder, like an irritating tic some short guys have. "While the boys are in town we'll go to my ranch. Do some hunting. Show the boys the sights. Well, good to see you, old boy, sorry about your old man." He clapped Hunter on the back with a plump hand. Hunters' thin shoulders shook at the gesture. A thin waft of perfumed after-shave floated around them. Max, thankful for her anonymity, had carefully eavesdropped on their conversation.

"So who's Sharky?"

"Scott Scofield. He's from a law firm in New York called Scofield, Jones, and Walters. You know SJW?"

"Sure I do, they're a pretty notable firm. Any relation? You're Jones aren't you?"

"Well, it's my uncle's firm, the notable Harold T. Jones. You turn over a rock in my family..."

"...And another lawyer runs out of the dark," Max finished for him.

"Something like that." Dark? He thought that was a peculiar adjective but he let it go.

"So, you do any work for them?"

"Oh no, they practice corporate law. That's how they got so big. They have branches tucked into many corporations all over America. They actually have one in Washington D.C. How's your sandwich?" To Max's relief, Hunter deftly changed the subject.

"Great. Wanna bite?"

Max could barely wait until after work to get back on her computer for some private research. The guy's countenance and manner played back in her memory. What about Scott Scofield? Did he say his friends at the table were Gilbert and Walters? From Washington? Maybe that was the Frank Gilbert that Mariah was always referring to. Mariah probably just knew his name and had never met him. What does that mean? Had she stumbled on to meeting them by pure accident?

She thought back to Gilbert. She'd barely noticed him. He had his head down. Just a curt, distant nod to Hunter. It was Sharky that had made the biggest impression, with his reptilian eyes, well-tanned and oiled skin and that large diamond pinky ring on his plump, manicured hand. He seemed more like a man of wealth and leisure than a hardworking attorney, probably because he had plenty of grunts doing the dirty work. Of course, big firm. He just lived off the gravy. So who were those other two guys? Hunter had said, Washington office?

She wished she could call Mariah. She glanced at her watch. It was already 8:00 PM. Still early. She was so excited at this new chink in the armor of the unknown. The man had mentioned a ranch; clearly there was a link between the place and these high-powered Washington and New York lawyers. She had no idea what that connection was but at least she had a strong lead to follow. With a sigh, she pushed away her extracurricular project and turned back to her work for the firm.

On a whim, too excited to sit still, Max picked up her phone and dialed Hunter's number. As she waited for the ring, it suddenly dawned on her: *They know Hunter, it's Hunter's uncle's firm. Hunter is Peter's best friend. Is Hunter the link?*

She didn't have to worry about it much before Hunter picked up.

"Hi, it's me, Max," she dropped those negative thoughts like a hot potato.

"Well well, surprise, surprise. Are you ready for dinner? Good timing I might add."

"Well, yes and no. My absolutely favorite band is playing tonight and I'm so sick of working I feel like I have been tied in here for weeks. Would you care to join me at a country bar way out in the boonies? We can eat too, they have food." It all came out in a rush.

"I would love to. Will there be dancing at this establishment?"

"Yes. And great music. The Lost Gonzos, they're friends of mine. I had promised I'd go, then I completely lost track of the dates."

"Sounds great. I'm still downtown so why don't I drop by your office and pick you up?"

"Good. As long as we can swing by my place so I can change. I'll be down in front of the lobby."

"It's a date," Hunter chuckled as he clicked off.

"Look," Max explained to Hunter on the drive out of town to the country bar. "I love to dance but I'm not Mariah. She danced modern

224

and jazz all through high school and college. I just like the music."

Hunter nodded, his gaze lingering. Max had changed into baggy Levi's and cowboy boots and her hair was down. Hunter hadn't been able to take his eyes off her.

"I'm excited you were up for this," she rambled, "This guy's an old friend. His band plays the best boogie-woogie dance music around. No one can sit still when he plays. I just want to move. I'm so stiff from being on the computer all day."

"You got it. Don't worry I'm a whiz on the dance floor."

Max wondered if there was sarcasm in the tone or just fact.

By the time they arrived at the Broken Spoke, the band was in full swing. As they approached through the dark gravel parking lot, the sounds of music and light spilled from the barn of a building. Hunter felt he was conspicuously dating a teenager, though she was a good ten years younger than he was, she looked much younger with her hair down. She still wore the turquoise ear buds and the black pearls.

She glanced up at Hunter as they entered the well-lit cavernous space. Couples were two-stepping and scooting across the floor like bumper cars on a mission. The music, as promised, was great, classic beer-drinking dance hall stuff. "I thought we should at least learn to dance together before we show up at your fund-raiser like a couple."

Hunter stood tall, gangly, all bones and awkward, his wire-frame glasses catching and reflecting the Christmas lights that were strung up around the old bar.

"Want a beer?" he yelled at her as he grabbed her hand and lugged her toward the bar.

"Of course," she yelled back. "I need food too."

They grabbed the beer mugs and headed to a red vinyl booth near the band. Hunter wiped off the split and taped up seat with a handkerchief before they scooted in on the same side. A checkered dress waitress came for their order.

"Two burgers with everything and curly fries, hot," Max said.

The waitress rolled her eyes.

"Spicy, I mean spicy fries."

"Gotcha, sweetheart."

Hunter wiped his brow; his face was taking on a pink glow in the heat. "Time to dance." He offered Max his hand. "Is Max short for something?"

"Like what?"

"Like Maxine? Or Maximilian?"

"Max will do."

The two joined the dance crowd for a two-step. Hunter was a great leader. All Texans can dance, Max thought, I should have known. She was pleased with his surety and assertiveness as they slid along the peanut shell and sawdust littered wood floor. They came back to warm beers just as the waitress brought their burgers, and two fresh mugs. They toasted and swilled the burning cold brew. Business was over, Max thought I'm on downtime now. Mariah sure keeps secrets about her acquaintances. She leaned over, loosened his collar and unbuttoned a few buttons. He surprised her by blushing a deep red. This guy was a real charmer, she thought, wonder why Mariah never mentioned him back then.

CHAPTER 33 *Fireside Peace Talks*

Hiking, climbing, running, swimming, and exploring, they had made both a playground and a training camp out of the wilderness. The community as a whole had grown more fit, stronger, faster, and lighter as they danced through their chores, classes, and events. Tristan took the knowledge he acquired from the Indians and passed it to select members. David and Mariah and the Inner Circle continued to train with the Indians. There was always free time for collapsing by the campfires at the end of long days.

Swimming-training involved holding your breath for several minutes under water, which increased lung capacity dramatically. Of course with these routines, lean body mass was on the rise. This was also due to the diet of fresh river fish, wild greens, nuts, berries, and corn. Tristan knew everyone in the community would have to be physically de-toxed, pure, and lean in order to handle the physical demands of the journey into the interior. The Indians would teach them serious survival skills but they had to have a group that would keep up with them in the first place. When they had begun, each coach would take a group for two hours. Then, a break before they'd switch groups. That meant four to six hours of physical training mixed with life training skills.

After the first months of this, when everyone looked like they were going to give up and go back to their TV sets, it clicked. Now they were enjoying the results of all their hard work.

David, Jody, and Jack would be team leaders on the trek into the interior. There was a mental transition that came with the physical sense of vitality and health each person imbued. People were strong, calm, and mellow with a heightened sense of self-awareness.

Tristan looked forward to the time everyone would be in the attuned mindset needed to accept the Indians' teachings. Then they would reveal their presence. After all, working directly with the Apaches was the goal. He looked forward to the synergy of both communities in a free interchange.

The silver tassels high on green stalks of the first corn caught the light. Peppers, green beans, and squash hung heavy on the vine. Onions were abundant. The harvest was greeted with eager anticipation as they finally tasted the fruits of their labor. Tomatoes were already fat and reddening on the vines. Watermelons, cantaloupes, and honeydews were still small but changing daily. Okra, a staple for all the stews, had to be picked daily while the little shoots were tender. Whether boiled in stews for gumbo, or battered and fried, okra was always delicious. More grains were maturing in the heat. They had red and white wheat, rye, spelt, and barley. Variety was necessary because some crops did better than others. Anya, Nikki, and Isabella preferred to cut the wheat grass and juice it; they consumed it as a drink, insisting on the instant energy it provided. The fresh picked harvests were carried to the central wash station for cleaning and distribution. They were then sorted into the two camp kitchens and the five main camp clusters.

Harvesting food fell into the category of garden chores. Sorting was a cooking team duty. The diversity of chores was great because they could dig a bed for new potato plants on Monday, and harvest green beans on Friday. It was instant gratification. The amount of people increased all summer as more folks arrived, thus there were more hungry mouths to feed, and more pickers available. It was the beauty of an agrarian economy. Many hands make light work. As more labor arrived, more food could be planted and harvested. Voila, more food for their increased numbers.

The newbies in small groups of twos and threes could join in with an established camp. Ten friends that came from Alabama began their own camp, choosing to set up beside a sugar maple grove in Painted Meadow. So they called themselves Maple Meadow. The original five clusters had grown. There were seven clusters total by the end of July.

* * *

Hazel looked around at her assembled youth. All the furrowed brows on the eager faces worried her.

"We are not telling you this to give you nightmares," she assured them. She was working with a bunch of kids after they had spent a few days reading the articles about global warming. "No, we have some ideas for solutions to all of these issues. We're trying to understand the miracles of our world, of Nature and how it's designed. The first thing to note is, all of us breathe oxygen and exhale carbon dioxide. What do trees breathe? They breathe carbon dioxide. They need it—thrive with it. So humans have a symbiotic relationship with trees. Actually, with all green plants."

"I have it," Sean said. "If we have carbon dioxide in the air, then we need more trees. More trees to use the carbon-dio stuff."

"Right. The trees need what we exhale, then they grow big and make more trees."

"So that's why planting trees is a good thing. Like Johnny Appleseed," Meghan said.

"Yes. All plants are a good thing. A necessary thing. Actually if there were no carbon, there would be no plants at all. They couldn't grow," Hazel said.

"No plants, no food."

"That's one way to look at it," Hazel said.

"I guess it's simple. Plant more trees everywhere to make up for the losses and stop cutting down the rainforest," Sean said.

"Someone better tell the president so he can start fixing the climate problem," Meghan added.

"Well, you guys write this down in your own words as if you were the president and could decide. Then, I will have all of this posted on our blog; Fireside Peace Talks." She smiled. "Don't worry, lots of people will see your solutions."

"Part of the solution is to stop pumping so many toxic chemicals in the air. What creates toxic chemicals?"

"Burning fuels from factories and driving cars," Sean said.

"We could drive less," Julia said.

"We don't drive at all," Michael reminded her.

229

"I know we don't here, but we used to. Everyone had a car."

"Would driving less help?" Julia asked Hazel.

"Yes."

"We could have more trains. There used to be trains in the old days. Couldn't we have lots of super-fast efficient trains to carry lots of people where they want to go?"

"Yes, that's a good idea," Hazel said.

"People need jobs, so they could turn the car factories into train factories and make more trains instead of so many new cars," Julia said.

"I think you have something there, Julia. Can you expand your idea and have a paper written by Friday for the blog?"

"Oh yes, Miss Hazel, I will be glad to."

All of these problems boil down to one main thing," Anya said.

"Yes?" Sean asked.

"Pollution and contamination. Wherever we turn to in our modern practices, we seem to cause some sort of contamination. Factories and cars pollute the air. Fertilizers and pesticides pollute the water. Rivers and streams are thus contaminated. That trickles down to all waterways and affects fish. Our society seems to make a lot of stuff that falls apart and then becomes trash. All that has to go somewhere. Buried in landfills makes it unseen and forgotten. So we pollute the earth as well. Global warming or climate change seems small compared to the daily onslaught of contaminates we seem to create. Since we began to live out here, I think it doesn't really have to be that way."

"I couldn't agree with you more, Anya," Hazel said. "As a matter of fact, speaking of trash, here is another huge problem. This is gigantic. Our consumer society has managed to create a giant island made of trash. This garbage collection is currently floating in the ocean. It's a mass of plastic, gasoline drums, and trash all wrapped up in tar made from the oil spills."

"Wrapped like a Christmas present in the tar of forgetfulness," Anya said.

The young faces looked up at Hazel, their eyes wide with horror and disbelief as she described this. This one was beyond them, she could see.

After a few moments of silence she said, "Don't worry about this today. We can think about the problems in the ocean tomorrow. Okay, off you go, I will see all of your papers on Friday."

She wished life in the real world could be simple. But she knew that by next week, she would be hearing ingenuous solutions or uses for the floating trash island. Hazel then went to find Paul. She was afraid she might be in a little over her head.

CHAPTER 34 *Cantaloupe - August*

Rob carried his precious bundle with him as he made his way to the Painted Meadow. When he got there, he spotted Chloe working with the boys. Sean and Michael needed special attention with their work.

"Hi Rob, what's up?" Chloe looked up as he approached. Her eyes squinted when she saw the baby in his front backpack.

"Josie let me take my little nephew, Mason, out for an evening stroll." He twisted his body around so she could get a better look inside his front baby pack.

"Oh, he's so precious," she said. "So alert."

"Yes, his eyes are huge, right? He takes everything in. Roxi doesn't even want kids. Josie's husband doesn't care so I decided I could be the favorite uncle."

Chloe was extremely relieved at this news. "For a minute I thought he was yours." She lost her mask of coolness as she gazed at the happy child. "He just warms my heart to look at him."

"I thought you'd like him. Do you have time for a stroll?"

"Why not?"

The early evening found the two walking down a wooded path. It was a narrow deer path that wound down beside a tributary of the main stream.

"Have you guys had supper already?"

"Oh yes. We have lots of teens living at our tent circle and they eat fast and jump up to go find friends. They have a kickball game going in the sunflower meadow. It's fun for them. Some nights I'm right there with them."

"Well, I'm glad you're not tonight. I thought you might like to meet this little guy."

Chloe handed Mason a small crystal. He gripped it in his hand and waved it around smiling. "He has his own language."

"Do you think we could meet up tonight?"

"What exactly do you mean?"

"I mean if I whistled for you around midnight, that's when everyone's asleep at my place, I thought we could perhaps have a midnight rendezvous?"

"Isn't it kind of dark by then?"

"The moon is still full. Last night the moon was bright as a searchlight."

"Well, what exactly do you have in mind?"

"I don't know. I just wanted to talk to you without all the people hanging about. You know, spend some time. Get to know each other a bit better."

"I like you. What can I say," she thought a moment, "Are you asking me on a date? Commune style?"

"I guess I am." He laughed. "Good then, I'll take that as a yes. I'll take him back to his momma for a feeding. Don't want him to go hungry on my watch."

Chloe watched the tender way he held the baby as he walked back to his own camp.

* * *

Chloe woke with a start. Had she heard something? A stone dropped, making a sharp noise on the tent wall. A low whistle. Sounds like a bird, a tiny strange bird. She strained her ears to hear in the dark. Nothing. A deep dark silence. Then a thump and another low whistle. She was wide awake now. She had slept in her jeans. She pulled a dark sweatshirt on over her white cotton t-shirt. She pulled her fingers through her wispy dark blonde hair; it had grown over the summer. Her heart beat wildly. What did this mean? Sneaking out at midnight at her age? She shouldn't be so excited. What was this long-haired hippie guy up to anyway? It was kind of thrilling, like being a teenager again.

He said he wasn't married. He was with someone, though, and

they'd been together for years. Chloe knew people frowned on her hanging with him. What was he up to? Should she go? Hell, she realized she didn't care. She liked him, and so what?

"Rob," she whispered when she was outside. "Where are you?"

"Over here," he whispered.

She could see his white tennis shoes glowing in the dark with the peculiar blue moonlight shining on them. He reached out with his large hand and grasped hers, pulling her along quickly. She trotted to keep up.

"Where are we going?"

"You will see."

They cut through the meadow and into the forest. After a ten-minute walk the path opened up to reveal a large meadow. No, it was a fully cultivated field. It smelled sweet. Her eyes were used to the dark by now. She saw abundant rows of plants, dark green leaves glistening in the moonlight.

"Hungry?" he asked.

"Sure, you know me, I'm always ready for more food."

"Well, he opened his arms wide, the feast."

"What is it?"

"It's a cantaloupe patch. We have rows of melons, honey dews, and cantaloupes."

"It smells so sweet." She looked hard at the field, her eyes adapting to the night vision. "This is fun."

They looked out over the rows that stretched on. The sky above was full of stars and a brilliant moon.

Rob set his backpack down on the ground between two rows and shook out a blanket he had in the pack on his back. The woven blanket was tightly rolled and it expanded as he shook it and laid it on the ground in the middle of the field between two of the rows. When they got settled, Rob reached out and felt the fruit until one gave to a gentle tug. The odor was pungent and sweet all at once. Chloe could see the ripe, coral-orangy fruit on his knee. He grabbed his pocket knife, and the firm ball opened up ripe and juicy, exposing the moist seeds in the center. He grabbed a handful and threw them on the ground. He offered her some of the ripe fruit.

"I know the gardening crews plant in many fields, but I wasn't aware you had one hidden over here." Chloe was watching him.

"Well, we've been planting and growing in a scattered fashion. So it's hidden and not obvious to the casual onlooker."

He then cut generous slices of the melon and offered it to Chloe. Her face became wet and sticky as she sank her teeth into the fragrant succulence. Rob had pieces in both hands. He was suddenly ravenous as his eyes met hers over the sweet melon.

Chloe took one look at his wet, sticky lips and face noting that his large hands were occupied. She launched herself at him, kissing the dripping juice from his lips. "You're always a bit hungry aren't you? This is a melon feast." Chloe said.

They opened some honeydews and ate their fill.

He smiled. Then they began rolling around, smeared and sticky with juice.

"What are we up to?" she asked.

"I'm not sure," he laughed. "We are all trying to figure that one out. Survival for sure. But you're fantastic. I'm having fun. How about you?"

"Yes, more so than I have had in a long while."

Rob lay back down on the blanket and stared up at the sky. "Makes you think, doesn't it? Being out here. How small we are. In the middle of such a flat place with such a big sky. I come out at night a lot because the stillness energizes me somehow. I just wake up and I'm excited. I wander and enjoy having the whole world to myself, while everyone else is asleep. It's so peaceful and timeless."

Chloe joined him, staring up too, trying to see it as he did.

"Hey I almost forgot, I brought a joint." He propped up on his elbows to light up, then the two lay together, smoking and staring up at the sky in the middle of the field.

They stared up at the planets and stars that filled the sky like an upside-down bowl. Rob then turned to her and took her in his arms, holding her close. He kissed her as if it was the most natural thing in the world. The wind started blowing and then blew harder. They kissed in a deep abyss of passion that could happen with two friends who never realized there had been so much held back between them.

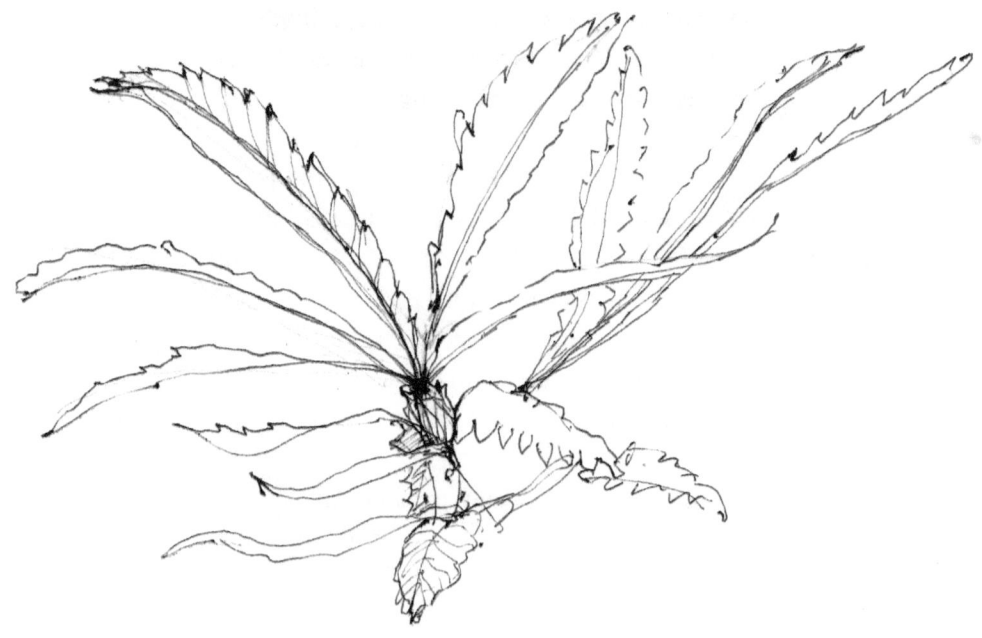

"Wow," Rob said. The wind was whipping the trees now.

"Uh-oh, look." Chloe pointed at the sky and the clouds moving past the moon that momentarily blocked out the light.

Rob saw dark cloud shapes silhouetted by the moon grow in number and move in front of the glowing orb. They both stared in wonder, too shocked to move as the moon came back out and then became hidden again. The wind was whipping, followed by a flash of lightning. More fire streaked across the expanse of sky. Then the wind gave a sharp blast. Chloe felt the chill like icy fingers. She looked up and stopped laughing as she watched the tree branches whip back and forth. She sobered up as she realized she was a bit tipsy and full for the first time in a while.

"What's happening? I'm cold!" she shrieked. Rob held her close for warmth. Then the first fat icy drops began to fall. Icy rain pelted her skin, stinging the sticky stuff away. She rubbed her mouth with her wet fingers. It was falling fast now. Lightning streaked across the sky.

"Summer storm. Where did that come from?"

They both jumped up at once and used the blanket over their heads to block the pelting rain. Rob grabbed Chloe's hand as they raced through the rain and lightning back through the meadow to the woods. Mud sucked thru his shoes as he sloshed through the mud to the tent.

"See you." He kissed the top of her head and dashed off. He was closing in on his own quarters when he remembered Roxi. This is bad. If Roxi wakes up, she will wonder where the hell he'd been. All he could do was pray she'd slept through the storm.

CHAPTER 35 *Harvest*

David only allowed the Inner Circle to harvest the secret patches of the Tree of Life. Harvesting was a concentrated process; one thousand Trees of Life would be harvested one field at a time once they reached maturity. At maturity they would be fifteen to twenty feet tall. Jet had demonstrated the process with a zeal borne of the vital importance of this crop. This particular seed was well adapted to this climate, however, the plants had prospered beyond expectations. Jet told them to hang a line from two oak trees and then suspend the plants upside down to dry for three days. They found they could combine harvesting with the weekly meeting.

After three days, the group convened with Jet to package the plants. With tremendous care, they sniped off all the little flowers and seed pods at the end of every branch and put them in very tight, woven baskets.

Isabella's group had fashioned the baskets for the purpose (so that the flowers and seeds were not lost in transport). The first harvest had surprised them, so they didn't have enough baskets. After that, everyone was prepared for the abundance and skill involved in the careful procedure. Running Wind and Daniel joined Jet in making swift work of the exacting task. They took all the stocks and remaining branches and bundled them tightly together. By the end, they made thirty bundles of stocks in all to haul.

The three Sacred Tree planting fields were further away from the other fields to maintain secrecy. After three days of hard work, ten people stood staring at the huge mountain of harvested produce. Now to solve a new problem—storage.

David suggested the schoolhouse, as it was the only place both dry and hidden. The downside was its location on the far side of Painted Meadow. Paul suggested he could commandeer a few of the *tamer* wild goats to transport the finished packages to the schoolhouse. They seemed to have a lot of secrets, David thought, for a community focused on Truth-telling as a motto.

Each time a field of the sacred tree reached maturity, they went through the same process. This became a great time of fellowship and camaraderie as the Indian brothers and the Inner Circle worked in tandem. Seven from each group were needed to accomplish the task. First in July, then in August, and later in September they would do it again. After each harvest, David set aside some choice picks for the Chief. That, he knew, was the Indian way.

In July, after the first harvest, Jet came with Lily to demonstrate some of the many uses of the Tree of Life to the Inner Circle. Then later Isabella incorporated the fibers they made into the weaving group as Nana Lola and Lily had shown her. She had lots of extra meetings with Nana Lola so she could get the skills down. The herb group led by Jack Java made cheeses using the fermentation process to go along with the variety of goat cheeses already perfected.

The Painted Meadow-Orange Group, all serious diehard vegetarians, were extremely happy with this grain-based cheese. There were different varieties. The basil and walnut-encrusted cheese was aromatic as well as tasty. But the fresh garlic, red pepper, and cilantro cheese was also very popular. Mariah was partial to the cashew, lavender, and cardamom, which although subtle was addicting. Cheese-making was a time-consuming process that took both skill and dedication. The seeds from the sacred tree were easily added to salads and sprinkled on yogurt. The seed inclusion was a necessary part of the diet due to the high protein content. Squash soufflé with a seed topping was a favorite dish that John had perfected.

Mariah knew the Chief's shirt had been made with cloth from the fibers of this flax-like plant. There must be some secret curing process they had not been privy to yet.

To normal people the hot July days were too hot for comfort, but somehow all at the camp were acclimating to the hot, dry temperatures.

For protection of their delicate white skin they all wore wide brim hats and the special skin crèmes developed by the herbalists.

* * *

By August they had broken the one hundred-member mark. This was the community's original maximum; the not-to-exceed figure. Now they had become a magnet. Word was catching like wildfire through underground networks. People came flocking in. The Inner Circle gave up on limiting growth. Some newbies were knowledgeable, eager to jump in and share expertise, and others were just manpower. That's the agrarian way, you welcomed man, woman, and kid power. Others had been out of work for months. They had been helpless and hopeless. Now they were glad to be here, working and focused. Life had a purpose again. Mariah watched as the sad faces of the lost, dirty children turned to joy. In a few weeks' time they were acclimated, happily unrecognizable from the pale apparitions that had first appeared in their midst.

"Isabella, how many are here now?" Mariah called to her daughter as they were working together making basil into pesto and mint into a form of chutney.

"About one hundred and thirty, but it's still summer. People are traveling. The new growth will stop in September, I'm sure."

"This was meant to be a test run. An example so others would know it was possible," Mariah wailed in amazement. "I guess we just let go and let God. We are obviously not the ones in charge here. It is not even our land. We are all squatters here."

"If it were our land we would most likely charge admission and try to make a profit. Ownership and capitalism are related," Isabella stated.

"Yes, maybe. But, we still seem to be able to feed all who join us."

"Of course we can. We'll have abundant harvests in August. Plus all the excess we have had all summer."

"Some of the foreclosed on families haven't seen fresh food in a while." Mariah chopped basil while Isabella ground pecans they would use instead of pine-nuts. "We won't be spending too much time trying to store the goods for later, at this rate of consumption." This was neither good nor bad, it was what it was. People were hungry now, so eat it now. Cross the other bridge when you come to it. Fresh was best in Mariah's world view.

"You're right, the little ones seem to blossom so fast. I thought it was the fresh air, but fresh food and a good three meals a day most likely has a lot to do with it." She stirred olive oil into the mixture. "You know Aaron? Jeff and Meghan's nephew? He's already ten. He watched me milk the goat the other day and was shocked to see where milk comes from. He was mesmerized. Now I have a new one on the goat team."

"I'm glad we are in the shade today making pesto. This fresh basil is having a calming effect on me," Mariah said.

"You're always calm. Wait, I can't believe I just said that. That would never have been true in the old days."

"Be nice. I am your mother," Mariah said, laughing.

Mariah and Tristan had thought about labor and growth early on when they were organizing the schedule. Based on the observation that gardening two hours, twice a day, six times a week worked for thirty people when they first arrived, then naturally they could extrapolate from there.

"We will just keep adding people to the teams. We keep the same routine, just add more labor. This will allow for the tilling, weeding, watering, and harvesting of more beds."

Thus the gardening team of three had grown to six by the time they doubled in size. By the time there were nine on the teams there were plenty of tasks that needed dividing. Now they were preparing the fall beds, as well as harvesting, weeding, and the latrine fill duty.

Planting the filled latrine trenches with baby trees was crucial as they reached the end of summer. The compost-manure filled trenches would be recycled directly into new life. Seedlings of the new trees would transmute the latrine field. The garden crew was also busy capturing seeds from the tomatoes, cucumbers, squash, and pumpkins. They tried to harvest as many kinds of seeds that they could, especially their favorite varieties. They also worked diligently on the compost. This was a big contribution to the land that they had found and lived upon. They would leave behind discreetly hidden compost piles. The only visible changes that would remain once they traveled to the interior were transformed soil and fruit trees. But who could complain about that?

CHAPTER 36 *To the River*

"How was your day?" Mariah brought a hand to shield the sun from her eyes. She peered at David from her perch reclining in the hammock. He was covered with grime and sweating through his clothes. It made her feel a bit guilty for being caught.

"Good. Exhausting." He began unloading the packs and shoulder bags he had carried his tools and supplies in. "You look comfy."

"I just got back from training and snuck over here." She lowered her voice, even though no one else was around, "and fell where you see me not five minutes ago. No seriously, the only time I'm ever alone anymore is on my way to training. I'm not sure if I look forward to the meetings or just the time away. Wait." She heard the voices of men in the distance. "Quick, follow me," she said.

David sighed and stopped himself from collapsing on a bench as she bounded out of the hammock and grabbed his arm. "Quick, let's prolong this rare moment alone."

He grabbed her wrist. "Wait, that hammock looks big enough for two." He was about to drop into it and bring her with him but her momentum had her moving with him attached. She took off on a worn bit of dirt through the brush.

"What's this, a deer path?" David asked as he caught his balance.

"A smooth way to the river. It's perfect this time of day." She continued trotting down the hill.

"What in God's name is the rush? I swear if I had collapsed you'd never have got me back up."

"I know the feeling. We're almost there. Voilà," she pointed.

It was an amazing secluded spot of river, kind of hidden in a weeping willow grove. "C'mon."

She pulled off her heavy leather boots, and began tiptoeing over the boulders. With no choice, he kicked his tennis shoes off and followed.

"I have so much to say all day and now here you are and my mind goes blank."

"It's okay, I don't think I can take in another thing anyway. So many new people. It's what we wanted. But it's a hell of a lot of work."

"Yes, but I never expected this. I mean, who in our extremely privileged society would want to rough it like this? It's still a minority, but it is surprising."

"I feel overwhelmed," he said.

Mariah was surprised.

"It's one thing to come out here, but to be responsible for getting everyone else settled." He smiled. "Thank God we have so many skilled and talented people. It really is amazing. These survivor types come with a lot of knowledge."

"Such as?" Mariah liked specifics.

"Building solar ovens, for one thing, and holistic dental care."

Mariah was jumping rocks to get to the large boulder that glowed rose in the late sun. She looked over her shoulder. "Come on." She stuck her tired feet in the rushing water. "It feels so..." then, bracing herself on the boulders, lowered to suspend herself up to her waist. "Co-eek-cold." Her lower body was immersed with her spine being pummeled with the rushing stream. The sting of cold water invigorated and numbed her. "Ah, that's amazing." She felt each needle of fatigue pulsing at the bottom of her feet start to let go. "I don't know why my feet get so tired at the end of a day. It's like all my fatigue just sails in at the end of a long week."

David joined her and Mariah reached over and rubbed his sore neck and shoulders.

"Umm, keep that up. I'm beginning to feel refreshed."

She turned her face up to the sun, and smiled. "Yes, darling it's finally Friday. I feel like I've been running a marathon all week. I was working on pure adrenaline for the first couple of months. Getting settled and figuring everything out."

"I figured it out," David stated.

"Okay, well, both of us deciding how to survive out here. Then you kept driving to all the nearby towns to collect more supplies and lead all the new people in. I'm so exhausted. Remind me why we did all this?"

"I think you were tired of the rat race. I was tired of traffic and I wanted land. Now we get to live out here together in marital bliss," David grinned.

Mariah laughed at herself. "Perhaps it's just the human condition. We couldn't just come out here by ourselves and enjoy the peace. We had to make an entire mission out of it. What's the matter with us?"

"What's the matter with *you*, you mean. I would be happy if it was just us."

"You say that now, but you would have been bored, not to mention annoyed that you had to do all the work yourself. It would be lonely if the world out there did fall apart and we had no one to share it with. Plus, like you said, look at all the skills. The musical extravaganza we do on the weekends is worth it. Can you believe we have Haley Erin from the Symphony?" Mariah was amazed at that.

"It's pretty cool who shares these kinds of values." David breathed in the fresh cedar air.

"Gerry has retired as principle dancer from the ballet. He's having fun working with the younger ones, reinventing dance," Mariah continued.

"All the dancing and music just makes everyone hungry." David shook his head. "I'm glad someone thinks about food."

David put his arm around her as she sat back up on the rock to let her legs dry in the sun. She leaned into his chest, the spot under his arm that fit her perfect. She listened to his heartbeat under his damp T-shirt. He felt so solid. Like a rock in a storm. His arm was warm around her shoulders. Mariah looked up at him, "Sometimes I feel as if all these forces are pulling us apart. We loved this place and we decided to share it. Now everyone pulls us in different directions."

David looked down at her. "Look, you are my calm in the center of the storm. As long as I have you to return to I don't care what I have to deal with all day. Plus, I love this kind of work. Hard work makes me feel alive." His arm tightened around her as his voice caught. "You, my girl, are my center."

They sat in silence for a while, each in the solitude of non-thought. Their minds full of the natural sounds around them. "You could spend some time in the fields with me, you know." David glanced down at her. "Things are about to stabilize now, we haven't had any newbies lately."

She turned and looked up into his eyes, so piercing in his tanned face, like aquamarine gemstones. "I could just go and live on a desert island with you." Her voice was husky. She cleared her throat.

"We are on a desert island, my dear."

She smiled. "Desert, as in one-hundred-degree temperatures? I have even learned to like your scruff."

He brushed his face self-consciously.

"It's soft now that it's grown out a bit."

He has no idea, she thought to herself as she studied him, how she truly felt. How much she loved him. *He just sees me running around, training, bossing people around. But I'm putty with him. Pure clay in his hands.* She leaned into him to prolong the moment of closeness one minute more.

"Hey, David, there you are!" Exuberant voices shouted above the noisy river.

"Sure, of course." He winked his quick wink at Mariah and grabbed her hand as the two jumped over boulders back to the rocky shore.

She let go of his hand to put her boots back on, then grabbed it again so he could pull her up. As she sprinted up the rocky slope toward Indian Point, she realized she was racing for home.

"Our prayer will rise up to the heavens with the smoke from the fire. All the wood will not die in vain. The sparks will be our messengers. The smoke of both our fires will find each other in the night sky—smoke woven with dreams unique as each dancer dreams. By these fires and rhythmic drumming we will hear the harmony of your tribe. We will dance until all dissonance disappears."

PART TWO

The Invisible Tribe

"You have come into our world. Our peaceful, humble, simple yet safe place, where we live in harmony and abundance. It is small and we are comparatively few. But what you see is what you get. We are free. You run to us."

CHAPTER 1 *The Dinner*

Max suggested meeting Hunter at the dinner, to keep things casual, but Hunter, being a southern gentleman, had insisted on picking her up. She was running late as usual when she spotted him through the dirty picture window of her second floor apartment. He pulled up to her building in a shiny BMW. She ran out, heels in hand, closed the door and locked it, before he could see what a mess she lived in. She hurriedly slipped on pumps, watching him emerge from his steel blue BMW. He looked around for the apartment numbers. She smiled and waved at him from the balcony, before running down to the car. He opened the door gallantly for her. She was dressed simply in a black sheath and a coral shrug she'd purchased for the occasion. She'd actually worn lipstick to match. Once in, filling the car with a sweet perfume, she sat back in the leather, took a deep cleansing breath and relaxed.

Hunter started the engine and turned to look at her. "You look absolutely amazing." He studied her with a quizzical look before putting the car in gear. He pulled out into the Friday evening traffic. Her heart skipped a beat right at that look. Something in his blue eyes told her more than he let on. She had never been looked at that way before. She could tell she was falling for him. She tried to keep her tone casual, like normal. She, the master of cool was falling for Hunter.

"Where are we headed? I forgot to ask where this special dinner was being held."

"Downtown of course. The Menger Hotel. It's an historic hotel where *absolutely everything* of a political nature happens." He drawled for effect. "You will like it, I have a feeling. Lot of history there."

"I won't know anyone. So what's my role?"

"Just stay by my side, and be your naturally charming self. And don't talk, of course. Ah, but to be seen and not heard."

"Such is the role of perfect children."

"And women. I wish."

"Really? You didn't strike me as the type."

He raised an eyebrow, "Yes, but we are in the South, you know."

"Texas isn't exactly the South. If I make a mistake just say I grew up on a ranch or something."

"You know what I mean, don't you?" He sounded alarmed. "Take your cues from me."

"Sure, if that is what makes you feel like a man, in control and all that. That should be a piece of cake. At least we have already established we know how to dance together."

"Perfectly. I'm looking forward to that aspect of the evening."

"That is probably the safest part. If the conversations get sticky just pull me on the dance floor. Will there be a band?" Max asked.

"Yes, that's the good news. You won't believe it."

"Try me."

"It's 'The Lost Gonzo's. They're your friends from the other night aren't they?"

"Well, yes. That's great. This is going to be a lot of fun."

"See, we are not all that uptight around here. Texas swing is all the rage. Our mayor loves the local stuff."

"Hurrah for us." At that she'd relaxed for the rest of the drive, determined to enjoy every minute of her time this evening. Despite Hunter's southern attitude surfacing.

They entered the grand lobby of the hotel. An army of solemn doormen, hostesses, and wait staff were on duty to direct the arrivals up the carpeted stair to the special dining room on the second floor. The comforting aroma of seafood bathed in butter, and baked rolls surrounded Max. Hunter wore black tie, of course. Most women wore long dresses, but some had opted for the shorter cocktail length like she had. She always went short when she could, to show off her great legs. There were a lot of middle-aged women rustling in pink and yellow satin gowns escorted by distinguished silver-haired men in black. Hunter was young for this crowd, she realized. It dawned on her belatedly, that he must be very successful to be in these circles. As they were shown to a table to the left of the dais, she recognized a few businessmen from local magazines and the paper.

There were several couples flanking the mayor and his wife, who sat at the table of honor. She realized the one who was the speaker was in from the office of Scofield, Jones, and Walters. They had met at lunch last week. The fellow diners at the table were an interesting mixture of politicians and businessmen. She quickly surmised people had paid handsomely for the privilege to be here tonight. The filet mignon was cooked to perfection and the seafood pastry had an excellent sauce. A waiter appeared at her elbow offering a choice of red or white wine. She nodded to the red. She felt the austerity of the crowd melting as the wine began to flow. The thick Texas accents were the first surprise as people began to relax and share stories of occupation and address. The severe and elegant silver haired crowd became less perfect as smiles showed silver teeth and pock marked faces. She even noticed the dandruff on the coat of the gentleman next to her.

"Where are you froum? How do you know Huntah?" People drawled at her. "He has such well mannehed childrin. How long have you two been datin?" Questions were hitting her all at once. She tried to make quippy answers or raise her eyebrows to keep from engaging in lengthy personal discourse. She managed to flip the questions back deftly as she nodded at the revealing tales that ensued.

Later on while mingling with the crowd, she heard a mans voice. "You don't seem his type."

"Come again?" She looked over at a short man at her elbow.

"You are different than his usual."

"Oh, we're good friends, I'm doing him a favor."

"Where did you say you were from originally?"

"Wow, that's a cool tie. Your wife buy it for you?" She said sweetly. "You don't seem the type to be so well-coordinated all by yourself." Her tone changed back to all business, "I'm from Houston. Why all the questions. Are you interested?"

"I could be." He let his gaze travel slowly up from her mini skirt and leveled at her nose. "If it's true you two are just friends."

"I don't believe you would let 'friendship' stop you from something you wanted." She reeled him in with a coquettish curve of coral lips, and paused for a beat before she hit him, fast and blunt, "But I'm not on the market." She stared hard at him, and then turned on her heel, ending the conversation with the last word.

"Hey, hey, I was just being frienley. I'm new in town and I needed someone to show me 'round," he called after her.

She slowly spun back on one spiked heel "Oh really? How new? You seem to know your way around."

Hunter appeared at her elbow. "Hi." He leaned in for a proprietary kiss on her cheek, simultaneously handing Max a glass of champagne. "Have you two met?"

"Not formally," the man was quick to extend a hand.

"Miss French, Mr. Scofield, our speaker this evening."

Max nodded. The name was familiar. "I've heard your name somewhere?" She cocked her head at him.

"Oh I'm flattehed," he replied, syrupy sweet. "My profession is a bit dry. I didn't know a pretty young thing like you would notice the news."

"Am I disturbing something? You two need a moment?" Hunter smiled, and then added, "Actually, Mr. Scofield, there are piles of people awaiting your benediction." He gestured to the people who had gathered around to shake his hand. Hands were thrust out in all directions. Hunter then guided Max out of earshot. "Was he bothering you?"

"Trying to, but I can handle myself. I'm a big girl."

"He's notorious, but I thought my friends were off limits."

"Maybe the challenge is what he's aftah." She spoke slowly.

"Forgive me. I'm sorry I told him your name."

"You didn't. I don't go by my maiden name anymore." She patted the arm she was holding.

"Oh, thank God. He's tenacious. He'll never find you then?"

"I will sic him on you if he does," she teased.

"That's not very respectful of our upcoming senator." Hunter chuckled as he steered her to the dance floor.

"Senator? No one told me. That's why his name sounded familiar."

CHAPTER 2 *Acting and Max*

"I'll be here for a week. I have some serious training to do after your little demonstration last time." Max's tone was flat. She'd already spent the morning relaying the events of her fund raiser dinner with Hunter.

"You are already in great shape," Mariah said. She knew a bit of competition was coming on. She was glad Max was back. She looked forward to her frequent visits.

"Get real. You know what I mean. I need skills." Max pulled her straight brown hair back into a ponytail. "Look at your abs." She lifted Mariah's T-shirt and poked playfully. "This speed climbing method you're using is foreign to me. Schooling in the use of medicinal herbs is crucial if we're going to survive out here long term. Not to say knowledge of wild edibles isn't vital. We could get hungry and poison ourselves!"

"It's been known to happen."

"OK. Got it."

Mariah opened the flap of the white muslin tent. Inside, light filtered in through a gauze-covered window, illuminating a colorful woven rug. There was a table and camp chair with lots of supplies scattered about. "Okay. Let's look at the list." Mariah cleared a place at the table, then sat down. Max took a seat cross-legged on the rug beside her.

"You've met Jack Java, right?"

Max nodded at her.

"He leads the Wild Edibles group. He takes everyone out about nine a.m. The Runners start about six a.m. right before breakfast. You could do both if you wanted to. Lunch is at one, we use the morning finds when we prepare it. At two p.m. the Spinners—they're a spin-off off of the weaving group—process the wool from the wild sheep and goats. The Weavers work the whole afternoon on blankets for winter. It's a large group of fifteen to twenty folks. Now that the stone ovens and spring houses are finished, the building group has morphed into the woodworkers. They gather around two and work through the afternoon, then at five we have a group hike or swim." She caught the look on Max's face. "No, this is more for R&R than hard core workout. At six we have yoga, meditation, and overall quiet time. Simultaneously, the dinner crews get going at the various tent sites." Mariah paused for a beat in case Max had any questions, but she just nodded for her to continue.

"There are seven main tent clusters," she singsonged. "You know that. Are you interested in learning new skills or building stamina? People attend about four activities a day. The athletes have a two p.m. swim class that focuses on underwater diving and breathing techniques. The potters meet after in the lower meadow about three because a lot of them swim. Pat Cooper found a place down near a cave south of Jade Cove that has wonderful natural clay. They harvest that to use in their pieces. A lot of the teens joined that group. There's also..."

"Okay, Okay," Max said. "I get the gist. Wow! I want to do everything. It would be smart to get in one of the predominately male groups as I'm single and all."

"This is not a match-making trip, I hope. Hey, I thought you liked Hunter."

"Later on that, are there any singles?"

"Yes. Lots. You get to guess which ones."

"That's not fair!"

"Well, how should I know?"

Max rolled her eyes. "What is the Acting group?"

"In the Acting group we practice things like archery, sword fighting, and even Tai-chi. Most often we learn how to understand and mirror animals. This way we can communicate with other creatures we share the woods with. 'Acting like' allows you to get in the animal's skin. It actually gets more sophisticated than that. Imitation is the key to communication. This is an early step in preparation for the shape

256

-shifting we will do later.

"We just started it recently. There are some devotees of the bow and arrow. Rob, our darling little brother, is leading that one, along with Paul. You know Paul, he has a very interesting background. He may be a little old for you, though."

"I like old guys."

Mariah ignored that. "They are very skilled, from what I hear. You have a week, right? You decide what your priorities are and go for it."

"I should take two weeks, now that I get the magnitude of what's going on."

"Can you really handle two weeks away from your precious life in the *real* world?"

"I think I have to. I wasn't kidding about the realities of winter."

"I know you're right. I'm glad to have you full time. There is nothing like family. Besides, there are some lost souls here who would benefit from more companionship."

"Really? Tell me about it."

"Well, we've been getting a lot of newbies. They don't have the history of those in our Inner Circle. We've been hanging out together for the past ten years. Our kids have grown up together. But these guys only have one or two acquaintances–they heard about The Ranch through word of mouth."

"So it's working? People are coming?"

"Yes, we use the written word. We write letters, you know, mail? David or whoever happens to be going into Lakeville posts them once a month or so. The word is out there, and folks are fascinated by our experiment. Maybe they bet on whether we are going to make it or not. I don't know." Mariah's heart raced as she realized their group was expanding while she was chatting away. "We also have the blog you have been posting for us. Thanks for that. "

"That's amazing in a way," Max said. "Never thought I'd be blogging under any circumstances...as a matter of fact."

"As I was saying, before you interrupted." She playfully patted Max's leg. Their whole family was notorious for going off on tangents. It was a rare occurrence that anyone could get from point A to point 'B' in a conversation. "They are lonely for those they left and searching in general. Don't get me wrong, these guys come with a lot of knowledge from different parts of the country. Some even knew Peter in the past. Various connections, you know." She took a sip of her strong camp coffee. "There's this one girl, Chloe, who has latched on to Rob. Check that out, by the way. He's being a good host. But you know he's been with Roxi for seven years and she's getting a bit pissed off."

"Uh oh, Politics in paradise."

"No, human relationships and interaction. Its natural, isn't it?"

"Depends."

Max was thoughtful. "You can take the humans out of the culture but you can't take the culture out of the humans."

"Right," Mariah's eyes glazed over as she thought of her own anointing. She used to agree with Max, but now she realized people can change. "Back to your training schedule. If you want my opinion, the Acting Group would be the best way to maximize your skills. Plus, it's mostly guys right now."

"That sounds about perfect for me. Say, nice digs here, by the way. "

"You're serious? I like it. It's minimal but has everything I need right at my fingertips." The two stood up and walked outside. "Think about coming here full-time." She embraced her younger sister. "I wouldn't mind having you at my fingertips too." She escorted Max out of her private chamber.

"Love you. Later."

Mariah grinned at her grown-up little sister.

CHAPTER 3 *Whisperers*

Max joined the Acting Group to learn how to commune with the wildlife at The Ranch. As decided, her 'job' was to be nice and friendly, especially to Chloe. Rob led the training. She rose before dawn and joined the others at the large oak tree off a narrow deer path a good ten-minute walk from Painted Meadow. Max was the last to arrive. Rob and Paul were there, along with Chloe and a few others Max hadn't met before.

"Good morning, Max," Rob nodded, his voice resonating in the predawn air. Rob really got the Indian vibe. Shirtless, barefoot with jeans hung loose on his hips. His humble straightforward gaze exuded calm. In the faint light Max could tell his skin was almost black from the summer sun.

"John and Sarah, two of the teens, have gone ahead," he said to her. "They both have a gift. Since you're new, I'll go over a few of the basics.

This morning you'll get to see the techniques in practice. Okay?"

At Max's nod, Rob gestured to several hoof prints.

"These are deer tracks. From the placement, it's a small herd. A buck, two does, and three fawns. You see here…" He pointed first to the buck and doe's prints, then moved to another, smaller one. "This print is almost the size of the three adults, but still bigger than the other two fawns. That means it's young, but no longer a newborn. Perhaps six to eight months old."

"Show off," Max teased, noting the curious look she got from Chloe. "Go on. I'm impressed."

"Sarah found this trail yesterday. These prints are fresh, made within the last couple hours."

Rob had taught John, training the old goats he had been intent on taming when they first arrived. Rob used the same techniques in teaching everyone else. This was the first time they would try it on a completely wild deer. Sarah, although young, had a lot of promise. He wanted this to work but really there was no guarantee that his Horse training methods from back home would apply now. "Since John began using the body language techniques on those old settler goats, everyone's been practicing daily. Sarah has shown the most hutzpah and sensitivity." Rob looked at the others with a wry grin. "She's been itching to try it out on something a little more wild." "She might succeed. Or she might just scare the herd off. This trail leads to a small meadow near the river. John is waiting at the edge of the woods. As we go to meet him, I urge you to keep silent. Then please sit down without moving a blade of grass. Keep your eyes open wide. Look for subtleties. John and I will then split off amongst the trees to back Sarah up. Everybody understand?"

Heads nodded, as they followed Rob single file. Max was first, then the two newbies, with Chloe and Paul bringing up the rear. The others had been practicing the graceful walk for weeks. A twig snapped under Max's foot and she endeavored to walk with more care.

John hovered, hidden in the trees back from the clearing. As they neared, they fanned out to stand side-by-side. Max observed Sarah, about ten paces out, sitting on her heels in the meadow. Sure enough, the herd was there. The river flowed along the far side of the meadow, and rounded the river bend. Max noticed that the meadow made a nice cove, with the forest enclosing the river on both sides. She guessed the meadow was a good couple hundred feet across, and slightly less than that from the river to where she stood.

Rob, signaled for everyone to squat. As she did, Max glimpsed John moving off through the trees to her left, while Rob did the same to her right. She glanced back to see that Sarah hadn't moved, and neither had the deer. They had their heads down, grazing on the green shoots. There was a magnificent buck with a full eight-point rack, and his two does near the river. Next to the does were twin fawns. One of them was nursing. The third fawn, the one Rob had identified to be a little older, was a short distance from the others, nearer to where Sarah was. She became a statue as her eyes focused on this young one. She gave an almost imperceptible glance to the left, and right. Identifying John and Rob's positions, Max thought.

Sarah edged to the right, staying low. Max realized she was moving around the clearing in a Tai-chi stance without getting any closer to the young one. Sarah was silhouetted against the predawn sky, squatting between the young one and the rest of the herd, a lead rope looped in her hand.

When Sarah stood, the young one looked up, catching her scent. Action. Everything happened at once. The young doe's glance darted from Sarah to the herd. Before it could move, Sarah flicked the rope out, keeping her shoulders square with the young one. The buck and doe dashed to the right, moving for the cover of the woods near Rob. Max couldn't see him but she guessed he squatted in hiding.

The young doe moved to follow, but Sarah flicked the rope, blocking its path. As she moved, she angled her body, her shoulders squared with the young doe. She kept it from bolting after the herd. Sarah and the doe were moving towards the river in tandem. Max realized it had only taken a few moments to separate the young one and Sarah ran parallel with the doe, moving from the center toward the river.

The doe angled right, and Sarah slanted toward it flicking the rope, constantly counter balancing the young one's every move. When they reached the river's edge, Sarah didn't close in. The doe angled to follow the river to the left when she saw she was blocked. Sarah dashed obliquely. Not directly after the doe, but back up the meadow slightly, and to the left, she changed hands as she flicked the rope out to the left.

Immediately, the doe skidded round and sidled toward the river, and back to the right. Again, Sarah dashed in a small semi-circle to the right, flicking the rope, and keeping her head high, shoulders square and strong toward the animal. Back and forth, down and back, the doe ran. With the swift flowing current on the one side, and Sarah on the other, they moved in unison. The doe constantly tried to escape, and Sarah just as diligently angled her body to block and flicked the rope to guide it back.

Max couldn't call it anything else. Sarah was dancing with the doe! She kept a fast pace, moving back and forth. The deer was tiring, panting and swinging its head around, looking for any escape. Sarah was out of breath too. She hadn't closed much distance between herself and the deer, but she had, with her body and the rope, influenced its movements.

Just then, the young doe dropped her head to the ground, its eyes all the while on Sarah. Her head was only eight inches from the ground. Sarah didn't stop moving, keeping her shoulders squared. The doe slowed down. Sarah closed the distance a little more, and the doe renewed its speed. With head raised it dashed around making a smaller circle. The doe slowed, trotting in circles with its head lowered to the ground. Sarah kept up the movement, but the doe stayed steady with its head to the ground. After another full pass, the doe started chomping down and licking its lips without eating, its eyes still locked on Sarah. Sarah slowed, and finally stopped. The doe stopped too.

No longer angled away from Sarah, the doe her head still lowered, licked, and chomped at the mouth. Sarah turned a fourth turn and looked sideways at the doe over her shoulder. With her eyes fixed on the doe, Sarah turned one step further away. The young one still stood, no longer trying to get away, even as Sarah turned her back to it.

Max watched as with Sarah's back still turned away, the deer took one hesitant step towards her. One slow step at a time, the doe moved forward. It was like magic. The doe was only a step away from Sarah's back. It stretched its neck and lightly rested its head on Sarah's shoulder like a friend. Max let out her breath in a gush. Her cheeks felt a little wet but she didn't dare move to wipe them.

Sarah's whole face beamed as she took a step forward, the doe stepped with her. Sarah angled to the left and the deer followed suite. Sarah then turned back to the right, and the deer joined her, following Sarah. It was amazing. She had the animal's complete trust.

When Sarah came back to the center she raised her hand shoulder height and stroked the deer's nose. While stroking, Sarah turned, with quiet grace and pulled a carrot from her pocket. The deer nudged the carrot, then chomped down on it. As it ate, Sarah scratched the animal's neck with one hand. Sarah raised the rope over the doe's neck. She pulled it gently into a loose loop. It sniffed at the rope, but didn't seem to mind. Sarah stepped in front of the doe and walked toward John. The animal followed behind with the rope loose. John glided up to Sarah, held out his palm, while the young doe remained still. The doe sniffed his hand while John stroked behind her ears.

Rob came out to meet them as they hiked, shoulder to shoulder, across the meadow with the young deer following.

"There you are little one," Rob held out his hand for her to smell. She did, Rob patted her on the shoulder. Then they climbed up toward the others, all speechless in reverence for this rare intimacy they had witnessed.

"Amazing is an understatement." Rob shook his head. "Sarah, I do believe you have the gift. John and I were ready to jump in and face down the buck if he looked ready to defend, but he herded the others off without a fuss." The deer flicked its ears toward him as if understanding every word. "You all can stand up now. Move slowly. Don't spook her now that she's warming up to her human friends."

"Wow!" Max breathed. She laughed softly at the mimicry.

"Now that was truly awesome," Chloe chimed in. "How did you do that?"

"That's my first time," Sarah looked delirious with a huge smile she couldn't contain. "I guess it works with deer as well as horses. It really works." In a rush she went on to explain. "I learned it from Rob, John, and Paul. Rob's teacher was a man named Monte Roberts – a real life 'horse whisperer', back when he worked with horses."

"In your case, 'Deer Whispering,'" Rob said.

"Mr. Roberts learned it from his full-blooded Cherokee grandmother, but I'll bet it's more ancient than that. Just like Rob teaches, it's all about reading the body, both for animals and humans. It's quite natural, actually," Sarah beamed.

Max gave Sarah a hug on her free side. Max could tell she was shocked by her success. By now, they were all gathered around the young doe, rubbing and petting her. She seemed a little frisky with all the attention, but she was standing fairly still. Max reached over and scratched her neck, marveling at how the animal leaned in at the touch.

"You noticed that when Sarah first stood up, and then during the entire running back and forth, she kept her shoulders square and facing straight at the doe?" Rob asked.

They nodded.

"That's an offensive pose when you move toward the animal. You're saying, 'I'm equal to you, and I can handle you.' If you stand still, with squared shoulders, you're being defensive, but also showing your equality. If the buck, or one of the mother does, had decided to charge Sarah, she would have begun hollering and waving her arms high, and John and I would have charged in if it didn't back off. It would have messed up her overtures toward this young one.

"You must be very careful with wild animals. They pick up on your scent. Sarah's practiced with John on the goats. They've tamed quite a few now, besides the nanny. If she'd been afraid, this little one would have smelled the fear and might have tried to bolt. Instead, you observed how quickly it responded to her movements. It had chances to bolt, but because she was so swift to counter each movement, it didn't.

"Body language is crucial, but so is knowing your own emotions. If the buck had charged, the worst thing to do would have been to turn completely around and run. She'd have been inviting him to chase her. If you aren't emotionally ready to charge back, hollering, screaming, and waving your arms, then you need to run at a diagonal, away from the charging animal, while always keeping a quarter of your body turned to him, with your eyes locked on him. Never let your eyes leave an animal that you think might attack you." Rob paused to demonstrate.

"This stance says, 'I'm paying attention to you, but I'm also interested,' if you're standing still. If you're moving away, it says, 'I'm paying attention, but I'm also leery of getting too close.' You're respecting its personal space and would like it to do the same for you. Another sign you may have noticed was when the doe finally lowered her head, she acted like she was chewing grass with her head lowered near to the ground, but she was not actually eating anything, and her eyes were tilted up on Sarah. She was saying that she's open to being approached and submits to you as leader. Deer, goats, horses, and elk all have very similar body signs. On the other hand, bears, cats, and dogs are predators and share a different kind of language."

Rob had been working with Jet, his Indian guide, to befriend one of the wild panthers that roamed the high steppes of The Ranch. Rob remembered all too well how the mother cat had screeched and advanced. Rob had backed away at an angle, keeping his eyes locked on her, with his position a good quarter turned her way. Thankfully, she'd been cool with him moving back. Jet had told him later that he needed to work on his fearless approach. Rob chuckled slightly at the memory. Fearless indeed, it'd scared him and he'd been sure if he had run away, that would have been it for him. He couldn't out run a panther, no matter how much training he'd had.

"Remember," he said to everyone, "caution is extremely important. Sarah's been practicing a lot. This is an extremely powerful tool, and as you learn the subtleties of all the different signs—how to identify tracks, droppings, and animal sounds—then you'll be able to understand more about how you interact with animals and with each other. But please, never go out alone to practice. Keep the buddy system, and as long as you want to learn, I'll get up early with you. Okay?"

They all murmured, 'OK's' and 'Gotcha's'. Max realized the sun was just coming up. She glanced down at her watch. The whole deer encounter had only taken forty-five minutes. Amazing, she thought, last week I was researching mergers and acquisitions and today I'm petting a wild deer.

"Now Sarah," Rob said, "I know you'll want to move around with your new friend. Perhaps take her back down to the river for a drink?" Turning to everyone else, he said, "How about we try practicing some of the stances? Paul and I will go over the body language with you, and help your postures."

Rob started by having everyone practice stances on their own. An hour later, Max was sweating, but she wasn't sure if it was from the movement or from intense concentration.

"Relax" Rob said when he came over to help her, "breathe, focus. See, you're tensing up trying to hold the stance. Let it be natural. Flow with the movement. Okay. Close your eyes. Try to imagine the buck facing you. Can you see him?"

"No."

"Do it again. Close your eyes. Now?"

"No."

"Just breathe in deep. That's better. Try again. Got it? Now turn and face him in one smooth motion. Just let yourself dance."

Max did exactly as she was told. She tried to relax her muscles, to imagine a charging buck, to imagine her holding her stance, to see herself being dominant. She stood calm, sturdy, shoulders squared.

"Ready."

"There you go," Rob whispered.

"Wow. It feels different standing like this."

"You were thinking too hard," Rob said.

"Oh, I was trying to do it right."

"Focus and tunnel vision are two different things. Let go of the outcome. Just try to flow with the movement."

"Okay, okay." Max took a deep breath, then circled her shoulders to relax the tension. "Hey, do you know that girl over there? She looks familiar."

"Chloe?"

"Chloe who?"

"I don't know, just Chloe, I guess."

"She looks familiar, out of context, though." Max looked towards the others, who were scattered about the meadow as they tried a new technique. They chased and circled each other, each appearing to take turns as the deer. It wasn't as good as Sarah with the doe, but they were practicing the movements, trying to learn and read each other.

"Keep practicing," Rob reassured, "and you will get it. That's a promise." Then, with hands clasped behind his back, he strolled on to observe the others.

Max tried again. She shook her arms, trying to loosen them, then focused on the tree and imagined it was a charging buck. As she looked at became bigger, big enough to obscure everything else in the scene. She could have sworn she felt her pulse quicken with fear. In her imagination she could only see a charging buck. Focus, she thought.

She squared her shoulders, leaned forward, and took a few strong steps. She was standing her ground. She could feel her determination rising. Success. This was fun and mentally invigorating, she realized. The morning flew by. She was caught up in flowing from stance to stance, practicing alone or with others, cocking her head, ever so slightly this way or that, using her eyes to encourage or discourage, feeling how the body flowed with emotion. She and Paul were paired up for a time. She felt her cheeks growing hot when Rob showed her different stances for how to be "inviting". She hadn't realized she almost always stood defensively towards men. Rob walked among them; pointing out different emotions he could read based on how they were standing and how they could pose to say something else.

Finally, Rob called it a day. "We will meet again in a couple of days, same place, same time. Good job, Max."

"Thanks. You are a good teacher. Perhaps you missed your calling."

He stared at her, amused. "What do you call this? This is my calling and here I am, doing it." He squeezed her shoulder. "I'm called by nature. I'm one of the most informed people out here. Stick with me, kid. I teach lots of workshops."

On the walk back, Max made sure she found herself next to Chloe. "Chloe, is it? I'm Max. I don't think we've met."

"No, we haven't. Hey, Max."

"You look familiar, though. Where are you from, by the way?"

"San Antonio."

"I thought so, I couldn't place it. I must have seen you at the Governors' Ball in Austin last year. Are you an attorney?"

"Me? God, no, I was with my ex-husband. She shook her head.

"He is. It's a past life thing. Wow, I haven't thought about him in a long time. Long, long ago in another lifetime. I had forgotten about that life."

"I hear you, out here, so far removed, it's easy to forget. Tell me, what are you doing hanging out with these out-of-work renegades?"

Chloe wasn't amused, "I live here now. I'm committed. Been here since June. I love it. And you are?"

"Oh, sorry, I'm Max, Rob and Mariah's sister."

"Okay..." She emphasized the 'K' part. "You are the one who works in San Antonio."

"Yeah, I come and go, but I'll be here for the next few weeks—see if I can take it. Tell me, you miss the old life back in town?"

Chloe gave her a strange look. "Like I said, it's like it never existed."

CHAPTER 4 *Dance Reverie*

The drums sounded a steady beat in the distance—pulsing like a solid vibration within the earth. Mariah floated on her back absorbing peace from the calm-as-glass lake in Jade Cove. She watched the hawk circle in the distant cobalt sky. She felt serene, as though one with the bird. He, floating the air currents, while she floated on the water. The sound that pulsed through the rock and the water like a distant vibration, snuck up on her. She had come to find early evening in the water the most peaceful times of the day. This was her kind of meditation. Buoyant and timeless, she felt held by the goddess herself. She was safe and coddled as a new born babe held in the arms of The Mother. This was the goddess's world. In the stillness, she could believe in the total transcendence and ultimate harmony of the whole planet. Perhaps their work here would lead to a totally healed and restored earth. Were Indians coming? Joining in with them this time?

Oh no, the Dance. Her thoughts turned to the fourth Dance happening that night. She had almost forgotten; she'd been busy organizing the learning units. It was clear Isabella had been true to her word, gathering the teens as promised to organize the Dance. They had all learned a lot as they tried to make the experience as close to a real pow-wow as possible.

In the month of August, Rob had been chosen to receive his anointing from Chief Nuage, Sunowa, and the others. All of the Inner Circle had gone through this individually throughout the summer. Tristan was first, when he went on his vision quest. Then she had been called. No one could have prepared her for what took place. She suspected each person's experience was unique and private.

The anointing had been a true awakening for Mariah. Her eyes and soul were opened. She saw her Indian brothers differently. She had insights into all the new people as they shed their old lives to join them. Her Life—her own role and *Life* itself—had felt amplified. More significant. Even the clothes the Indians wore (she had assumed were leather) were really a dense felted fabric from the tree of life plant. These newly evolved Indians had never been hunters. They were lovers. They reaped what they had sown. They formed and fashioned with magic hands from plants they had grown. Creative hands. She had never known of this plant before. She couldn't have truly realized it. The thick ultra-soft suede and beaded dress Chief Nuage's wife, Swan Cloud, wore for the anointing Ceremony was actually fabric formed from this plant. Now she understood that man could keep evolving spiritually and creatively. The Apache Indians from the lost tribe in the 1880's had evolved in this new way. They were enlightened. They lived in harmony with all Living Things. In the modern world, the one she had forsaken, it was only the machines—computers, cameras, technology—that had evolved, were *still* evolving.

After Mariah, David, Isabella, and Jack Java had been chosen, each had returned empowered to take on new roles with conviction. For Isabella that role was the preparation for the fire ceremony.

Finally, in the month of August, Rob had been called. His anointing was to be an initiation of sorts. He had been chosen to lead the entire ranch community in this final step of preparation, much like the role of Shaman. Indians have a chief to lead physically, and a shaman to lead spiritually. Jet worked together with Rob to prepare the sacred herbs and the special tinctures included in the anointing oil.

Mariah noticed Rob came back from this experience very much changed. His face shone with light, his bearing erect and his voice patient as a teacher's. Mariah had noticed changes in her children, but they had always been evolving in that direction. Their anointing served to set them firmly on their paths with confidence. With Rob, who had lived much, the transformation was profound.

She rolled to her belly and swam smoothly through the water to the rock ledge, her arms slicing the surface in clean strokes. She used her momentum to push herself past the rough edges of rock. When she stood, she squeezed the water out of her hair. Her jean shorts and oversized white Henley had been lying on the warm rocks; they felt good against her cool skin as she pulled them on over her suit.

Long grasses shown like silver swords in the evening light. The leaves on the pecan trees had a lime green pulse in the breeze. Since she was already late, she hopped the rocks along the stream bed, thinking it would be the quickest way to the pow-wow circle. She moved swiftly, using her body in the new silent way she had mastered over the past few months. She soon rounded the bend and could see the medicine wheel laid out in the dry grass meadow.

Many people were already gathered in the circle around the fire. A few folks still waited to be smudged before entering. She floated down the dirt trail and joined the line. People were somber. The loud drumming, now a determined call, thrumming in her brain. More people hurried to join the circle. Smoke and the scent of sage hovered over Jack Java and his son John as they teamed up to smudge each participant. The sun was low on the distant horizon, the sky a large expanse of brilliant color. About a hundred people were gathered around the fire circle. They all focused on the ceremony that was about to begin, turning expectant faces towards the fire.

CHAPTER 5 *Fishing*

David was determined to enjoy Sunday as a day of rest. He walked away from camp towards Big Rock, the wide pool closest to the main house. It was the place he fished to find some peace and quiet. Although he no longer kept the fish, it was peaceful to watch them in deep water. In the pale gold of the afternoon he noticed a lone figure up ahead on the river bank. For a moment, David just watched the silhouetted shape casting about in a rather messy fashion, trying to make out who had beat him out here. As he grew closer, he realized with a start the short-haired guy with spectacles was Hunter Jones.

"What are you doing here?" David asked.

Hunter tossed a beer can over his shoulder. "What are *you* doing here?"

Despite his casual manner, David could see he was visibly startled to see another person in this wilderness.

"You look bummed," David replied instead.

He noticed Hunter was aimlessly fishing around his cooler for another beer with his left hand. Empty cans were strewn about in the tall wheat grass.

"I never come out here. I miss him," Hunter said. "We were best friends. I thought it would be hard, but, hell, it's been over ten years. This place brings back countless memories. Crisp as yesterday." Hunter stared out at the babbling stream gleefully churning over rocks as if all was well in the world.

Unsure how to respond, David let that sink in, while he prepared his line for a traditional fishing effort.

"Wait, what are you doing here?" Hunter asked again.

"Well..." David slowed his speech as he sorted in his mind what to say. "You do remember me, right? I'm David Agnelli, Mariah's husband. We met at one of Peter St. George's gatherings."

"Yes, of course I do," Hunter groused. "Your hairs grown a bit and you're a bit scruffy but I remember. Hell, like it was yesterday. Good to see you!"

David studied the unshaven face and hollowed eyes. "We were camping in the neighborhood. I thought I'd come by and do some fishing. Didn't think anyone else would be around. Mind if I join you?" David asked, even as he sat down on a nearby rock. Hunter didn't reply, and the two fished in tense silence for a while.

"No one comes here," Hunter broke the ice. "His family used to, but now they rarely bother. That's why there's ample fish and game."

"So, Hunter, tell me, what's life like in the big city?"

"Big city? You're from the big one. You ought to know." He cast out again against the current. "The war. The gas prices, the banking industry, money, or lack of. The country. The whole country is a disaster. I came here to get away from it all. My wife left, went to San Francisco. Said Texas was too small town for her. I can see why Peter didn't have one. A wife I mean. Yet, it could be dangerous to live out here alone..."

"I know what you mean."

"My Dad died this year. I'm supposed to take over his practice. Now I'm flooded with too much information. Texas oil; money barons. God, oil is big business."

"Are you going to camp here?"

Hunter looked around. He finally cast out.

David surmised his thoughts must be full of Peter and the old times. There was a soft splash as the line hit the water's surface, then a comfortable silence settled between the two men. They heard a hawk scream as it circled the endless blue above. David watched the bird float the vortex. They tuned in to the chirping of the crickets and hum of the grasses in the faint breeze.

"God, I thought Peter was crazy." Hunter broke the silence. "You know, going loony out here from too much solitude. Now I realize when I'm out there, I had bought all the bull-shit 'they' want you to.

You know, the buzz of the world. Fell for it all hook, line, and sinker. It's hard to be brainwashed if you spend eighty percent of your time out here in nature. Hey, have ya'll set up camp?"

"Well actually, if you can keep a secret, we have." David looked long and hard at Hunter while he made his decision. "I think Mariah might miss me about now." He thought about what he was doing, "If you're willing to stay, I'll take you back with me."

Hunter shrugged and pulled his line from the water.

David helped Hunter gather all his supplies and empties. They trudged in an awkward silence towards Indian Point. When David heard the sounds coming from the first camp he began to question his decision. Too late, he thought, as the people saw them approaching and waved. David introduced Hunter to everyone, watching as Hunter's blue eyes lit up and a slow smile of understanding spread across his face. He glanced at David, and David nodded.

"Where's Mariah?" Hunter asked.

"Let's find her. She's at the upper camp."

The two strolled in silence through the camp sites. David let Hunter take it all in. Small groups of people were gathered under trees, busy with one task or another. Tents scattered in small clusters, maximized shade in the large expanse of prairie grasses. There was a concentrated hum as supper prep was underway. When they trudged up the hill to Indian Point, they saw the cooking fire was already ablaze. A few feet away, Rob prepared a colorful array of roasted tomatoes, corn, eggplant, squash, and peppers, while Mariah sliced a loaf of bread into thick slices. She smiled when she saw her husband, then drew back in surprise when she recognized Hunter standing next to him.

"Catch anything?" Mariah greeted David as she walked over and kissed his cheek. "Hey, Hunter, long time. Great to see you." She gave him a welcoming hug.

He clung to her as if holding on to a lifeline.

"Have a seat, a log rather." She gestured at the sumptuous array of log seating. David got her pun; belatedly he realized she meant Hunter was today's catch.

Hunter dropped on a log as bidden, and awaited the explanation. His wide blue eyes looked up into Mariah's green ones. "Okay. Ayn

275

Rand huh? You have come a long way since we met. Anarchy. Freedom. Self-sufficiency. I don't think so."

"I wanted to tell you. But you're a high-powered lawyer for heaven's sake. How did you find out?"

"I didn't. This is a purely spontaneous, random visit. To say nothing of illegal." He saw the look on her face and waved his hand impugning her crime. "Believe it or not, I get it. The world is crumbling out there, and no one seems to know how to fix it. We need a fix. A savior. A new solution."

"There's a little more to it than that," Mariah said. "If you can't beat 'em, leave 'em. That's our solution. Here, Rob's got dinner tonight. Let me show you around." She led him down a narrow path and across the stream. "Let's start with the weaving area first." They strolled through Painted Meadow, passing the Blues and the Orange clusters. At the Yellows, Pat and Jody Cooper's area, they sampled a fresh tortilla warm from the stone ovens.

"Save a bit of it," Mariah said as he was about to take another bite. He lowered his hand. "Sorry, just a suggestion. Cheese at the next stop."

At Robin's tent, they were in time for a plate of fresh goat cheese rolled in sun-dried tomatoes on a plate of fresh basil. Hunter sampled a bite of goat cheese on his tortilla, grinned and nodded his approval. Robin sent them on their way with a plate to have with their dinner.

The weaving area was between the next two camps, in a grove of pines. The trees were tall here. Bright Navajo looms leaned against them with a slow burning fire to one side. A girl, her hair in braids down her back, was at work at one of them, her face a study in serenity and concentration. The piece was a good size, with shades of white and beige with a ribbon of indigo spaced throughout. For a moment Mariah and Hunter stood quietly watching, amazed at her skill and patience.

Nearby, a slow-burning fire had brought a large soup pot to a boil with a dark liquid. Mariah spoke softly. "Sarah is boiling plants to make natural dies for her fibers. I think that may be blackberries–which is what they use to get the indigo color. Onions make yellow and rhubarb makes red."

Hunter followed her hand as it travelled to a long branch lashed between two trees, from it hung skeins of yarn in various colors. There were also dried grasses and some natural fibers that looked like jute or hemp. Some were brilliant yellows and golds, while others were rustic reds, pale purples, and even a deep cobalt blue.

"Plants have different color possibilities," Mariah said. "It begins with lots of experimentation and guidance from those knowledgeable in the craft." Hunter looked thoughtful as they moved on.

"We have a quiet period after the work day and before the dinner hour. Sarah is not on any specific task tonight. She's making headway on her project."

"Task?" Hunter looked at her sideways. Is this some sort of commune or other?"

Mariah laughed at the implication. "No, not a commune—at least not in the way you probably mean it. But it's communal living. In order to make it work we have to be very organized. It's not like we can run to the corner store or call a plumber whenever we want. In terms of daily life, we have the chores necessary to keep this place functioning. Such as water, fire, and sanitation issues. Kind of like any small town, the utilities are provided for a fee. We do it ourselves. Or the fee is the labor plus time each person donates to keep the system working."

Hunter listened, clearly impressed, as Mariah explained their schedule of work slots and teams put together for the various tasks.

"Then there is a whole matrix of 'classes' where we learn survival skills and how to make things, such as the weaving workshop and the pottery place. In the beginning the same task rolled around about once a week. Every day you had something different. Cooking lunch, cooking dinner, meal clean-up, and wood gathering are a sample of the types of work. It's simple but it has to be done. With new arrivals the volume of work increased but so did the labor supply."

A burst of fire caught their attention. Hunter gasped in alarm as the flames burned in the dirt, surrounded by nine onlookers.

"Oh, that's the Raku firing – one of the efforts of Pottery Place," Mariah said. "I'm a bit surprised too, I thought they usually did it on Saturdays. They have created quite the assortment of pots and bowls, which you will see at dinner."

"I take it you all eat together?" Hunter asked.

"We have communal meals twice a day six days a week. On Sundays, each camp is on its own. Like I said, Rob is making our camp's dinner tonight, and you'll join us." She raised the plate Robin had given them and smiled. "And now we have fresh goat cheese as part of the appetizer."

"By fresh do you mean she made that stuff?"

"Of course. How else do you think we would get goat cheese way out here?"

"I don't know, buy it in bulk and bring it in? Okay, okay, but *how* does she make it? I know you are just dying to tell me."

"You know this place has always had old goats hanging around?" She paused while he took it in, "The animal group managed to tame a few so we corral them for milking. Wait, Hunter, I don't think you quite get it. We are generating over seventy percent of what we need. We don't just go to the store. We have been out here since April, figuring things out. What you see is what we grew, scavenged or gathered. We try to figure it out, or do without. Plus, new people are joining us at the rate of six to eight a week, and they bring stuff with them as well. Some of it we can use, some we can't. Part of our sanitation job is taking the unnecessary junk back out. Lots of trash comes in from the outside world. As for us, we're not generating much trash. We burn wood for fuel. Everything we grow has its own packaging. The seeds we reuse. We compost organic stuff. We bury anything we cannot utilize in the compost piles. We have different grades of compost piles. Most everything can be reconstituted to mix back in with the soil."

Hunter's eyes scanned the campsites with new interest as they walked. Colorful bowls and plates were arranged on rustic picnic tables. Colorful gourds hung from trees. Hammocks and woven blankets were scattered in shady areas near the trees. People went about their tasks and visited with one another in hushed tones. At one camp an array of fish was hung over a smoking fire to dry.

"Hey, Mom!"

Mariah turned to see Isabella hurrying over to join them, a curious expression on her face. As often happened these days, she was struck by how grown-up her daughter looked, and how beautiful. Her auburn hair hung loose to her waist. Although her clothes were simple, she wore some amazing jewelry. She had an elaborate woven necklace at her neck and three or four bracelets on her tanned slender arms.

"This is Hunter, Peter's best friend from long ago. Hunter, this is my daughter, Isabella,"

Isabella smiled and held out her hand. "I've heard your name a time or two. Nice to finally meet you."

Hunter looked from Mariah to Isabella and back again. "She looks like you exactly, from way back when." He pointed to her necklace.

"That's an interesting piece you are wearing."

"Oh that's a new one, thanks."

"I take it this is your own design? Do you sell your work?"

"Sell? God no. We don't need money here. But I do trade for things. Sometimes for special pieces from the pottery group. You know. It's fun. We barter and trade stuff. Or I just keep it. Some things are hard to part with."

"I'm still digesting the fact that you all are here. You have established a whole new community. I'm in a bit of a shock."

Isabella laughed. "You sound like the newbies." She looked at her mother. "Anyway, I came to say dinner is about ready."

"Sounds great, honey," Mariah said.

"Are you just visiting, Hunter? Or are you thinking of staying?"

For a moment Hunter looked startled, then he recovered, "I don't know about that, but I would like to stay the weekend if that is okay with your mom and dad."

Isabella said, "Wait until you taste our cooking before you make a decision."

"Do you want people to come here?" Hunter asked Isabella.

"Yes, we do. It's a different life, for sure, but it grows on you." She paused to study him for a minute. "I know it's not for everyone - Aunt Maxi doesn't live here more than three or four days at a time—but you were Peter's friend..." She looked down at her bracelet.

Mariah broke the awkward silence by finishing her daughter's sentence.

"... We think you'd fit in perfectly here."

"A girl, her hair in braids down her back, was at work at one of them, her face a study in serenity and concentration."

CHAPTER 6 *Humble Feast*

Mariah, Isabella, and Hunter chatted on the climb back up to Indian Point. There the picnic tables were arranged near a roaring fire.

"No one knows we're here. We've been very private," Mariah said. "How long?"

The group gathered around the fire, the smell of food intoxicating.

"Since spring. I guess that is about five months. Easy to lose track of time out here."

Hunter's mouth dropped open. "I had no idea."

"And what about you? How are you doing now?" Hunter's haggard appearance hadn't escaped her notice. Mariah gestured for him to join her as she settled on a cedar log.

"My wife left me two years ago." He sat down on the log seat beside her. "Some rich guy bought her better presents. And my dad died. I have the practice, but no freedom." He shook his head in disbelief. Looking around, he took it all in as new awareness dawned on him. "I can't believe you pulled this off."

"Well, we have a lot to be thankful for." She squeezed his arm. "You know I wanted to tell you. You did a lot for me back then."

"How was the tour?" David said as he approached. There was an unmistakable note of pride in his voice.

"I'm still taking it all in," Hunter said.

"You could help us a good deal if you wanted to join us. You're well acquainted with The Ranch."

Hunter nodded.

"The hard part is coming and going. Most of us never leave."

"You met my sister Max? She's with us this week," Mariah said.

"She never said a word. It would be great to see her," Hunter said.

As if on cue, they heard Max's voice. She came up the trail from the river, a few teens in tow. When she saw Hunter, she stopped short.

"Look who's staying for dinner," Mariah called out. "Hunter, I believe you've met my sister Maxi?"

"Max." Max growled under her breath.

"Yes, Mariah, I feel right at home now. How is Maxi today?"

"Just fine thank you." Max joined the circle, unable to keep the wide grin from her face. She greeted Hunter with a hug.

As Max and Hunter caught up, Mariah checked on Rob to see how the vegetables were coming. She grabbed some pottery dishes and utensils and set the old wood table. Isabella brought wild flowers for the centerpiece. The abundant blooms spilled out of a Raku pitcher. The group of nine people gathered around the table and warmly welcomed Hunter, then clasped hands in a prayer of thanks. Hunter felt a surge of electricity around the group. Then with big smiles they all sat down.

Hunter bent over and put his face in his hands. "Peter was right. He longed for this. There is great clarity in the hermit lifestyle."

Everyone froze and there was a split second of dead silence. Hunter was overcome. Then they passed the platters of roasted veggies piled high and well-seasoned with garlic and lemon. Boisterous noisy chatter ensued. They had corn tortillas, a salad of mixed greens, sweet potatoes, and Robin's fresh goat cheese.

"Hmm, Indian food," Hunter said.

"We do have a good bit of squash and corn, but no beans." Mariah looked up and stared at Hunter. "You're a red Irishman. What do you know of Indian food anyway?"

"Hands off, he's mine." Max tagged Mariah.

Hunter couldn't help but crack a smile, the first he had in a long time.

"We used to eat a lot of fish," Rob said. "But now we have tons of veggies to mix with wild edibles."

"I spend a lot of time in the garden. I'm glad Rob is such a great cook," Roxi said.

"I thought I'd miss hamburgers and stuff," Isabella said, "but you'd be surprised how quickly you get used to a new way to eat and live."

After every drop of food had been consumed, Hunter rose from the table. "I think after such an unexpected feast I should help with dishes."

"Nonsense." Max shot up fast. "The girls will do it."

Anya saw her chance, "It's a lot of dishes Mom."

Max shot her a look, but Mariah, who loved delegating, realized this wasn't the time, instead said, "Okay, teamwork."

Mariah washed the pile of plates. Everyone else dried, cleaned, and put everything away. The girls cut up, giggling and dancing as they worked. Mariah laughed as she watched them. "Wow, you guys are in a good mood."

"Hunter, how old are your boys now?"

"They are away in college."

"Perhaps they can come for a visit?"

Hunter tried to picture his preppy sons at The Ranch. "I think Brandon and Brice do deserve a trip home for a change."

Mariah and David went along with the fact that Max and Hunter were acting like casual acquaintances. "You know we'd promised to run to the Cooper's for dessert. Are you guys okay finishing up?"

Max took the towel off her shoulder eager to escape being alone with Hunter. She called out, "Wait for me, I'll come too."

Hunter grabbed her hand. "No stay, I'll help you." He waved to Mariah and David. "You guys enjoy."

"Max. You didn't mention 'The Ranch' last time I saw you," Hunter said when they were alone.

"Huh?" The bowl in Max's hand was already dry but she kept wiping. "Oh, that was weeks ago."

"From the looks of it, you guys have been out here a while." He glanced around, "quite a long while."

"How could I say anything? You're a lawyer and a friend of the family. If I told you anything..."

"Pay me a dollar."

"Huh?" Max set the bowl down, and reached into the pocket of her jeans. "Not sure if I have a dollar. We don't need money at The Ranch. But maybe...Yes." She pulled out a smooth black stone and handed it to him. "Will this do?"

Hunter slipped it into his shirt pocket. "It will have to. Now you can tell me. Everything. Start at the beginning. Mariah is married to an Italian and living in Idaho? David Agnelli may be Italian, but Idaho?"

"I thought you'd met David before. Look, there's not much to tell. They've been out here all summer and I drop by for visits now and then."

"Your kids live here."

"Yeah, it's summer. It's an extended summer vacation. They like camping. They're teenagers, for heaven's sake."

"Look." He sat down and patted the log beside him. "I've got all night. Come sit down. Start at the beginning."

So she told him. Some of it. All about Houston, the evacuation, and living off the grid. "They are having an off-the-grid lifestyle experience-experiment. Lots of folks do it. Some call it the *simple movement*, like the *slow food* movement. Just stepping out of the rat race and living consciously. It actually is very exciting. I don't know if Mariah told you but new people are coming all the time, sometimes from as far away as the East coast. Others were friends of Peter's from way back. Or friends of friends."

He shook his head. "I never knew. I never come here. It was too painful."

"Why today?" Max waited and let it all sink in.

Hunter shrugged as if he didn't know himself.

"By the way, on my drives out here," she said, breaking the silence, "I noticed some ranches have super high brick formal entrances with high wrought iron gates. On further inspection, I noticed high barbed wire like a prison. Had you ever noticed that before?"

Before Hunter could reply, Mariah dashed back up to grab a bowl of blackberries she'd left, she popped one in her mouth. She offered the bowl to Hunter and Max. They helped themselves.

She watched the two, then feeling she had to explain things, said, "Peter sacrificed to preserve this land. We are trying to pick up where he left off. So far no one knows we're here." She sat down at the table, "I mean if you found out, Hunter, it would be a sign that word had leaked out in the wrong circles."

"Your saying I'm in the wrong circle?" Hunter acted surprised. "Are you saying I'm somehow involved with the 'wrong people'?"

"Well, yes, aren't you?" Mariah asked. "What we are up to isn't exactly kosher, squatting on someone else's land."

Hunter sat in silence for a while. He'd finished his tea concoction and they didn't have beer here. He needed a beer. "You know I can help you guys," he said after a while. "I mean, that is why you hang out in San Antonio so much isn't it? He glanced up at Max. "You are trying to dig up information. I know this place. Very well. Peter was my best friend. You guys are trespassing." He held up a hand, "I do not blame you."

Max was smiling. "I know you can. You will? Actually help us?"

"Peter was my best friend, and I think he would be happy that you're here. Yes, I will help."

Mariah stretched out her hand. "Then come, meet the Coopers. Follow me," she invited.

With Hunter following, they stepped out of the circle of light from the camp fire.

"I know the way in the dark by heart."

They were plunged into darkness. Mariah grabbed Hunter's hand and placed it on her shoulder, then led the way down the crooked path. The stones had a bluish glow in the dark. A few minutes later they came upon Meadow Yellow Camp, where a large group had gathered around a fire. There were a few people Hunter hadn't seen before; including a baby boy Rob was bouncing on his knee.

Hunter was jovial. "Wow, you guys have a bigger social life than I do in San Antonio."

Mariah laughed, "That's the point. We have extreme poverty and simplicity, yet in community. We pull together. We solve problems."

"You guys have problems? All my headaches disappear on my way in to this place. And once I'm here I never think about the real world."

"Yes, I remember. But for us this has become the real world. This is now our world. There is no going back anymore, but it does have its own set of problems."

"Here, lie on my couch and unburden yourself."

"Not those kinds of problems," she laughed. "They're physical, day-to-day survival stuff. Not so much psychological or stress related."

"Go on." He was eager to hear about this radical lifestyle.

"We solve problems, we invent things. Everything is solved with the materials at hand. We talk face to face. No e-mail necessary. We are a community with like-minded goals and contrasting personalities. We have discovered a harmony in the work- play involved in survival."

"We are waiting out the economic storm here. There is a lot to learn."

"Tell me, what are your future plans?"

"Like I said, it's sort of day-to-day here."

Max chimed in. "Guess what I'll be doing here all week? Training for this environment and deprived lifestyle."

"Deprived?" Hunter looked surprised. "You certainly eat well."

Pat Cooper showed her dessert array. "Four-star gourmet with all organic ingredients. Nothing has to be certified. It's all fresh picked."

Hunter was curious, "Consequently, what happens—If? What's the next step?"

"We don't know," Jody said. "In the language of your world we could say, we're creating a coexisting, sustainable lifestyle. It's very one day at a time here. We don't have all the answers. But, forgive me here, didn't Mariah show you around already?"

"We've evolved a lot," David added.

Hunter pressed. "You've either learned a lot or you knew a lot before you came out here."

Jack said, "I thought I knew everything. I've been studying phenomenon for thirty-five years. I tried to be completely prepared. But finally we just had to jump in with both feet. It's impossible to completely predict the things you have to be prepared for. There are surprises."

"You can say that again," Mariah said. "Like that Josie came out here pregnant. She said it was for her child."

"Who's Josie?"

"Our youngest sister. She's twenty-five and she should know better."

"That little one was born out here?" Hunter nodded at Mason, bouncing on his Uncle Rob's knee.

"Yes, Mason's our community's firstborn. He'll grow up knowing only this way of life."

Hunter looked around at the baskets, weavings, and circular array of tent structures, then his gaze returned to Mariah. "I still can't believe no one told me."

"Hunter, when I first came out here, I wanted to prove the truth about Peters' death. You made it clear to me in our brief lunch last year that you were completely over it—not concerned with the *why*. I just had to know. Now I can never prove my theory, and I know I can never avenge his death. He was a pacifist, as we are. He lived without fear. I'm trying to do that. I may be inept at solving crimes, but I can adopt his lifestyle. You know? Pick up where he left off. If you ever want to join us, just say the word."

Hunter laughed. "I'm tempted, I'm sorely tempted." After a beat he said, "Mariah, you are referring to the theory that Peter's death was not random. But the case was solved. The boys did time. It's over, an open and shut case."

"So you said." She took a small bite of her blackberry desert. "Now, back to joining us...?"

"Well, now, it seems nice for a vacation," Hunter back pedaled, "but the truth is that while things aren't perfect, I have a decent lifestyle. A lot of perks. You know? This seems novel and charming; you have an authentic thing going here. My kids are used to a certain lifestyle too at this point. They're in college, and I'm still supporting them. I can't just think of myself."

"Right." Mariah kicked herself for betraying obvious enthusiasm. "I guess David and I are extremely fortunate that our kids are right here with us. They thrive out here." Mariah kept the rest of her thoughts about the secret tribe to herself.

CHAPTER 7 *Fireside*

"Why would Hunter suddenly just show up at The Ranch after all these years?" Mariah said. "It's been over ten years and he claims he's never been back."

After everyone was tucked into their tents for the night, the sisters sat together at the campfire with a few stragglers. "I don't know," Max mumbled.

"Did you tell him that we were out here?" Mariah pressed.

"Of course not. Give me some credit. I'm using him for information."

"Did you ask any suspicious questions? Do you think he just followed you?"

"I thought of that but I've already been here a week. There's something else, Mariah. I've seen Chloe before. I don't mean to be paranoid, but under the circumstances I'm naturally suspicious."

"What do you mean? Where have you seen her? In San Antonio?" Maybe that was how Hunter knew about them.

Max shook her head. "No, at a political party in Austin. She looked extremely familiar. I had to say something to her. She mentioned that her ex was an attorney. I have been racking my brain ever since. But it came back to me. She was married to Hugh Harlan's nephew. He was too young to be made partner at the time and he was in way over his head. Then I found out he was the nephew. Mark Fox was his name. It just dawned on me today."

"You lost me. Who is Hugh Harlan and why is he important?"

"You know, he's a politico. Ran for governor a few years back. He lost that race but he's still around. Anyway, it's weird she turned up here of all places. She's a socialite, or at least she was at some point."

"Well, now she's all about Rob. Treats him like her personal guru. He has taken to this Indian Inner Circle thing pretty strong. Everyone says to leave him alone, he's a big guy."

"Yeah, well, he certainly looks the part." Max smiled thinking about his tanned skin and long braids.

"That's our brother. He's very committed to the Inner Circle, even more now that he's become a leader."

"Leader? Our little brother?"

"Since his anointing."

"Anointing?" Max was lost.

Mariah nodded. Later she would have a lot to explain.

"Rob has grown into his position. Now he's become a teacher. He really has copious knowledge from all the books he's read. You know?"

"You think that's what Chloe's drawn to?" Max all but guffawed.

"Who knows?" Mariah said. "All will be clear in time."

"Aren't you the wise one."

Before Mariah could open her mouth to reply, a voice spoke from the darkness.

"Are you two talking about me?" Chloe came up so suddenly that neither one noticed.

"We were talking about Rob." Mariah's tone was neutral but the implication was clear.

Chloe didn't bat an eye. "You probably think it's odd because he's your little brother. But he is an amazing person. He's extremely enlightened. You should talk to him sometime. He has insights on many things."

"We talk." Max offered, "You know he hasn't even been to college."

"That makes him even more amazing. I have a master's degree in philosophy and he can out debate me. I bet you think it's just sexual attraction. But it's way beyond that. I'm way beyond that."

Mariah said, "What Max or I think is irrelevant. Roxi has been feeling left out. Who can blame her? You guys seem to spend a lot of time together."

"Look, I don't know what goes on with those guys after dark. That is their business. But I would say he's outgrown her. I thought this crowd was beyond high school." She grinned, a perky flash of white teeth. "Got to go." She waved a finger wave.

The two sisters watched her go. "Guess she's right," Mariah said. "Who knows what's really going on between Rob and Roxi? Or Rob and Chloe, for that matter. We've all had to shed old behaviors since being here. Maybe he's shedding his old relationship as well. I'm just being protective, based on his past behavior. But maybe he gave that up with his smoking habit."

Max laughed, "Miracles do happen."

CHAPTER 8 *Run Away*

Today, gathered inside the crystal cave, Mariah could hear Jade Springs far below. Mariah inhaled the cool musty-dark of the sacred space. Indian elders took turns sharing wisdom, so that no one in particular would be seen as the guru. Their numbers had reached one hundred and forty by now, including families, couples, and lots of single adults, and teens. Once Hunter had left, the Inner Circle of David, Mariah, Tristan, Jack Java, Rob, Paul, and Isabella were eager to escape to the crystal cave for another Indian elder instruction.

"You want to run away from the mess your people have created in America. No you cannot." Chief Nuage's dark eyes were shadowed beneath his thick silver brows.

Dead silence greeted this firm pronouncement.

Mariah knew most of the tribe they had met were wise ones. Today, her heart was glad but still intimidated by the presence of Chief Nuage. He looked fierce, his arms crossed upon his chest with the great mane of silver hair floating thick over his shoulders. He wore only the simple feather Isabella had made for him, beaded in his hair. Everyone sat in a loose circle on the cool stone floor. The flash of red against the soft blue sky caught her eye as a bird flew past outside. For a flash, the red cardinal distracted her.

"You can't just run away," Chief Nuage continued.

"What do you mean, 'our people'?" Rob interrupted, amused. "Our government has done these things, and I think we've shown just by being here, that we reject them."

Nuage stared him down while a stillness settled over the small gathering. "Are you the president?"

"No."

"Did you ever run for president, or even try?"

"No." Rob flushed under his gaze and looked around.

Chief Nuage began to pace. "You are a white man, a white patriot in a patriarchal society and it's *your* country. You have every right to participate in the democratic government of America."

"Well, everyone knows that's impossible. You have to be a player to be in the game."

"My point is, that instead of changing the America you have, you have all left. Run away."

Silence.

"Is that not obvious?" He turned, and stared them down one by one.

"You have come into our world. Our peaceful, humble, simple yet safe place, where we live in harmony and abundance. It is small, and we are comparatively few. But what you see is what you get. We are free. You run to us." He looked around, his voice hoarse. "You run to us," he whispered.

"Well, yes. When you put it that way," Rob conceded.

"I'm simply stating facts. To help you, I simply show you the actions. The positive actions you can take as you move forward in this new life. We choose to live like this. To live with the land. To honor everything we always knew to be right and true. To preserve our race, our culture. But more than our race; the earth. Our awareness of how to live upon Mother Earth.

"Our decision ensured that we are still here now, after all these generations. Our youth know the way. Our youth know the truth. They know the difference between right and wrong. They know the story that preserves the truth. The Way. They know who they are, where they came from and what the work is." He paused. "One day they will do the *great* work and move into the scorched earth to heal her."

Mariah shook her head. He clearly had no idea all they had sacrificed to come out here.

In the stillness that followed, while the last echo of his voice hung in the air, Mariah thought she heard the sound of water running deep within the cave. The tinkling sounded hollow. The crystal walls flickered, reflecting the few simple torches they had lit during the meeting. She was curious as to the depth of this cave. She was well aware of the mysteries and the unknown aspects that surrounded them daily. Secrets. Soon, if things went smoothly, many mysteries might be revealed. She knew this was the time to speak up. She pulled her focus back in to address Chief Nuage.

"I love the earth. I love this earth." Her hands clutched the bits of dust and rock from the cave floor. She let it slip from her fingers. She forced herself to search his eyes. She shook the cobwebs from her head. Her voice broke as she explained. "I always have. It was born into me, this devotion to place. The feeling of the energies of places. It's simply how I came into the world. I know in my gut, as odd as this crew is, the desire is sincere. In my old life, I kept running into people, in surprising places, who resonated with the fact that something was *wrong*. We decided not to participate. We could not perpetuate the myth any longer. Only by stopping abruptly in our tracks to try something new—only by action, by becoming what we expounded, could we discover things. We didn't even know if it was possible.

"I mean you don't know," she went on. "There is no scorched earth out there. Not in America. It is far away. This country is filled with beautiful homes, and stores, resorts, hotels, and landscaped living communities. Everything looks beautiful, abundant... on the surface. It's only when we looked deeper, into the core, that we found the rot. But the moment we recognized it, we planned to get out. Yes, it took ten years to get untangled from those lives. Now we are here. Like new babes we know nothing. We must learn a whole new way. We embrace this knowingly, with the understanding that it's much better than living as before. Living on the surface of life. Hearts and minds shut as our country attacked first one country than another. That is where the scorched earth is. We can't see it. But we know it. America, our great country, with its motto 'Let Freedom Ring,' is responsible for much of it. It absolutely sickens us to know this —it sickens me to say it. The news media has taken on the qualities of a movie: faraway and cinema graphic." She waited while her words had their affect.

"I don't think we are running away. We are running to. To you—to the Earth Mother. To sanity, truth, and understanding."

For a long moment, Chief Nuage said nothing. "Yes." Another long silence. "I see." He turned his back, broad and strong, folding his arms tight across his chest. "Evidently all of you could see beyond the illusion."

"Yes." Mariah let out a held breath. "And we searched for a bit of earth that was real, alive, and untouched. Even this place is no longer untouched because Peter's blood is here. We are looking for his murderer." She mumbled the last bit.

Chief Nuage turned back toward her. "To what end?" His voice thundered in response.

"To know the truth... for answers... for why." Her throat hurt from trying to push the words out. Words and thoughts that lay bottled up inside.

"Evil is why." His voice was low in his throat. A guttural growl spat out the words. "To taint this place. To make you run away from here. To ensure you would not come back. The blood of the innocent to guard the door."

"I came back." She held his stare.

In his anger, Chief Nuage appeared young again; a great warrior in his prime seemed to be standing before her.

"I had to leave a place who's citizens let a Texan who drinks blood from the skull of Geronimo become president of our once great country and run wars all over the world. Who knows who's really in charge out there?"

He shook his great silver mane of hair as he interrupted her, "They do not have the skull of Geronimo. They have another poor dead man's skull. What magic they are up to, I do not know. What power they think that gives them I can only imagine. But they seem to have plenty of power for now."

There was a long silence. Then, just when David nudged Mariah's arm as if to leave, Chief Nuage spoke again.

"It's time for all of you to have a community anointing ceremony." Everyone looked at each other. "It will be held before the next full moon." As they finally grasped his meaning, in assent, all moved silently from the cave and into the blazing sun that awaited them outside. Mariah watched until everyone was gone.

"Chief Nuage, this place has been tainted...Now."

She pressed a gift in his hand, a small earring made of copper and lapis lazuli. "Thank you," she said softly.

She emerged from the cave and stood facing the great cliffs before her and the river below. It was well worth the climb, she thought. The rest of the troupe was already winding their way down. Bits of laughter and voices carried up on the wind. She observed the speck of red, the bird on the craggy bush. Maybe she had a guardian. Her eyes teared as a big involuntary smile hurt her cheeks. They didn't have to fight the entire American government. They just had to live here, one day at a time.

CHAPTER 9 *Rain*

It had rained for three days straight. By now the consensus was that it may never quit. Activities were on hold. Everyone had crowded into any dry spot they could find. Many had gone to the central cooking/washing area in the Painted Meadow. It was the closest thing to a structure they had erected. They had constructed it with two tall poles opposite two existing trees. The solid rock wall of the cliff effectively blocked wind on two sides. But it was open to the river on one side and the meadow on the other. When the rain didn't let up, they broke up in clusters. Some went to the nearby caves. For the first time overcrowding was an issue, and after three days it had rubbed nerves raw.

The blistering heat had continued well into September, hovering around one hundred and four degrees. The rain immediately cooled everyone off. Steam rose from puddles every time there was a break in a downpour.

Chilled for the first time all summer, Mariah sipped hot tea while she thought about their situation. They had learned much from their Indian brothers. Wisdom Discussions were held at least a couple of times a month. Sometimes they were organized, like the one at Crystal Cave. Frequently they happened spontaneously as after-dinner talks at Indian Point.

Most of the Inner Circle dined at Indian Point, and their discussions sprung from the stew of ideas that had become their life. Everything they did at The Ranch offered an alternative, and a challenge to society. There were no schools or churches. Yet many of the same questions about the meaning of life remained. *Who am I? Why am I here?* We all have different backgrounds, from Jews, to Christians, to Hindi. Survival was clearly more important than issues of religion, yet thoughts about God were in people's hearts even more so here, on the edge. *If the worlds' systems don't work anymore, and we need to create an alternate way, then what of religion? Do we need a church? A place of worship? How do we do that universally? Can we revolutionize that too?* The talk was stimulating and inspiring. No one had answers. There was much discussion. All were trying to find the right question.

Perhaps when we ask the right question, the answer will appear. Just let the process of nature and the rightness of being here inspire them. They were close to the heart of The Mother, trusting that she would provide for, and nurture them. She would keep them safe, daily.

Soon conversations drifted to happy talk of miracles that appeared like gifts in each other's lives. The way of worship evolved into extended families coming together and sharing their insights. They shared the personal ways each felt God's presence. All were eager to share these happy surprising moments. Mariah liked to call it a miracle listing. Some became aware of grace that had occurred years before that they hadn't quite recognized. This increased their awareness of how close God was in their new venture; guiding them by dreams and inspiration, new-found friendships, and surprising alliances. Perhaps He had been there throughout their entire lives, people soon began to realize. It took being here now to recognize that. The wisdom discussions, once begun, happened every weekend—whether or not an Indian Guru dropped by.

In two weeks' time they would have the sixth full moon dance and the community anointing ceremony. This ritual would mark everyone's conviction to move into the interior. After that, all would learn directly from the Indian tribe that had befriended them. It seemed everyone enjoyed the rituals, or celebrations of the new lifestyle.

With all the rain, feet sucking mud was everywhere. This last test of Nature impacted the whole community—make them or break them. The whole scene reminded Mariah of the crowded apartment scene in 'Breakfast at Tiffany's'. Would Holly Go-lightly bale or stick it out? She wondered. She wanted everyone to stay. The diversity of their group made things interesting. You can't only have serious hard-core wilderness-types. Where would the humor be in that? She certainly didn't want to end up living with a bunch of Marine-macho super pragmatists. In fact, she much preferred the dreamer-positive thinkers. They worked a little less but the joy and inspiration they brought was a gift in itself. She knew they needed all these super-prepared survivalists. She half-suspected they were glad the world was falling apart, allowing them to use their skills and all that gear they had invested in. She laughed to herself, remembering when the Indians first noticed Ian's vibram sole toe-shoes.

"War paint on his feet?" They asked. "You have some strange practices in your world."

Got to have some whimsy or the place would not be balanced. She buried her head in her hand as loud voices echoed around the cave. But they stopped fast as one of the young ones told the two teens to practice meditating in silence while focusing on the sixth chakra.

Good advice, Mariah thought.

To date there were almost one hundred forty-four solid members, all eager for initiation. Another twenty-two had decided they couldn't hack it. They quit for a variety of reasons, but none had made the decision lightly. It was no small undertaking to move away from the consumerism and creature comforts of the real world, and those who could not, often saw it as a failure. Mariah viewed it as a reflection of human nature, in all its simplicity and complexity.

More than anything, she was grateful for this organic weeding out process. The next step would be their most challenging yet. The community planned to leave this wilderness as they found it—full of nature and empty of mankind. The only dwellings were the main stone house and garages, which housed all the vehicles and equipment. There was also the rebuilt schoolhouse and the one log cabin. There were still remnants of the cedar fences that had enclosed goats and gardens from one hundred years ago. All new traces of their presence should be eradicated by the time they left.

Fifty members had already been anointed at previous full-moon ceremonies; ninety-four would be anointed at this one—the largest

renewal of their commitment together to date. Mariah was psyched. For many people, it had begun as a vacation, something to try on. Soon many found it intoxicating. Life had become simple again. With a structure that balanced productivity with freedom and nature, the days flew by in a flurry of hard but satisfying work. Friendships were formed based on cooperation and a shared vision. It made it difficult to quit. No one had to pay cash to come to The Ranch, but if they wanted to stay, they had to sacrifice old baggage.

The nine trusted Inner Circle members convened at David and Mariah's campfire. "Okay," David said as he paced, "here it is, the moment of truth we've been waiting for—training for these past several months. Our Indian brothers have deemed us worthy of joining them, and just as we disappeared from Houston under the cover of Hurricane threats, we're now going to disappear deep into The Ranch. It won't be nearly as tough, as we've already let go of the outside world. Still, it will be a challenge." He paused, "All of our other friends have joined us coming from afar—New York, Virginia, Tennessee, and California. We have evolved into a strong company over these past months. We have been invited in, deemed worthy by our Indian brothers. Now it's time for the long awaited step." His breath caught as he choked up. "We are actually going to vanish into the interior, one cluster at a time. Anyone that is not trustworthy can't go in. The Indians have kept their presence here secret for over one hundred years, since 1888, and we're not going to blow it for them. They shape-shift, that's how they could pull it off. We will learn to vibrate at a higher level, use the 'Mercabra' breathing. We will be able to transcend illusion, and heal the planet with our loving work and new found wisdom. Which includes, of course, how to survive at a much higher level. But it will take time. Be patient with yourselves. I know we are ready!"

CHAPTER 10 *The Invitation*

"We are going to a place of healing, a place of transcendent transformation. Who is allowed in Paradise?" Rob said, drawing himself to full height as he addressed everyone. His mellow voice held just a trace of Texas.

"The Anointing Ceremony has its roots in the Jewish culture. Yet the practice dates as far back as the Sumerians and the Babylonians. The time of Yom Kippur, still practiced annually by Jews actually means 'The Day of Atonement.' Yom Kippur is traditionally held after Rosh Hashanah in the fall. It's a type of spiritual cleansing. Throughout the year, as humans pick up the baggage of doubt and deceit, or fall into various temptations, they in a sense are feeding their demons. Where demons reside, God cannot. Truth cannot. A society, a legal system, is hard to maintain if the population becomes ruled by their demons. Thus the ceremony of anointing is a time of atoning for past transgressions. A complete purge of all the demons that have taken hold over the year. Each person then enters cleansed, enlivened, released, with ones conscious clear, ones burden light. Those who are too attached to these bad habits are generally outcast from the group. Thus the term outcast was for those outside the City walls.

"A group, to be truly free, must be self-governing. Yet if a person's vision is clouded, and their heart crowded with competing voices, they cannot rule their own mind and heart. Thus through the anointing process, the group conscious stays clear, as each individual is clear. Just as the daily habit of the Japanese, to honor the home as a sacred space, is to remove their shoes at the threshold, and leave the dirt outside where it belongs.

"You can see it clearly in a community that has abandoned these practices. Where Christ and Truth fill your soul, there is no room for darkness. To the degree that one is light, so is he lighter. When one is illuminated, one becomes as light as a feather. It's not that the demons aren't there; it's that they grow weak if they are not fed. The hold is lessened. The high-mind and heart are free to rule the body once more.

"The Anointing must occur before everyone enters the Realm of the Indians Sacred Home. Indeed, the way we eat, coupled with physical training, has prepared us all well already. Had anyone of us tried to be anointed while many addictions and habits still held sway over the body, the results would have been disastrous.

"You have made choices, and you have done the work. You have done the inner work, for you all have battled your own issues to come this far. You have all changed in terms of material things; of greed, of lust, of jealousy.

"All are pretty equal here. We perform the same work. We dine from nature's table. Still this anointing can be frightening. Even damning. One must be mature enough to face your inner demons. You will see nightmare visions of buried trauma. You may see sins of the fathers. You may come to know truths and insights about yourself you do not want to face. All these things can happen in the process. In the baptism of fire, you will die to self. I assure you, you will die. Your ego will be blown away–shattered to smithereens.

"Each of you has mastered Self, enough to judge whether or not to undergo this cleanse. In short, I invite you to this baptism of fire and water from the bottom of my heart. With tears and weeping I implore you to do this, to take this gift, experience this release. To make yourselves pure vessels to be welcomed into Paradise on earth." Robs voice dropped just above a whisper and Mariah strained to hear him.

"But this is no soft water that will gently wipe away your sorrow. This is hot and stinging. Strong like stones. Pain like you have never felt. Pain in dark places inside you that you may not know exist." His voice rose with his intense emotion. "I must implore you, and yet my words fall like feathers on your ears. Until you fall into the circle of your personal anointing, you may not believe a word I have said. The decision is yours. As I beg you to embrace this fire and be cleansed,

I must also tell you to run back to your old ways and ignorance. For ignorance is a type of bliss. However, I'm convinced that the gift of self-knowledge, and I have *lived* to tell you, is the most profound joy you will ever experience on this earth."

The silence was deafening at Rob's last words. He stood before them humbled, yet tall as a tree headed towards the heavens, and utterly still, as the very air held its breath. The birds and crickets paused in the stillness. A big sigh sounded in unison. Only then did the group begin to Aum.

Rob told everyone that the ceremony would be held in three days' time. All those that chose to leave must do so, as all who stayed would experience it together.

As his elder sister, Mariah knew much of Rob's story, although until now she had never guessed the depths of his struggle. He had battled demons, she realized, lain side by side with darkness. And yet his intelligence and knowledge was great. She was surprised he had been entangled to such a degree. Now with the muddy waters of confusion gone, his innate wisdom shone thru his intelligence with a bright intensity visible through rich hazel eyes. Eyes that she knew had once been almost black with darkness and deceit. His deceit had always been turned on himself, not others. It was himself he'd hid from. Running from a destiny he suspected God had always had in mind for him. Thus he had truly become the wounded healer.

* * *

Mariah looked over at her daughter. Isabella was playing an instrumental version of 'Yesterday' on the guitar. Was she longing for the old days? She hadn't even been born in *those* old days—the 60's and all that stood for. She studied her a while before interrupting. Isabella had flourished at the Ranch. Her thick auburn hair had grown down to her waist. Today, beads and a single feather were woven into several braids that wound around to frame her face. She was lithe and strong, with lean muscles—the kind acquired from their challenging swimming and climbing regimen. She was one who trained with the Indians and it showed. "Isabella."

"Mom, what's up?"

"We look like a bunch of campers here for a long weekend?"

"Sort of...In your dreams," she laughed.

"Then after the long weekend we will have to disappear. Without arousing suspicion of anyone in the surrounding towns. I'm not sure how to do that."

"We can practice sleight of hand like magicians do." She concentrated in that way she had when she put her mind to the task. "I know, we can leave like we came, in colorful trucks and vans, shouting, hollering, and singing. You know make a general ruckus, so they notice us. Even though they ignore us now, we know the small town folk are aware something is going on out here."

"Peter always had piles of friends out here when he was alive and they generally ignored him, and them," Mariah said.

"Then we can sneak back in. We still have some vans here even after all the trading and bartering that has gone on. All we need is five drivers to leave with the radio blaring. We have to create the illusion that we have left, and then—snap." She snapped her fingers like a gypsy fortune teller. "Dissolve into the interior. Some will have to begin hiking further into the wilderness while others make a lot of noise leaving. One minute we are here, next we are gone, vanished." Her eyes widened at the prospect.

Mariah considered. Everyone had served a purpose. The last unit who wanted to leave, which included Roxi, could possibly drive all the remaining vehicles out of here. During the next few weeks everyone was on their own about whether to stay or go. Mariah knew some would opt to leave. The vans could be stuffed with all the things like coolers, plastic tarps, extraneous stuff not needed in their new life in the interior. She knew there were plenty of Mexican Americans over by the Frio River who would welcome a vehicle. Keys, no plates, and a little bit of gas left in the tank, would make it possible for someone to adopt it for a while. A note might help, to allay thoughts of stealing these godforsaken dinosaurs of the modern age. That was a good idea. It would solve two problems at once.

"Good idea. I think that will work." She gave her daughter a squeeze and a pat. "Thanks, hon."

CHAPTER 11 *Max and Chloe*

"I'm in love with Rob. It's not what you think." Chloe went on in a rush. Max and Mariah had finally squeezed in the dreaded talk with Chloe down at Jade Cove. They had the place to themselves.

"I know those guys you mentioned the other night. That's what I have been trying to tell you."

"Whoa," Max said.

"You know, those savory characters you met at that fund-raiser dinner? The speaker, Scofield, my Father in law, Hugh Harlan, is a big golf buddy of his. I've heard enough. They're all alike."

"Few secrets around here I guess," Max said.

"Not a lot of walls here. Anyway, they have never done anything for me. We may be related, but family is not what matters to them."

"Related?" Max asked.

"Hugh Harlan is my father in law. I can explain. The main thing is no one matters to them. That is what's so creepy. They are not fully human in the way we understand it. You can't understand, you're all about family."

Max looked at Mariah, Max thought Chloe was too tied-in to be entirely innocent in her involvement with the group.

Chloe continued. "I'm glad to be able to talk to you guys, I hate knowing all of this. I had thought once I was here I could just forget that other world ever existed. I will gladly tell you what I know. "

The three women found a shady ledge that overlooked the cool expanse of green water and dusted off the pine needles. Max nodded for Chloe to continue.

"It will be hard for you to relate. This place is all about family, extended family, community. The ego is such a powerful force. These guys only care about the game. And fame. How you play the game. That's what matters. People don't matter because all the people on earth may die and they will still be here ruling according to their plan."

"Plan? What plan? Now we are getting somewhere," Max interrupted.

"They have a plan to beat death." Chloe stared down at her knees, her legs dangling over the edge.

"Oh, that plan," Max chuckled. "We are all on board with that plan. Isn't that typical? Baby boomers don't want to grow up."

"Or get old." Chloe's face was set. "I'm deadly serious here. You must know what you're up against. They have spas in Switzerland, hidden in remote mountain villages. These are all set up with refrigerator tunnels embedded in a stone mountain. It is connected to embryonic research labs.

"They're involved in a type of dark sorcery. They have invented potent serums. They plan to inject it into their own bodies. They use human tissue from unborn babies. This will extend their life, vitality, and appearance. These hyper-expensive serums are like the 'Elixir of Life'. It's part of all the stem cell research the government's been sponsoring. They have a blank check for funding research. They have hidden laboratories and keep all their discoveries secret. But they have created an elixir that reverses the clock, extending their life span twenty years at a time.

"These guys that have been around are still in charge. They do not plan to hand the mantle of responsibility to anyone. Not to their spoiled progeny, that's for sure. They are the epitome of selfishness. They care only for themselves and power. Power and control is what drives them. That's why there are so many sex scandals going on. They need lovers, as they don't share the elixir with their wives. It's a completely patriarchal world they're after. No one knows their real age. They never get old enough to retire. They simply go to the spa and disappear for a month in a frozen tunnel in a sleep state.

"They don't care about people at all so the wars can go on endlessly. It's all about population control and preserving the world's resources for themselves."

306

She had their attention. Max and Mariah both watched her face intently.

"The elixir of life is then carefully administered. I don't know where or how. I heard it all third party. I pieced most of it together. They gave up on their progeny long ago."

Mariah studied Chloe's face. She was smart. She'd been playing a hard game. Mariah spoke, "Whew. Thanks for sharing. These guys are nightmare Frankenstein's." Mariah patted Chloe to calm her.

"The other concern we have," Max broke the silence. "Rob has a family, a woman he's been living with for years. Why did you latch on to him? Seems like you just slid yourself into someone else's family."

"That's not fair! He's not even married. It's not my fault," Chloe said.

"Well, no one said life is perfect. Here on earth, as a matter of fact, it's messy. The thing is, Roxi is considering leaving. Now all this information turns up about you. How do you know so much?"

"I told you, I heard things. In my former life as the unhappy pretty face attorney's wife, I knew things. It's not a fun role. Treated as dumb as a doll and vacant as a model. Especially now with the increase in women attorneys. I started doing my own research to follow through on the bits and pieces I overheard. It's rather amazing what people talk about to each other when you are supposedly a deaf, dumb, and blonde 'trophy'. He had no idea how out of the social scene I was. As in, not cut from the same cold cloth. I have the right breeding but different values."

"When were you going to share your info?"

"Why would any of you idealists want to know that sordid stuff? Spas in Switzerland? Reclaimed fetuses. Recycle and re-use. That's why abortion has to be legal. No one wants to waste such valuable DNA. The illegal abortions of the past led to the unborn babes lost in garbage cans and toilets. Of course the media campaign against morals ensures a continued supply of abortion victims."

Chloe had her hands on her hips. She looked back and forth at the two speechless women. "The more attorneys you know, and the more you know about the legal system, as I do, the sicker you feel about our current society. That is why I appreciate life out here so much! The

307

sanity out here is amazingly refreshing and rational. Pure nature—wet, hot, nasty, buggy, sticky or divine. It's all real. Solid. I'm glad to be here." She emphasized each word as she spoke. "I love it here."

"Are you a spy?" Max asked. "This is our humble way out of the rat race. There are no millions to be made here. Just life in community."

"Spy!" She threw her hands up in the air incredulous. "Didn't you guys hear a thing I said? These guys are born of scum and to scum they shall return." She plopped down, spent and disbelieving.

"The simplest thing is for you to depart with Roxi. When she leaves you should go too." Mariah was diplomatic.

"I want to stay here. I want to be here."

Max studied her face, "Prove it."

"How? Can't you just take my word for it?"

"I want to. You're bright, obviously educated. Why here, why us?" Mariah asked.

"I'm not one of them. They don't even seem human to me. Cold, callous, unfeeling. So selfish it's diabolical. That's it. When I visited my father-in-law, I felt a cold vacuum. His presence was like a vampire sucking blood—*life*—right out of you. I could feel the warmth of my very self being sucked out. Everything was perfectly smooth on the surface. Gorgeous vast home, impeccable interiors. And just cold. Air-conditioned and cold. Blood sucking feeling. I always felt exhausted when I was in his presence. I remember dinners. The table set perfectly. The flowers, the candles, the food looked perfect. But the taste—sawdust in your mouth. No interesting conversation, not a thing out of place, like a stage set. His wife said not a word and every bite washed down with wine or liquor. Yes, we washed the food and the conversation down the same way." She looked distraught, clearly infuriated.

She caught her breath from her monologue while the two women stared at her. "Prove my loyalty, you say? Okay, I think I have an idea. I know how to do that."

"Good." Mariah waited a beat. "You know, what you are describing rings a bell. I read somewhere that the Fallen Angels could have material bodies. Then they can be on the earth in positions of power and wreak havoc. They have cruel hearts, no souls at all."

"Just like I described. That fits. I don't even want to think about them. That's why I'm here. I had forgotten my sordid past. It gives me the creeps to bring all that up again. I hate to think the behavior I described is human. I'll just think of them as soul-less aliens."

"Are you kidding? A chilling thought." Max tone betrayed her skepticism. "Those in power are an Alien race, and no one knows it?"

Mariah shot her a look. "Well, humans are born with free will. No one ever said humans were incorruptible."

"Don't you see? If Peter's family is in with these guys, then this is what might have led to Peter's death. Let's say then, they already know about this place, its virgin nature, its thousand hidden springs." Mariah paced as things clicked into place. "We don't want to be in a battle either. We want to mind our own business. Live, love, and survive. Believe me, it's the last thing I want, but we need your help."

"I want to be here, and I can prove it. I still have ways to access inside information." She faced Mariah, eyes clear.

Max's eyes gleamed as comprehension dawned. "Your ex."

Chloe nodded, "My ex."

Mariah was surprised she would go to such lengths. "Well Max, can you two work together on that?

"That's totally in my league," Max said.

"Chloe, it's your decision. Sleep on it. There is no going back if you decide to stay. You have to be sure," Mariah explained.

"Then I'll go back and check out Hunter. It's time Hunter and I had a heart-to-heart anyway," Max said.

"The great Hunter Jones," Chloe said. He's got a rep as a brilliant young lawyer. But he is a quiet one. Hard to know about him."

With that Mariah slipped carefully from the ledge into the cool water. Chloe and Max followed. Mariah took long smooth strokes as she swam to the far shore. Was she swimming with the enemy? If so, she may just lead Peter's killers right to them.

She took a breath and swam deep. All the tensions of the conversation melted into the water. A peace enveloped her as she breathed and stroked, cutting a wave through the calm water. She felt at home she realized as she kicked deeper beneath the surface. When she emerged Max and Chloe were laughing by the dock like old friends. Mariah resolved to be cautious next time she saw Hunter. Time would tell.

CHAPTER 12 *Bed Chamber*

The sinewy female form was silhouetted by the early light filtered through gauzy curtains. Hunter's voice spoke out of the darkness, "You're up early."

"Couldn't sleep," Max remained staring out of the window. She inwardly jolted at the sound of his voice.

Max had a lot on her mind. Most of the puzzle pieces had begun to come together once she and Chloe went through the names, dates, and alliances. Once she knew 'the who' and 'the why' she could have become super busy. Too busy to see Hunter anymore. In truth, much of her hunches were mere speculation. She now had to cross-reference some details. She had been almost scared to visit him. Now that she was this close she didn't want to know. She wanted to side with David and Tristan and say, "Peter's dead. We can't bring him back. Life belongs to the living. We may never know the truth."

After he had found her out at The Ranch she had successfully avoided Hunter. Now weeks later, she had been curious and he had been lonely. Lonely and such a gentleman. And she'd missed him. Now they were clearly in too deep. Things had become complicated. Boy, and she had so streamlined her life. He had no idea about how much she knew. He hadn't said anything. She had found most of her information through her superior hacking techniques pieced together with Chloe's information. Hunter wasn't aware of her intelligence.

Now it had become personal. The truth about Peter's murder was not on his mind, she was sure. But at this point, it was on hers all the time. Could she talk to him? Should she?

Hunter broke the silence. "I've missed you. It's been a long time."

Max hesitated. "I've been busy."

"Where have you been? Have you been spending more time out there?"

"Yes," she sighed.

"I said I would help you. You haven't even mentioned The Ranch all day. I meant that."

"I have been training a lot out there. I needed to play catch-up."

"What do you mean, training?" He moved to the overstuffed armchair, and pulled her down on his lap.

"The lifestyle out there is rugged and demanding. Those guys live outdoors like a bunch of gypsies. High heat now, and later it will be cold. Especially at night. In terms of foods, it's like an extreme diet. It's just different," she shrugged. "Somehow it's getting harder to switch back and forth." She patted his hand where it lay. "Yet, I missed you too. I didn't want to admit that, even to myself. I have enjoyed our friendship. It's been lonely for me, doing research, writing reports, and meeting deadlines. Josie and Mariah having all the fun with the kids, doing all the creative stuff." She paused before she added, "You know, I was focused on work. But since our paths crossed, work has become a lot less appealing. I look forward to our time together. Our walks, our runs at the park or even just late night dinners. When our schedules agree, that is." She punched the cushion.

"Ouch, you're strong. I didn't mean to make you angry. It's fun for me too. It's different for me. I'm married to my work. I've always been that way."

"Is that why your wife left?"

"Ouch. Maybe. Probably."

"Me too. Married to my work." At least she had been before she met him.

"Well, then, I guess it's mutual."

Max shrugged, and continued to stare out the window. Not really, she thought.

"Come back to bed, we both need our sleep. Tomorrow will be here whether we are ready or not. So, no strings?"

That stung. She hadn't seen that coming. "Roger that, no strings." Her voice was flat. She had read him all wrong. She couldn't believe what she was hearing. Guys were all ass holes. She knew that, she had two kids and no husband.

"Well, are you coming back to bed or what?"

Max unfurled her limbs from the chair and studied his form relaxed against the pillows once more. "You got me."

Hunter woke her up with a gentle nudge. She squinted her eyes open. "What time is it?"

"Seven thirty."

"You're already dressed."

"I let you sleep. I have an early meeting. Take your time; I made coffee, help yourself to anything in the fridge. Just lock the door when you leave."

"I'm embarrassed. Can't believe I was this tired."

"Today's paper's on the table." He bent and kissed her forehead. "Have a great day, lady." On second thought she hated nice ass-holes. They were so easy to fall for.

The door closed softly behind him. With a whiff of musky aftershave, he was gone. *Lady?* Max jumped out of bed and ran into the shower. She cursed the icy blast she needed to jar her to her senses. Five minutes later she was out. She toweled her hair, hopped into her jeans and grabbed her sweatshirt before she ran into the kitchen. As promised, Hunter had left nearly a full pot of coffee. She brought the steamy black stuff to her lips, pausing to plan her next move as she savored the pungent aroma.

She pushed the door to his office gently. Coffee still in hand she entered his dimly-lit private study. His computer beckoned her from the large cherry wood desk. Max flexed her hands as she prepped herself to begin. Finally alone with his computer, she couldn't believe her luck. All in the name of good. *I'm one of the good ones.* She scooted in closer and settled in to her work.

He believed her a lot. He believed she was a research assistant on a big Houston case and needed records based here in town. He believed she was overworked and underpaid. Here goes: Scott Scofield, Frank Gilbert, and Hugh Harlan. One at a time she followed her hunches and leads. She cashed in on favors and typed furiously. Her stomach rumbled. She checked her watch, it was time for food.

She ransacked his fridge for some stuff, finding English muffins, lox, jam and cheese. She boiled some eggs while she assembled it. Then, plate loaded, she went back to work. After another hour she sat back considering her discoveries, and tendrils of connection between the three men. Why did she think they were connected? Because she had seen them together; as well as Chloe's Intel. She'd assumed they were colleagues, but the connections, on paper at least, were practically nonexistent. She had only found them on a hunch and a leap to connect the dots. She suspected these three were connected, but they were careful, very careful. Maybe the connection was just one piece of information they alone knew. She was out of time and she couldn't prove a thing. What about those ranches with the rings of barbed wire at the top like a prison? Hunter had never answered that question. He was always nice, but evasive. While she was at it she'd search that too.

When she searched them individually she found plenty of dirt. These guys were completely over-extended in all of their dealings and business investments. It seems they had incurred a huge debt. All of their businesses were leveraged. They seemed to be masters of the debt game.

She recalled a friend of hers raving about being a millionaire. On paper, it turned out. One million in debt. One million in debt plus interest is a logarithmically cosmic negative number.

There tucked and folded, as though casually, beside Hunter's computer, she spotted it. She hastily opened it and glanced down. She stopped typing and looked hard at the map. She stuffed it in her jeans and went back to the screen. She froze for a minute deciding what to do.

Countless events for these men seem to have backfired or dominoed. Some of their predictions had been off. They were placing their pawns and setting the stage. It was so close, but not there yet. Max could see it wasn't all there.

Max turned everything off, and hurriedly stuffed her skirt and heels into her large shoulder bag. She ran a brush through her wash-and-wear hair. Her silk blouse looked fine with jeans. She slipped on her loafers, and then wrote a quick note to Hunter before setting the alarm. She knew she'd stayed too long for one who had a job to go to.

She drove quickly to the small apartment she'd rented in town. She was going to have to make some decisions fast. She decided the best idea was to get all the information to Mariah and David ASAP. She would then explain why she had to quit this San Antonio charade. She could quit her job. She had saved plenty of money. No the job was now the least of her worries. The enormity of what she was on the verge of uncovering increased her panic. These guys were malicious, desperate men, cold-blooded murderers. They wouldn't hesitate to execute the son of a colleague, or orchestrate the collapse of business associates, and they most likely had already done so. She would warn them, but she couldn't name names. Not yet. Not until she had proof.

CHAPTER 13 *Top Down*

Max was shaken. One minute Hunter was telling her this was a casual affair. And the next she had finally connected the dots. She had no more reason to stay in San Antonio. She had been fooling herself. There was no way to have it both ways. She knew she had to pack and leave her apartment. It was a small month-to-month affair anyway. No biggie there. But she wouldn't be back. She grabbed her cooler from the hall closet and stocked it with the ice, food, and drinks she would need for the journey. She wasn't sure of anything now. Hunter was her friend. She'd stay friends. She wasn't sure where his loyalties lie. But she would keep it friendly.

Stay focused, Max. Her job had been to collect information and she had. But she wouldn't be finished until she had delivered it to her sister.

She packed all her clothes in her suitcase. She didn't want to leave a mess. Anything she didn't need she could give away later. She moved quickly, her heart raced from all that morning coffee. She didn't care. She pulled into Starbucks to get another one for the long drive. Just get out of town she told herself. I'll have plenty of time to think while I'm driving.

"Would you like something with that?" The clerk looked expectant.

"Pumpkin bread to go please."

"There you are."

She smiled. She dashed to her car and leapt in. She loved her cherry red Chrysler convertible. The weather was perfect; she could drive with the top down and the music blaring. She stuffed her pony tail into a baseball cap so it wouldn't be blown about in the wind. She was off. Girl on vacation. I'll call Hunter before I'm out of the service area, she thought. It's common courtesy to let him know I'll be out of town for a while. A long while. Hope I get his voice mail.

She replayed her findings in her mind. There was a company she had never heard of, Covington Interests, LLC. Headed by a Mr. Hugh Scott, CEO. Was that an alias? It seemed to be connected to a lot of well-known establishments. It must have a huge debt. There were a lot of spin-off companies listed. Real-estate development, import-export. It was difficult to get the idea of what the company actually did. The law firm that represented them was Randall, Jones and Jones. Frank Gilbert was a partner with the firm. Oddly enough, his name wasn't listed on the marquee, which was why his name hadn't come up before. He was also the link to Peter. He must be a kind of low profile guy.

Her mind flashed back to what she knew of the men. Had she ever been properly introduced to them? Had they seen or noticed her? Maybe not.

"It seemed all a game to them. How you play the game. That is what matters. They made the rules they changed the rules. Knowing this, we know they are ruthless." She recalled Chloe's description of her ex- husband's colleagues. Regardless, she bet they wanted this land, sooner rather than later. Max was sure of it.

Thank god Chloe had put her on the right trail. Too bad these guys were all around Hunter.

Let's see, she mused, there was first the lunch, then the mayor's fund-raiser dinner... This was the moment when it hit her. Her heart skipped a beat as she remembered. She had fallen for him that night. The perfect gentleman, Hunter.

CHAPTER 14 *Texas Oil*

Miles flew by while Max was lost in thought. Back-out plan. Economic attack. Scofield had noticed her at that diner. If she revealed this knowledge, could it backfire? She decided she would not name names. She'd keep her speculations to herself.

Would they be able to harm them at The Ranch in some way? She hadn't found enough facts to confirm her speculation. She still needed more information.

She refocused as she realized she was close to the turn-off for The Ranch. She had to strain her eyes to see. It was difficult to find hidden and overgrown as it was in late summer. She squinted in the waning light and prayed that there was more to hide their whereabouts than a few wild shrubs. Her heart pulsed as she made her way, fording the streams to find her friends at Indian Point.

* * *

"Okay, chances are you've never heard of these people." Max had everyone's attention as she stood by the picnic table sharing her news. "Very low key. What they all have in common is that they own Texas ranches. I'm speculating that this nameless group has a plan. This is what I have managed to piece together:

"Someone has been indirectly financing the war on terror myth. The whole plan seems to be to escalate the Middle East into such a state that the value of oil is increased on the world stage. Now that these guys are satisfied with the record prices for oil, they plan to come in and save the day by offering to drill their precious reserves. Of course drilling is very expensive, and until now, cost prohibitive. They have to tap into the limestone pockets. Not only are there record prices for oil, the lobbyists in Washington have succeeded in grabbing government subsidies to defray the costs of drilling. Presto, they can sell oil to a captive market."

The inner circle was gathered around hanging on Max's every word. Mariah glanced at David. What was Max talking about? Oil? She was confused.

Max took a breath and went on, "Their trump card is a *new peace plan*. Bring the troops back. Withdraw from all involvement in the Middle-East. And access our own US oil, thus rescuing the world from the oil crises and the endless war at the same time. They become heroes and billionaires at once."

"That's wonderful. I guess," Mariah said, deflated.

"I'm not sure if the fame is not just as important to them as the money," Max said.

"That solves a lot of problems," David nodded absorbing her news. "They are the good guys after all."

"Yes. It would seem so," Mariah said.

No one said a word, as they pondered this new information. The fire was quiet too, resting. Suddenly the fire whooshed to life as David placed a dry log on the flame.

"Guess where this Texas land with all the oil is located?" Max broke the silence.

"I don't know. West Texas?" David asked.

"I have a map of the territory," Max said, pulling it out of her bag. The three piled around the picnic table.

David pulled the lantern closer, casting a yellow glow on the map. "Wait, that spot you've marked?" David pulled out his glasses to study the topography of detailed hills and valleys. "That's right around where we are now." He looked up at Max. "Are you saying those guys own ranches near here?"

"That's exactly what I'm saying. From what I can tell, two of them seem to border this land. I wanted you to look at this before I jumped to conclusions. Both ranches are quite large, and both were bought at the same time by two different companies."

"These ranches are miles apart," Rob said.

"Why that is unusual, is that all other ranches are owned by families. The fact that two Houston companies decided to purchase land out here within a few months of each other is suspicious." Max told them. She had just realized her worst fear—this news explained the motive for Peter's murder. "Furthermore, I found a large survey that linked all three of these vast holdings into one bundle. It's dated about the same year as Peter's death. I have the geological survey right here. I made a copy this morning before I left San Antonio. In red you see the pockets of oil hidden below the limestone."

Jack Java pushed his way in to peer closer.

"The new infrared technology allows them to photograph the earth to locate oil before they drill. See, these lands have these dark pools? It's not water. I see one here, and another here. But here, the mother lode, the big sea of oil is here." She pointed.

David stared, eyes wide and mouth open. "I know this terrain. I've been studying the maps just to get oriented. It seems like we are in a vast wilderness of sameness. But that's here. That spot with the huge lake of oil is on Peter's land."

"That's why I came straight here. That's what I feared," Max said.

Mariah said, "I think I finally understand why Peter was murdered. For this." Her finger pointed at the map. "For this oil, hidden on his land."

Max nodded. "The adjacent piece was bought by Frank Gilbert, Peter's brother-in-law."

Mariah said, "Gilbert was married to the sister who died of an overdose of meds six years ago. I believe her name was Ruby."

"Yep," Max said. "That is the only name I could dig up. I couldn't find anything out about the company, Covington Properties or some such. It seems to be a spin-off of a vacation resort—like for corporate weekend getaways."

"Peter had controlling shares of the land," Mariah began. "If they bought Gilberts' land, do you think they made Peter an offer and he wouldn't sell?"

"The other caveat is the price they paid, pennies on the dollar. Very suspicious."

"Do you think Peter knew he was in danger? Would he have had any inkling about the oil?" Mariah asked

"I doubt it. He was completely focused out here," David said. "He knew there was a whole civilization here and he didn't want to disrupt it. I don't think he paid attention to politics. He spent his inheritance restoring this land, taking care of it, being here. Drilling would destroy water and then on down the line, no one would be able to survive."

"Well, no one has made any move to come out here for a long time," Mariah said. "I guess it will take some years before the oil demand reaches the point for them to begin the process. They will have to begin on their land first. That's about twenty miles away."

David shook his head, "That is still too close for comfort."

Max said, "I guess we have motive. We understand now why someone wanted Peter out of the way. Yet, it seems like a long shot to murder him way back then. No move was made to purchase or take possession of his land. That seems odd."

David said, "Perhaps they jumped the gun. Got Peter out of the way before they needed to."

"Wait a minute. Peter died the same year as the Gulf War began," Mariah said.

"That was when George Bush Sr. was president," Jack said. "He had big interests in oil, in fact, he owned Zapata Oil. That's a Texas company. It was bought out by somebody. I don't know who."

David added, "And all the talk back then, was of the New World Order and blood for oil. Those discussions have resurfaced again twenty years later. Aren't these guys getting old? Perhaps they have family and a legacy."

"Maybe the war and all their plans didn't unfold as they had hoped, and they are only now, able to continue their original plan," Rob added.

"Which company was he with?" Jack asked.

Max was calm now. "It's perhaps not a big conspiracy or anything. These guys are just reading the world stage and playing their assets into the hand they are dealt. They are just businessmen. Anything in scarce supply and high demand is more valuable. They may not even be murderers, just bystanders benefiting from a death. Think about it. Back in the 70's and 80's oil wells were pumping oil out of the ground twenty-four- seven. Then they got the bright idea to stop. While fuel use all over the world escalates, their assets remain. For example, the oil consumption on the world stage has increased tenfold since the 80's. We have a captive market. These guys are in a waiting game. The hitch is, now they are getting older."

"Who are *they*?"

Rob said in his patient tone, "Put it this way, like Max said, they are just businessmen. They are not crooks and they don't get their hands dirty. But why buy it from the family if they don't have to? Peter was the one who lived out here and worked the property. With him gone, no one's the wiser, especially as the properties are at oblique angles. Why spend money you don't need to spend?"

"Who? Mariah demanded, "Do you suspect anyone? Do you have a name? A hunch? Someone in government or business? It's a huge holding. It would cost a small fortune if it was for sale. Why buy what you thought you could just take?" She rephrased, "In other words, this is a vast territory, and with Peter gone no one is out here to stop them from *stealing* what they need."

"My bet is since they used a local to do their dirty work before, they would not be personally involved this time either. If they are at all suspicious of our presence here, they would delegate the job, and go on with their lives, business as usual. Just go on about their big important, decadent lives. Once the problem is taken care of, they will get a phone call. End of story," Rob said. "They sound too high powered to get their hands dirty."

Jack stroked his whiskered chin. "When you put it that way, Chloe could be their perfect little spy."

"Here we go again. That's true, except she stays here and never leaves," Mariah said. "Max and Hunter are the only ones that come and go anymore." She turned to her sister. "Now that you quit your job and moved out of your apartment you might stay here. Does Hunter know that, by the way?"

"No. I had to just go. I couldn't afford to ride the fence anymore once I knew without a doubt the danger involved. It's hot or cold, in or out. I realize I panicked and made hasty decisions, but I found it harder and harder to live both lives. Hunter didn't tell me any of this himself. I just found out and came straight here." She gave Mariah a sheepish look. "I was getting too attached anyway."

"Hey, do you see what I see? Look at the relationship of the two properties. They are adjacent. Yet there are no roads connecting the far west corner to the main highway. I mean someone could access Peter's land directly from the back corner and no one would know," Mariah said.

"They could be doing it now and we wouldn't know the difference. They may not even care that we're here. They might be too busy to notice us," Rob said.

"We are too busy to notice *them* for sure," Jack said.

"Conspiracy theorists just love 'they' and 'them'. No one ever knows who that is," David said.

Rob gave him a dirty look.

"They could view our activity as a diversion for the village. While we are busy here, no one would notice their activities in the back door," Tristan pointed out.

"I really don't think anything has started. It all depends on the war and economics. But you know these are just my hunches. It's all speculation really. I didn't dig any deeper once I found the maps," Max said.

"Let's assume nothing is happening now. Can we just get on with our plans? I think the less we know the better."

Tristan looked at his father. "Perhaps we need to speed up. If we disappear, no one will ever be the wiser. Max, do you have any idea about timing?"

"Now would be good in my opinion. Why risk it?"

CHAPTER 15 *In Process*

In the early morning, as Mariah finished her meditation, she stood at the edge of the cliff looking out at the vast expanse. She felt renewed from the invitation they held earlier in the week. She anticipated the group anointing; already feeling enthused with a new power as she surveyed the valley. Her thoughts focused on the exodus to the new lands. She shoved Max's dire facts about the evil oil cartel to the back of her mind. Then she spotted a figure down below approaching a camp in the lower meadow. Who is that, she wondered as she studied his movements. The person seemed familiar. With a start she realized it was Hunter. What was he doing here? That was fast. Ah flies do like honey. As she jogged down the narrow deer paths back to her compound she considered the situation.

"David, there you are. I just spotted Hunter in the lower meadow. I think he's here to visit Max."

"Strange, don't you think?"

"It's super bad timing. Here we are preparing for the exodus." She looked at her husband. "Do we tell him?"

"Where is he now?"

"I don't know, Max probably took him down for a swim. Alone. Do you think he was suspicious at Max's abrupt departure?"

"I honestly don't know," David said. "It's probable he knew all of the information Max just discovered the whole time."

"Hard to tell. She researched his colleagues using his access codes, mostly following hunches or suspicions. He may never have asked the same questions, never looked beneath the surface. He most likely didn't want to know. We have a broader perspective and everyone in those circles are suspects to us."

"I realize I'm giving him the benefit of the doubt. I'm a pretty good judge of character. He was Peter's best friend and yours too!"

"We wanted to know the truth." Mariah spiraled up from her cross-legged spot on the ground and examined one of the woven blankets. As she stroked the colors, the softness of the wool calmed her. "It's just... Hunter showing up at this moment, the timing is uncanny."

David's tone was a warning. "Mariah, now that you know how close Hunter is to the oil guys, you realize we can't tell him the whole story."

"I hate to face it, yet he belongs to that world. He's a big deal in town," Mariah said. "Let's just lay low and see what he does. I mean, what made him come out here after all this time?"

"We need to find out." David was focused on the next step. "No loose ends."

"We'll say we are returning home since it's the end of summer." Mariah decided. Anyway, we were planning to make a show of it to fuel the small town rumor mill."

"Yeah, it's a good idea. He doesn't have to know what we're really up to," David agreed. "If he thinks we left, he won't be obliged to tell the St. George family that squatters are hanging out here."

"Do you think he would? I thought he was too good a friend to betray us."

"You're probably right," David said. "It's Friday. We'll leave he and Max alone to enjoy the weekend. That gives us a couple of days to prepare. Then we'll head out Sunday afternoon."

"Okay. Good. I guess I will get on with the rest of my day then."

"Not so fast." David grabbed her arm. "Where are you off to now?"

"No place special. What do you have in mind? "

"I was just wondering. Just don't go too far."

"I do need to let Max in on our idea. I plan to grab a quick breakfast at her camp. Is that okay with you?"

"I promised Rob I would work with the Acting Group this morning. I'll catch up with you later."

She pulled him to her and kissed him lightly on the lips. "Sure?"

He smiled. "Of course."

He left soon after, but Mariah lingered, having thought better about interrupting Max and Hunter's visit.

* * *

It was evening before she went to find Max.

"What's up? Specifically, what are you and Hunter up to Max?"

"I honestly don't know. It was a shock to me that he came today. I just tried to act normal," Max said.

"All of this information you've discovered—has he known it all this time?" Mariah asked. "I'm not sure if we can trust him if he has."

"He says he can help us."

Mariah shrugged, "We're planning to move to the Interior. You know, soon we'll break camp."

"Everything is moving so fast. I didn't realize..."

"Fast?" Mariah almost squealed her impatience. "We have been here a long time. We have settled in. Actually, we are established to the degree disappearing seems impossible. Nevertheless, we have learned everything we can second hand. Soon we will be living it. Who would stay out camping through the winter?"

"Are the winters bad?" Max asked.

"Cold and wet. Uncomfortable. But there are caves. I've explored some of them around here. I can't wait myself. I can't wait to see how everyone handles the change."

Max looked wistful. "It's hard for me to let Hunter go, we had an awesome day. It's quite mesmerizing, like a day of magic. Rather timeless. Being out here is otherworldly."

"Tell me. Where did you go?" Mariah had never known her sister to be so conflicted.

"Everywhere. We hiked to the place where the petroglyph cave drawings are. We climbed to the top of the plateau. We dined on wine and chocolates and other goodies. We actually took a long hike up the creek draw after lunch. He loves this place. He knows it well. It's like he leads a double life. His world in San Antonio is quite a contrast. Then, we swam naked in the spring of course. It felt good. Icy and chill you to the bone. But so clean and crystal. Magic water. We discussed everything."

Mariah watched her sister's face, animated and full of peace as she

326

spoke. She's falling in love, she realized. A warm breeze blew in from the southwest stirring her hair. They both breathed in the warmth of the last breath of summer. The soft gauze clouds took on a pink glow and there was a rare hush as the day shifted into evening.

"I know you will have to listen to your heart to decide what is best," was all Mariah could think of to say.

"I'm pregnant."

"What! Max the waters don't work that fast."

"It's true." She shook her head.

"How long? When did you know?"

"I suspected when I moved out of my apartment."

Mariah moved to put her arms around her sister. "You didn't say anything."

"I wanted to be sure. Sure where I stood with Hunter."

"Is that why he came out this weekend?" Mariah realized she was prying.

"No. Yes, I mean he knew I left abruptly, but he doesn't know why. I need to end it. I don't want to let you guys down. I haven't really solved the issue of who killed Peter yet. I have all those suspicions but... I'm serious. I can't go back to the city now. I need to stay out here with you guys. Actually it's best if I take a break from Hunter right now. I don't trust my judgment when I'm around him. After all, I found all that information when I was using his computer. His uncle's firm has that branch in Washington; Randall, Jones, and Jones, the one that Frank Gilbert works for." She paled. "He's one of them. I don't even trust myself right now. These leads were blocked to me when I tried other computers. I have access codes. He has higher access codes. What is clear is that he knows them. I don't know how well he knows them, if it's just business or social. Whatever we plan to do we must act soon."

"I agree. I want you to know that we are working out a detailed plan to help cover all these possibilities. You're worried someone will figure out you tapped into all that private info and they will want to know why? In your condition you don't need that kind of stress. It's best for you to lay low, stay out here."

"We have to find out the truth. I didn't want to name names earlier, but I met Scott Scofield. He's involved in a big way and he's a politico, as well as a ruthless businessman." Max was miserable. Mariah could see that. "Would you go?" Max finally asked.

"What do you mean?"

"You go back to San Antonio with Hunter," Max said. "Pick his brain. He said he would help. Hold him to it."

"That's crazy." Mariah did some back peddling. "No, I can't leave. Absolutely impossible."
You could hear the air in the silence. "I have so much to do. David needs me."

Dead silence followed as Max's face fell in utter dejection and hopelessness at the situation.

"However, I got you in this mess in the first place. No, I mean yes. You are absolutely right. If we are the ones concerned about Peter's murder, we should not give up until we know for sure." Mariah paced and clapped and spun around.

"Stop you are making me dizzy."

"Oh, I'm sorry. How are you feeling? You really are with child aren't you?"

Max laughed. "Not so good. But it will pass. Out here with some peace and rest." She waited a beat. "You will do it. Won't you Sis?"

"I have decided. It's my turn to go to San Antonio. I'll say I plan to escort Chloe and the others out. I'll meet up with Hunter and pick his brain. Then if he can help us that will be a lifesaver. In the meantime you'll be here to rest up and decide about your situation."

"It's not a situation, it's a baby."

"Right." Pause. "That way you'll get a chance to be with your daughters and help them with this new transition." She gave her sister a sympathetic look. "By the way, don't be so hard on Hunter. Just because he knows them doesn't make him one of them. He knew Peter better than any of us. I want to remain optimistic."

"Mariah, you have got to find out which side Hunter is on. I found these files in his home office. He knows these men. It's not clear if he's in league with them. He can't find out I stole all this info. That would imply I'm using him to find stuff out about Peter."

"Which is what we are doing."

"I guess things have gotten out of hand."

"You and he have a lot in common. It's natural." Mariah took Max's hand.

"I'm on a slim footing with him already. If he's on our side he would want to avenge Peter's death. Just as much as we do."

"These are high powered men—future senator and all that—It may be difficult for him as well. The murderers have already been convicted and served time; case closed. The St. George family seems to be satisfied," Mariah said.

"That's true. There are a lot of what-if's."

"Don't you worry. I'll go to San Antonio, hang out, win his trust. See what's really going on."

"Good. That's a big load off. Do what you can, but don't make it the biggest priority. By all means, don't sacrifice all you have going on here. I'll keep training—between morning sickness that is."

"Did you tell him?"

"No. I don't want that to be the reason, if he decides to join us."

"You're being noble to say that. I couldn't do it," Mariah said.

"He made it clear it was just a fling."

"Fling! Why did you guys have so much fun together then?" Mariah saw Max's face light up at that thought. "You rest up and think positive. This place is like a resort. All the good healthy food and no stress."

Max smile was weak.

Morning sickness or love sickness? Mariah thought. They both made you feel queasy.

"Truly, I'm grateful," Max said. "I don't want to cause problems between you and David."

"I can do this. Just think after six months of living out here, even I'm suddenly having one last visit to the 'real world.'"

"Correction, *surreal* world," Max said.

"Right. And then I will be living this way for, I hope, a very long time."

"You were such a city girl."

"Was a city girl. It will be like a huge culture shock."

"It's not just the contrast, but things are changing. The way things were are changing visibly. I don't want to disappoint you. You'll see for

329

yourself."

Mariah looked wistful. "I think I'm ready. Been a long time since I've seen the outside world."

"You won't like it like you used to," Max said. "It's changed, or you've changed. Both I think. You can't see it with the old eyes once the curtain has been torn down."

"No going back, really," Mariah conceded.

"That is what they say."

* * *

Mariah hummed all thru the dinner chores, while her helpmates teased and bickered in a pleasant camaraderie. She was wide awake inhaling the bit of cool air that was settling in as she joined her family back at Indian Point. She looked thoughtful as she observed her two men conversing by the fire. "You know? I could do it." Mariah burst in with an off-subject interruption.

David turned to Mariah looking puzzled. She hadn't said much, had just been gazing into the fire. "Do what?" David asked.

"Take Chloe and the eight or nine others who are not committed back to town."

David frowned, clearly surprised by the idea.

"You have so much to do here," Mariah explained. "You are supposed to lead the Exodus into the interior. The harvest will be our gift to the Indians as a trade for their hospitality. That leaves you to head the core team—Jack, Pat, John, Rob, Jody, and Isabella on the exodus to the interior. We can't risk being discovered if anyone follows us back from town."

David and Tristan just stared at her. Mariah wasn't sure if that was an agreement or not, but her mind was made up. With much to do, she disappeared straight into the sanctuary of her tent.

* * *

"What's up, Rob?" Mariah looked up as her brother came in.

"Roxanne can't quit cigarettes. I mean she's having fits. She's packing."

"I know, she told me. How are you with it?"

"No one could have made me give up all my vices. Somehow I did

330

it. It was my choice. I can relate to her. Anyway, I've been spending a lot of time with Chloe. It's not my fault she's always hanging around me, but it gets on Roxanne's nerves."

"Chloe follows you around like a puppy," Mariah agreed, "But you don't need to encourage her."

"I'm not. Well, she's good to talk to." Rob was defensive. "Besides, she's older. She knows what she's doing."

"I'm sure she does." Mariah put her hands up. "Not my business, I know, just a bit of sisterly advice. Anyway, I'm going to take the last trip back to San Antonio, which will be our last chance for winter supplies. Then Joseph or Jet will help me get back to the interior. Roxi can go with me, I would appreciate the help. Maybe all you two need is a little break? She can come back in with me or not, whatever she decides to do."

"Will it be dangerous for the group? I mean if she decides to leave this late in the game?"

"I'll be glad to talk to her. It would be too late to come back if she changes her mind again, though."

"That's a relief. There is only one danger then."

"What on earth could that be?"

"If she talks. She's mad at me."

"She won't. She has worked too hard with us to want to blow our cover. She loves you and just because she can't live with you doesn't mean she'll be vengeful."

* * *

After Rob left, Mariah sat for a bit, staring at her dusty bare feet, contemplating Rob's news. She reached up into mountain pose to stretch the kinks out of her back. Just last year Rob wouldn't have been willing to let go of Roxi. Now he seemed willing to shed her along with his other habits.

Mariah slipped away from camp, down to the stream to bathe. She carefully navigated the rocks and the steep climb down to the water. She could hear some happy children's voices in the distance floating above the splash of waterfalls. Rob was sincere. She knew that. He was such a handsome guy. She'd never seen him look healthier. He was thriving on this lifestyle. Roxanne, not so much. For years she had followed him everywhere, through lots of poverty and struggle, yet she couldn't follow him to a life without cigarettes and beer. Chloe's pursuit of Rob had just been a symptom of the real problem. Now with Chloe hanging on Rob's every utterance, he'd seemed to have gotten over Roxi. The trouble was, Mariah didn't completely trust Chloe. She knew Max was on top of that. She shouldn't worry. Nevertheless, the thought nagged her.

The male ego is a funny thing, my male is probably starved to death for attention by now, she thought. She laughed to herself. Her feet hit the ice-cold water and jolted her back to reality. She smoothed the pure water over her face, neck, and arms, marveling at how this paradise had become her reality. Some folks couldn't see that. They might see lack while she focused on abundance. Anyone who wasn't sold on this life could head right back to civilization if that's what they truly wanted.

She heard a bird call in the distance. She squinted her eyes and shielded them as she searched the cliff-face for David. Her face burst into a grin when she spotted him coming quickly down the hill in cutoffs, towel over his shoulder. She was sure he would eventually see reason and happily consent to her plan. It seemed that they were always pulled in different directions based on the needs of the whole community. She'd make it all up to him, she vowed. They were here together now. Once I get back, I won't be going anywhere she'd promised him.

"Don't even think you're going to bathe without me," he ordered. Then he smiled.

Laughing, she splashed water at him as he tried to grab her and exchange some wet kisses. They used Dr. Bronner's soap to bathe. Mariah washed her dark hair and rinsed it with cupfuls of the ice-cold water, then they scrubbed each other's backs.

CHAPTER 16 *Conversation*

"Max said you wished she have a nice trip back to San Antonio," Mariah said.

"Yeah after seeing her with Hunter I realized I had been missing something." David didn't look up.

"I don't understand, David. It seems you've forgotten that I'm planning to go to San Antonio."

"You're right, I had forgotten, or overlooked that detail is more accurate. I thought you would change your mind once we were close to the time."

"I've already worked out all the details with everyone. The nine leaving will not return. It's my duty to get them out safely. Then I'll go on into San Antonio for our winter provisions. If Roxi changes her mind at the last minute, she can come back with me. Joseph has promised that someone will help me get back to the interior." She saw a storm brewing on his features. "We've already discussed it. Admit it, David, my plan makes the most sense." Mariah was rolling up her sleeves to do serious battle. She was not prepared to disclose Max's situation this early on.

"I'm not for it," David interrupted.

"Come again?"

"Absolutely not," David was adamant.

"Wow, you sound so definite," Mariah said.

"I mean it. No. No discussion. None of your little conniving conversations."

"You sound like a dictator. At least be open to a conversation."

"I'm not a dictator, I'm just your husband. I miss you when we're apart. Now I plan to settle in and enjoy peace with your company included."

"Thanks, since you put it that way."

"Besides, you are a bit naïve," David said.

"I beg your pardon?"

"You are naïve. An open book. You don't have boundaries like normal folks. Being out here has made you even more vulnerable. I realize you let your guard down so you can commune with nature, and be open to your little friends, the Indians."

"Little friends? You sound jealous," Mariah retorted.

"I always go along with you. What you say, what you think, your latest intuition. Christ, we came all the way out here, didn't we?"

"You're a leader. It's your destiny to be here and do this work. Everyone looks up to you, respects what you say. You are about to lead everyone on the biggest step we're going to take." Mariah was fuming as she paced about. "How did this happen?" She wailed. "Why are we fighting now?"

"You are so naïve. You're vulnerable, you trust total strangers. You go around spouting your theories about reincarnation to anyone who will listen. Half of the people don't even take you seriously."

"I haven't been talking about that at all lately."

"Come on, you know some of your brothers and sisters won't come out here because they think you're a pagan."

"Explain?" *Pagan*, that thought amused her.

"If you didn't open your mouth in front of the wrong people they wouldn't know any of it," David said.

"Well what's wrong with that?"

"For one thing, if you actually think the world is about to collapse, you would want those you love to join us here. Not drive them all away with crazy theories and strange visionary rhetoric."

"I didn't know you felt that way." Mariah was miffed.

"I've lived with you for years. I'm used to it."

"Maybe you should be the one going. Not me. But I don't understand why you would want to come back. If that's the way you feel."

"I'll think about it. Don't worry. Seriously think about it."

"I think I will take my sunset stroll by myself, thank you very much. See you later. I need to go commune with the woods now."

"That's just like you to go run off in the middle of a discussion."

Discussion? Mariah thought to herself as she marched off 'Dictator. Materialist. Patriarchal master.'

With her back stiff, Mariah, stomped away to take refuge in the solace of her tent. There in the peace and cool of the white interior, she took pen in hand to write. With a deep breath, she began. Writing always helped her divine some reason in this world.

Mother

I'm a woman
I'm black
I'm a slave
I'm a second class citizen, piece of property
In this white man's patriarchal world.

I'm a possession,
I'm a trophy
I'm a piece of decorated art
I'm a second class citizen, piece of property,
In this white man's Patriarchal world.
It's about to change,
I can feel the change
As I shed my skin of your perception,
Limitation, under estimation.
You think I'm mad because I am a woman,
Don't go to doctors,
Don't have insurance,
In this white man's patriarchal world.

I am mad woman, psychic healer,
Transcendent master, shamanic leader.
I know my way.
I know The Way.

In this white man's patriarchal world.

It's about to change,
I can feel the change
I can sense your pain as I let go
Of your suspicion, your perception, superstition,
My incarceration, inclination, full gestation, hibernation,
In this white man's patriarchal world.

I'm the earth,
I am dirt,
I am dug out, dug up and raped.
For energy to fuel this
White man's patriarchal world.

I'm your Mother
Can't you see me?
I try to heal all I know.
As I cover all the open wounds
With clover flower abundant blooms.

Dogwood spring,
Lilac tree,
Wisteria vines encircle and entwine.
I can bind you with all of these
Cover you with pungent smells
Rock you to sleep in a cool night breeze.

Can't you feel it changing?
Hear the changes.
Surrounded by love,
In this one, beautiful, world.

CHAPTER 17 *Compassion*

It was late afternoon when Mariah heard the flap of her tent open. She was lying on her mat, and although she was facing the other way she knew who it was. She turned around and looked at David, silhouetted by a ring of golden sunlight behind him.

"Hey," he said.

"Hey."

"Look, I was expressing my opinion back there. You didn't have to run away." He moved beside her.

Sitting up, Mariah spoke with a glint of humor in her eye. "It wasn't *'opinion'* I was running from, but my own disappointment. Here we are trying to transcend and evolve and vibrate at a high level, and you slip into some foreign, controlling, manipulative, passive-aggressive behavior. And what's worse, I still care."

"Mariah?"

"Seemed like you were expressing yourself, that's true." She studied his clouded blue eyes. "I needed to be alone for a while. I thought if I let your words hang in the air you would hear yourself more clearly."

"So, refresh me." He was great before an audience. In some moods he became the man of few words.

"Refresh you what?"

"My words."

"Do you remember our talk at all?" Mariah asked.

He took her by the shoulders and spoke directly to her face. "I just don't want you to go." His touch was firm but gentle. "That's simple."

Mariah shrugged. "I'm flattered. Ah-huh and you said 'No, No. No. NO. NO'. I know that's not a discussion. It's a statement." She raised her hand. "I've considered your request. I understand you don't want me to go. That is, however, a negative request. I would like a positive request. What would you like me to *do*?"

David answered quickly, "Stay here."

Mariah made a pinched-lipped smile, "Yes, but *to do*, here?"

"Lead your troop into the interior. Carry your load. Help us get where we're going."

"Can't someone else do that?"

"Huh?"

"Lead my troop. The way I see it, Max can handle that. And while I 'carry my load,' who will resolve the matter of Peter's murder and the oil drilling threat in San Antonio? I know you could. You could carry that off well. You are capable of finessing such a complicated diplomatic task. You should go back with Hunter." She moved behind him and rubbed his tight shoulders.

Mariah waited as her words sunk in. David shook his head. She could tell this idea did not sit well at all. She sat in front of him as he kept shaking his head. "Mariah, first I don't think you can resolve all of that in one trip. And you don't have to. Peter died a tragic death. He died young. Healthy—wealthy—he had it all. Try as we might we can't bring him back."

Mariah felt inadequate as he said the words she didn't want to believe. However, she didn't want to give up before she had even tried. All she wanted to know was the truth. She took a deep breath and tried again. "David, you have become the leader of this community, and as leader you must be the one to guide everyone to the interior. This is what we have been waiting for since we got here." Even as she said the words, Mariah realized she had been waiting much longer than that. She had been waiting, on some level, since the night in the teepee. "In that slot you are irreplaceable." Mid-sentence she had a new realization, as she caught David's expression. He was actually afraid of this next step. "Wait. Is that it? Is that the real reason you don't want me to go? You don't want to lead alone?" She studied him. Perhaps he was not as sure of himself as he seemed. Cool and confident in that laid-back friendly way he had, no hurry, no worries.

He paused, "I would be lying if I said I wasn't nervous. I mean, this is *it*, Mariah."

"I know. But you *can* do that. You are great at that. I can see you would like to have me by your side. You've been the one to welcome the newbies and lead them here. You have spoken at our monthly gatherings. The people admire you and take direction from you. They fall into place beside you." She took his hand. "You are the leader because you lead by serving. Why do you think so many are in the gardening group? Yours is the welcoming smile everyone recognizes. I know you want me by your side. I'm already there. I'm with you every step."

He was about to speak but she squeezed his hand to let him know she wasn't finished.

"It's just dawning on me now. I always thought your destiny lay in your art. Yet, in your own words, the quality of the art produced is a reflection of *the soul* of the person. You worked on your personal life: integrity, responsibilities. Art success seemed easy for you—winning awards, getting gallery directors to believe in you and show your work. You have natural charisma. I'm the mopey loner. Too intense for most. I spend hours alone. You are born to lead."

David sat speechless watching her talk. Finally he said, "You are my wife."

"I know. I'm glad to have that honor, but I'm still me." She got up and stretched. She realized she was stiff from the intensity of the dialogue. "You are scared. You're scared to step up now. Well, don't be. Do it your way. You always say lead by doing. Just go. It's almost time. Isabella and Jody have organized everything. All you have to do is go. They will follow. But I must make sure things in San Antonio are managed properly, otherwise everything we've worked for could be at risk."

"I will miss you." David spoke with resignation.

"I will miss you too. Can you name someone who could do it for me?"

He didn't hesitate. "No one. You're the one that has to finish this." David gave her his best wounded look, followed by a hug.

339

CHAPTER 18 *Friends*

Everyone in Painted Meadow turned to face Mariah. "We are prepared to discuss the logistics with you." As Mariah cleared her throat, her eyes scanned the crowd, and she could see the supportive faces of David, Jack, Tristan, and Rob. She sensed their rapt attention disguised by their casual stances, as they scattered amidst the crowd. "The Exodus to the interior must be obscured with the noise of leaving. As we arrange the groups for our transition into the interior, we must create the impression we are all leaving for good. This is an opportunity to pack all unwanted clutter into the vans. "

"Can you explain exactly what you are going to do with the vans?" Fred asked.

"Good question. We'll place them on old dead-end roads in the countryside near the Frio River. There are a lot of families there, and we have a few things that might be useful to them. We'll just leave the keys and some gas in the tank."

"Maybe with a note," Jack added, "Like, 'Please help yourself before the police impound this vehicle. Have downsized my life. Keys under the mat. Have a nice day.' "

"Or, 'Today is your lucky day,'" someone joked.

"It's a great idea," Hazel said. "People who are homeless can actually wait out the winter in a van."

"When people leave unwanted furniture by the curb, it usually disappears before trash day." Meghan spoke from experience.

"My grandmother once furnished her whole house with other people's castoffs," Max said.

"That would be my grandmother," Mariah teased.

"I had a friend that did that with half-dead plants. She landscaped her whole yard practically for free. It was a wonderful garden. Took up the whole backyard." Stacey smiled at the memory.

A voice spoke out of the crowd. "We left Mehico for the American Dream." Mariah looked to see who belonged to the quiet voice. She spotted José and beckoned for him to step to the front. Thanking her, he moved to the front and turned to face the group. He held his hat before him as he spoke, "Some ideal of the American dream, the only true democracy."

As if America invented the concept. America, the embodiment of freedom. Mariah thought.

"But actually we realize we love Mehico. You guys don't have it any better." The group listened attentively to José. He was a small man; his hands twisted his hat as he spoke. He was a hard worker, capable of accomplishing much. "We long for our homeland, our families, our cousins. It is just the murder, drug lords, and corrupt governments we were trying to escape.

"You have it all too. All the same corruption in your government from what you say. Your country is so big you can't feel it breathing down your neck so close to home like we can. America is bigger. Everyone hides out in their own private backyard barbecue.

"May we please take one of the vans? We have decided to return to Mehico. You have given us courage to stand our ground. We are going to go back to our own country, show our neighbors and friends. You have truly inspired us. It's amazing what everyone accomplishes when you work together."

The group was scattered around on blankets listening attentively to the sincere man before them. Then shouts erupted from the crowd. "You can do it, Jose'. Good Luck. We will be rooting for you."

Mariah and David shared a look. "Yes, of course you can take the van."

A woman wearing a floral pattern dress that swung from her large frame as she rushed to give Jose' a huge smothering hug, spoke up. She was weeping, filled with mixed emotions. She smeared her tears from her face onto her fingers. "I lofe you guys. But you have it harder than we do back home. We have our houses and our goats. Thank you for letting us leve here this summer." She held her José's hands in both of hers. Together they strolled back to their spot in the group.

Not knowing exactly how to take this, they all gave José and his wife, Ruth hugs. "We have our own families to go back to." Ruth's eyes were red and glistening, but her white teeth showed as she smiled. Once everyone had quieted down they went back to their discussion.

"My van smells a little like patchouli," Jeff said as he flashed a grin, "but you guys are welcome to it."

Mariah gave him a stern look but she was smiling. "Just don't leave anything like pot or illegal substances in there. We don't want them to have any problems."

She turned back to the couple. "This is going to be risky. We put the title in the glove compartment but we blanked out the names of the owners. You certainly won't be able to take it across the border."

"Not all of the vans are going to be given away. Since Vince and Vera are leaving separately they each are taking one with them. They're giving the others rides back to San Antonio and Uvalde where they can find the way back home or on to their respective next adventures," David said.

"In conclusion, that gives us three, Hunter, Roxi, and I, along with the eight that want to return, we will have eleven. That should work," Mariah said.

"How can Hunter drive a van? He has his own car," Hazel said.

"You're right. The sixth car will make our exit seem larger. Two per van and Hunter in his own car."

"Shouldn't Max go with you?" Jack suggested.

"No she's trading with me, she will take my group in to the interior so I can go," Mariah said.

David looked at her in shock. "Wait, we're leaving you behind?"

"I'll catch up," Mariah said.

"And Chloe? Did she decide to stay or leave with you guys?"

"She and Max are going to work together. It should be fine," Mariah said. "Hopefully the locals will assume we all left after a summer season of fun. I think we just have to act rowdy and fill up at the local gas station with music blaring, windows open wide."

"I'm game. I can totally do that." Roxi looked cheerful.

Matt laughed. "Yeah, I'll have one of those loud boisterous fights with her. Just like any red neck couple would."

Mariah cut her eyes at David. "It's not only red neck couples who fight."

David squeezed her hand. "C'mon, I said I loved you. I'll just miss you."

"Me too," she said as she gazed up at him.

"You can use my car for your trip," Max offered. "I don't need it now."

"Wow, thanks, that is amazing." Mariah knew, that for her sister, this was a significant sacrifice.

"Sounds like a plan," David said, his unsmiling mouth was a grim line.

"I'm a bit nervous," Mariah admitted.

"Just a bit of acting, Mom," Isabella offered. "You always said you dreamed of being an actress."

"That's true," she said, squeezing her daughter's arm, "I just thought that coming out here meant I was leaving theatrics behind me."

* * *

The sun on the horizon seemed unusually large and red as it sank, touching the yellowed dried grass with streaks of fire as it slipped over the edge, leaving a glowing twilight in its wake. Everyone had gone to help prepare for the Anointing Ceremony, except Tristan, who had offered to keep an eye on his cousin Mason. Tristan laid a blanket under a tree and placed the baby down on it. He picked up the old guitar he'd brought from his tent. A lot had happened since he had learned to play when he was twelve.

Nearby, Joseph's cousin Daniel sat cross-legged, listening to the plaintive notes that seemed to hang in the air one at a time. Mason crawled to the edge of the woven blanket. His big grey eyes were wide at the sight of the Native American resting by the tree. Tristan lost in thought, strummed his guitar.

Tristan could hardly believe the time had come. In just a few days they would begin the biggest transition of all - the metamorphosis into the interior. Quite a feat to make the impact of one hundred and fifty people disappear. A guide would be there to meet his mother when she returned; it's not like one could rely on geography and maps to get here. Tristan wasn't completely convinced Mariah's trip to San Antonio was necessary, but he trusted her instincts. After all, she'd been the one to get everyone to The Ranch. This community was her brainchild. David would lead with the first group. Each of the Inner Circle members would lead each camp in succession. Anticipation had been building for the past week.

He thought about Roxi, who would be leaving with Mariah. She'd better be sure about her decision; it would be terrible to realize she had made a mistake, only to be locked out of their community—and away from Rob—forever.

Even if the world didn't collapse, Tristan preferred this way of living, even as he acknowledged that it wasn't for everyone. He had grown to like Roxi and hoped she would be part of the exodus, just as he'd hoped Hunter would decide to join them. He was well, aware, though, that when it came to Hunter it was much more complicated.

"Tristan." A voice at his elbow spoke, jarring him from his reverie.

"Daniel, you startled me."

"It's time now for you to receive the most important gift."

He placed the guitar on the ground beside him. "But the group?"

"They are in capable hands. David, Rob, and Jack will handle that. The chief needs you to come now."

Tristan nodded, then reached over and scooped Mason into his arms. "I will bring the child to his mother, and then I'm all yours."

"Don't worry about Mariah, we still have our scouts. When she returns I will go personally and ensure she joins us safe and unharmed. Time is moving fast. It's time now for your biggest task."

CHAPTER 19 *Chrysalis*

The man-made world seems flat and empty, a dull, lifeless place, when our vision is suddenly clear. That is how it came to Mariah. With clear vision, you can see beyond the illusion. In contrast, Nature, 'God's World', is full of song and sound. The birds' song. The roundness of the air. The tip of wind upon her cheek, that barely blows her hair. The shadow of a tree branch waving in the freshest breeze. God's world is round and full.

The first light was just breaking over the hill when they came, streaming in twos and threes from all directions to meet in the open east side of the meadow. There was a quiet buzz as they fanned out in a large semicircle and laid their mats down. The sun grew higher and the round orange ball was large as it sat on the crest of the hill. All faced the glow, hair tinged in red highlights of sun, faces turned upward as they assumed a cross-legged yoga pose. Awaiting transformation, Mariah realized.

Rob waited for them to get settled. "Welcome. It has been three days since I invited you here for this special Anointing Ceremony, and I assure you, you have made the right decision in accepting. We are about to go to a place of healing, a place of transcendent transformation. Who is allowed in Paradise? As promised, after today, nothing will be the same again."

Rob met the gaze of each person. He continued as though born to this new role. "Let me remind you, the anointing must occur before anyone in the group enters the Realm of our future Sacred Home. Yet, if a person's vision is clouded, and their heart crowded with competing voices, they are unable to rule their own mind and heart. Thus through the anointing process, the group conscience stays clear, as each individual is clear. Thus the ceremony of anointing is a purge. A purge of all the demons that have taken hold over the year. Each person then enters cleansed, enlivened, released, with one's conscience clear, one's burden light."

Rob paced as he spoke to the attentive crowd, quiet in the morning light, "All those in the world want to be in the gated community. They desire exclusivity. I invite you all to stay and hide behind your walls. Lock yourselves in. For you have all tasted corruption and dined with her at your table. The demons have run the show, *are the show,* in fact. Why are the 'men's clubs' next to the burger joints? So a gentleman can have *it* on his lunch break in the middle of the day. And still be back home at cocktail hour in the evenings, his wife none the wiser.

"Why the missing children? Where do they go? A society that sells its children; hunts zoo creatures; celebrates whores and prostitution; takes mothers from there babes. That place is demon- lover possessed. RUN! RUN I tell you.

"Some could say we have our own club and are creating our own world, but to quote my teacher, 'we have run from, but not away. We have run to. To a *new* way. RUN I repeat. In all that murky darkness how do you find the light?" His words, harsh in the soft light of morning, hung in the air. He searched the crowd as though looking for the answer.

He spoke softly, "Read the rules of Christ; *'Love God,' 'Love one another.'* Say *NO to false gods or demons.* Three guidelines. Say this as a mantra."

Again, silence wrapped them like a veil, as all waited.

"All of us must purge our demons. They are not allowed in, to the place we are going. The anointing oil is prepared. It's made with flowers from the Tree of Life, olive oil, cinnamon, and special herbs. I have it here. All who are ready, let us be anointed." He lifted the flask full of amber liquid up into the air.

"We do this today to mark the eve of our departure, our Exodus into the interior. As we attend the Anointing Ceremony together, we are in the stage of the chrysalis to be sure. This new life is our transformation.

"We are venturing deeper into the forest, where we will create another, more hidden abode, complete with many gardens and our new homes. Once we arrive, we shall celebrate with feasting and dancing at the full Moon."

Rob led the group in meditation in the great meadow. Six helpers moved among the gathering with the anointing oil. Helpers placed oil on the front of each forehead and back of each head. A small bowl was passed with cotton swabs. Each person took turns anointing the breast bone of the person next to him. Everyone wanted transformation.

* * *

That evening, after dinner, Mariah was once again in the solitude of her white tent, pen in hand. On the table before her was her journal, the chronicle of their journey thus far. She ran her hand along its soft leather cover. How would she explain this latest event? She studied the thick, white, blank, page before her, in this book she had received as a gift from David on their trip to Italy. She was wistful as she recalled the distant memory. She considered the extreme intensity of Rob's words. Just a few weeks after his own anointing he had already stepped into a radically enlightened self. She herself was different.

She wrote, *"This is perhaps a messy attempt, a clumsy effort, from a true heart that gets a vague glimpse, sometimes razor clear, of the truth. Like seeing through a camera lens, twisting into and then out of focus. But in my nature I run towards beauty and sunlight. I turn my head from the dark demons of the underworld."* She lifted her pen and pondered Rob's words. He had followed a brutal path in his life. He could speak to aspects of the human condition of life on earth she could barely imagine. That was most likely why he had been chosen by the Indian elders to lead the Anointing Ceremony for the entire group. She pondered the differences in their upbringing, she, as the eldest, at the top, and he among the youngest of their large family. Was this the reason his notions of love and family and loneliness were the opposite of hers? What joy she felt to witness his healing. His healing had helped him to quickly blossom into the wounded healer that could reach out with compassion to many people.

She closed her journal. She had plenty to do before she headed to San Antonio with Roxi. She gathered a few belongings to take with her. She took the leather journal and carefully wrapped it in her white shawl. As she packed, she convinced herself it made sense for all to leave at the same time. But maybe David was right and she should just stay here. But no, she should go with Roxi. They, together with the vans full of extra stuff, would all depart at once. Hunter needed to believe the bulk of them were leaving and only one small contingent would stay to clean up the land. As it was getting late, she stepped outside to check on her own family.

In the black night, Mariah was surprised to see Tristan, hands clasped behind his back, pacing. He was clearly waiting to talk to both of them. She glanced at David, speckled in light and shadow by the fire, and then nodded for Tristan to spill it.

"I spoke to Joseph about the next level of initiation," he began. "He said it will take about a week." He paused.

"And...?" Mariah asked.

Tristan rushed his speech, "But the process will be very different and more serious."

Mariah raised an eyebrow. "More serious?"

Tristan nodded. "He said I must travel and find some kind of special device, truly valuable. He said it was a gift for our people. In the past, all of our times together have been close by in Texas. We practice a kind of shape-shifting, like to soar above the earth with the Hawk. It feels wonderful. This will be different. I will be travelling with Daniel.

This trip is a great honor." He spoke with a light humor in his voice as though to diminish the gravity of the situation.

"Go far? Shape shift? Travel? Did I hear this correctly?" Mariah asked.

"I was afraid you would make a big deal about it, but it's fine. I'm excited really."

Mariah and David were speechless.

"All of my training has prepared me. I have shape shifted before. It's awesome. You would love to try it yourself someday, Mom."

David turned to Mariah, "I suppose you're just going to let him go?"

"With my blessing," Mariah replied calmly. "And yours too, I expect?"

"I am ready for this," Tristan told his father. "I'm just not sure what they mean by a gift—I think it may be an invention of some sort."

Mariah studied her son. She was still shocked by how much he had matured. "When do you leave?"

"First light."

"We'll be heading out in different directions about the same time," she replied.

David's face looked pained. "With Mariah gone I was looking forward to some father son time."

"I know Dad, me too. It seems everything is happening at once. Hopefully the exodus, and Mom's trip, will go smoothly and we'll all be together again soon." Tristan's eyes glowed as he tried to describe the importance of his mission. "I think the special gift is something crucial for our survival in the new lands. Also, I don't think it's an accident that we're being used in these final days for tasks we must perform alone. Isabella is leading the teens; even you two will have separate groups."

Mariah, smiling, pulled him into a hug. "I am proud of you. Tristan, please be careful."

David, still looking a little shell-shocked, wrapped an arm around him as the family gathered around Tristan trading hugs.

"I'll be back, you know."

"Well, everyone's leaving me to do all the work, I see," David

"*The battle is in the mind of the thinkers. There are the thinkers and the thoughtless. The thoughtless are those who walk on autopilot— who follow.*"

observed.

"Not everyone." Isabella patted his arm in mock sympathy. "I'm here, Dad. You know you can handle it all but I'll help."

David managed a smile. "Thanks." He looked at Mariah and Tristan. "At least we're going to the same place." He reluctantly felt a twinge of admiration. "Okay, you both have my blessing. It will be hard with both of you gone, but what a reunion we'll have when we make it to the new territory." He smiled. Mariah loved his smile. He then opened his arms wide and grabbed each into a big bear hug.

Mariah was lifted off her feet with his embrace. 'She shouldn't go', her thoughts panicked in her head. She should stay with her family. Do this thing together like David wanted. She closed her eyes to remember all of them more clearly. Her husband and her son.

After discussions long into the night Mariah had assured him not to worry, that somehow his fears had just come to the surface all at once. "We have all gone out on a limb. If you get struck dumb with fear now that you are in the middle hovering over the abyss, it's the worst. Don't look down or back. You must look forward to the world you are trying to create. We never know for sure what's around the next bend." This was the biggest leap of faith so far Mariah thought. "I need you now most of all. I need you to believe in me. We each have our role. You're leading the whole group into the Interior. I have one last trip to San Antonio. Who do you think should go, if not me?" Mariah asked.

"You're right. I'll just miss you." David stuck his hands in her pockets and pulled her close. "Promise me you will be careful and you will be fast."

The next morning Mariah rose early to grab some breakfast. As soon as she reached the dining area, she felt it—something had shifted. The Anointing Ceremony, she realized, had brought everyone closer. There was an afterglow on all the shining faces, a new bond, something deeper than friendship united all. Yet she was leaving. Had she made the right decision?

Everyone ate quickly, then returned to their various camps to pack the essential. It was time to go. David walked Mariah to the van, made her promise for the hundredth time to be careful, then he kissed her lightly on the lips and helped her inside.

After everyone had taken off, the camp was quiet. David did a few sketches of Tristan before he left on his quest. Tristan played his guitar in a way that made David realize he would miss both of them. "It's amazing how much you've changed in the last six months," David said. "Not that you weren't a wonderful person when we began this trip."

Tristan looked up with a wistful smile.

"You are really growing into manhood."

"Good, thanks. Mom was getting pretty far along in the work. She received a lot of training from both 'Runs' and Jet. Don't worry about her or me while we're gone. I'm sure she can take care of herself out there. She has a lot of techniques now. She is prepared for the battle."

"Battle?" David wondered aloud.

CHAPTER 20 *The City*

Mariah headed to the main highway in the red convertible, behind Hunters Jeep, on the long grassy road thru the Ranch. Vans loaded to the gills followed behind. She saw in her rear view mirror, the vehicles snaking behind with windows open and arms hanging out in clouds of dust, as they drove through the meadow. It reminded her of the school bus adventure of the original California hippies when they traveled out to find land in Tennessee. It seemed as long as a wagon train. Roxi and Matt were in the van behind her. Hunter would be convinced they were all leaving. He threatened to be the biggest leak in there escapade—family-friend and lawyer that he was. Finally, they squealed into the closest town with windows open wide, music blaring, and tambourines shaking. She could tell by the way they were ignored, they had made there point.

They gave each driver a map to the drop-off point, to be picked up later, by Vince or Vera. While in the parking lot, they made a show of kissing, hugging, and squealing good-byes as the promised radios blasted from open windows of the beat up vans. Mariah whooped it up with tears, speaking over-loud, and lots of hugs all around. The girls waved good bye as everyone took off for points north and various small Texas towns. She hadn't been faking it. She would miss them all.

After the last group left, Mariah patted Max's now-dusty red Chrysler. She noticed a guy with greasy long hair under a dirty cowboy hat leering at her. He looked her over with a familiarity that gave her the creeps. He grinned and shouted obscenities to harass them. She hoped she hadn't inadvertently invited such unwelcome attention. Of course they ignored him, and she and Roxi coolly joined Hunter in his air-conditioned Jeep Cherokee to confer about the travel plans. They would follow his lead on the drive to San Antonio. Roxi walked over to the market to grab some Marlboro's. Mariah glanced over and was unable to suppress a shudder.

After Roxi crammed more supplies into the cooler in the back seat she muttered, "Ass hole," under her breath. "Let's blow this place."

With unspoken assent from Mariah, Roxi took the wheel. Neither Mariah nor Roxi had driven for months and she thrilled to be in the driver's seat.

Mariah was worried about facing 'The World' alone. She was extremely glad Roxi had joined her. As the miles flew by, Mariah glanced over at her companion. Sun hit the golden lights in the thick, chopped, brown hair that framed Roxi's strong featured face. She was an action person, tall and strong. She had given her all at The Ranch and had the muscles to show for it. Her outfit of white tank top and khaki shorts hid little. She was a doer not a talker. She was exactly what Rob had needed, someone who took care of things, while he devoured books, dreamed, and pontificated. Opposites, Mariah observed. Clearly he had needed more conversation. In Chloe he had found someone similar to himself in his intellectual acumen. Well, you never knew. As we grow, as our lives change us, and we, in turn, act on our lives, we change. Life is unpredictable. Isn't that refreshing?

The two drove in companionable silence until they arrived in Kerrville. They pulled into a small, dilapidated, vintage gas station. They got fuel and more ice. As Mariah climbed back into the passenger seat, she spotted a long-haired cowboy leaning against a dusty powder blue pick-up truck. He tossed a butt and got into his truck as Roxi pealed out of the weedy lot.

Mariah turned in her seat. "Does he look familiar? Or am I imagining things."

"That guy back there was weird, huh? Very un-cool of us," Roxi said.

Mariah sat silent as a heavy sadness felt like a lump in her gut. "I don't know why he shook me up. I've been in the wild too long. All my guards are down. He just took me by surprise. Something so lost and evil about him."

"I know what you mean." Roxi patted her knee. "Cheer up old girl, soon we will be in the city and I plan to have some fun." Roxi wanted to check on some old friends in San Antonio. "Maybe there is work there, and I won't have to go all the way back to Houston." She was bright with anticipation.

As they drove, Mariah felt pensive. She studied the myriad of bracelets that ran down both of her arms: blues, aquamarines, jade, agate. She began to realize that the open sensitive vibe she'd cultivated in the wild had to shift. As the miles flew by, bringing them gradually back to civilization, she stared out the window. She watched as the trees and beautiful vistas were being replaced with one tacky billboard or building after another. She shuddered. They know not what they do, she thought with sadness. Roxi still wore the toughness she'd come in with, and hadn't shed during her months in the wilderness. Mariah was struck by how she and Roxi were having such different reactions to the same environment. They were just outside of San Antonio when Mariah had an idea.

"Why don't you take the car," she said, "and I'll ride the rest of the way with Hunter? That way you can head off with your friends."

"Really?' Cause that would be great."

"Yeah, go ahead. You've helped a lot already."

When they saw the next gas station, Mariah stuck her arm out the window and gestured to Hunter that they were turning in. He pulled his Jeep up beside them with a questioning look.

"I'm coming with you," Mariah told him. She handed Roxi Max's cell phone, "Call when you get done and I'll give you directions to his house."

"Wow, we get the car and the cell." No one had cell phones at The Ranch.

"Only the best for you," Mariah chuckled. Then she grabbed her back pack from the backseat and carried it to Hunter's Jeep. "See you later."

Hunter's trusty Jeep had fully functioning air conditioning. After months with nothing but the river to cool her off, Mariah felt like she was sitting in a meat locker. She reached over and turned off her vent. On the drive through town, Mariah stared in silent shock at the gas prices that had doubled since she'd left Houston. A lot of gas stations were abandoned with unsightly weeds taking over the pumps. Those still open were charging twice the price as when she left Houston. People were picketing at City Hall. Homes had For Sale signs in front of them and some houses were boarded up.

"This landscape's changed," she remarked.

"Lots of factories have shut down. People have lost their homes. The Mississippi flooded last summer, and that created a ripple effect down river."

"The protests. Is that about the war?" There seemed to be an air of despondency in the people as they carried their signs.

"The Government's talking about a draft. Tons of folks have become more active in the anti-war movement. Anyway, the cost of oil has put a lot of stress on the economy. I forget you have been out of touch. It went like this. First the war effort put a big demand on construction materials like steel. This had a trickle-down effect on construction, making construction costs rise. We were in a building boom so construction didn't stop, everything just became more expensive. Loans were higher, thus costs rose. This translated to less house for more money. Finally people collapsed under a huge debt burden. Then factories and plants laid off workers, lots of factories had to close because demand for products decreased and then... foreclosures. When new houses wouldn't sell, the prices dropped because builders couldn't get out from under the huge amount of product. This meant all the existing houses were over-valued. Suddenly a family of four may owe more on their home than it's worth in the marketplace. It's as if the economic picture is caving in from different sectors simultaneously. No one has discretionary income, so car sales fell off, and that was followed by more massive layoffs." Hunter sighed. "Everything seemed to be spiraling out of control. You wonder how long it can continue."

Mariah nodded her head. She was too tired to have this conversation. They were silent for the rest of the drive through the suburbs of San Antonio. Hunter pulled into the driveway of a white columned affair set stately back from the road on a spacious lawn of mature oaks. He ushered Mariah into the dimly lit entry way to the quiet hum of air conditioning. Their steps were muffled on the plush white carpet. *What is this, a museum or a mausoleum?* Mariah thought, almost afraid to step into the pristine place.

"Make yourself at home," he said, breaking the silence. "You and Roxi can use the two bedrooms off the landing upstairs."

"Thanks." Mariah grabbed her pack, took a deep breath and bounded up the stairs. "I'm going to get cleaned up. What are you up to today by the way?"

"I'll be at the office all afternoon, but we should be able to meet around six-thirty for dinner."

"Sounds good." She turned and waved from the landing.

"Relax. I want you to enjoy yourself while you're here. I'll put an extra key on the table."

"I'm in shock about all the changes in the city. Just trying to take it all in. I will be A-Okay after a shower." She lied.

"Hey, we will have fun tonight, all right? Explore the town," Hunter said.

What a nice guy, she thought. *Relax? In the shock of the apparent changes, Hunter must be numb or blind. Then she remembered he was still part of this world.*

"Thanks for everything. See ya, don't work too hard."

Once upstairs, she dropped her pack on the bed and found the attached bathroom. Moments later she stepped into a steamy shower. By the time she heard Hunter pull out of the driveway she was already lathering her hair. Twenty minutes later, she dried herself off in one of Hunter's fluffy white towels. Downstairs she found a phone to call Roxi on Max's cell.

"I'm jazzed to be back in the City," Roxi chirped. "Max had the right idea, enjoying the best of both worlds." Mariah heard voices in the background, then Roxi said, "I'll come pick you up when you're ready."

"I'm all clean now, but we have plenty of time. You can grab a shower when you get here."

"Perfect. Just give me directions."

Later, as they pushed a cart through Whole Foods, Roxi said, "Sure

357

was nice of Hunter to let us stay at his place."

"Yes, it certainly was," Mariah said absently. She told Roxi how she spotted the red-neck's pickup after getting into Hunter's car. "I feel a bit safer staying with someone. Then again, who knows if it was the same guy. Was that a coincidence or do you suppose we were being followed?"

Roxi shrugged. "Don't know. What's up with those two, Max and Hunter, anyway?"

"You know, Max wants to spend time with us at The Ranch now. And she's giving him some space. Absence makes the heart grow fonder? Or something, I hope. Actually, I think he will be heading out there sooner rather than later."

Roxi laughed. "To each his own. You're right, I can tell Hunter loves the place. But me, I need to plant my feet on some solid concrete."

Mariah said, "I can relate, I used to be like that. Back in my twenties when I did the whole New York thing. You ultimately have to go where your heart leads you, or me, I do at any rate. I absolutely thrived in New York. I bought the city mystique for a while. I loved my job, the excitement, and the people. I thought I had outgrown my Teenage ways. But at the core, I have always been passionate about Texas. I think David and I gravitated together because of it. We have that bond. I miss him when we're apart. He is absolutely married to the land. It suits me fine." Mariah stopped abruptly, her eyes wide.

"Hey Roxanne, there's our guy again." Mariah pointed to the dusty truck, clearly out of place in this uptown Whole Foods parking lot with shiny black SUV's and silver Cadillac Escalades of the local clientele.

Roxi looked genuinely nervous, "So he was following us."

"What time is Hunter supposed to meet us?" Mariah asked.

Roxanne glanced at her watch. "He's supposed to meet us at the juice bar in five minutes."

"Okay, let's head over there." Mariah's eyes darted around as the two glided through mountains of colorful produce and fragrant lilies.

"Hey girls," Hunter said from behind them, making them both jump. "Did you find everything you need?"

Roxi grinned, "Finally. We spent half our day sitting in traffic."

"That's life in the city." Hunter studied the two tanned ranch escapees. "You clean up good."

Hair shiny, clean blue jeans, and white T-shirts made them look almost normal.

"Hunter, seriously, someone's been following us. I'm sure of it," Mariah said. "Big cowboy guy. Goofy grin, funny teeth. We saw him in Lakeville, and later when we got gas in Kerrville. Now his truck's here. Doesn't look the type to wander in to a juice bar. He may stay in his truck until we leave. Can you get a look at him?"

"Roxanne and I will go pick out some melons outside. She'll point him out. Mariah, you stay put," Hunter ordered.

She headed for the juice counter, and ordered a shot of wheatgrass. She downed it, then buried her head in a Yoga magazine. She tried to look inconspicuous.

"You shore are a cute thing in those tat blue jeans," a low gravely voice drawled in her ear. "You should wear 'em more often. When daddy lets you out, that is."

Mariah started as she looked up. She got a close-up of dirty pores and blackheads in pasty white skin. Stale beer breath hit her in the face.

"Who are you?" Came out of her mouth before she could stop herself.

"Well let's just say I know Peter's friends. I look out after their interests, shall we say." He was up and moving before he added, "If you know what's good for you, little lady, you should leave the ranch, keep your mouth shut. What's gone is gone. Let dead dogs lie. Get my drift?" He tilted his hat before he disappeared behind a display of bottled water. Mariah sat rooted to the spot. Seconds passed, she didn't know how many. Hunter and Roxanne raced up.

"He was there." She pointed to the seat beside her. "And he knew about Peter."

Hunter raced past to catch a glimpse of him.

"What did he do?" Roxi asked.

"He grossed me out," she shivered. "He boasted with some empty threats. Should I worry? Can he do anything in broad daylight? Something about dead..."

Roxi looked incredulous.

Hunter came back. "I just caught a profile. Split second. But I have an idea. We can't talk here. Come on, you girls follow me. I'm in my BMW."

After checking out, and loading the groceries in the trunk, Roxi and Mariah followed Hunter as he maneuvered through side streets. Finally, he parked in a little known pull-off by the San Antonio Riverwalk. A great oak tree, with boughs hanging to the ground, nearly hid the old stone terrace and steps that led down to the Colorado River. The three descended in silence.

"Okay. Like I said," Hunter began, "I only caught a glimpse, but—I don't know how to say this—but the guy resembles one of the three boys who killed Peter. What did he say?"

"Something about dead dogs," Mariah said.

"Anyway, two went to a jail in Uvalde, and the third was under age, considered a conspirator, he went to a boy's juvenile home. Let's see, that was thirteen years ago... the youngest boy would be thirty years old now." His eyes went dark with anger. A big boy, but still a country red-neck. It was a tragedy and a travesty of the legal system. They only got five-year sentences—For murder, cold blooded murder."

"I heard about that. They would be free now." Mariah trotted ahead as she spoke, the others jogging to catch up. "My theory is that it was not some random killing, that someone else hired them. Someone who didn't want to bother with a professional hit man. Sloppy, in my opinion." She shook her head. "They just enticed some wayward boys who would do anything for a few bucks. I never thought much about the guys who pulled the trigger. I was always concerned about the brains behind the shooting. What if I was wrong? And it was just random evil?"

"Someone certainly wants to scare you," Hunter said, pulling out his cell. He started typing.

"I mean, random evil is worse. Killing for no reason. Killing for the sake of death. He caught me alone and disappeared when he saw you guys coming," Mariah said. "He said something about dead dogs. Gave me the creeps."

"Peter had two black dogs," Hunter mused. "Wow. Peter's two dogs were still alive in a shed at the crime scene. No one knows how they got in there."

Mariah remembered seeing Peters dog Samson on her last trip, that had been seven years ago. Hunter handed the phone to her, so she could see the results of a Google search.

"Here's a picture of the three guys from back then."

Mariah studied the photo. He had longer hair, more meat on him now. "The big guy looks like him. He is actually smiling in the photo."

"Okay, this is scary," Roxi wailed. "A peaceful trip camping in the wilderness for a few months, that's one thing, but now, I don't know. There's a lot to give up when you live a life like that. I'm fond of Rob, but I didn't sign-up for all of this. Now we're being stalked by a goon. Guys always stare at me, I'm used to it. My blonde hair and my boobs get 'em every time. That's why I got good at martial arts."

"You are? That's amazing. Which one?" Hunter was intrigued.

"A little karate, some jujitsu. It's for self-defense mostly." Roxi displayed her bicep like a boy would.

Hunter appeared momentarily fascinated. "But why would anybody follow you, let alone Peter's killer? Perhaps Roxi's right. No one knows you guys are out there. I nearly had a heart attack when I ran into David out at Big Rock." Hunter's voice caught. "I was having my own private grief session. I was grateful to see familiar faces out there. It was like the old days. Camping at The Ranch. Just as if the place had been waiting patiently for us all to come back." He continued, "It gave me the feeling that whatever we have been doing in the intervening years—isn't even real. The Ranch is what's real, what's important. I'm certain no one in Peter's family knows you are out there. If they even suspected they would call me."

"It's the same guy from Lakeville. He had to have followed us. He knew about Peter. I'm sure of it." Mariah was shaking, her teeth chattered as she spoke. "But Roxi, you're much tougher than I am. If you are worried then we must be in some kind of danger."

"Let's just take care of the essentials. You guys are welcome to stay at my place as long as you need. You can lay low for a couple of days," Hunter assured them. "That will give Roxi a chance to find a job and a place. And Mariah, you can have a nice city fling."

Mariah smiled at him, grateful for his attempt at humor. The three began to relax and enjoy the walk along the river. The sounds of Mexican bands floated across the water as they drew near the more commercial end of the famous Riverwalk. Mariah's brain tried to sort through the facts. The businessmen Max had been stalking on the internet, couldn't be connected to these wayward lost boys. Had they acted on their own after all? Was she trying to force the facts to fit like square pegs into round holes? These boys, with no motive, had apparently killed and been arrested, confessed and served time. Now they were out and on the streets, free as birds. Apparently curious about she and Roxi. Were they stalking her now? Yet the oil men had some kind of motive. Why did he mention the dogs? Peter's dog was gone now, at least they had never seen a dog in the six months they had been there. Her mind pondered as they walked amidst the growing evening crowd of gayety and laughter.

They strolled along the Riverwalk, taking in the festive noise of the crowds and competing Mariachi bands. Soon the overwhelming smell of Mexican food got to them and they opted to eat at a place with a raised stone terrace and stone tables with large yellow umbrellas.

"Margaritas anyone?" Hunter offered.

"Tequila!" Roxi exclaimed.

Soon, over chips and spicy salsa, with a pitcher of margaritas, the mood turned festive. At least it did for Hunter and Roxi. After scanning the crowd for their strange stalker, Mariah forced herself to enjoy the familiar sounds of her old life. It felt strange. The drink was too strong and too salty.

"I do feel much better now," she said. "I didn't think I was the paranoid type." Ravenous, she embarked on her meal, only to push it away after a few bites. Taste no longer justified putting junk into her body.

"Hey, you gonna finish that?" Roxi asked.

She looked at what was once her favorite dish, chicken enchiladas. "You know, I'm not so hungry. You go ahead Roxi. Help yourself."

Mariah watched in amazement as Roxi dived in, and then washed it down with another margarita. A dark-skinned young man gallantly asked Roxi to dance, an invitation Roxi gleefully accepted, leaving Hunter and Mariah alone.

Hunter waited until she was out of earshot, then turned to Mariah to continue their earlier conversation. "Peter was a pretty tough guy," he said, his voice low, "but the one thing he feared was that some company would tap The Ranch's oil reserves. You know, make his family an offer they couldn't refuse."

Mariah looked up, shocked. "Wait, you think there's oil on the Ranch?"

"Yes."

"Peter thought so too?" She sipped her margarita.

"Yes, he was a geologist, remember. He kept mum about it, but he knew. That's why his mother deeded all her Ranch shares to him. He has the controlling shares. Behind his laid-back exterior, he was brutally aware of the devastation drilling for oil would create. His dad disagreed. That's why they stipulated that the land couldn't be divided. One person has to own the whole thing for it to be sold. Sharky..."

"Wait," Mariah interrupted. "I've heard that name before."

"He's friends with Peter's brother-in-law."

"Wait, is his brother-in-law Frank Gilbert?"

"Yes. Sharky and Frank used to tie firecrackers to cats' tails, a real pyromaniac in his youth. Everyone called Scott, Sparky. Later, when he became an ace at stealing businesses someone changed it to Sharky. That fit. The name stuck. They grew up together, then Gilbert married into the St. George family. When Peter's sister died, all her assets, including her share of The Ranch, went to him. People forget that, because he's from here and never showed much interest in The Ranch." Hunter paused to take a sip of his margarita.

"As I was saying, Gilbert and Scofield both have big interests in Exon. They have been trying to get the mineral rights for years. Since Peter's death no one's been there to keep an eye on the place. I'm afraid Scofield may make a move with his drilling plans."

"Wait, I thought Frank Gilbert was a lawyer."

"He has a law degree, yes. It's complicated."

"Why now? Peter's been out of the picture for years," Mariah questioned.

"Simple—the price of oil. This is all new to me. I want to help you."

"But how?" Mariah asked, "How can you help?"

363

"Mariah, Mariah. Sometimes I wonder about you and Max. She was quite pissed at me last time I was there. Like she doesn't trust me. You and I go way back. You trust me don't you?" He took a long sip of his margarita.

Mariah nodded. "I'm listening."

"When my dad passed, I got all his clients and all his documents. I began digging into the files, once Max took off so fast after her last visit. Anyway, what I found was very interesting. It seems those in the oil business have been hoarding American oil. They could get Saudi oil cheap these past few decades so they halted Texas drilling and waited. The value of oil has never exceeded this current high. It's ten times what it was in the 80's. I'm speculating that the companies couldn't justify the expensive drilling procedures needed to get below the limestone to the pockets. So my research tells me."

"Why are you telling me all of this anyway?"

"Why?"

"Yes, why now, after all this time?"

"Like I said, I have been familiarizing myself with my dad's clients. This is all new to me. I'm speculating. As I have been tying up loose ends, not everything adds up.

"In fact, you guys may be in some kind of danger. Are all of you actually leaving, by the way? I know most of the group left, but I imagine they will all come out to try again next spring and pick up where you left off, especially if some of you guys tough it out for winter."

"What do you mean?" Mariah shrugged, noncommittal.

"Well, Max gave up her apartment and she moved out there and started 'training' with a vengeance. You tell me. Why would she do that unless she was joining you? Suffice it to say, I think you are all in a bit of danger."

"To answer your first question, yes. It's true, everyone left except our family. We plan to tough it out for winter. The others may come back in the spring. David and I sold everything. We have nowhere to return to. We have to make it work. We will be hiding out in caves." Mariah ignored his grim look. "No one will know any of us are still out there."

Hunter shook his head and took a nice long sip of his Margarita.

"What are you trying to say? Do you know something?" Mariah laughed engagingly.

"I'm still digging through files. These aren't savory characters. For example, they keep kangaroos, antelope and elk it seems. Ranch retreats for the fat cats. Big game hunting like an African experience. You spotted that goon-cowboy guy. Perhaps someone is having you watched."

"It's not just a coincidence we keep spotting that guy?" Mariah took a polite sip but her mouth was dry.

"C'mon, what do you think? Don't take my word for it. You are the one who stirs up all the conspiracy theories. Running around asking questions. Asking me."

She bit her nails. "Great. Exotic hunting grounds attract people who like to kill. Like the cowboy. He must be a regular out there. Maybe he works there for them?"

"You are so sarcastic," Hunter laughed. "It's just a front. There are several estates out there like that. Huge stone entrance gates, high fortress-like fences. They charge hefty fees for folks to come hunt exotic game. An 'African experience,' they call it. The big difference is the wildlife is all fenced in."

"Like shooting some tame creature in a zoo!" Mariah's heart hurt. She could picture the warm brown eyes of a trusting gazelle facing the cold barrel of a shotgun. "That means they have guns."

Hunter rolled his eyes. "They're hunters, Mariah. They probably have a prized collection of guns. Anyway, that's it. I think Gilbert has been biding his time. His oil partners, a lot of Houston oil money, come down and hunt whenever they can get away. Peter's dad was always ready to sell out. Peter worked hard to keep his place pure, a habitat."

Mariah's face fell at the matter-of-fact way Hunter spoke.

He realized he sounded flippant, and tried to redeem himself. "Look, I'm on your side. But I do think the guy you spotted, and Peter's murderer, are one and the same. He has served his time and we can't touch him. Why is he following you?" He shrugged. "Tell you what. Don't go back yet, stay at my place for a while. Enjoy civilization, but lay low."

"You are serious?" Her voice rose in question.

"You are welcome." He spoke in earnest.

"Well thank you then." She stirred her margarita with the paper umbrella stuck in the lime.

He nodded, "The moral of the story is, Peter single-handedly tried to keep the place pure, a wildlife habitat."

Among other things, Mariah thought sadly. Had Peter told Hunter about the Indians? For all she knew he had and Hunter thought he was keeping his friend's secret safe from her. She was wistful. As much as she wanted to, she couldn't tell Hunter. It was Peter's secret. Mariah was quiet for a beat, and finally took a long swig of her drink.

"Yes, and he did it. Alone. He did it bravely, with grace and without reward."

"Just for the sake of it." Hunter finished his drink.

"Whew." Roxi, reeking of men's cologne, plopped down into the chair. "I'm hot now. Margarita time."

Hunter's eyes met Mariah's. "We had some good times in Austin back then."

"You two. Be careful on memory lane." Roxi gulped some margarita.

"Hey girly," a cowboy pulled Roxi back on to the dance floor.

"I'm off." She waved at the two lonely hearts.

Mariah watched them disappear into the crowd. "No one asked me to dance."

Hunter raised an eyebrow, "In the old days you would already be on the dance floor."

"We didn't see each other much that week. I borrowed your ten-speed and had a blast going all over Austin. You were the perfect gentleman." She batted her eyes, trying out her old moves.

"Too perfect. My one regret." He picked up the pitcher of margaritas and refreshed their glasses.

"I admire you for it. And we're friends forever." Mariah hefted her glass to his before taking another sip. The icy goblet gave her a sudden chill.

"Back to planet earth. With all that is going down now, you should stick around another week. Hopefully, Cowboy will get bored and forget about you. I do want to help you, if I'm able." Hunter rose from the table and extended a hand, "In the meantime, would you like to dance? This slow one is about my speed."

Mariah's smile lit the night. "I thought you'd never ask." The two moved through the crowd to the strains of 'The Girl from Ipanema.'

CHAPTER 21 *Tristan's Quest*

All was quiet as Tristan woke up in the semi-darkness and packed a few essentials to take on his journey. He hiked the two miles to his usual meeting place. Daniel's lone form etched a dark silhouette on the cliff against the sky beyond. He turned as he heard Tristan approach. His white teeth glowed as his face broke into a smile.

"I think you are right, your group is ready. Those that do not wish this lifestyle will find a new path." Daniels liquid movements had him standing in front of Tristan in a seamless motion. "We are strong believers in the free will of all species," Daniel continued. "Many nations must live on this great circle of earth. The weak have left. The strong are warriors for peace, for harmonious co-existence with the earth. You must travel back with me. Our Chief will give you one more key of knowledge."

"I'm ready." Tristan's face was serious. Tristan's mind matched the early morning fog. In a semi-daze, in the semi-darkness, he followed Daniel.

With one foot in front of the other, soon, he and Daniel were on the cliff above the Blue Spring. Daniel made a swan dive into the pool. Tristan sprang up into the air, arms outstretched, and formed a perfect arch before curving towards the deep blue water. His body broke the surface of the cold water and all went silent as he plunged into the depths. Tristan swam swiftly behind Daniel, his body like a dolphin's as he followed him into the tunnel that waited hidden beneath the rock ledge, thirty feet below the surface.

Daniel swam fast. Tristan followed. The tunnel glowed a blue green. Sunlight shimmered through the lime green ferns. The greens moved into the rich teal of deep water. The two young men passed orange and coral fish, silver trout, and crystal rocks. Tristan's speed was almost as fast as Daniel's now. Although he wasn't conscious of it, his body had transformed into a dolphins. He glided through the darkening tunnel. His bright eyes trained on his friend, allowing his mind to go in sync, and thus pull his body to the destination that awaited him.

His mind blanked out for a second. And then splashed in the rushing waters of a river. Cliffs rose up high on both sides as he surfaced once more in human form.

"Here," Daniel said. Tristan swam toward a rock and pulled himself out. The day was blue, seamless, and brilliantly hot.

"Where are we? I've never been here."

"No."

"Okay." Tristan shook the water from his hair, laughing as he gazed up at burnt orange canyon walls.

"Chiricahua, Arizona," Daniel said.

"Our Chief's here? I thought he lived... Never mind. What do I know?"

"He does," Daniel said. "He's here to show you something."

Tristan panted as he rested on the rock beside his friend. He caught his breath and let the sun dry his skin. "We traveled at Dolphin speed?"

"Precisely."

"Okay. Let's get on with it. I'm hungry."

"That's no attitude. I guarantee that even you will forget about food today."

Daniel's eyes traveled the rock face of the endlessly high canyon wall towering above them. Tristan stared up until his neck hurt.

"Well if you're ready, we climb."

So up they went, hands and feet scaling the cliff. Their tan bodies hugged the wall, sweat glistening in the bright sun. Tristan was soon bone dry. No trace of water left on his shorts or hair. The sun scorched his back. He felt he'd soon become a petrified form on the face of the cliff. Still, Daniel's form above him kept moving higher. The wind whipped against Tristan's body. Now, afraid his grasp wouldn't hold him long, he kept on. It looked like they had ten feet more to the top, when suddenly Daniel turned around, his face alight with a grin. He slipped into a sliver of a crack in the wall.

Tristan followed into the dark slice in the canyon. He felt the gush of cool air from within. His sweat-soaked face tingled at the sudden coolness as he reached the spot. His bare foot groped its way to a secure foothold. The floor of the cave was spongy soft, covered with moss and pine needles. Daniel's eyes glowed, still smiling. Tristan concentrated. The two moved steadily ahead into the blackness. Their bodies, silhouetted against the sun, partially blocked the afternoon light. A startled bat flew out from within.

Tristan moved with caution as the two walked in silence. The sound of the river down below was dimmed by the distance. Time stood still in the endless sameness of the dark world they entered. Some moisture oozed from the walls accompanied by a dank, musty odor. Tristan walked in faith into the darkness before him. As he rounded another bend, he saw a faint glow ahead.

His pace quickened. A bell tinkled in the distance. As they moved closer Tristan became aware of a hum. Then the tunnel widened out before him and he found himself in a great hall—Tristan figured about twelve feet wide and twenty feet high—but he could not fathom the length because it seemed endless. The sides of the hall were lined with books, crates and boxes, stacked full, and piled high. As they hastened forward, he spotted rolls of papyrus lining a honeycomb of cubicles. The frayed yellowed edges of rolls tied with leather and gut strings, stuck out unevenly from the cubbies. Tristan noticed that the earlier mugginess had given way to a crisp coolness. He realized from the turns and twists they had taken in the tunnel, both vertical and horizontal, that this chamber was in an air lock deep within the canyon wall. Finally, a dim form became visible ahead. As he grew closer, he saw the figure was an ancient man seated on a platform hewn into the rock as if he was waiting for their arrival.

Tristan's eyes focused on the works that lined the walls. He walked slowly, staring at the titles. He abruptly stopped in front of the ancient red skinned man. The Ancient One was dressed in long woven robes, his long grey-white hair combed cleanly back from his wide brow. His hand gestured to the surrounding records.

Tristan's voice was rusty. "What is all of this?"

"I believe your people call this, *The Lost Hall of Records.*"

Tristan blinked at him, and the Ancient king nodded gravely.

"I don't believe it. This is awesome. The Hall of Records from Atlantis," he breathed a whisper.

"It's all here."

"My Uncle Rob goes on about them, the lost secrets of Atlantis, the Hall of Records, and all that. He says various archeological groups have been searching for years."

He laughed softly. "Your uncle is correct. Many have searched, but only those with the purest of intentions are allowed to find. The lost secrets of Atlantis, there are some who have searched long and hard to find them."

"Do they contain the reason for the fall of Atlantis and the ultimate destruction?" Asked Tristan.

"Ah yes, and more, much more. The secrets are here; the facts of the Great fall. The two great destructions were recorded, and all the records of the destruction were preserved. The fall was great, because their achievements had made them high above any other civilization."

Tristan felt the eyes of the Ancient One boring into him as he spoke.

"The mighty fall harder and further. How God loved these beautiful people. They had it all, physical beauty and mental clarity. A perfect race, they knew little of illness or disease. Their bodies could heal quickly. Their strength and grace made them masters. The temple priests and priestesses fell out of sync with the scientists. They were not a warrior people, so when there was a conflict, resolution was essential. Enough." His voice had risen in timbre and strength, its vibration echoed through the tunnel.

An abrupt silence followed. He continued in a quiet tone. "The main reason you are here now, is to obtain the blueprints for a very important invention. You need it to save your planet in the here and now. The blueprints and diagrams, all the information you will need to build the machine, are here."

"Which invention?" Tristan tried to take it all in.

"The Torus."

"Excuse me, sir?"

"The Torus, the Dynamo-eterna Apparatus."

"That must be similar to a perpetual motion machine," Tristan guessed.

"To solve the energy crisis on your planet," Ancient One explained.

"My Planet? It's yours too." Tristan realized belatedly, that was a cocky reply.

Ancient One's eyes blinked in slow motion as he looked hard at this teen child. A mere boy really, about to step into manhood. Tall and tan and a bit overconfident—or perhaps just friendly? With good intentions, the Ancient One decided. He had traveled far on faith and had walked nearly five miles in this dark tunnel. Yet he stood here before him, fresh and ready with a gleam of humor in sincere eyes.

"You see, the planet must survive if mankind is to continue to evolve. The people are not finished yet. They have not evolved sufficiently to move into the fourth dimension. And yet, you are about to destroy the very Earth that is your home in the 3-D universe you reside in. Hence you need, shall we say in your terms, an Energy-Wheel. It's an 'otherworldly' invention that can keep your Earth safe for you to be able to continue your evolution process. There was someone born in the twentieth century that had the gift. Tesla made many inventions. Way beyond the others, he was extremely close. He was playing with the wheel and the magnetic forces. He nearly succeeded. But alas, it was not to be." He sighed, clearly recalling a longed-for time. "It's hard to fathom the greed and power-lust motivating many on your planet.

"There is an incredible amount of energy on earth: Chemical reactions, electrical reactions. People keep using fire for destruction." His voice was strong as it rose in power with a passion bigger than his stature. "To blow things up instead of to make things happen. You could be flying interplanetary by now with the amount of energy you have learned to unleash. Sadly, it's being thoughtlessly squandered. Blown up. Destroyed for no reason." The Ancient One's voice dropped to the smooth, mellow baritone of Tristan's grandfathers, comforting to his ears. Tristan waited, not daring to breathe. He didn't want to miss anything.

"But still, no one directs it. They just point firepower at human life and blow it up. Human Life!" He fairly shouted now. "Human life is the only thing you cannot create."

Spittle hit Tristan in the eye. Yet he dared not move.

"That is why it's the thing you should never destroy. Power over another human is The Great Sin. People always debate over what is the greatest way to anger our God?" He stopped abruptly, waiting for the echoing cacophony to subside. In the stillness he continued in a whisper.

"Well, God forbade even himself from controlling, or dictating to humans. Don't you think He of all of us knows best? Yet, does He tell us?" Silence surrounded them in the cave.

"No. Because of Free will. Freedom. We would be mere puppet extensions of Him, if it were otherwise. Can you have a relationship with a mannequin?" His voice dropped to a hoarse whisper.

Tristan waited, enchanted.

"Yes and no," the Indian chuckled as he answered his own question. "A bit boring." He shrugged his shoulders. He had reverted back to the comforting grandfatherly tone. "Nevertheless, my son, if God does not deign to force His will upon us, why do you suppose people try to do that to each other?" The black eyes bored into Tristan's.

The silence extended and Tristan knew he didn't have the answers.

"Since you know exactly what I am speaking of, you know the world you are living in has not evolved... yet."

Tristan nodded, his own eyes wide open.

"Part of evolving is to become like God. And God would not hurt one of his creatures. Therefore -"

"I see. I get it," Tristan shouted, interrupting as the logic of the Wise One's speech penetrated his thought process. "So as long as we— mankind—force our will upon others, we will always remain like gods with a little 'g'. Gods in our own eyes only."

"Yes." The Ancient One sat back in his chair and took a deep breath. The Ancient's black eyes glistened like obsidian as he watched the illumination take hold. "And forever stuck on the material plane. While the singing and rejoicing and true joy goes on in heaven, Earthlings remain blind. What you need today is the Dynamo-eterna." As the echoing sounds resonating in the cave subsided, silence ensued.

"On another matter, Human life is destroyed on your planet at an unprecedented rate. Children, gifted children, that need to be born to take your planet further in the evolution, are denied entry by their Mothers. Souls are searching for the opportunity to arrive, while their very life is at the mercy of the will of the host Mother. The love a mother has for her baby and that a father has for his son, has always been the model for God's love. Yet mothers on your planet kill their own unborn, before even their first smile is seen. How can a planet survive that practices genocide on its own?"

"It will be a miracle." Tristan glanced around the room at the files. "But what does all this have to do with Atlantis?" Tristan felt old for his years. Everything was making so much sense but what could you do? What could he do?

"The egocentricity of Atlantis was astounding, thus the destruction. Does that sound familiar?"

Tristan's head was spinning. He knew everything and nothing at the same time.

"That sounds harsh, I know. The destruction was a product of their egocentric behavior," the Ancient One said. "I don't mean an outside force bestowed punishment."

Tristan saw how this could be possible with the endless circle of life, death, and rebirth. Could you ever get off? Atlanteans had been brilliant, and yet they had missed it. It's like the fine crevice in the canyon wall. You could miss it. The fine and narrow way. That was always *the way*. He thought about Jesus. He stood there contemplating this outburst of old and new information. Jesus gave his own Life. He did not take life.

The Ancient One looked at Tristan calmly. "Where do you think you are?"

"On the earth. Somewhere. New Mexico?"

He was patient. "How long did it take you to find this place?"

"All day?"

"Try sixteen years. You have been preparing for this meeting for sixteen years. Time is relative. You are on the earth. That's true. In the past, present or future? In a parallel universe? But you are here. And here are the records. No one has found them until now."

"I didn't find them. I followed Daniel to you. You found them."

The Ancient One patiently studied the man-youth before him. "I have always had them. But you need the Dynamo-eterna to save the planet: the Earth, your home, our Mother, our Sustainer and life-giver." He spoke with reverence as he said Her names. He looked Tristan straight in the eye and held his gaze as he spoke the next sentence. "Through whose laws and principles you can find the solution to the issue."

Tristan stepped up on the stone platform, upon which the Ancient sat, his legs crossed yogi fashion, the scrolls placed by his side. Tristan sat down beside him and carefully untied and unrolled the fragile paper.

Daniel grabbed Tristan's arm. "Tristan, we have to go."

"Look at all of this. People are looking for this info." Tristan held his ground.

"You need to get the gift and bring it back. Timing is important," Daniel insisted.

"I can't leave here." Daniel was crazy if he'd think he would do anything other than sit down right here.

"Mariah won't know how to find the others. I promised Joseph I would help her."

"But here it is. I don't even know how we got here."

"It's not time for you to know everything."

CHAPTER 22 *Exodus - Tree of Life*

Everyone had been working since dawn at The Ranch. They had one more load of the Tree of Life harvest to deliver to the schoolhouse. They were finally ready for the trek into the interior. This is what Mariah had long referred to as the exodus. This was the point of no return. The no return rule was for the privacy of the Indians, in order to keep their location hidden. Everyone agreed they were not interested in being found or starving to death and trusted that this new location, deep in the territory, would keep them out of the flow of normal traffic.

With Mariah and Roxi gone, things were strangely quiet. Or maybe it was just because they had taken the few rowdier malcontents and chaos lovers with them. Without them, everything had an air of peaceful contentment and calm. Packing had become much simpler with the extra stuff gone.

That morning, Rob and Jack had taken a group to harvest the remaining produce, along with the Tree of Life. Jack was curious to see how their friends planned to use this mysterious, obviously native plant once they finally arrived at the Indians' home. It was an amazing harvest. No sooner had he and Rob found the hidden field, than they realized they were glad to have extra manpower. They bundled and loaded the goats up as they had done when they harvested the two previous fields. Sarah loaded the deer, she had trained, as well.

Paul looked up to see Max hovering outside his tent flap. "What's up?" He ignored her strong tan legs exposed in her running shorts. He noted her crossed arms and knew he was in for something.

"You have quite a mess in here."

Paul wiggled his eyebrows. "I guess I pretty much moved in for keeps."

"Looks like you have been here for years. What did your apartment back in Houston look like?"

"There was a path." She is bossy but I like it, he thought.

"Let me guess, from the door to the fridge to the coffee pot?"

"Plus I had cats."

"You mean piles like this and cats too?"

"Let's not think about it."

"You look overwhelmed."

She is softening he thought. "You're right, I can use some help." He tucked his thick curls behind his ear and shoved up his wire rims.

"Not to worry, organization is my specialty." Max squatted on the floor and began gathering and sorting. She glanced up. "If I keep going, will I find a bedroll somewhere in here?"

He blushed.

"I'm sorry, I didn't mean, Gosh. It just looks like you sleep on papers. Tell you what, I'll do this, but I think Rob needs more help at the schoolhouse with the latest harvest."

Paul looked doubtful.

"I typed all of these articles up, remember? It's in the computer. And it's safely in the cloud. I also printed hard copies–just in case Mariah's right after all."

"I want to keep the drawings. The kids. They are so visual in their understanding of everything."

"I get it." Max scooted out of the way. "You go on. I needed your brain and now Robbie needs your muscles. And a little help with her." She looked through the tent flap, out across the meadow. She could see Chloe in a tangle with Rob. Trying to pull him along. He didn't want to budge. "Do me a giant favor. I'm supposed to keep an eye on her."

* * *

"Chloe, what are you even doing here?" Rob jumped as she grabbed at his elbow.

"I came to help you guys," Chloe sing-songed.

He looked at her thin, frail-looking frame.

"I'm small but I'm strong."

Rob shook his head, hands on hips. "No." His stance was solid, unmoving.

"I heard storing this was crucial. Timing is crucial. Let me help." She whined a little. "What do you have, some sort of secret?"

"Secrets? Us?" Rob gave a robust laugh. "Hah, of course not." He steered her around and back towards camp as he spotted Paul strolling toward them.

"You do have a secret, Rob. Don't you trust me?"

"I do trust you."

"Then let me help, let me go with you."

"Of course. Perhaps next time. Don't you have things to pack?"

Paul joined Rob. He walked around the piles of bundles, inspecting. He tightened the load in a few spots. He popped the goats rump and it scurried off. Rob jogged to catch up.

"We all downsized, remember?" She was calling after them as the two headed quickly down the road. "You need my help."

Paul turned around, walking backwards, he yelled, "Max could use some help with my stuff if you have time." To Rob he muttered, "How many women do you want to piss off in one day?"

Rob said, "Chloe? She'll get over it. Roxi? Now that's another matter."

"I never had those kinds of problems."

"Max is doing your packing? I would look out if I were you."

Paul adjusted his glasses and patted the last goat on the rump.

* * *

The Potty crew had already filled up the latrine trenches and planted trees. After every one left, Jack and Rob planned to finish up the last vestiges of cleanup. Then they would await Tristan's return.

Now the place was packed, cleaned, and sorted. All the tents and supplies had been transformed into small bundles, colorful bound packages in various sizes designed for carriers of all ages. There was one for each member to carry. They had downsized to normal backpacking equipment size. Some of them had handmade packs of sticks and ropes in the same fashion as the commercial counterpart.

It happened without fanfare, after lunch, in the sleepy part of the day. David gathered the first two groups—his and Rob's, while John, Isabella, and Sarah, went to get two others.

"Are you guys ready?"

"Well, yeah." Julia rolled her eyes.

There were no young ones in this group, just a mix of teens and aging hippies who would be able to travel efficiently. John helped Isabella and Sarah, with their packs. With little sound, under the cover of cricket chatter, the somber group left the clearing that had become home. Nikki, Anya, Ian, and Jonothon, formed a single line as they moved onto the deer path through the brush. David's group was ready when they joined them. He'd been stalling all morning, hoping Mariah would show up.

Hazel reminded him, "She's not supposed to come yet remember? We need to be gone. Vanished. Not a trace in case anyone follows her in."

Rob hugged David. "Safe journey. Hopefully Tristan and Mariah will be back at the same time. I will join you as quickly as possible."

David looked around at the place they had called home for six months. The grass was worn out; it matched the rest of the crispy drought-ridden growth that surrounded their cliff-top site. Pat and Jody led two groups, allowing Jack Java to remain with Rob. They would meet Joseph at the crossroad, and he would guide them to the final destination. The seven groups were to stagger their leaving by half a fist by the sun, thus the hubbub of departure would not make such an impact. Still their travel was heavy footed and boisterous.

David used a walking stick to keep a rhythm to their march. He understood the land they were headed toward looked a whole lot like the Blue Spring, but it was a long way beyond it. He'd heard the waterfall was large and majestic. He looked forward to the new life they would lead as they trudged through the rocky roads and the dry stream beds.

CHAPTER 23 *The City*

"Mariah, look, it's late. You two should turn in," Hunter said as they walked into his house, "You look exhausted." He gestured to his office, "I've got some work to do."

Roxi didn't have to be told twice. "I get to sleep in a real bed!" She said as she trudged up the stairs, "See you guys in the morning."

Mariah went to the kitchen, filled a glass with tap water, and brought it to her lips. She spit it out, grimacing. What a shock, all the chemicals, chlorine, and chalky taste was foreign to her. "Do you have filtered water?" She called to the closed door of Hunter's office.

"In the fridge."

"Thanks." She opened the subzero, noting it was fully stocked with things she hadn't even dreamed of in months, and reached for the pitcher. She poured two glasses and went to the office door.

"Can I come in?"

Hunter swiveled around in his office chair as she opened the door. "I'm glad you're here. I wanted to continue our conversation but I was unsure about Roxi."

"You're right. She doesn't know a thing."

He gestured to a chair. "Like I said earlier, I have been familiarizing myself with my dad's clients. I have a few suspicions. While I have been tying up loose ends, it seems not everything adds up. I know you and your sister are up to something."

Mariah laughed, "Well, as I mentioned, we plan to set up in a few caves to prepare for winter. That is why I came to San Antonio. To get winter gear, Hi-tech sleeping bags, and a few strategic items. I agree, the fall is great, but everyone had to go before it got too cold.

We bathe in the waterfalls now and you know about the solar shower we constructed. We're not equipped for the winter months," she said.

"Look I want you to know that as soon as I have some inkling of what's going on, I will share it with you, Hunter said. "Just lay low here. Give Cowboy a chance to forget about you. In the meantime relax." He stood up and held her shoulders, looking her straight in the eye, "Now it's late. You look more than exhausted." He opened the office door. "You go on to that real bed up there. I'll see what I can dig up."

Mariah's heavy thoughts slowed her steps as she climbed the stairs. Why was he finally talking to her? She already knew much of this, yet hearing it from him made it seem like he was on their side, and maybe he was. Would he really try to help them in the long run? Could she trust him? Why did Max seem to doubt him? She didn't even want him to know about the baby.

The next morning, Mariah, a cup of hot Java in her hands, sat with her feet tucked up in the chair. Her legs were curled into the oversize T-shirt she was wearing. "You look rough. Late night?" She asked Hunter.

"Well yes, but I'm used to it." He grinned as he poured a cup.

"It's a beautiful morning. Mind if I check out your pool?"

"I'll join you. Fresh air will do me good." Hunter and Mariah strolled to the walled yard by the pool. "You have a secret," Hunter said.

"Yes, it's a big one." Mariah was surprised he was so observant. "Do you already know what it is?"

"I have an idea. And that's why I want to tell you my decision to go back with you. I can swing it. I want to go. It's where my heart is."

Mariah's eyes shot up and she hugged him. *If he only knew.* Max will be extremely elated about this. "I'm glad. I think you belong there, as unlikely as that seems. It's just that I don't think I will see anyone I used to know again. It's giving up a lot."

"I keep focusing on what I'm gaining. Let's be honest, the way the world's going, this way of life won't be sustainable much longer. Your way may be the only way."

"All paths lead to the same center. Eventually," Mariah said.

"That may just be the way we all need to be."

"The secret," Mariah interrupted. "Do you already know it?"

Hunter was pensive as he organized his thoughts. "Peter and I had a talk when he suspected someone was trying to kill him." He paused to look at the red hibiscus blossom, his hands in his pockets. He turned now to face her. "He tried to tell me there were Native Americans living on the land."

Mariah just stared at him, a white rose in her hand.

"I didn't believe him then," Hunter said. "I still don't."

She shrugged. She wasn't quite sure what to reveal at this point.

He continued, "I thought he was delusional, paranoid. That was our last conversation. Then he was murdered. I never told anyone. Have you any reason to believe that might be true?"

Mariah watched him steadily. "I don't know. It seems possible, the place is mammoth. I guess Peter was the only one who knew for sure. And we can no longer ask him."

"And if so, could the Indians have been the ones that shot him?"

Mariah's mouth dropped open, she pricked her finger on the rose. What next? "Yeah right." She could humor him and ignore that. It could explain the bit about the dogs, she thought. "We're just trying to survive. We do live there and we're trying desperately to keep that a secret." She studied the tiny drop of blood and resumed the stroll.

"I know. It's just that since Peter died his words have haunted me. The fact that their real meaning might have eluded me bothers me. And then of course, he was concerned that someone may have wanted something from him he couldn't give. I did absolutely nothing," Hunter said.

Mariah looked at Hunter, deeply conflicted. "I am very serious. It's all coming down now. I'm glad you will join us, but I've got to be back in two days. It's imperative." He seemed genuine, but did she gamble their whole community on it? Finally, she sighed. "There is something else, Hunter, something you have to know if you hope to join us. We're planning to live there...Permanently."

Hunter's jaw dropped in surprise, then Mariah saw his eye dart toward the house. Roxi had not emerged since the night before.

"She doesn't know the big picture. She's been on the fence about staying for some time. Rob knows, of course, but he kept it from her. It

382

had an effect on their relationship, and now you see how happy she is to be back in civilization."

The two strolled in silence for a few minutes. "Hey, this is a beautiful place and all, but I'm going stir crazy." She looked around, taking in the scene of pool, blooms sparkling with dew, and the myriad of shrubs edging the perfect green lawn. The right amount of large oak trees shaded the impeccable carpet of green framed by wrought iron. "It's an old neighborhood, isn't it?"

"Very," Hunter said.

"This place is perfect. Not a thing out of place. I've personally slaved to have such beautiful landscaping. You have a yard guy, don't you?"

"Yes. I know what you mean. It bugs me too."

"It's a bygone era, really. This place is like a cozy little womb, and you don't know what lies beyond the hedges."

"It's what we all aspire to, a good place to raise a family, and then the mortgage and the lifestyle exhaust us so we are content to rest in our carefully laid garden. We don't have enough energy to notice anymore," Hunter said.

"Like a graveyard of carefully laid plans," Mariah laughed. "But it's not real. In a way it's part of the matrix. Eventually you are so frazzled on the treadmill, you don't realize you are only treading water."

"We're in America; far away from the rest of the world and the wars, turmoil, and suffering."

"People end up with such a malaise and ennui because, I think deep down, they sense it's an unreal illusion. But on the surface it's so pretty." Mariah stared at the elegant lawn, manicured flowers, and flagstone around the quiet chlorinated pool. "It looks perfect here." She paused, "Changing the subject, you are going to take me back to the north entrance of The Ranch right? It's only a five mile hike to the jeep from there."

"Mariah, you don't get it." He took her by the shoulders and faced her. "I'm coming with you. Now. For winter. I know the cave system. There's a big one above Jade Springs on the south side of the canyon."

"Wow. You believe us?"

"All I ask is that you give me more time. Then we can go together."

Hunter tossed her a towel. "This is for when you finish your swim. I know you are itching to get in." He added, "Hey you know you can stay as long as you want. I just want to be sure our old cowboy friend forgets about you."

Mariah had been staring at the water distractedly. "I'll meet you for breakfast in an hour. Thanks." She looked up at his face, calm yet worn with a lightly veiled sense of the years caring for all those he loved. She felt half apologetic for all the judging she'd just landed on what he'd built his life around. His kids were away in college, and his wife had left him. Only then does the whole thing seem pointless. Hey, that's a thought; the very society that built its economy on perfect families, spread a materialistic dogma that sanctioned a fifty percent divorce rate. Divorcees were the ones left, suddenly questioning what they'd built their life around. The discontent was a result of the artificiality. The lack of connection some felt. Like Hunter. Would he miss his neighbors? Had he even seen them lately?

Mariah pulled off her wrap. She placed one toe in at a time as she immersed into the temperate water. Hunter watched her fit brown body, in her one-piece black suit, as she slipped into the water. Her thick black hair plastered to her back. Opposites attract, I guess. She looked like an Indian. He was fair and red haired. She'd always fascinated him. As he watched her, he realized he couldn't let her go. Not just yet, anyway. He liked her here, right here.

After her swim and a shower, Mariah found Hunter and Roxi in the sunny breakfast room off the kitchen. "I'm making omelets," she announced as she pulled out the eggs, onions, and peppers from the fridge. She chopped green peppers and onions. And sneezed.

"I'll help," Roxi said. "Got a cold in this heat?" She began grating sharp cheddar with gusto.

"I guess it's the AC. Gives me a chill." The oil sizzled as Mariah poured the golden liquid into the hot skillet. "Back in Houston I had one of these every morning."

Roxi gave her a curious look. She was quiet as she chewed.

"Did you decide?" Mariah asked.

"I can't go back." Roxi's eyes were on her omelet. "It's not for me. I thought it was."

"You are sure, aren't you? I know you've given it a lot of thought. Meanwhile, we need a plan about our cowboy."

"I'm afraid he's dangerous," Hunter said. He dug into his omelet, cheese oozing out of the sides.

Mariah rolled her eyes, "I'm trying to be careful and discreet, but at this point what can he want? I don't want to get so distracted I lose focus."

"Roxi, how did it go with your friends? "Do you think you will stay in San Antonio?"Hunter asked.

"I'm not sure yet. I think I may use the time to travel a bit before I settle down." Roxi turned to Mariah. "When do you plan to head back?"

"I want Mariah to stay put for a while at my house. It will give me a chance to check things out," Hunter answered for her. "I'm hoping time will make it safer to go back unnoticed. I want to put my fears to rest. What are you doing today?"

"I'll be getting supplies for my new trip, my new life," Roxi sounded enthusiastic.

Mariah wondered if her bravado wasn't masking some of the hurt she felt at leaving Rob behind. "I'll go with you," Mariah offered. "I have a long list."

"Well, I'll run into my office and put in an appearance, late as usual," Hunter said.

"What happened to your WASP work ethic?"

"I don't know, I seem to be losing my grip on the rat race. Bad timing, as I'm making more money than I ever have before."

"I bet you have no time to spend it either."

"How did you know? You are right once again, Miss Mariah."

CHAPTER 24 *Tristan's Quest*

"You brought me. I want to stay. I need to." Tristan glanced up at the Ancient One's stone countenance.

"You're letting your emotions control you. I have to keep my promise to Mariah. I must go and find her," Daniel said.

"No. Not me. This is too important." He would leave it, if Daniel spoke truth.

"You are my responsibility."

"Please. I am in a room with all of this." He gestured to the piles of scrolls and manuscripts. "It's a once in a lifetime experience."

"I brought you." Daniel was firm.

"You go," Tristan said.

"Your anointing is still new," Daniel said.

"I can make it. Don't worry about me. I will make it back."

Daniel felt betrayed. He couldn't believe his young friend thought he could survive the trip back alone. "You will have to shape shift on your own."

Tristan gazed longingly at the pile of scrolls he'd selected. He stood taller, banishing all traces of self-doubt. "I can do it. I have to do it." He spoke with certainty. "I do not see an alternative."

Daniel stood erect. He looked Tristan in the eye. "OK my friend, you do understand I must go now? Mariah cannot be left long wandering on The Ranch without a guide."

As they unrolled the three parchments, a soft bell rang. Daniel helped weight the corners with stone.

"You are a great friend Daniel. Go and be well," Tristan said.

Tristan studied the markings. Some were iron red in color and seemed to be similar to Egyptian hieroglyphics. Others were blue and grey with a yellow stain embedded in the paper helping to illustrate the work. The bell rang again, just a tiny silver sound.

Soon Tristan was deep in conversation with the Ancient One. He suspected this wise man was more of a Shaman than a Chief. He remembered Rob saying that the Atlanteans had a priest class as well as scientists. It was this priest class that carried the wisdom of Atlantis by boat to diverse shores of the Americas, as well as to Egypt.

"The Roman Empire," the Ancient One was saying, "is the model of evolution the earth population is stuck in today."

Tristan studied his dirty bare feet. He laughed ashamedly to himself. "I guess you are right."

"Imperialism still rules the day. You live in a warrior culture. How many wars are going on right now across the planet?"

Tristan looked around at the magnificent ancient interior. He almost expected to see a high tech command center.

The Ancient One studied his face. "The mind of a highly evolved human can divine more than your technology can ever tell you. The human mind is a living organism, and like all others it needs sustenance—that which nurtures. Life is its Food, as well as other humans, animals, and nature. A diet of pure technology can kill the soul. The soul breathes through your mind and body. There are those on your planet that understand this. These people seem to be called backwards, third world, low tech or indigenous, by the western hemisphere.

"These people—shamans in India, sacred healers in Arabia and Afghanistan—they know. The Russian seers know. The Irish druidic priests had such knowledge. Some in your modern society know too—these are the 'intuitives' or 'psychics'. Many imbibe in alcohol or drugs, to hide from, or numb their awareness. To hide from their deep soul that is in constant battle with the scientific evidence of your highly technological civilization. There is a lot of power that can be very hard to handle, when one is not prepared, or properly trained. Some drink because your culture gives them no space to use, or even understand their gifts. The battle between the soul and technology is ongoing.

387

To think is not to know. Atlantis as we knew it, is gone forever. But Atlanteans are not."

This thought piqued Tristan's interest. He laughed to himself as he pictured many folks looking for the Lost Records of Atlantis so they could decipher from old texts and cryptic messages. The Atlanteans themselves, have been alive all along. What better way to learn than at the feet of the wise ones? Still, he looked around, eager to get his hands on this treasure trove of wisdom.

"God is a merciful God. The One True God is a merciful and Loving God. His Love can heal this world and all of her people."

Tristan sat cross-legged upon the cool marble floor as he read through the scrolls and tablets. The Ancient One had left him some time ago, and he was a lone figure in the grand room. Time became timeless in the velvet depths, as flickering fires illuminated the room. As his eyes grew accustomed, he found it was bright enough to read by. As he looked around the hall with its tiled marble floor and classical columns, he unexpectedly connected the Atlanteans to Ancient Greece. It's as if the Greek culture took off from where Atlantis had stopped.

The Greeks were obsessed with beauty and form in the three dimensional world, perhaps because it differed greatly from the spiritual plane they had come from. The Atlanteans were beautiful, but had sought a more scientific advancement, their minds hungry for gnosis, or knowledge. They had achieved perfection in their physical form. They had clear ideas of aesthetics. Now they were ready to move beyond. They wished to transform the 3-D universe they had found themselves in. They lived simply, content with the blue Mediterranean Sea, and the blue sky overhead. They were fascinated by boats that could float on the water. As they studied the ethers and the birds, they longed for a new kind of ship. As the scientific community became more obsessed with the power of the intellect, the priests, and priestesses became wary. The wisdom-knowledge of their culture must be protected, maintained, yet hidden.

Power and greed ultimately blinded the scientist class of Atlanteans. Supremely enlightened beings, the priest class had warned the scientists. Advising them in an effort to prevent the schism. In the end, technology prevailed. The misuse of these energetic extremes totally destroyed their world.

The Atlanteans speculated that it would take centuries for earthlings to evolve to a spiritual-intellectual height capable of responsible use of such massive power. Thus the priest class preserved this knowledge. Sacred teachers and priestesses were elected to journey to different lands. They travelled by boat, then dispersed throughout many nations. To the ordinary citizens they were like gods. The epitome of physical beauty, poised and graceful in bearing and attitude, the Atlanteans became teachers. Thus they managed to preserve their wisdom. They adopted the role of Druidic Priests, Shamans, and Medicine men in many societies.

They hid the records in at least three diverse locations. The left paw of the Great Sphinx in Egypt was one place. Somewhere in the Caribbean was another. Here in the cave of the Great Earth Crater, is the third.

Thus, the knowledge was protected and available for the future time when Earth's people evolved. The wise ones instilled the knowledge in the hearts of those who could 'hear' to fuel the evolution. This power would eventually be used to benefit the earth, not destroy her.

Unfortunately, the Atlantean scientists were left behind, and eventually lost, in the sinking of Atlantis. Those that stayed on the earth had their own hard road to travel. The mass of humanity had scars from a hard life of tilling the earth for sustenance. Atlanteans are from the stars. These regal beings now had to humble themselves in order to assimilate with the population. The descendants of that race continue to be called by the stars. They search the sky for answers, and are often overcome by the feeling that they don't belong here. Yet, at the same time, the earth accepted them into her bosom; nurturing, honoring, and sustaining them. Today, those most respectful of the earth and her blessings are these Atlanteans, grateful for a home that feeds, nurtures, protects, and entertains them.

Ancient wise one revealed all of this to Tristan. He sparked his mind to stretch, opening as he read the scrolls and examined the hieroglyphics. Tristan recognized the similarity between the cave drawings he had often studied at The Ranch, and the illustrated markings on the parchment.

He felt unsure and gazed into the deep grey eyes in the wizened face. As he felt the generous spirit and open heart, he suspected his guide was an Atlantean Shaman, living through the generations to guide the people. He also knew all beings were interconnected, and were here to help, share, and evolve together. The Ancient One saw us as One, when we didn't know enough to see each other that way. Ah, *the Law of One*. Now he understood.

Tristan finally realized that crystals illuminated each torch. And the crystals had absorbed the one light and reflected it back in many facets. He bent his head back to the page and began to read. As his mind opened, and he attuned to the strange mixture of pictographs, hieroglyphics, and detailed drawings, he realized what he was meant to know. As his mind opened to receive the new insights, it hurt. It was painful to keep opening up. Yet, he wanted to know, to grasp it with a real comprehension. He was no longer satisfied with the vague glimpses that had contented him in the past.

Fire was crucial. The initial fire generated a light, which was encased in a crystal structure. The crystal didn't burn but contained the flame. This flame-encased crystal, generated enough energy to heat a home in winter. At another scale it could run a generator. A medium-sized unit could propel a type of car. The problem, Tristan could see immediately, was that the design of cars in our world had been all wrong. This car, the car he saw sketched on the parchment, was small and streamlined— like a chariot without the horses. Well, this surely wouldn't work, not in our modern age. It was all so ancient-looking. And then he noticed the drawing of a kind of hovercraft that could float over the water. The crystal heat generator was creating a steam cushion beneath the craft that was then powered across the water with a crystal engine. The interesting dilemma was the crystal, the flame, and the oil, were all used to create the energy system. Only a small amount of oil was needed to power the system. The sun's energy was used to ignite it. The magnetic pull of the metal element set it spinning.

The sun is extremely powerful, he thought. The generator the Atlanteans made in their ravaged past was huge. He surmised that the misuse of this invention is what led to the demise of a great civilization. This was clearly the missing piece since all the records had been sealed. The history books skipped the Atlantean epoch and went straight from cavemen to fire—Stone Age, Bronze Age, Iron Age, followed by the Egyptians, with no mention of the huge leaps made en route. Yet still today, much wisdom of the Egyptians remain a mystery. Finally the Greeks and Romans are considered to be the cradle of Western Civilization. Everything that cannot be understood by the Western mind is considered a myth. We can discuss everything from dragons to Greek gods, and believe it's all fantasy.

At long last, Tristan looked up and noticed his host's grey eyes watching him. He had no idea if he'd been studying for days or hours, so absorbed had he become. His host was totally taking him in. The eyes watched him and knew him. He felt himself being read like an open book. He felt naked and exposed. His first instinct was to hide, to cover up, but the compassion that accompanied the gaze allowed him to relax. He opened into this loving gaze, and allowed the deeper conception in. It was an exchange; an exchange that made him richer, bolder. He realized the Ancient One was imparting wisdom and depth. This gave Tristan a template to understand the strange signs and symbols that lay before him, like reading a new language. Hebrew and Chinese also look like delicate drawings before they come alive with meaning. It was as if the Ancient One had given him the key to understand the language.

He responded with extra mental energy. If his mind burned brighter, he would absorb more. The brain is a muscle after all. The burn he was feeling increased the capacity for more. The Ancient One smiled and then he grinned. The old cracked lips parted to reveal surprisingly perfect white teeth, and his eyes teared with joy as he laughed. It was such a moment, Tristan laughed too. Much tension left his body as he did so. Then Tristan became aware that the space on his forehead was opening up wider, and his brain no longer hurt. This new opening allowed him to digest more. His heart warmed as if filled with love. It burned and glowed within his being. He was renewed. Awake. Clear. Yes, that was it. A passion for new wisdom was born within his soul. It instilled in him a love for the Ancient One and the cave.

After a long silence, Tristan's mind was full of questions, thinking, calculating, and computing. It was a while before he realized there were no words being exchanged. Only ideas. This felt something like mind reading. Instead, his heart filled to bursting with Love and an emotion that felt like adoration.

When Tristan spoke, his voice sounded low and raspy in the silent cave. "The Ranch is full of crystal caves."

"You are right."

"You are concerned about the destruction of all the crystals in the lustful excavation for oil."

"Yes."

"People are fighting over the wrong 'Gold.'"

"Yes, the value system of those on the planet has become misdirected. Or perhaps out of order. Gold is valuable, but not the most valuable thing in this world. Also, there are other ways to make energy rather than robbing the earth of oil. Relationships: Human Life, is at the top of the list. Everything else, including energy, is just in service to that."

"Energy... Energy. Energy." Tristan savored the word.

He thought hard. He knew this was a clue. The most valuable thing in the world is relationships. The energy of that—human energy. Power, freedom, and evolution, involve people in relationship. Material fuel is just there to support us while we continue in relationships. Yet, in the quest for power, due to oil domination, we quickly destroy relationships, the world, and especially human life.

Human life is the only thing with any real value. And water is the only real necessity. It is a mean trick to entice humans to destroy virgin water supplies, while mining for oil. Oil is not actually necessary for human life. In fact, it's poison.

Tristan felt there was a battle happening on a cosmic level. Here is their perfect planet Earth, in the solar system. The one place that can sustain life on the third dimension, a perfect playground—a stage for the biggest drama—human evolution. The game is: *Will the beautiful people that have incarnated on the planet manage to destroy the place before they have a chance to evolve to the next level?*

The clock is ticking. Time is running out. The forces are all around, smiling, and cheering us on. And one in the bunch is a trickster, confusing the game. Stacking the deck. Stealing the script. The ones that know—the Atlanteans, the guardian angels, the grandmothers—are here to help, guide, and nurture, while we keep bumbling around. We're as slaves to our lower natures. Energy is here, we already have energy. That's a big trick. Like the one getting people to buy water.

"Revealing ourselves to you and your family is not accidental. We are patient. We have been waiting a long time. It is now time." My gifts, to your mother through you, are these blueprint diagrams that explain the Dynamo-eterna. Take them, along with this small crystal model of the light machine. From this, you should be able to extrapolate the other sizes you need to move forward. It's time to join the Atlanteans and move forward in a new era of peace and harmony."

"These drawings and writings, are similar to the ones at The Ranch," Tristan said, laying a gentle hand on the parchment. "Were those written by the same people? Is The Ranch connected in some way to all of this?" He searched for the right question. "I mean, are there more people from Atlantis here?"

"Where do you think Joseph, Daniel, and their family are from?"

"I thought they were from here, America. American Indians?"

"Where do you think Atlantis was?"

"In the sea, it was an island and fell into the ocean after the explosion."

"Yes, the Atlantic Ocean. It was a long time ago."

CHAPTER 25 *The City*

Somehow, despite all her misgivings, Mariah relaxed into the rhythm of early morning swims and leisurely breakfasts. She enjoyed long debates with Hunter morning and evening. He seemed to keep very flexible hours for a lawyer. She explored his library and found he had books on many fascinating subjects. She knew she had to leave soon and this was just a breather from her *real* life. With the cowboy on the loose, it was safer to stay put, she told herself. No sense in wasting time. She would read, catch up on stuff. The days flew by.

At first, she had mentioned the trip back to The Ranch, daily. Hunter always seemed too preoccupied to discuss it. She was working on patience, so she vowed to go with the flow. The reason for her extended stay almost forgotten, thoughts of The Ranch became displaced with the lure of all the fun of the world. Hunter was a charming host. The nights soon filled with trendy dinners in cool night spots, and dancing at the Riverwalk after. When she spoke of leaving, he laughed and hugged her, and out they went to another quaint bistro to meet yet another acquaintance, followed by salsa dancing.

* * *

Mariah stayed in shape by adding long bike rides through the hills to her morning swims. She hadn't realized that over a week had flown by and Hunter had revealed nothing new. She had even gotten snoopy and tried to search his office. Perhaps she could find something out about Covington Group or Properties, something Max had mentioned. His office was locked. Another dead-end.

Now she was done. She'd been patient with Hunter when he said they would leave soon. She was finally tired of his treadmill-spinning friends. All clones of the Texas frat guys she'd avoided in college. The city's tinsel had rusted now. Super loud music blared without sense or substance, assaulting her psyche at every turn. Noise with a beat. She couldn't hear herself think, let alone others. She stepped out of the loud café. It seemed between the music and the roar of the espresso machines, she couldn't hear what people said. When she went outside the traffic noise was deafening.

"Has city living always been this loud?" she wondered.

"Come again?" Roxi asked.

"Never mind." She grinned, "Point taken."

She buried herself in Hunter's house, seldom venturing into town any more. The point was to stay in hiding until Cowboy lost interest or left. After her morning swim, she shut herself into Hunter's library and poured back through the shelves. Through the rows of dry topics, she thought she might find something interesting. She found herself making stacks of clever titles. She hadn't read a book at all at The Ranch, they'd been so busy.

She embarked on her pile, selecting one, "The 'Seven Secrets of Solid Success." She studied the cover, the jacket, and the introduction. That's nice. She was sure she had gleaned all the book had to offer. She looked for the secrets and read them. Next one; nice topic, nice cover. She read briefly, but found no substance. As she went through she found herself bored by what surely would have interested her just last year. "The Conspiracy of the Twin Towers"; "Green Homes of the Future"; "Concrete Spaghetti Nightmares" or "Why the Freeway is not Really Free." Finally, she chose the book on green homes, sat down on the couch, and tried to read.

Her path was different now. Her raison d'être had changed. Her world had become entirely hands-on. Had she dumbed down and lost any sense of culture? She hoped not, but she couldn't deny that the wisdom she had gleaned from her Indian friends, even Running Wind, who was the most physical of them, made much more sense than these dime store insights. She had experienced life first hand with a front row seat. At the Ranch, she had a new epiphany each morning, and operated from a concrete sense of inner knowing. In comparison, her old world seemed superficial, dated, clearly dying. She had been seduced by the death throes. It's as if there was a living presence at The Ranch; a voice that was silenced here among the dilapidated buildings and perfect suburbs. Everyone here seemed to be going through the motions. She feared she must have been like this; walking through life half-asleep. Now she *knew* better.

The future was being created now. Her life was on a new trajectory. Completely unpredictable. How would her own story unfold? What was happening at The Ranch now? Had Tristan found some new truths or ancient secrets? Would they be able to survive the winter? What did the Indian's home beyond the cave look like? She kept staring off into space.

BAM. The book in her lap dropped to the floor, startling her.

Hunter looked up, "You make a lot of noise."

"Oh, sorry."

"Just kidding. I was watching you, ah, 'reading'. Anyway, I'm planning to run out for dinner at Tim Wagner's house. Love it if you'd join me."

"In that case, how can I turn you down?" She dreaded the idea of going out. "Just take Roxi. I'm too busy."

"She's off with friends." Hunter paused as he studied Mariah's face. "C'mon. It will be fun."

"No thanks. I've already had some."

"What's wrong, Mariah? You stayed home all week. It's not good for you, and it's not good for my ego."

"When you put it that way," she said, forcing a smile. "Just this once."

"It'll be fun," he replied. "You'll see."

"You have to meet Tim," he insisted. "He's just ripe to join your group."

Now he was whizzing her off in his BMW, the sun low on the horizon. That's how he always got her, she realized. For the good of *the cause*. Like she was some sort of evangelical. She wasn't. She was a loner. Yet, she fell for it every time.

"He lives out on the lake. I promise it will be fun."

Fun, fun, fun, fun. Everything for Hunter was either important (work) or fun. She masked her thoughts with a smile. She'd become secretive. She hated judging others. It would be so easy if fun still mattered to her these days.

Now here she was, out of place, as everyone jockeyed and flirted and made tasteless jokes. The girls seemed strange, so much make-up. Sprayed, tinted hair, altitude-altering heels, and short skirts glued in place. Barbie dolls. That's what it was, they all seemed like Barbies. Had she never noticed that? Shrill laughs coming from faces with no eyebrows finished the picture. Do these guys admire, respect these women? Did the women even care?

She felt, oh-so-awkward, when someone addressed her, as a guy was doing right now. "Who, me?" She pointed to herself and mouthed the words. She balanced her plate of spanakopita and mini-quiches. She hoped she looked apropos. A tanned dark-haired man in black jeans was quickly by her side. "Do I know you?" she asked, a bit put-off.

"Hi, I'm Chip." He stuck out his hand. "Now you do. How about some fresh air?" He opened the door, smoothed her outside, and snagged a drink from a passing tray in one motion.

"I'm Mariah. I'm not really here. I don't know anyone, I came with Hunter Jones."

"Quite a tan you have there. You're just visiting, I take it?"

"Yes, I'm a sun worshipper, I'm outside a lot."

"Me too. I ride horses."

"That's nice. I used to. Dressage."

"Oh really? I'm a show jumper. It's what I do. Train, ride, ride and train."

Mariah smiled. A genuine one for the first time in a while. They talked horses.

Someone came up, took his arm, and dragged him off. He glanced back at her with a strange look.

She liked it better outside. She had no idea where Hunter had gone off to. She hung on the sidelines of a green edge of lawn, watching the sun slip orange behind the black silhouette of oak trees and disappear.

Someone was talking to her. *Babble babble...* "Huh? Oh, excuse me, yes. I'm just visiting," Mariah said.

"What do you do?" a woman pried.

"I'm a maid."

"Come again?"

"Clean houses—other people's toilets, that sort of thing." Great, got out of that one she thought, as she watched the pert, painted lips freeze and fade, and the girl quickly waved at someone and left.

"No Ingleze," she told another person. This was getting a bit exhausting, this meaningless chitchat. She slipped off her sandals and wandered barefoot in the wonderfully cool grass. Her face turned to the sky, she watched as stars came out one by one. Hello, friends, she thought, how I've missed you. Venus low on the horizon, so intense.

Then the band started up. The squeak of the amp reverb announced their presence. "Oh God save me," she thought as she covered her ears. "Hunter...?

Mariah looked around. She must be the odd man out. No one seemed to notice the band. Some guests made a feeble attempt at dancing. In general, the talking just got louder. The whole effect was a loud din with a drumbeat, set off by the singer's wailing, coming from the mike on the backyard stage. "Never again," she whined. And in that moment, she completely understood Peter. It finally dawned on her. He had been wealthy. He had it all. He could have hung out, and partied his fortune away. But he had chosen to live an almost hermit-like existence at The Ranch. His Ranch. Her savior, her sanity. Inside her, something snapped back into place.

She went back inside and tried to enjoy the party, as every nerve in her body rebelled at the discord. She found Hunter at a table with a group of friends. As she listened to their banter she found them interesting, knowledgeable, and opinionated. Knowing no one, she slipped into observation mode. One guy, a powerful big person, was drinking his glass of wine as though it were Coke. Someone handed him a joint and he took that as well. Then he passed it on, only to light up a cigarette. She watched as he gulped wine, smoked, took a hit of the joint as it came around, all between sentences.

Multi-tasking, she observed.

A tall elegant woman offered brandy to a few of the guests. He grabbed that up too, in his large fist, and downed it as though it were a shot. His talk got louder and angrier as he warmed up with booze and smoke.

She glanced at Hunter. "Is this one of your friends?" she muttered under her breath.

"Oh yeah, a high school buddy. He knows everyone around town." He swirled his brandy in the snifter and sipped as he enjoyed the aroma.

Hunter was a refined gentleman in contrast. She tuned back in to the cheerful banter, trying to ignore this assault to her senses. He talked a good talk this guy. He was saying all the right things. He could fit in with one of the rough-around-the-edges Ranch types she had grown so close to. He was down on the government and down on society. All in all, a pessimistic world view, she realized. Is that how they sounded, she and her friends? She wondered in horror. As she watched in disgust the consumption—the smoking, the drinking, and now more food—she realized the difference. It was clear that there was no positive action or even intent for change here. Just *life's-a-bitch* banter. The large man kept flicking his ashes into the overfull ashtray, oblivious of the butts that fell over the edges. Oblivious. The word stuck in her head. Entitled and oblivious: The New Generation. She felt sick and hung-over all at once, just watching this guy. She shuddered.

I must be such a Puritan, but I don't care. I would rather be a Puritan. I was such a social butterfly, or at least I thought I was. But perhaps that too was just a diversion. Maybe I don't really like people as much as I thought I did. Her thoughts trailed off. Mentally, she tried to catch them. The harsh bang of the drum, and the electronic buzz, surrounded what might be a nice male voice, but he pushed out the syllables of the song in a forced attempt at coolness, or distortion, or both. What's wrong with the purity of a simple voice? Her ears were saying, "EECK. Help me, please." Where is the escape from this land of Chaos? I must get back to The Ranch. No more excuses. I have to get back to the garden." And then, she heard the strains of Crosby, Stills and Nash's,, '*I Have to Get Back to the Garden*'. Someone was strumming it on a guitar. She could just hear it like a light whisper under all the other noise. Like a miracle.

CHAPTER 26 *Aqua-Buena*

The group hiked in a steady rhythm. Isabella jogged back a bit to reach John who was bringing up the tail.

He grinned at her and his dimples showed. "Good to see you, girl. Thought you forgot about me back here."

She smiled back, and flipped her long braid back over her shoulder. "I'm worried about Mom."

"How so?"

"Well, if she's stuck in San Antonio, and Tristan is supposed to join her at camp when he's back... I mean, it's all timing. What if it doesn't work out?"

"What makes you think she would get stuck?"

"Dunno. Just a feeling."

"Faith. We are each doing our part. We're all gonna wait for Tristan at Aqua Buena. He'll come."

"You're right."

"Of course. About a lot of things."

"I'm worried," Isabella added.

"You're cute when you're worried."

"Are you flirting with me, John Java?"

"Wow, I never thought about it like that. I guess I missed you. All I see is everyone's backs."

"The path is a bit narrow." She glanced down at the narrow ledge they were climbing during their banter. "I'm serious. I'm gonna run back to camp. See what's going on."

"What if no one's there when you get there?" John asked.

"I have a sense about these things. I've got to go back."

"Isabella."

"What?"

He grabbed her hand and pulled her to him. He kissed her hard on the mouth. She wrapped her arms around him. "Be so careful."

They held each other tight. She smelled that good outdoor odor he had, mixed with peppermint soap and patchouli.

He took off his bandanna and wiped her forehead. "Keep this."

"I will." She tied it around her head like a headband.

Isabella ran off with feet that had been kissed by the wind. Her heart pounded as she ran. Was this worry or excitement? She was full of feelings these days. She couldn't get the smile off her face though.

* * *

They had hiked for days. Marching with a steady pace and rhythm that carried them through the overgrown creek draws, high up on the ridges of hills and down again. After a long, steady, uneventful push they finally arrived at their first destination. The campers were quiet as they spread out amidst the fields of grass and scattered boulders to rest. This was the designated half- way point. David and six of the groups were gathered here at the place his friends called, 'The Aqua Buena.'

David stood at the top of the cliff, staring hard into the far distance. From his perch he could spot any new arrivals, yet he knew those he most longed to see would not be coming. Mariah had not yet arrived. David wasn't really expecting Tristan to be done with his Vision Quest yet. Mariah, on the other hand, was a different matter. It was supposed to be a quick trip—basically drive to San Antonio and back. Piece of cake. What had happened? Had she gotten lost? He looked out over the huge expanse of territory. He saw endless hills, prickly dense woods, and boulder-strewn creek draws. The territory had always been more wilderness than "ranch," and full of mountain lions, wildcats, and birds of prey. They had traveled in a large group making enough noise to scare off anything unwelcome. Now Mariah was out there, with only Joseph or Jet to protect her.

Where was she? Hadn't he done everything he could to make her happy? He'd come out here to the wilderness, and listened to her dreams and visions. He had believed her stories and intuitions. He had

401

walked with her, listening to her sometimes wild imaginings. They had trained together, and studied at the feet of the Indian elders. He had applied the practical teachings they taught. She soaked up the more esoteric thoughts. He'd worked hard meanwhile, but he'd done the work he knew. He did what he was good at. It was hard work but he did it well.

He'd dug the hard earth. He'd planted, harvested, and grown food. He'd gone back and forth for supplies until he was dizzy. He'd been a good father and a good husband, hadn't he? Now at the last minute, just before their dreams were to be realized, she'd dashed off back to the city. Why?

He'd organized the group well, and left on schedule. She had promised she would be back. She'd promised the Indians. Joseph and Jet said they would escort her safely to the secret 'Cave-Spring,' place of the eternal spring. She had learned techniques to travel swiftly, as had Tristan. Perhaps she was already there? It had been against his better judgment. He hadn't wanted her to go.

From his spot on the cliff he could see all of them spread out in the field in small clusters. The place buzzed with a mixture of anticipation and exhaustion. It was a ton of people once you had them all in one place. He could hear the whine of some children punctuated by the laughter of others. One group started playing guitars, and others gathered around to listen. He headed back down the cliff.

David forced a smile as he strolled among the small clusters. Watching the other families sharpened the pang for his own. He realized Isabella was gone too. He prayed they were all right.

When Tristan arrived, they would have the first meeting to divulge the presence of the Indian guides. The Indians had been close to his heart since he was a boy; Tristan was the one to tell their story. Then Sunowa and Daniel would finally lead them to their new home. David had anticipated this special moment all summer, and he wanted to share it with Mariah, damn it. He would wait for Tristan. Hopefully, they would arrive together, making their family complete.

CHAPTER 27 *The City*

"The research has paid off," Hunter enthused late that night after they returned. He poured Mariah and himself a brandy.

"Tell me." Mariah toasted and sniffed the rich aroma of Benedictine and Brandy.

"The fact is, all the Texas oil guys want to drill in Texas now. They have financed their lifestyle knowing the value of their oil reserves will make them billionaires."

Mariah stopped him, "Wait. Hold up. They? Who are they in the first place?"

"Scofield, Gilbert, and their associates. But Scofield is the dominant force. Let me back up here. The new radar devices...wait; I have a map of the territory." He strolled to the imposing oak table floating in the library like room. He retrieved a document from his breast pocket and carefully unfolded it, smoothing it out flat on the table. "When they get the terms they are looking for, I'm afraid they plan to begin drilling," Hunter said. "Here is the geological survey." He gestured at the map spread out on the table. "The new infrared technology allows them to photograph the earth to locate oil before they drill. Drilling for oil used to be random. No longer. With this device they can locate the hidden oil pockets prior to drilling. It seems the quantity at The Ranch is substantial. Once they make the initial investment, they can tap into acres of oil reserves. I see a large pool here, and another here. There are two or three small ones. That spot with the huge lake of oil is on Peter's land. To them it was a giant trust fund that they didn't have access to."

Mariah strolled over and stood casually beside him, peering over his shoulder, trying not to appear too eager, while trying to decipher the marks on the worn paper. This was clearly the original that Max had copied.

"But it's land they do not own, they have no rights to it," Mariah stated.

"They seem to have purchased the adjacent property. They call them game reserves. Ranch retreats for the fat cats. A great cover, big game hunting."

"Like an African experience." Mariah finished for him. "So it's true."

"As I was saying, Scott Scofield uses his place as an exotic hunting ground. It justifies the huge fences like a compound. Tall fences with barbed wire and spikes at the top. They say it's to keep animals in."

"But the real reason is to keep nosey people out." Mariah waited, he'd shown her the same map Max had found, all be it a newer version. A little drink and dancing had opened him up. What was he playing at, she wondered? What did he want from her?

"Precisely. No one knows what's beyond the gates."

Mariah sat, brows furrowed in concentration, as she took all of this in. She knew most of the story by now, but she was surprised to be hearing it from Hunter. "How big a group are we talking about?"

"Scofield is the leader. I speculate his plan is to access the ranch from the adjacent property he purchased."

"That's what all the power lines and roads that we see parallel to The Ranch entrance are for?"

"Yes, he'll start on that side." Hunter was matter of fact.

"Hunter, you know that will totally destroy The Ranch. Drilling for oil at Jade Springs will pollute the water and the entire ecosystem with it. That is the headwaters for a major Texas River. You know that."

Hunter shrugged noncommittally.

"You of all people should understand!" Mariah all but shouted. "Uncontaminated water is crucial for all the creatures and the people living out there. Without water the Ranch is a mere wasteland. We need water to survive." Mariah was furious. She couldn't hide it. "How can you be so casual?"

"Fresh water is a commodity since flooded farmland managed to fill the entire Mississippi river with lots of chemical pesticides," Hunter agreed.

"Fresh water is a birthright. Now it's at a premium."

"You're in grave danger." Hunter cut her off. He sipped his brandy.

"Come again?" She was stunned. His change of tone was abrupt from good ole boy to serious.

"These are desperate men. You and your theories are right after all. This is a high stakes game," Hunter said. "They wanted Peter out of the way. He wouldn't go along with any kind of drilling plans, or selling out. Those boys that murdered him took the fall even if they were paid pawns. I did some research on cowboy."

"Research?"

"I had him tailed. He works for Scott at the Game reserve. If your hunches are right, there is the connection." He took another sip. "How does it feel to be right?"

"Awful. Hunter, can you stop them?" Would he? She wondered. It took long enough for him to believe her. Whose side was he on?

"I don't think so. Come here." He escorted her to his large computer screen. "I was listening to your arguments. I searched at first to disprove your theory. But now I have evidence. Look at Mr. Scofield's companies. He's completely over extended and in debt. He has gambled everything on the plan for oil to skyrocket when we focus back on Domestic oil. They all have."

Mariah stood behind him, looking at the computer screen. There were several flow diagrams. "I don't follow."

"See all these companies?" He pointed to the diagrams. "These all belong to him and his partners. Different partners on different deals. All over the world. Each company leveraged, one against the other. Each one is dependent on war, or oil. If both stop at once, he'll be desperate. I've been working on this," he added. "Its a bit unethical for me to share this."

"How do we stop them from drilling? I feel powerless. Peter would want to protect the Ranch." For the millionth time Mariah was tempted to tell him about the Indians living out there in secret. They were the ultimate pacifists. Once her group went into the interior they would be powerless to stop anything. Without water the Indian tribe would die out. She said, "So this is the real reason Peter was murdered?" She looked straight at Hunter. "For the oil on his land."

"After all the time on computers, searching maps, and records, here we have it." Hunter shook his head. "I don't want to believe it."

Mariah knew the Indians and the land were in imminent danger. "You are trying." She shuddered. Hunter was naming names. Max had been speculating. "Thanks for this. Why are we toasting with such grave news?" Mariah paced, swirling the golden liquid in the crystal snifter. "Hunter, first Peter was in danger, because he owned the land. Now the land is in danger. Who is to protect it? How can these men be stopped? Distracted or delayed?" Now Mariah felt like a caged animal. She paced bounding thru the spacious room, back and forth.

Hunter stood holding his brandy like a delicate gentleman, waving slightly, about to be shattered.

"Sorry. It's just cruel. Cold blooded and cruel," she raged on. "They corrupted those boys too. They were so young and now, since the crime, they have no real future." Mariah stopped pacing and dropped back onto the couch, the down pillows sucking her in deep. She realized he hadn't known, but he did now, and it was a shattering realization. It's like Chloe had said, wash it all down with liquor to hide the bitter taste of truth.

"About you now," her eyes searched Hunter's face. "You're free to join us. You have certainly done your due diligence and pieced together the who and why of this horrendous crime. I feel as though I owe you."

"I could try to keep them distracted with Alaska. Any place but Texas."

"Alaska. Good idea. That will give Tristan time to get the special invention."

Hunter's mind twitched at the use of the word 'invention.' He raised an eyebrow and refilled her glass.

She convinced herself that Hunter was a very valuable asset to have on their team. He would return with her, she was sure. Max would be pleased. She owed her sister this. Max could tell him her news about the baby.

"As long as we're sharing," Mariah took a rather nice sip, "Tristan is working with some people on an invention. He left after I did. It's

406

something that will help us thru the winter months." She sighed, winter seemed very far away. She had no idea how much time they had.

Hunter was thoughtful as he took in her news. "In that case, I think I should stay here and keep an eye on things. Monitor their progress. Put a few legal hurdles in their way. They won't know I put it together, or told you."

"Very noble of you, like a spy. In that case," Mariah inhaled the golden liquid, she had been swirling her brandy, "you need to know we're going deep into hiding. So deep that if you try to join us later—if there is a later—Max, my family, and I will be beyond you. We think the world is not sustainable. We truly believe that. I can't *beat around the bush* here. You must choose. It's a sacrifice and a reward at once. Let go of one thing, gain immensely. The shift is occurring. All of us alive today are *living* thru it. With one foot in the old world and one foot in the new, when the split/shift occurs—you will be torn in two. You do the splits until you decide. One side or the other. The chasm between the two has been growing. Like the gorge in Taos—deep and wide and long. I've made my choice. I must get back right away."

Hunters face was grim as his shoulders sagged in defeat or resignation.

"For heaven's sake, Hunter, I don't know why you would want to have any dealings—casual or professional—with these men. *The men who murdered your friend.* The men who are trying to control all the oil in a world that runs on oil. Obviously they are part of the *Evil Elite*. My friends and I made our choice because we believe all the power is soon to shift. I beg you to consider all your options. While you still have them." Mariah put her glass on the polished mahogany desk. She wasn't going to betray Max's confidence. "Good night."

Finally back in her room, Mariah dug frantically, searching for something in her pack. Her fingers brushed a softness, stuffed way down at the bottom. She pulled it out. It was the white shawl she had treasured so much back at The Ranch. She gasped as she pulled the downy cloth to her and buried her face in the smells, mixtures of cedar camp smoke, and lavender. When she touched the shawl her fingers froze. Emotions flooded her being, as memories filled her with an unattainable longing and loss. She missed David's arms around her at night.

I've been *Anointed*, for heaven's sake, she suddenly remembered. I'm a NEW woman with fresh eyes. Of course this world reeks of dishonesty. Of course it reeks of unreal smells, sights, and sounds. Why had she second-guessed what she knew to be TRUE?

She recalled the last conversations she had with David. It was the night before she left The Ranch. He had given her his blessing, his love, and his body. His arms had held her and comforted her all night long. She had embarked the next day with confidence and the positivism of her own strength and sureness. He had trusted her, against his own concern and instincts, to keep what he loved close to him. Yet here she lay, in this unfamiliar place, night after night, while who-knows-what was going on back on the beautiful land. She must have amnesia or something. Who was she fooling?

She had justified her behavior, determined to win Hunter over, so he would join them. He was going nowhere. Instead he was keeping her here. She was afraid to go out alone. There was always someone with her. He never argued with her. He always agreed. Yet they had not gone back to The Ranch. Give me a few days, he would say, I'm on to something. What he had found out was devastating.

She now knew *who* killed Peter and *why*. But she couldn't stop them. She couldn't fight them; sue them; convict them. She belatedly realized this battle was way beyond her. The illusion that she could stop them had nearly cost her The Ranch. She must trust and call upon the legions of angels to make her path clear—straight back to The Ranch and her people. Her beliefs and her actions must unite and become as one. There is power in that, she knew. And peace.

In the end, peace and power became her mantra. Peace and power she focused on. She wrapped herself in the shawl and then she slept deep.

That night at 2:59 p.m., New York City blacked out. Three other cities—Boston, Philadelphia, and Chicago—followed at two-hour intervals. Los Angeles was still alive because she he had a lot of wind power. Alerts went out across the country begging everyone to use less power, so the reserves could build, and New York could get back on. The wake-up call.

"That's a wake-up call," Mariah said the next morning. She clutched a chunky yellow mug in her hands as she sat, her legs curled into the chair. "You look pale. Late night again?" She asked Hunter. Her coffee gone cold, she stared at the lukewarm liquid in the cup.

"Well yes, but I'm used to it." He grinned as he poured a fresh cup.

"Scary news. I can't say I'm surprised, just amazed it's happening so soon."

"The ripple effects of New York's blackout will be trickling through the country for weeks." He put two spoons of sugar in his cup and stirred absently.

She stared at him thoughtfully. "Peace and power."

He glanced up at her. "What's up?"

"I'm leaving today."

CHAPTER 28 *Land-Rover*

"Roxi's going to go ahead and drive me back to Lakeville. I have to hope Cowboy's lost interest by now."

Hunter studied Mariah's face. "Look, I can drive you in the Jeep. He's already spotted your vehicle."

"No. It's a long trip. You're busy."

"No, I want to. I insist. Max's car will remain in the garage. It's like a red sign. Staying here like you've done may have convinced cowboy you're not a threat."

"That was our plan. You think he's lost interest by now?"

"He may be a spy and not intend real harm," Hunter said.

"Wow. Texas isn't the Wild West anymore is it? There are way too many of us for a shoot-out. Peter was one guy easily removed it seems. Killing a wayward band of hippies would be impossible or messy."

Mariah turned on her heel, rinsed her coffee cup out in the kitchen sink, and headed upstairs for her backpack. She put one foot in front of the other. Don't lose focus, don't debate him, just go, she told herself. She headed to the car, where Roxi was already waiting. Hunter locked up the house and joined them.

As they drove out of San Antonio on that grey day, now late September, there was a chill in the still air. Mariah had loved San Antonio when she had spent the summer here, but as they drove out, they passed yet more closed gas stations and boarded-up houses. For sale signs began to look like "to vote" signs, there were so many in front yards. The overgrown lawns and shaggy landscaping gave a forlorn look to once fashionable neighborhoods. The world was already changing, she realized. She could only hope to God they weren't too late. After all, just how long can you ignore the signs and still plead ignorance? Hunter stopped the car at a burrito shop and she jolted out from her reverie.

"Hey, I'm not that hungry."

"You have to eat something. They make a mean *huevos con pappas* with bacon here."

"All right, peppers and onions, no bacon, okay?"

"Gotcha."

"I'll take two," Roxi chimed in, "And keep the bacon on 'em."

Mariah was convinced Roxi would go back to city life with all its perks. "I appreciate your coming on this trip," Mariah said. "It's not too late to change your mind. Are you sure you want to stay in San Antonio?"

"Yeah, I'm cool. I'm not cut out for that Wild West stuff. Anyway, I can say I knew you when."

Three hours later, Mariah had almost dropped off to sleep lulled by the sun glaring on the windshield. Her head jerked up when Hunter, spotting Cowboy, tapped her knee.

"Where's he been hiding?" Her parched mouth went dry.

"Maybe here in Lakeville. He may have been waiting to see if we'd reappear."

Mariah wondered at this coincidence. Why had she trusted Hunter? How could this guy have known their timing?

Roxi scooted closer to Hunter. "Look, I've been thinking. Maybe we should have a change of plans. I don't think we should leave Mariah alone out here. Mariah and I should go together, I'll get him to follow me, and then Mariah can make it back undetected. I can double back and make it to Lakeville, you can meet me there. I'm the blonde after all. I'm the one he likes."

Hunter glanced at her hair and shook his head. "Dyed blonde. I don't like it. Is this the best we can do? We can all go back to San Antonio together and completely confuse the guy."

Mariah shook her head. "No, I must get back. Now. I've been away too long." She was tense and frustrated. She'd had it. She was ready. It'd taken six months to really be sure, and now she didn't want some weird

411

obstacle to hold her back. The longer she was away she worried that The Ranch might not *let* her back, that the gates to paradise might be closed. And what if Daniel didn't show up to lead her to the others? Oh no. Why had she left in the first place? A terrifying thought took hold. What if it's like *Pandora's Box,* and that *Ranch-Indian* world isn't quite real. It had become real to her. What if it involves a quiet lifting of the mist like in the *'Mists of Avalon'*? She didn't care if it was actually real. It had become her world and she wanted back in. When she remembered she was trained to remain calm, she took deep breaths, closed her eyes and focused on being back at The Ranch with everyone. She pictured Tristan and Isabella, and David. She had to get back to the Garden. She hummed the song.

She knew she lacked patience. Yet, this urgency was real. "I'm already way overdue. Tristan is probably back."

Hunter stared straight ahead, but his ears perked up. "Tell me about Tristan. Where did he go?"

"I don't know much." The wind was loud as it beat against the Land Rover in the silence as everyone pondered the situation. "Oh, Tristan—he loves technology, so he was invited to go to New Mexico to work with a think-tank there."

"Really? White Sands?"

"All I know is that it's an energy device." Mariah shrugged distantly. She was pulling away from him.

Hunter dropped it and drove expertly, rounding the turns on the back roads off the main high-way.

"Maybe I'm just paranoid." Mariah twisted around to look out the back windshield. "He's not following, so I guess we're okay. Still I'll probably just hang at the main house as though I came for a retreat week."

"No, Roxi protested, you'll be a bug in a fish bowl."

"What's he gonna do? Shoot me like he did Peter? Then he can do real time because he's an adult not a minor." She looked disgusted. "What does he want anyway?"

"Maybe he's just a goon."

"I'm sure of that," Mariah laughed. "But whose? If he takes Roxi as bait, she can lead him completely astray."

"I am up for that," Roxi said.

"He's not following us," Hunter said, "because he knows where we're headed."

"I can grab the Jeep the family keeps at Peter's house to get back to our camp. If I move quickly, I'll be gone before any undesirable person like Cowboy shows up."

"I will play decoy. I can meet you, Hunter, back in Lakeville," Roxi said.

"Wait, Mariah, what are you going to do about the oil problem, the drilling and all of that?" Hunter seemed genuinely concerned.

"I had hoped you were using your 'golden son' touch on that. But in the meantime, for our part, we will pray and Dance about it. If we pray and dance, it shows we trust in the Earth Mother, and in the power of good over evil. I have to live like that. I can't, we can't, none of us can live in fear. When you get that, you *will* want to join us. Not just two-step your way around the truth. I look forward to that day."

"Mariah, I just don't think it's going to be that abrupt." Hunter said. "Evolution takes years. Conspiracy theories have been around for decades. Today isn't that *final* day. Sorry."

Mariah held her tongue.

Max had joined their group. If he ever hoped to see her again he would have to make a decision. Hunter drove in silence knowing he knew too much and wondering if he was crazy leaving these two so far from civilization.

"Hunter, look, there's a turnaround. We can walk from here. We can take a short-cut to the house."

The two women jumped out almost before he pulled to a stop, eager for the next phase of the plan.

"I don't know when I'll see you again, Mariah," Hunter called. "Give Max my love. I will visit you guys come spring!" he saluted.

"Thanks, peace and power," she said.

"Lakeville," Roxi muttered.

"Sure, be careful."

The two women hiked swiftly up the bank and over, disappearing behind the scrubby trees. Hunter watched the brush a moment before turning the truck around. He drove through the tunnel of live oaks, headed back towards what had become the disquieting landscape of the twenty-first century. He'd avoid listening to the news, he thought, until he was back in the city. It would be all about blackouts he surmised. Better to prolong the sanity of this timeless place. He scared up a few wild turkeys and watched a shy fawn follow his doe deeper into the green-blue dark of the woods. The twenty-first century had turned into the unknowable; the landscape of the future, bleak.

He realized that over the thirty plus years he'd returned here, time and again, he'd changed, but nature was predictable. Solid. The stocks he'd invested in, once sure bets were now a mystery. His wife had shocked him when she left. The kids were busy with their own lives. No one could predict when the shortages would stop and the plenty would return. Banks were foreclosing on thousands of homes. Businesses were declaring bankruptcy. The middle class was being squeezed on both sides. Losing. Losing homes, jobs, marriages the war. They had even lost the war, although few knew.

So why was he headed back to the chaotic civilization he no longer believed in? Something had to shift. Or maybe it already had. God, how he had missed The Ranch. He had quit coming for a decade since Peter's death. One tragedy drove him away, another tragedy—his wife's abrupt departure—drove him back.

"Crazy hippies," he said aloud. He shook his head.

Then he spied the truck tucked off in the brush. He kept driving, eyes focused. The plan was underway. The Cowboy was on to the girls and they knew what to do. He'd meet Roxi as planned, and then he'd decide.

Hunter suddenly remembered all his stocks, his life savings. All the company investments will rise with the *Evil Elite*. And fall if they fell. He was invested right with them whether he liked it or not. If they went down he went down. He had to have it both ways. Suddenly, he made his decision. He turned his truck in the direction of Indian Point. He told himself he was being responsible for the women's safety. He told himself that for once he was being heroic. He would let everyone know what was up with Cowboy. The girls had been gone twice as long

as expected by now.

CHAPTER 29 *Breaking Bread*

Jack and Rob walked once more around the now forlorn campsite. They had filled the compost toilets in the woods and gone over the site for all debris and signs of life. Only one small white canvas lean-to, and the fire circle remained.

"We should try to make it to the Petroglyphs tonight," Jack said.

"I don't know what happened to Tristan," Rob said. "We have to wait for him."

"I'd like to make it there tonight, but it's some hard going up that cliff and we'll need the sun to make our way."

Jack looked at the sky to gauge how much time they had left.

"What! Are you guys still here?" Tristan's voice was jovial as he appeared suddenly from the woods.

Jack and Rob's heads jerked up. They both gasped in relief. "Tristan, you knew we'd wait for you," Jack said.

Tristan slapped them on the back. He was clearly a bit out of breath. "I was counting on it." He dropped his bundle down by the tent and leaned one-armed on a maple tree. Breathing hard through a big grin, he reached for their hands. "Let's give thanks for this special day before we leave for good."

* * *

Hunter's truck bounced across the field, over a road, obscured by years of overgrowth. He knew he should be careful. Not arouse unnecessary suspicion or draw attention. He parked at the lower meadow and hiked the small trail up to Indian Point.

Hunter's foot dislodged a stone as he trudged up the bank. The rock bounced down the cliff from rock to rock before landing in the water. As he turned and watched it fall, he realized how quiet it was. When he crested the top and came up to the center of Indian Point he encountered three figures in a circle, faces turned up to the sun. Rob, Jack, and Tristan sat cross-legged in a yoga position, all in a silent meditation. Not sure what to do, he waited. Tristan nodded to him and he found a place on the circle. A chime sounded from the crystal bowl Rob held beside him.

Hunter quieted his thoughts—racing since he'd dropped the girls off in a kind of possible danger. What were his motives? He breathed in deeply to still his thudding heart. He felt the sun warm his cheeks and joy filled his entire body. The bell sound rang again as the meditation concluded.

Then Tristan broke a thick round loaf of spelt bread and passed it to his brothers. Tristan offered Hunter a piece of the thick dark stuff. He nodded his thanks. The three were jovial, smiling with their mouths full, as they spoke of the adventure before them.

"Where is everyone? Is David around?" Hunter addressed Tristan.

"No, not now, he's off," he gestured toward Jade Cove.

"Wow, forgive me for staring but with your tanned face and interesting dress you seem rather like a native."

Tristan extended a moccasined foot. "You mean these? Comfort itself, the only way to travel."

"What's going on here?" Hunter put his hands in his pockets and glanced around.

"Well most folks have packed up and left before winter sets in. It's natural. We expected it. Not so gung ho after a few chilly nights. I thought Mariah was with you? What's going on?"

"We had a little problem in San Antonio."

"Let me offer you a cold drink and you can tell me all about it." Tristan pulled out a flask of the brewed sun tea. He poured it into metal cups. The cold liquid sweated the metal with icy dew drops.

They sat on a cedar stump under the shade of a maple tree as Hunter briefed them on the stalking cowboy. He decided to give only the briefest update. "So," Hunter concluded, "everything's fine now. I thought I'd stop here and check things out."

"Whoa, *cowboy*?" Tristan asked.

"We were followed. Roxi and Mariah were followed to San Antonio by some red neck guy they call Cowboy, dirty hat and all. Anyway, Mariah didn't want to lead him back to the real camp so she hung out in San Antonio with me until things cooled down. I just wanted to explain the hold up. All is good now."

Tristan just stared at him, thinking, *and I'm not to worry?*

"I also want to talk to you about another matter." Hunter shrugged and continued, "I understand you are working on a special gadget or energy system?"

Tristan spiraled up out of his position and stretched. He nodded for Hunter to follow him. Jack and Rob left the two alone.

"Where did you get that idea?" Tristan poured more tea.

"Mariah, your mom, mentioned something. She was quite vague. I'm intrigued."

"You are intrigued are you?" Tristan mulled over this turn in the conversation. Hunter was full of surprises. "Well she wasn't there. I have just come back from a trip. I will tell you one thing about it. It will most definitely revolutionize the way we use energy."

"You see, Mariah asked me to work on something for her, while all of you are gone. I thought I should make you aware of it. I think we have determined that Frank Gilbert and Scott Scofield, and their associates plan to drill for oil on land near here. I had hoped to discuss this with David but as you have the invention, it's better that you and I have this conversation."

Jack noticed Hunter still sat with Tristan and joined them. Tristan nodded as Jack sat down. "Now go on, I think you need to catch us up."

"OK, then." Hunter took a breath, "I discovered that the owners of the nearby ranches are planning to drill for oil. I told Mariah, of course."

"Go on."

Rob came out of his tent, similarly garbed in a colorfully woven tunic, and cotton drawstring pants, his feet clad in moccasins. "Will someone tell me what's going on out here?"

Hunter then outlined the theory he had pieced together. Jack poured everyone more iced brew. He passed around the rest of the manna bread

Tristan was silent, looking down at the dirt. When he looked up, his green eyes focused on Hunter. "Perhaps you should tell us more. We only know bits and pieces."

"Agreed. Frank Gilbert has the ranch, thirty miles to the north of here. He had studies done in the area with the radio-x-ray sonar machine that was developed in the early 90's. Gilbert discovered there were deep oil pockets on much of the ranch land. He then encouraged Scott Scofield to buy up available land in the area. He purchased a section bordering the west side of Peter's ranch. While going through their due diligence they discovered the bulk of oil was in fact on Peter's land. They tried to purchase it but of course Peter wasn't selling. I just found all this out recently." Hunter stuffed a big bite of bread in his mouth and swallowed some tea. "The fact is, they have been sitting on this information."

"You come bearing bad news. Perhaps everything hinges on timing," Tristan mused. "The invention I am speaking of is a new energy machine. This machine—engine—will make oil obsolete."

Rob and Jack looked at each other in surprise, but kept quiet.

"When you speak of drilling for oil, it's an exercise in futility. They can drill and destroy land. Pollute the water and create a huge mess on the landscape with their trucks and expensive drilling machinery." He studied his hands, "And, suddenly America has plenty of oil reserves. Abundant oil." He looked straight at Hunter. "Catch is, by that time, this simple invention will have trickled through the grass roots culture." He took a bite of bread. "No one will *need* oil any more. Everyone on the planet will have simplified, streamlined, downsized, and reignited their relationship to the natural order of things."

"Your point?" Hunter asked.

"Then what? When everyone has caught on that we're no longer oil-dependent, what will they do with all that oil?"

"Hold on, you're losing me, what do you mean- '*no longer oil dependent*'. The world is oil dependent. That's a fact."

"Okay, let me back up. This little machine will revolutionize the way we use energy."

418

"Alternative energy? We already have solar power, wind power, and methane digesters. We are still an oil-energy economy," Hunter said.

"Yes. I mean, solar power has been around since 1957, but it hasn't changed much in that time. Solar collectors aren't that efficient. Everyone always contends we lose a lot of energy in the transfer. This small invention is light-years beyond that. It will bring power into homes all over the world at a scale that everyone can afford."

"That's impossible."

"Well, it may have been in the past but now it's not. What I'm saying is that soon, with this invention, we no longer will be oil dependent. Since I know this, I could say tearing up the Ranch would be futile. Specifically, as those already in the oil business have all the oil they can ever use, they don't need the mega expense of obtaining even more."

"I don't know exactly how your invention works but if it works like you assume it will..." Hunter put up a hand to stop Tristan from speaking. "I hope you're wrong, but you have the notion that if your invention reaches the world, it will finally end the need for oil?"

"That is true. It will. It will solve the energy crises, and the need for oil for fuel will stop." Dead silence followed the assuredness with which Tristan spoke.

Hunter's eyes were wise, engaging behind his wire frame glasses. "My concerns are purely distribution. Here you sit, in the middle of nowhere. With apparently a great invention, I don't know how you have it, but you guys are full of surprises. Tell me, how do you intend to patent, manufacture, and distribute your invention?"

Tristan went along with Hunter. He had only mentioned a small bit of information about the invention. "It sounds like you have some suggestions in mind?"

"I do. If you distribute this thing yourself, and stop the need for oil on the planet, what do you think will happen?"

"Oh, I don't know. When we stop being oil dependent, I imagine a whole list of things will occur. Blood for oil, hence the war—will stop, troops will come home, energy costs go down, resulting in more money in the hands of the people. Shall I continue? Resources back, self-sufficiency and small villages will be viable, rural areas will be independent. Third world countries will be able to connect on computers."

Hunter's eyes squinted as he listened. "Well then, those in power; the banks, the oil barons, will lose a lot of their wealth. The banks will crumble, and then so will the whole economic structure of America. If not the world."

Tristan countered, "So? What has that to do with us? We wish to live peacefully out here in the wilderness. We hurt no one. We take nothing from anyone."

"Well, now our future senator, Scott Scofield and his buddy Gilbert are ready to make their move and begin drilling."

"That's crazy, it's cost prohibitive. A highly expensive and unnecessary venture."

"So they must convince a lot of investors to begin the process. If they begin to drill at The Ranch..."

"The Ranch!" Tristan stood abruptly. "They can't do that!"

"That's true, but they need oil."

"But the oil will be worthless to them, once this invention surfaces on the market." He paced with rapid strides clearly his early cool was lost.

"My point exactly. They don't know what you and I know about your invention. If you give it to me, I can sell it to them to manufacture and distribute. Then I will put your name on it. You will have royalty checks forever. You will be rich. You will have riches beyond your wildest dreams."

Tristan stopped and gazed at Hunter. His calm returned as he looked around at the blueness that enveloped them, with just a tint of pink light on the horizon. The breeze chilled the air. The birds were deep in a cacophony of song. He opened his hands to his surroundings, "And if they begin to drill, what will that do to this land?" His face was impassive. "To this pure spring water? The innocence that surrounds us?" He leaned against a tree as he spoke. "We're coming full circle in this discussion."

"If they purchase the invention from you, you protect the human race from complete and total economic collapse. That way you stop them from drilling. You are the hero." Hunter felt confident as he explained. "Do you have any idea what kind of life money can buy? At your age, you would be an overnight millionaire. Women, power, ranches—hell islands. You could own all the wilderness you ever dreamed of."

Hunter became desperate as Tristan remained calm and impassive at suggestions of fame or finances. "Don't you see? The economic collapse will trickle down and hurt everyone. The farmers, the workers, the housing. How will anyone survive without the world as we know it?"

All three men crossed their arms and looked at him. "The way we are. It's not the same. It is other. But it is possible. We are still alive."

"Hah! See if you last two full years. One year is nothing," Hunter challenged.

Tristan spoke, trying to make his thinking clear. "Hunter, you say you want to protect humanity from this economic collapse that you say our invention will create. You're blind. The world is already imploding from an economy rotting from the inside out."

Hunter fumed. "Oh come on. Without distribution and financing you cannot even bring your little machine to the market."

"Your point here? I thought this was good news. There's no motive for anyone to drill at The Ranch. If you know how to reach these guys," his voice trailed off.

Hunter paced. He was mad now. He skulked away, his shoulders hunched, his back to Tristan, while his head pounded. He could think on his feet, he would solve this thing. When he turned around he had an idea, "You need these guys, Sparky and Gilbert, and you need their financing. Come with me back to San Antonio. I will clean you up; put you in some normal clothes, and present your ideas to Sparky. Hear my words—this 'invention' of yours will never see the light of day without substantial financial backing."

"Clean me up?" Tristan was amused.

* * *

Isabella paused in the woods and let her breath catch back up to her. She could hear voices ahead at camp. She turned her head and there was Jet. He stood erect and his solemn gaze held hers. At that moment, she knew she was here for Tristan and her mom was in good hands. She knew with certainty, as they made this transition, each of their steps was protected or guarded. With Jet's nod she continued toward the clearing and waited.

* * *

Jack stood up beside Tristan, all five-foot-seven of him.

"But humor me a moment and hear me out. You say you can 'protect' the world from economic collapse by stealing this invention from me." Tristan saw the indignant look on Hunter's face and put his hand up. "It's a humble, small thing. It is simple. Just a gadget, really. But I wonder, why you? You are our friend. Why is it your job to protect the economic machine? Do you think you have the power to protect humanity? Like you alone can control what will happen? The movements of destiny are already in motion. These men made their choices long ago. Do you think that I believe for one minute these guys have the welfare of the healthy capitalistic system on their minds when they orchestrated the current fiasco?

"If you were to place your finger upon a leak, the pressure will build somewhere else and the damn will still explode if it is meant to do so. So if you let nature have her way -"

"Not nature," Hunter interrupted. "It's scientific invention."

"How do you know?" Tristan studied his face. After a long pause he said, "No, it's working with nature, with the natural flow of things. So when nature has her way, and the economic machine crumbles and collapses, it is only a purging. It's to sift the weak from the strong, the chaff from the seed. Mankind will survive, will grow, will flourish, and be better for it." Tristan stood. It was time to end this debate.

"No man can sit like a king and order the whole world about at his whim and survive. There is a Divine order, natural laws like gravity. Lots of stuff can run on the one law of gravity. Picture a world without gravity and you can imagine the result. Gravity is limiting—we cannot fly—and yet an ordering device, that makes order out of chaos. The laws are here for a reason."

Isabella was observing the scene veiled in the trees. She gaped at Tristan, he sounded so wise. Tristan noticed her, "Hey why are you

422

here? I thought you left with Sarah's group?"

Isabella shrugged. "Mom wasn't back yet. I was worried for her so I ran back."

"Well, you come with us then, we will be ready soon." He turned back to Hunter. "Hunter, it's not too late for you. You too can join us out here in our strange wilderness," Tristan said.

Hunter looked lost, less sure of himself. He looked around. The whole place had been full of hippies and children, a sort of gypsy camp. Now it was clean and quiet with this small band remaining. These guys were serious and organized in a quiet way. They were all tan and lean and strong. Not a round fat one among them. A handsome group, he thought. What was he doing? What was he saying, trying to get them to sell out?

"Hunter, all you have to do is ask them... your colleagues, to retest the area. It may have been years since they tested. Things could have shifted, leaked out. They will applaud you for the suggestion. Then if you can guide them elsewhere..." Tristan let his suggestion trail off. "My point is, they can only drill at one place at a time."

Hunter was silent for a moment. "Okay, okay. Perhaps they could drill on Scofield's section first. That's a good thirty miles away from here. That's the one with the exotic animals for hunting."

"That sounds diabolical. If you can influence them to begin their mad drilling anywhere else, we can benefit from the time it gives us. We will have a chance to move forward with our invention." Tristan studied the pale face before him. "In our way, in our time. You can be a big help to us Hunter, but you must choose. You simply cannot have it both ways."

Why would they have exotic animals out here? Isabella wondered.

CHAPTER 30 *Glass Jar*

Mariah ran straight into the house and locked the door behind her, then stood, frozen, in front of Peter's hat rack. Memories flooded in from times past. The last time she had been in this house, it was as Peter's guest. She strolled through the familiar rooms. She realized the family still used the place, so it had most of the conveniences she remembered. Her feet echoed on the flagstone floor of the dormitory they had spent so much time in. The curtains and blinds were shut, making the house an echoing tomb. For all she knew, no one had opened the house for the season.

Get a grip, she told herself. She'd get exactly what she needed for unforeseen circumstances. She ran through a mental checklist. She had thirty minutes at most to load her pack, grab the four-wheeler, and head out.

* * *

Roxi opened wide the metal barn doors that hid The Ranch vehicles. Roosting pigeons scattered at the noise. She squinted in the darkness. The sun slit dusty rays of light through the barn slats and she found the Jeep. She dusted off the seat, found the key under the mat, and on the third try it started. The faster she was on the road, the more likely he'd be to follow her.

Cowboy heard the Jeep before he saw it. It turned at a fork in the grassy road by the old school house. He scrambled up in his seat, started his truck and followed. He rubbed the dust around on the windshield with a dirty rag. His teeth were banging out of his head on this rocky excuse for a road. Those girls are in a hurry, he swore, as he tried to see through the dust-refracted sun rays blinding him. He grabbed his binoculars from the seat. He peered through the greasy lenses. They turned again. Where are they going? He gave his truck more gas. He wasn't going to lose them. Silly chicks. He peered through his binoculars, and saw a flash of blonde hair under a ball cap. She thinks she's a tomboy, I'll show her a thing or two. Wait till I get a hold of her. His tooth hurt, a throbbing pain that reverberated through his skull. He took another swig of the Coke beside him. He glanced down at the sack of stale donuts. What he needed was a pretty woman to make his breakfast. He ran his hand through his thick hair as he bumped along. Wait. There is only one chicky in the Jeep. Where had dark eyes got to?

Mariah jumped on the four-wheeler, her pack awkward with supplies. She stomped on the accelerator and gave it gas. It didn't start. After three futile tries she hopped off to check for gas. Empty. She took off her pack and left it on a metal barrel. She searched the shed and spotted a gas can in a corner covered in spider webs. Praying that it would be full, she grabbed the can, filled the tank, and checked the tires. She took a deep breath, telling herself to stay calm as she hurried. She pulled out into the yard. The coast was clear as she drove down the path. The sky was fall blue. The straw grass rustled in the breeze as it had for years. She was almost home free. Smiling at her near panic she recited her checklist. Then she realized she'd forgotten the pack. She circled the four-wheeler back to the house. Parking by the back door, she ran back into the house, unsure where she left it.

Cowboy took another swig of the flat syrupy black liquid. "Where's our girl?" He said aloud. "Is this a trick? That lawyer guy will throw me back in jail. I'm not going to fall for that." He ground out a scorpion absently with the toe of his boot. "Dangerous place. I ought to leave these girls out here. They can die of natural causes without my help. Then my job's done." He heard a noise in the distance. "Gotcha. Glad I'm a patient man."

Mariah charged back in the kitchen. A stab of pain in her heart froze her where she stood at the thought of Peter. Her eyes darted around the kitchen. Then she heard it. The distinct sound of a truck in the distance.

"Roxi?" She hoped. "No. She wouldn't come back here. Oh, no." She stood frozen at the thought of her next move.

CHAPTER 31 *Cowboy and Mariah*

Cowboy pulled the truck up to the house and stopped next to the four-wheeler parked by the back door. He knew she was inside. And he knew, she knew, he was back.

"Stupid girl." He decided to wait a bit. Crickets baked and crackled in the late afternoon sun. He got out of his truck, crouched low by the wheels, then he pulled out his blade, and sliced two of the tires on Mariah's vehicle. "Maybe she can just have a nice slide down into a canyon. When she tries to go she can't go far." He glanced around, satisfied there was no one else here. "One down. I'll be back little lady jest you wait." He climbed back into his truck to pursue his next victim. "I'm ready for a beer."

Mariah stayed very still inside, listening to the sounds of him leaving, her heart beat fast again. Her breath caught as she tried to calm herself and slow her racing heart. She counted as she breathed deliberately. "I'm fine. He hasn't touched me. He can't touch me." She wondered what he'd do now. He knew she was here alone. She listened to the truck sounds disappear into the distance. Once she was sure he'd gone, she went back outside to the four-wheeler. She noted the damaged tires. *Screw him,* she thought, *I can walk. It's even better now that it's getting dark.*

She realized she had left the pack in the barn and went back to retrieve it. As she reentered the house she locked all the doors once again. She leaned with her back against the door. Roxi had him on a wild goose chase by now. Mariah could only pray she was safe.

She rummaged in the cabinets and found a couple cans of herring fish steaks and a can of green beans. She listened to the sounds of The

Ranch as the light faded to grey outside. Pausing by the window, she studied the steel grey sky dimming to charcoal.

She remembered the time her family had spent Thanksgiving here. She couldn't quite place who had come—her Dad, her sisters, Kate and Kristen for sure. She'd brought several college friends. Dad had his entourage with him, along with Bill and Matilda. It was their family Thanksgiving, not Peter's family. Everyone had pitched in on the cooking. They had made a feast. Kate had made spanakopita from scratch. Mariah had made her famous desserts. She'd gone hiking on the cliffs earlier that afternoon before the feast. She remembered leaning over the edge into the bitter wind. The wind was so fierce it had held her up.

Later, when she was back indoors, in front of a blazing fire with plenty of food on her plate, the experience made her appreciate everything all the more. The contrast of the brutal weather made the warmth of family and belonging twice as good. She wished she felt as secure now. Peter had lived right here, eaten his meals in this kitchen. He'd had his last thoughts right here. He'd stepped outside thirteen years ago. That cowboy was the one who had blown him away.

One of the three teenagers who'd been there had pulled the trigger. It only took one gun to kill. Peter wasn't afraid that day. He didn't know. He walked out the door to greet his visitors. You always hear the impending arrival long before someone arrives. No one can sneak up. She realized this was all repeating itself right now. Cowboy was out there somewhere. She could be afraid. Or was he chasing Roxi? But he would be back. "This is dumb." She kicked herself. "What is he gonna do now? We think of him as harmless because he has done nothing but stalk us thus far. But now we're both out here alone, separated, with a known killer. Or maybe he's a chicken. I think I'm counting on that."

Once you've taken a life, it's easier to do it again, or so she had heard. But she felt at peace. She didn't know fear anymore. She had to focus—Peace and Power. She pulled her sense of purpose and her mission back into the task at hand. Medicine, just in case, she'd gather some essentials. She changed her clothes into jeans and thick socks. She padded into the living room, quiet accept for the wind whistling through the windowpanes. She perched on the window seat and

428

watched as the stream below rushed past. She began her list, the pad resting on her knee. Soon she found herself staring out the window at the water crashing into rocks below. It is easier to kill, once you have killed. She loved this place. Peter had loved this place.

CHAPTER 32 *Tristan and Hunter*

"You do have a plan." Hunter was using his fatherly tone.

"We may, but under the circumstances, I'm not telling you about it, considering who your friends are, you wouldn't want to know," Tristan said. "What would they think if they discovered you knew all along about the eventual downfall of oil dominance?" He noted Hunter's pained expression. "If you want to be one of the good ones, entice them to focus elsewhere. It will give us the chance to make a go of it. We may not succeed." He shrugged.

He got up and Hunter felt the warmth of Tristan's palm on his shoulder.

"We must try. We must see our task through. Surely of all people you can understand that? After all we have lived through, after all we have become. This is our destiny." He looked deep into Hunters' eyes as he spoke in a soft voice. He tried to speak beyond the man's ego, to a place that welcomed an inner perception.

A warmth flooded Hunter's insides in a very unfamiliar way. It was a feeling he recognized but had not experienced in decades, maybe since the birth of his children. Hunter saw Tristan was offering him a way out. An offer of peace, without a condemnation of what he had been about to do. He thought he should take this olive branch.

"Okay, Tristan, I see I cannot budge you. In that case I will take my leave."

Tristan wrapped his strong arms around him and gave him a hug.

Hunter nodded to the brothers and hiked back towards his truck. The four looked at each other, and each silently wondered: *Who was*

Hunter, really?

Tristan dropped some of his bravado as he watched Hunter's back slink down the trail and out of their camp. Who did this guy think he was? Would he do the right thing eventually? Even after their lengthy conversation he realized he had no idea. Why had his Mom spent so much time with him in San Antonio? He let out a deep breath as Hunters form disappeared. He hoped she was safe and would make it to camp soon.

He turned to his friends, "We must continue with our packing. It's time to catch up to the others."

"We can start at first light," Jack suggested, "and make it to the Petroglyphs for breakfast tomorrow."

"That sounds perfect," Tristan agreed. "I've grown accustomed to our spot here. I will miss this piece of woods."

"There is a lot of land here," Rob said. "Do you really think Hunter will come back?"

"Oh yeah, he will. He longs to. I just don't know if he will come to realize it in time. He's still caught up in saving the world as he knows it."

His statement hung in the air as the four stared off to the southeast in the direction Hunter had left. The sun slipped over the horizon, staining the sky red.

"Why didn't you tell him about the Indians?" Rob asked, "And the fresh springs and the total destruction that unleashing the oil will create? How about our truth pact?"

"I'm sure he knows about the springs and the devastation. He knows much," Tristan replied, half to himself. "The Truth. Yes, it's a universal law that solves many things. But remember, the secret of the Indians isn't ours to tell. They can reveal themselves to whomever they choose. They chose us. He will know the truth in time if he's meant to."

Jack raised his eyebrows. "Tristan, in our new technology we have ways of knowing what happens on this land. When we arrive at our destination we'll have our first dance with our new brothers."

"There is power in that. It will be a new kind of protection for us," Isabella said. "It's not us alone who wish this land to remain pure and untouched, to preserve the fresh water and fresh fish, and life-giving minerals to grow our plants. The great Mother Earth herself protects all of us, and this is her gift to us."

"The drilling is a huge concern," Jack said. "If they dare to drill and destroy it's tragic. But there are so many 'if's'; if the investors don't loan money, if the radar equipment gives a botched-up picture. How can they convince anyone the oil is still underneath eighty feet of limestone? Electromagnetic waves can be altered by intention."

"Thus we dance," Rob said.

"Thus we dance with our intentions," Isabella agreed.

"With our brothers," Tristan said. "When we get there."

"It's a long way," Isabella said.

"Yes. With us as the last group, we can pick up any stragglers," Rob said, "perhaps we can pick up Mariah."

The cloudless red sky darkened to indigo blue as the small group worked around the camp, rolling their bundles and erasing the fire. Tristan could just make out the cliff ahead as full dark descended upon the quartet.

"She's in good hands. I saw Jet. He will look out for her," Isabella said.

Once they settled in for the night, Isabella knelt on her red wool scarf, a starry blanket of darkness as her backdrop, and sang. The words rang clear in the night air. "*In my backyard, there's a ship that sails the sea...*" Isabella could feel silent support all around her, as sure as the stars that beckoned in the sky above. It helped her know that she was listening and doing the right thing. With that she knew she could watch for the signs of the hawk or the dragonfly and could guide Tristan, Jack, and Uncle Rob. They would be swift to Aqua Buena to join the others.

Their conversation died out with the sun, and Isabella's song lulled them all to quiet. Tristan felt Indian Point's magic surround him like a warm hug. They would be up and on their way in the still dark morning. Tristan stared up at the sky, watching as stars and planets pierced the darkness. Thoughts of the journey that lay before them colored his dreams with a sacred sleep. By the first hint of dawn on the horizon, they would reach the Petroglyphs. They held new meaning for him now.

CHAPTER 33 *Cowboy and Mariah*

Mariah didn't know how long she sat there, mesmerized by sounds and memories. The window before her was pitch black and she couldn't see a thing outside. She stared at her reflection mirrored back in the surface of the black glass. Her black hair, pulled back smooth, framed a face, open, almost innocent. Deep inside she felt wise, yet ageless, with much to learn on the path before her. She sat as though glued to the spot praying for her family; thinking, digesting, and readying herself for this next transition. She had pulled herself out of the quicksand of twentieth century life. Now she was in the thick of battle. The adrenaline of the chase made her momentarily forget she was finally headed into the deep—the forest of no return—into the interior to join with her Native American friends. All of the people she had met and befriended were now well on their way. And yet she would make it, only when and if, destiny somehow allowed it. She had waited for the cover of dark because her hawk trained eyes held the advantage. It was inky black outside now. Yet still she sat. The narrow way, she mused. Had it been her destiny only to invite and to lead people to the threshold? Was she going to pull off this one last ordeal? Of course she was. Breathe in the air of the possible. Fill herself with sureness. Courage, plain and simple, that was the word she sought. *Courage.*

She found her mantra again, *peace and power*. Harnessed energy feels like power. Power held together under a thin veil of peace. A harnessed force vibrating at a huge velocity. This was the unified-self theory she had arrived at when she had been imprisoned in the ennui of Hunter's cocoon.

A wail, a moan, an inhuman cry, snapped her back to the present.

She ran into the kitchen—the direction from which the sound had come—and peered into the darkness that enveloped the house. She'd left the shades up. She was actually glowing like a bug in a jar in the glass house. She turned the inside lights off fast and flipped on the outdoor floods. Nothing. Those lights were busted. She turned on the side porch light. A thin pale light trickled out to the yard and she saw a form sprawled on his belly in the grass. The voice whimpered and wailed.

"Help me." The cry was desperate.

Her first instinct was to run out and see. And then in her mind she flashed on Peter. Peter had run out to see the visitors without a thought or hesitation. Her hand flew to her mouth as she realized Cowboy was wriggling on the very spot that Peter's body had lain so long ago, soaking the earth with his blood. The huge blonde man lay on the ground, sprawled on his belly. As he twisted, the light hit his face. The guys face was white, with black sockets for eyes. His hands like claws grasped at his throat, tearing the grass, holding his leg. She stayed rooted, watching through the back door window. He screamed again, that fearful animal cry. It sounded of fear and anguish. Mariah could no more stand by and watch, than leave.

"What are you doing out there?" she called out.

"Help me. Please? Help me?"

"What are you doing, stalking me?"

"I'm gonna die. Help me. A snake, a rattler, my leg. I'm gonna lose my leg. Or die. I'm dying out here."

She felt no fear from this lost-soul cowboy wriggling on the bloody earth, on the spot of the bloody death that had claimed Peter. "What would Peter do?" She knew in a heartbeat, she knew. She came out and stood looking down at him.

"Look if you're sure it's a snake bite you will die. It's just a matter of time. Let's see, they will have to amputate your leg for starters. Shall I call an ambulance?" Her tone changed abruptly. "You got a gun? Show me your hands."

"Back there."

"You're stalking me without a gun?"

"Look I'm just doing what I was paid to do. I wasn't planning on

434

murder. But I don't want to die. Please?"

She shined the flashlight in his face, and around the ground where he lay. Cowboy's face was streaked with tears and dirt. His watery eyes streamed. He's just a boy, about thirty she guessed. "Look, you don't want to die out here in the field in the middle of nowhere far from any town. Let's get you up to the light. I can handle snakebite. Do you have a knife?"

His response was another scream as pain mingled with the fear of death. With her pulling, and his scooting with his other leg, they managed to get closer to the light from the back porch.

"I'll need your knife," she repeated.

He pointed to his hip pocket.

"Okay, now put this between your teeth and bite down. I have to get some stuff from inside."

In the kitchen she boiled water while she searched the cabinets for something she could use. She returned to him as he lay on the grass. Now she was all business.

"There now, you have to trust me and you have to calm down. I'm going to get the poison out first. I found plenty of stuff here."

After some tense concentration and work on the area, she'd managed to cut a large hole in his jeans. "I think we will be able to save your leg. Now, are you going to tell me what you're doing out here in the yard?"

"I was paid to watch you and follow you. And report back what was going on."

"I'm here having a little vacation. I have a project I'm working on and I needed some solitude to get it done. Suddenly, I have a vehicle with slashed tires and now I'm just as stranded as you are."

"What about the other girl?"

"Hey, you're on my turf, I'm asking the questions here. So you're not supposed to kill me? Just make my life miserable?" She nodded at the sliced tires.

"No. They want to know what you're up to. I told them I wouldn't do another murder. That was a nightmare."

"Whose nightmare? Not yours, I hope you realize."

"That was a long time ago."

"Do they pay well?"

"Not enough to die for." He choked the words.

Mariah brought her mouth to his hot flesh and sucked the poison out as Jet had instructed in survival training. She spit it out in the metal kitchen bowl. Mariah suddenly had a strange sensation as though Peter were here, watching. Peter, standing quiet with his hands in his pockets leaning slightly. He was helping her heal this boy. It was his way of forgiving his killer.

After a bit, Cowboy's agonized cries were more of a whimper. He said, "Did you know him?"

"Yes. He was a great friend. I had been camping, but the weather is turning colder. I decided to move inside."

The late moon rose and shone down its blue light on the two by the porch. The pain began to ease and cowboy calmed down. "Who are you? Why are you helping me?"

"I'm a healer," Mariah said simply. "Healers heal. We've got the worst of it now and you've got to rest."

"The pain," he moaned.

"I'll see what I can do." Mariah rolled her eyes toward heaven. This was a good candidate for drugs.

* * *

Roxi was watching from the darkness. Mariah and Cowboy. His moans were interrupted by the two talking. What a baby. When Mariah went back in, Roxi went around to the back door and rapped on it.

Mariah turned with a *now what* question in her eyes, "Roxi," she breathed. "Am I glad to see you! You scared me at first."

Roxi tiptoed as she entered mouthing, "What the hell happened?"

"Snake bite."

"What do we do with him?"

"Look, I know there are some pain killers in the medicine chest. We'll give him enough to knock him out for twelve hours. He needs the rest anyway, help that bite heal."

"Good idea. Get me his keys and I'll get his truck. I spotted it back there in the brush. I'll give him a ride far away from here after he's knocked out. By the time he wakes up he won't know where he is. I'll leave him in there. No keys. No gun. He won't bother you anymore. You'll be able to make it out of here."

"That's a good idea."

Mariah went back out with a wool blanket and a glass of water.

"What's your name anyway?"

"Jared. Thank you, ma'am. I am grateful."

"Your keys," Mariah extended her hand. She then handed him the pills. "May your pain be gone. The magic pill," she announced.

He greedily gobbled up four.

"Hey, save one for later. It will help you sleep."

"Why are you helping me? I could have died out here."

Mariah studied him for a long moment. Then she said, "Two deaths don't make a life, you know. I'm doing what I can. You have got another chance at life. See that you use it well. All you need now is rest. The worst is over." She covered him with the blanket.

It'd been a long time since anyone had tucked him in for the night. It didn't matter that his bed was a field under the stars. It felt good. Then he blacked out.

By the time Roxi came back with the truck Jared was out, his body a complete dead weight. The two girls heaved and shoved Cowboy into the back seat of his truck. Mariah tucked more pills in his pocket. Then she grabbed Roxi's arm and gave her a big hug.

"Do you need anything?"

"No, I'm good. I think I'd better get a move on while he's out."

"Please be careful."

Roxi went around and scooted in behind the wheel. Mariah picked his cowboy hat up off the ground. She dusted off the grey felt. She laid it on him, watching as his eyes flickered and were still again.

Mariah went around to Roxi, "He slit the tires on the four-wheeler so I have to walk."

"No you don't, I left the Jeep in the meadow."

Mariah let out a held breath. "I'm ready to be gone from here. Thank you, thank you."

"You should be able to make it now."

Mariah hugged her hard. Relief was palpable. "Wow Roxi, thanks. I'm going to miss you. You will make it? We gave him enough didn't we?"

"Sure, I'll be fine. I *will* be fine," she assured. Roxi melted into the hug, her eyes moist.

"You sure?"

"The wild west isn't for me." She wiped at her face and tried to smile.

Mariah looked up at the sliver of moonlight. "Thank you Roxi," she smiled through her tiredness. Beyond exhaustion now, she felt a calming energy all around her. She was wide-awake, and she was going to make it.

Once Roxi took off, she went back in the house, straightened her mess, grabbed her pack and headed out. She strode swiftly along the cedar tree path to the meadow. The moon lit her way. She had to walk along the streambed for a bit, and then turn left over the rise and the trees opened up to the field. The boulders along the stream glowed with a blue light.

As she walked to the Jeep she thought about Jared. Mariah's heart had stopped racing once she had poured her energy into her work. Healing took complete focus. It calmed her and sustained her. Now that it was over she felt buoyed and powerful. Sure of herself. Cowboy had taken Peter's life. The snake had attacked. And she had healed. She could no more stand and watch someone suffer than she could inflict suffering. A sudden jolt of fear went through her. Oh, what had she done? What would he do when he woke up miles from here?

Mariah found the Jeep and grabbed the keys from her pocket. What a good sound, she thought as it started on the first try. She estimated it would be a good ten miles before she found her guide. It would be either Jet or Daniel. She was sure he'd spot her before she found him. She was most likely now a week behind schedule. But we're all on Indian time.

Mariah had no clue how long she'd been walking. She'd parked the Jeep below Indian Point. Now she put one foot in front of the other on the path toward her future. Why had Hunter been so curious about the invention? The thought nagged at the back of her mind.

"Wa-hoo! Wa-hoo!"

The gentle call, blended in with the night noise interrupted her reverie. "Jet," she breathed his name.

"Wa-hoo." Jet glided up beside her and took her hand easily in stride. She stopped and reached up to hug him. His shoulders felt strong and sure. What a comfort. Mariah followed Jet with a blind faith. She was thankful to be alive, now, too exhausted to question anything.

CHAPTER **34** *Aqua-Buena*

David heard the familiar bird call in the distance. Tristan! David was, once again, perched on the cliff high above the plateau, endeavoring to spot them. Sure enough there was Tristan, moving smoothly, his golden limbs floating through the heat-hazy air. Three figures followed close behind him. Even at this great distance, David noticed the group was full of boisterous camaraderie. He saw the energy from here. *Grateful* was an understatement. His heart sang at the happy sight. With a pang, he realized everyone was here but Mariah. He rubbed his eyes to clear his vision. All of the groups were now accounted for at Aqua Buena. His joy and elation at seeing Tristan was suddenly tempered by longing. Only men followed in his wake. Wait, here his sweet Isabella was running ahead with her head held high. Their family was almost complete once again.

Tristan was back, elegant and taller, it seemed to David. "Good to see you, son," David said, and then embraced Isabella, Jack and Rob. "The others are waiting for you over there." David had called a meeting to be held in the meadow as soon as he had seen Tristan in the distance. The three embraced. Tristan recapped with David what he would say.

With swift strides, Tristan commandeered a large rock as an impromptu stage. With the bit of elevation it gave him, he looked out at the crowd. He addressed the expectant faces before him.

"I'm sure you're speculating about all the ensuing changes. You know why we've moved. Here's a bit about where we're headed. As you know, we were too close to the places used by visitors. We entertained many guests this summer. As a matter of fact, if we had relocated earlier, some of you would never have found our group. But our group, our new tribe, now one hundred and forty-four people, is perfect. We have moved deep into the interior. That feels good, *is good*. We have broken camp and left our gardens and fire circle. We have made a home of sorts in a nomadic way. Yet we're still on the move. Those who ultimately didn't jive with the strange minimal simplicity of the new lifestyle have left. May they find the peace they seek.

"I have been on another quest. Soon each of you will have the opportunity for your own Vision Quest. Actually this entire trip is a sort of quest." He spread his arms as he spoke. They were wide as wings, as if he wanted to hug the whole group at once. "Right now I have something of..." He paused as his voice caught, "great significance to share with you." There was a stony silence as he tried to compose himself.

He motioned to David, Rob, Paul, and Jack. "Dad...my friends, will you join me?" They came from different places in the crowd and stood at the front of the group flanking Tristan. He continued, "We have shared all of our skills for the past five months. We have studied, practiced, and learned teachings to impart to all of you. I know you have worked hard, but hopefully you have had fun too." He surveyed the serious faces of the group gathered around. His words were being lifted and carried off with the wind. The chill gusts made folks gather close together, forming a tight circle, to hear what he was saying. A flurry of fallen leaves twisted up in the chill wind. Isabella pushed her blowing hair from her eyes as she listened. Pat and Jody nodded their encouragement.

"What I'm trying to say is, that a group of us have gotten this information from Native Americans, who have been generous enough to share their ways with us. They have lived here since 1880, and they wish to share our journey."

Jack Java spoke up. "Actually, the tribe of Native Americans who live on this land are with us now. They are a lost tribe and this is their home." He watched the crowd to see if there was a flicker of comprehension. "Look around you, they are right here. They are among you." He gestured towards the wooded grove of cedars that flanked the meadow.

"They will lead us on the journey to the new Cave-Spring where we will make our home," Tristan said, picking up the thread. "With them," he added to clarify. "From now on you will be taught one-on-one. Each family will be guided in the arts of survival. Perhaps more appropriately termed, *the art of life*.

"Our education will be swift now. We're very close to our new home. Tonight we will rest here. Then in the morning with a fresh start, we will continue to our new home at the celebrated Sacred Cave-Spring."

People turned to look at one another. "What is he saying? They are with us now?" They looked around and noticed that quite near, next to their friends, were other friends. Quiet and erect, still, hidden in the shadows of the tall trees, there were others. They were dressed in colorful woven shawls over thick shirts and breeches. Somehow they were there. They stood, quiet as trees, as if they had been there all along. Folks soon realized there was a lot more going on around them than met the eye. That perhaps they just hadn't been conscious of it, but the presence of these new people seemed both comforting and familiar."

Tristan addressed the group, "Are there any questions?"

One man raised his hand. He was standing by a tree and staring as if mesmerized by an apparition.

Tristan nodded for him to speak.

"How did you meet them and know they were here?" He asked.

A woman with a toddler on her hip spoke up. "Why do they want to help us?"

"How long have they been here?" someone shouted.

Everyone was asking questions at once. It became a noisy din as people jostled.

Tristan had to shout above the stirring crowd. "These are all good questions. I have many answers. Why don't we set up camp and gather around this evening's fire? All of us, David, Jack, Rob, Paul, John, Pat, and Jodie, can tell you some stories. That will be the best way to address your questions."

"Good idea."

Tristan hopped down, light as a gazelle on his feet.

Together everyone made a swift pile of stones to circle the fires for the night. Tristan's group set up a minimal camp of bedrolls and lean-tos. Then they gathered around the fire to eat. Soon many voices were raised in song, with drummers drumming. Everyone was mesmerized by the unsuspecting additions, staring at the newcomers, they spoke little. Families hushed the little ones.

The older ones gathered around the fire to listen to a new song as the Indians drummed and chanted.

"That was a huge burden off my chest," Tristan said.

David patted him on the back. "Son, you did well. It's a hard concept to share. Everyone's too tired and shocked to say anything."

"They are most likely relieved to know we have help and are not trying to do everything on our own. Only ten of the natives joined us tonight. That's not enough to alarm anyone."

"I'm glad we waited until now. I had planned to spring it earlier. But then I realized I should wait for you," David said. "This way, we're all together."

As the parents settled the young ones, Tristan joined the teens at their fire circle. He sat cross-legged and warmed his hands in the blaze; his palms open with his fingers spread wide.

"Do you remember Thanksgiving? We still celebrate it. One of the most fun, low stress, enjoyable celebrations we have. Can anyone tell me about the first Thanksgiving?" Tristan asked.

Michael Alexander spoke up. "Well, when the first pilgrims from England had survived their first year, they wanted to celebrate with a feast prepared from the harvest. It was the custom of the Native Americans to make peace offerings and give gifts in gratitude. They also traded and bartered as a matter of survival. Breaking bread together meant a truce."

"What kind of truce, do you think?"

"It meant, we will share our land and game with you. You are welcome to share this wealth with us."

Tristan smiled at his cousin, and picked up the story as others began to gather around. "That is the origin of Thanksgiving. It's part of the Native American culture to give thanks. Everything nature gives to them, plants, animals, or a good hunt, they in turn give thanks. It is called honoring the Sacred Source. The Earth Mother. Somehow, European Americans, didn't learn that lesson. Of course, history has taught us that any kind of truce once made was completely broken. All promises to the Native Americans were eroded. We won't rehash the gory details of wars and murders, as more settlers came, and more countries laid claim to the Americas.

"But the intention of the Native Americans—the Iroquois Nation, the Cherokee, and the Choctaw—was always one of teaching. They knew we were completely ignorant as regards survival on this abundant land. With the language barrier, they were unable to communicate, or teach us, *their* way. Yet, they knew how to thrive. They had lived out here for one thousand years or more. Yet, we have managed to destroy the prairie, the buffalo, and countless other sensitive ecosystems that were thriving, providing sustenance for these Indian brothers of ours, in a mere two hundred years."

"The massive battles that ensued were a necessity of defending their wives, children, and homes. They weren't possessive of the land itself. They didn't lay claim to the land. The land is held sacred to them.

"In the spirit of co-existence, on this lonely planet in the middle of the galaxy, in our tender ecosphere, the Native Americans have offered to take us by the hand, and show us how to really live—to live with Nature, in harmony."

Tristan continued, "There is much to learn and experience. We have been invited to do so on these sacred lands. Lands they have kept private for one hundred and thirty years. Our new friends have great knowledge. They were unable to communicate their methods long ago because it was completely natural to them. They couldn't verbalize or communicate their ways. But now, all that has changed. All the basics we have mastered will be put into play to deepen our perceptions."

Rob nodded, "We had to keep mum about it, because we wanted to purge our group, to make sure we had the largest inner circle we could, before revealing excessive secrets. We didn't want to compromise their presence here. Now, as we move deeper into the interior, our tracks will disappear and no one will know we're here. Of course, there are a few tricky pieces. Mariah has been left in transition since her trip to San Antonio. One of the scouts will bring her to join us soon."

"There you have it. Tonight let us sleep with the sun. We have one more day of travel to Cave-Springs," Tristan concluded. He turned to Rob, "Mariah's not here?"

"Surely she will be here soon," Rob said.

The flames reached high towards the indigo sky. An Indian summer breeze chilled the air. The gathered circle of friends held hands in silence. Tristan knew they were each grasping the news in their own way. Each would come to enlightenment in time. He felt chills at the thrill of contained excitement. He was ready for the changes he had yet to fathom.

CHAPTER 35 *Cowboy*

Cowboy-Jared opened his eyes and stared straight up at the rusted spot on the ceiling. His tongue felt thick in his mouth, his throat parched.

"Water. Where am I?"

He sat up. His head throbbed. He regretted the move. This was his truck. It was morning. Which morning? That must have been some party last night, he thought, but he didn't remember it. Parking lot. Everything ached as he crawled out and planted his boots on asphalt. He threw up.

Roxi was tucked into a booth in the diner. It was early, six a.m. Both hands hugged a mug of black coffee as if it were a life support. She didn't know the name of the dusty town she'd landed in. All towns look the same at 3:00 am. Even Motel 6 looked good at that hour. She'd driven long into the night. Putting at least three hundred miles between Cowboy and his target. She'd blown her Lakeville meeting spot, but she didn't care; she didn't trust Hunter anyway. He was a lawyer after all, one on the other side. Now she could abandon her ward and use his truck, or just leave him be, truck and all, then find her own way home. She was too exhausted to be hungry but she had a vague notion she should eat. Maybe she'd find a truck driver and catch a ride back to the nearest city. Her fingers shook as she fumbled through her purse for a cigarette. The door banged shut, and she looked up. Cowboy, covered in dirt, grime, and yuck, limped up to the counter.

"Water," he mumbled. A middle aged waitress, Nancy, according to the plastic tag pinned to her pink uniform, complete with stained apron, put a glass of water in front of him.

"Coffee?" After a moment she let out a big sigh. She said, "You should have a doctor look at your wound."

"You think so, little lady?" He winked in an attempt to lay on the charm. "I'll get to that," he said, as he pushed a greasy hunk of hair behind his ear.

Roxi's ears perked up from her spot in the booth to follow their banter. She realized he'd awakened far ahead of schedule. Now what? She hadn't even snagged a trucker yet. She hid low in the booth and peeked out from her hair. He was unbelievable; winking at the waitress. A flash popped in her head, she still had the truck keys in her jeans pocket. The waitress was offering Tylenol to Cowboy by this time; she could see he was definitely in good hands. She looked totally taken in with his sob story as she arched one drawn-on eyebrow.

Roxi jumped in the truck. The smell of diesel assaulted her nostrils. She punched the accelerator and gave it fuel. She felt strong, in complete control behind the wheel. As she backed up to pull out, a ray of new sun shot through the dusty window into the diner, illuminating the Cowboy at the counter. He tipped his hat.

"Wa-hoo!" Roxi shouted as she hit the highway, the morning sun on the rise. Sunlight shimmied on the endless miles of flat Texas road stretched out before her. It was okay. They were going to be okay. She knew Mariah was safe, and Cowboy wasn't even planning to go anywhere. She threw her half-smoked Marlboro out the window. Her hand went to the radio to find some music to drive by.

CHAPTER 36 *Metamorphosis*

Anya climbed the cliff over the deep spring-fed pool with ease. She placed one foot in front of the other on the narrow path high above the water. The packs of extra weight demanded a more cautious step. Anya kept her body close to the cliff wall, and then stepped gingerly over the foot wide crevice without looking down. She followed John as though connected and the others were doing a good job of mirroring that. There were ten teens and a few others in this group. They had succeeded in trekking behind, and ascending above, the waterfall. This last leg of the hike took the first group over seven hours. Water pounded loud, a deafening sound. It welcomed them, although it drowned out there whoops, cheers and joyful laughter.

Anya caught her breath as she pulled herself up and swung her legs over the final rock ledge. She stared in awe at the magnificence that greeted her. The waterfall plummeted a good thirty feet. It fell into the cool depth of the crystalline pool. The brilliant white limestone that lined the pool, made a perfect resting spot. Wide flat stones like a series of tables surrounded the water. The light was strong and bright. An occasional cool breeze off the water chilled her sweat-drenched neck.

The second group arrived soon after. They found the first arrivals napping around the water like lions after a hunt. Max was leading this one. She had worked hard to catch up with Nikki, Anya, and the rest of the teens. Competition with teenagers was alive and well. Pat would be here soon with the third group.

"The land of milk and honey," Max breathed.

"Well, certainly water," John replied. "Where's Isabella? Is she with your group?"

"I'm not sure. Looks like she's taking after her Mom, disappearing acts and all," Max answered.

"I'm here, I was just helping Mason a bit." Isabella ran to John's side.

"This place has a wonderful lushness to it. It's fragrant," Josie said, fanning the water spray that tingled on her skin. "I would love to swim, but I'm too tired to peel all this stuff off me."

"You grown-ups. We girls are prepared," Anya said as she, Michael, and Nikki dropped the bundles off their sticky backs. Anya and Nikki jumped right in. John stepped back to watch as Isabella made a perfect swan dive. Michael, stepped on, yelped. Sarah, more cautious, waded in.

The land was formed in a way that allowed several tributaries to come in from the surrounding hills. The meadow a couple of hundred yards away was to become their new home. This had been the Indians' home for the last one hundred and thirty years. They had lived, gathered, and fished from this piece of paradise. Further down were the headwaters, where a wall of springs with water gushed out and spilled down moss-laden rocks.

"Here we have the Sacred Cave-Springs," Tristan said, inhaling deeply. "Paradise Found."

Max and Josie glanced up in unison. As usual he had arrived quietly. They smiled their greetings at him.

CHAPTER 37 *Emerald*

The warmth of the sun on her face brought a smile to her lips, as Mariah lay peaceful, and more content than she had felt in days. Her eyes still closed, her mind tried to play back the movie in her mind. She had been dreaming. The thoughts were a tumble of sweet sadness, and familiar faces of friends she hadn't seen in years. Her eyes popped open, she stared into the brilliant blue sky of midday. A dragonfly buzzed by her forehead. She swatted as she abruptly sat up, startled.

Where in the world am I? She propped herself up on her elbows, and noticed the rich hues of the Indian blanket covering her while she slept. *This is a beautiful blanket,* she thought, stroking the soft texture, *but how did it get on me? Am I having blackouts?* She realized she was surrounded by trees on three sides. She lay on the soft grassy meadow at the edge of a forest. Her head arched around in all directions. There was an emerald green stretch of clear cold water by her other side.

She gazed at the sunlight sparkling diamond tips on the mini-waves. Life was good. The breeze blew a waft of sage smell up from the Indian blanket. She was alive, she realized, as she stretched and looked around in awe at her strange surroundings. That's what the miracle was. She was alive; alone, warm, content, and alive.

She had endured the ordeal, defected the conflicts, and survived. The Garden had let her back in. Yippee! She was here. Life was good and nothing else mattered. She began imagining how she would live on nuts, persimmons, kumquats, and berries, by the shore of this emerald lake. The thought contented her. As she got to her feet she realized how stiff her body felt. She dropped her clothes and stepped slowly through the mossy shore into blessedly cool water. She swam deep with her eyes open, stretching every muscle as she kicked and did the breaststroke. Her mind went through the mental checklist:

Gather wood for the fire before dark; try a new recipe with the herbs she could find in the new location. As she pulled herself out of the water, a shadow fell across the rocks. She looked up; Jet was standing there, accentuated by his long, dark, shadow.

Ah, Jet. His hair hung like a long black cape down his back. His skin glowed bronze from the sun. His face looked grave. It made Mariah want to laugh, just to cheer him up. His green eyes showed concern as he watched her before he spoke.

He handed her the blanket. She gratefully wrapped herself in the reds and blues. She shook her head swiftly to free her hair of water.

"Jet?" Her voice was a question,

"Do you remember?"

"Huh?"

"Do you know where you are? Or why?"

She tilted her head to knock water out of her ears.

"Do you remember your name?"

"Name? The blanket began to slip. She wrapped it more tightly around her. She began to shiver a little bit in the sunlight.

"Follow me; I have a fire ready in the woods."

"I like it here."

He walked away. She stood stubbornly. She gazed longingly at the water, although it was now too late to go back in. She shrugged as she gathered up her clothes. She glanced up to see him moving into the teal green darkness. She thought it better to follow him now, ask questions later. The grass was cool and soft between her toes. She stopped and lifted her heavy wet hair from her back and squeezed the water out. The wet droplets chilled her as they fell across her back.

Peace and power, the words echoed in her head, like a lost friend. "Wait, I'm coming." She tiptoed, gracefully dancing up to his side. "You look so serious."

Soon he paused by a fire, he motioned to the dark opening in the cliff, barely a cave. She slipped inside to change. She ran out to get back to the fire's warmth, fanning her hair as she gazed into the flames. He stood still as a sentinel without speaking. His chamois shirt looked soft and touchable. She vaguely wondered why she never noticed how handsome he was before. She stood on tiptoe to kiss his cheek with a feather light touch. He turned and gazed at her with soft eyes. He pointed at the fire. She turned to look, to see what he was seeing. She stared at the warm, orange flames; mesmerized by the lick of red, yellow, gold, and blue that glowed on the old wood. The smell of cedar filled her nostrils. Memories came with the smell. Thoughts of her dad, loving the fire.

Where was he now? Long gone she sensed with sadness. *And Peter and his Ranch, gone too*. She stared longer as the day around her faded and the air grew chill. *Why was Jet being serious?* He was killing the mood. This was a mood of magic and wonder. A kind of anticipation had taken over her. Something was about to happen. A great mystery would reveal itself, she was certain. If she spoke it would blow it. It was in the air. She watched his still as stone profile, unwilling to intrude on his thoughts. The light fissured across his features. What was happening? As she stared back at the fire she tried to concentrate. The cedar smell, the smoke, the flame. Her brain was in a fog. Some thoughts were knocking, trying to get in. But at the same time she didn't want to know. The peace. The peace was amazing. Her children. She had children. *Where were they? And David. Where was he?*

This place. *Where was she?* It seemed familiar, but she knew she had never been here before. It didn't really matter, she liked it here. It was peaceful. She could stay, if only she knew where her family was, knew they were safe. She turned her face toward Jet, her eyes full of questions. He clasped both her hands in his big brown ones.

"You must trust me now, Mariah. If you are ready, we must prepare to leave soon. First we will eat." He opened the leather pouch he had tied to his waist. He extracted a piece of cornbread and honey with some goat cheese. "We have already come a long way. But we have one more step on our journey." A new anguish replaced the happy glow.

"It's the others."

"Yes. It is. The time we have shared is precious to me and I shall treasure it always. The others need you. As hard as this is for me, it is time." Then he opened his arms and held her. "As much as I want you for myself," His voice trailed off, the words lost in hair that smelled of sage and gardenias.

She wasn't sure what was happening to her but she could sense something different in him. The way he held her. The way she was beginning to feel in his embrace.

She jerked back at once. "Jet, I do trust you. But how long have I been here. In this meadow?"

"Not long, not too long."

"The past feels like a fog to me. I feel perfect, content and warm here now. I don't even feel like me. Not the old me." She pushed him away, "What are you saying? I have not been myself. I know we were friends, are friends. Nothing has happened to change that." Her voice rose in a bit of a panic. "Has it?"

"Oh, no. I was waiting for you to wake up and come to yourself. I know you trusted me. But I dared to hope." He blushed, "but no. I was merely waiting. I can see that it's all my mistake. Still, you did need the rest. I can see I have harbored some wishful thinking." He choked on his mumbled bit of a speech, "The others need you." She clung to his embrace. His soft clothes were velvety against her cheek and breast. He held her shoulders as he gazed down into her face. Her gold-green eyes were penetrating, almost fierce. "It is good. You are ready I can see that. But it must be your choice. I cannot choose for you."

"I understand."

He motioned for her to sit down. They sat cross-legged facing each other on the blanket. "Where is everyone? Your friends... and mine, for that matter?"

"It's just us in this place. For a bit."

"How long?" She waited while the silence hung in the air. "Why?"

"You were tired. We came here so you could rest before completing the journey. You seemed fine and happy for the past few days. But you were partially drugged from the snake venom. I have been feeding you a vegetarian diet of herbs, corn, and also a special milk from the cactus that should revive and cleanse you. It's almost as if a type of amnesia had come over you. That is the only way you could truly rest. You have been through much. Now that you have begun to remember you want to leave."

"How long? How much time have I lost in this state? In this

contented fog?" Her voice had grown louder as she became panicky over the missing hunk of time.

"It's okay. Relax. Enough time. You needed this rest believe me. Your energy has changed. You have changed. You have become, I don't know how to say it, but Indian. You have become one of us."

Shadows of concern flickered across her face like light through a butterfly's wing. And then they dropped like a cloth. The pure countenance of serenity came back upon her features. It was tangible. Her old mantle of worry and tragedy fell effortlessly away, and left her clear-eyed, and knowing, with an inner sense of peace. She listened to his melodious voice telling the story of her days in this strange paradise. He held her hands still from the scrabbling in the grass they were doing. The warmth from his touch immediately flowed through her palms, and flooded into her heart, and head. She felt a calm clarity within and without in the very air around them. She allowed herself to look once more into Jet's clear green moist eyes. With a start she realized they mirrored her own.

"You have been under my care for some days and nights. You have swam and sunned and rested. Climbed the hills," he gestured expansively, "fished for our dinner. You have grown tan and brown..."

"As an Indian." She finished for him. She stared longer as the day around her faded. The pond became silver in the last light before an indigo night seemed to steal over the place.

She was already tan and fit, but now she felt softer and supple too. Her eyes glowed green with the dark ring around them that made them mysterious. Her dark hair glowed with a reddish halo. He played with her hand now, as if reading her palm. His long thin fingers stroked delicately as they traced the lines. The connection was electric. She tingled all over but did not dare betray the fact. A new understanding began to dawn on her, about how close they had become.

"Do we need to go back? Everyone's surely left camp by now."

"You remember."

"I think so."

"It's like we're twins. You and I are more alike than you know. To me you will always be Wind Angel."

"Wind Angel?"

He smiled and shrugged, "It is what all of us call you. You will rest this night, and in the morning at first light, we shall leave this place."

All the fight had gone out of her. All that argumentative spunk seemed far away now, like she was watching her past self from a far distance. *Peace and power* her mind chanted. And yet this was her real self. Her true core was calm as polished stone. Tonight she was just Mariah, or perhaps Wind Angel. She could get used to that, cross-legged by the fire, under an indigo sky, somewhere on The Ranch.

CHAPTER 38 *Gathering*

The silver ribbon of a stream carved its way, shimmering on a stone bed lined with ferns, moss, and crystals. David sat on the cliffs above Cave-Spring. He found comfort in high spots. He looked out over the vast distance of the space that surrounded their new home. As though expecting something, every so often he gazed up and out far. His two children, Tristan and Isabella, were together there by the water, bantering like they used to. Things were almost back to normal.

* * *

Mariah held Jet's hand as they walked. She stepped lightly on the rocky path. They were in a creek-draw, following a lazy waterway with only a single thread of water. The sun in the distance beckoned through the darkness of the woods. A ray of sunlight hit the silver thread and shimmied. As they moved closer, her grasp on Jet's hand, as though to a lifeline, was hard and sweaty. Her heart pulsed.

Dark, silhouetted shapes, moved in and out of the sun path ahead. Everything was just patterns of dark and light. Her heart beat fast and her eyes couldn't focus. Her feet kept marching. This path of pine needles and leaves was soft now. As her eyes concentrated on the dark shapes, her heart jumped to her throat. People, those dark shapes were people. Her people? They seemed familiar, here in this strange magic place. Her pace picked up. The shawl wrapped around her cotton dress billowed about like wings, as she ran towards the light. She dropped Jet's hand and ran full out.

"Wind Angel," Jet said as he watched her run.

She stopped suddenly, as David's back was solidly right in front of her. She was suddenly shy. Worried, and so close she could see his distinct form. But was she here on the same plane as he was? Breathing the same air as he? She almost cried with hope and desire. He didn't seem to be aware of her presence, her nearness. She approached gingerly. She stretched her hand out to touch his shoulder. He brushed at his sleeve, still talking to someone down below that she couldn't see. She grabbed his arm more firmly.

"David," she spoke aloud. He turned and looked, their eyes met.

"You!" His voice caught. "You are here. At last." He opened his arms and held her close to him. Mariah wrapped them both in the white shawl and they stood, cocooned.

Tristan and Isabella looked up from the shore below. They were at the deep pool of Cave-Spring.

"Look, she's back!" Tristan said, as he pointed upwards.

There they were; both parents. David and Mariah were as one form, a dark shape against the cobalt sky. They watched the strange unmoving monolith of form of the two in a strong embrace. Tristan turned to Isabella, "She's here. She's back with us. We're united again."

Isabella was ecstatic. "I knew she'd make it. It was the *when* I was worried about." Isabella's neck arched as she threw her head back and stared up at the two of them. She put her arm around her brother, and sighed. Then they looked around at their group lounging by the deep pool.

The waters were transformative, they knew that. They loved watching the surprised looks on people's faces as they experienced the crystalline healing power. Tristan was glad that absolutely nothing was planned for the next three days except feasting and dancing. Their cousins, the Native Americans, were hosting them. Everyone was on their own time to rest, wander, and revitalize.

"Tristan, in all this excitement, you have never shown us the gift you received on your quest," Isabella said.

"Oh, yes." His eyes lit up. "I was waiting for Mom to be here."

On the cliff, Jet gave David and Mariah a blessing, and the two thanked him, as they renewed the vows they had made long ago as newlyweds, and again in New Mexico. They were about to embark on a new life together.

"Did we just renew our wedding vows?"

The two kissed and then turned. For the first time they were aware of the others gathered below by the spring. They held hands as they scaled down the cliff.

Beside the shore, a grove of weeping willow trees framed large limestone rocks, bleached white, and smooth from the sun. Mariah grabbed her two kids, Tristan and Isabella, and held them to her.

"You made it back safe!" she exclaimed, as she looked at Tristan. "Thank you for leading your group through safely, Isabella. I'm proud of you, both of you. We're all here." She was ebullient as she glanced around. "I feel absolutely blissful to be here." She squeezed them both again. "We're all lost together, in this forgotten place, with this forgotten tribe." She then found a spot on the edge of a large rock, and placed her tired feet in the water. "Oh Tristan, I nearly forgot, what was the gift or the invention? Did you get it on your last quest?" Mariah's eyes darted around at a lot of blank faces.

"The Dynamo-eterna, I have kept it safe for your return," Tristan said. "Ancient One told me to bring it to you first; and no other. A lot has happened around here. First, once I got back to Indian Point, it took three days to hike here."

"Tristan's become the wise leader," David explained.

Mariah's eyes questioned her son.

"The gift was more than a simple object. It is the blue prints and instructions for a new way to solve the energy issues on our planet. I need to go get it, so you can see for yourself." He took off.

"Oh, Isabella, David, have I been on a trip! I was afraid I wouldn't find you. I have been walking for days it feels like. All the days melded into one endless trek. I have lost all track of time. I'm so glad to be here." Her eyes looked out to the endless blue above their heads.

Isabella said, "Our Indian friends are hosting us. Tomorrow is the full moon and they have prepared a great mysterious feast. It is wonderful. They have all but disappeared for days working on it. It seems to take the whole village to prepare the feast. We're left on our own to explore. And this water is transformative. Transcendent or something like that. How do you feel now that you have been sitting here awhile? With your feet in it?"

"Awake. Totally awake, revitalized. I feel clear. The food from the harvest, were you all able to pack it and bring it here?"

"Oh, yes, it's all here. They were shocked when we presented it to them. They are shy, but you could see their delight at the bounty of fresh food. I can't wait to see how they prepare it."

"Aho," Tristan greeted them, holding a small bundle wrapped in a soft cloth in front of him. Isabella spread the cloth out on a stone platform. Tristan laid the crystalline, cube-shaped object upon it. The jewel-like box was ten by ten by ten. Tristan's face was calm, with a deep sense of satisfaction. "This is a scale model," he explained." One physical example."

The base was made of slate, but the other five sides were of alabaster. He opened the top and removed a small stone from within. When he fastened the lid back in place, the three prongs of spun silk filament ignited into a light. The whole cube pulsed and glowed. "When the three prongs touch we have light and heat. To the right is brighter, to the left it's weaker."

"So, here it is." Tristan looked up from this precious object. "I have it now. What do I do with it? Where do we go from here?" He looked from his mom to Isabella then David. No one spoke.

"It's tiny," Mariah said.

"This is a light generator. The real gift is the blue-prints for the perpetual motion machine, I have yet to construct. Yet, it's hard to imagine this has all the power generating force they say it does. I have all the blue-prints for both; Rolls of diagrams on parchment. They're in my tent." He gestured over his shoulder. "The irony is, we don't need it. We've learned to live this way, by the sun. The night is a welcome rest after a busy day. A campfire under these brilliant stars is pure tranquility."

"Unfortunately, the world out there is still trying to blow its brains out over oil," Mariah said.

"The Ancient One saw us as One, when we didn't know enough to see each other that way. Ah, the Law of One. Now he understood."

Rob greeted Mariah with a brotherly bear hug. "I'm glad you're safe! It's been a long couple of weeks. Eventful ones of course. It's just that Hunter showed up right before we broke camp."

"He did? I didn't realize that."

"Tristan, Jack, and I were at Indian Point, stalling, awaiting your return. He said you had a hang-up with someone named 'Cowboy,' who had been stalking you and Roxi ever since you left The Ranch."

"That's true, but I didn't want anyone to worry."

"Tristan can catch you up on that conversation. He said you had it under control, so we went on."

Mariah's eyebrows shot up at that one. She'd felt quite threatened.

"After a few days of travel we all showed up here. Tristan and I brought up the rear with all the stragglers. You still hadn't showed. David's been practicing faith and not letting on, but I know he was concerned. I swear that man's a saint."

"I'm glad to be here now. What I went through was necessary for my growth. I'm prepared to truly *be* here. Not just in body, but in mind and heart as well."

"And Roxi?"

Mariah looked at the dirt when he asked. "She was a great help." She looked straight at him. "I couldn't have done it without her. She was my back up when dealing with Cowboy. I will tell you the details later. I couldn't have done it alone. You need to know she wanted to go back. She's happy for you, and she's where she wants to be."

It was a beat before Rob had his voice back. He didn't speak. Mariah continued, "So your group has been here a while? Tristan mentioned you hadn't had the welcome feast. Or the sixth Dance yet."

"Right on cue, that's right. We were waiting for you. And the full moon of course. The Moon is full tonight. And see you made it after all." He offered her his arm as he added, "Let me show you around." He continued as they walked. "Tristan found the Hall of Records from Atlantis, you know."

"No, I didn't know that. He's modest. He didn't exactly explain his trip to me. He just showed me the gift, the invention."

"Well the 'gift,' as you all refer to it, is from the Lost Hall of Records from Atlantis."

"Wow, come again, can you explain that twist to me?"

"Of course I can." As he spoke he led her to a shimmering pool of spring water surrounded by bone-white rocks, making the perfect stone enclosure. "Step into the rejuvenation pool while I explain."

The air was chill. Mariah noted the soft steam rising from the water and acquiesced. She spread her shawl and removed her dress exposing her black bathing suit beneath. She lowered herself into the warm water. The force pummeled her arms and shoulders.

"I'm sure you're aware many groups have been searching for the Lost Hall of Records," Rob continued."

"I think since Plato first spoke about Atlantis," Mariah agreed.

"Many thought Atlantis was in Greece, in Santorini. But Edgar Cayce, the sleeping prophet, asserted in his readings that the American Indians, he termed them the red race, were the original Atlanteans. He said Atlantis had disappeared in the Atlantic Ocean, and placed the lost continent near North America."

"Seems like it would be hard to lose a whole continent."

Rob chuckled, "You have a point there. Regardless, Tristan shape-shifted and followed Daniel. He ended up on a cliff, and soon found a cave. He wasn't at all sure at that point where they were. He assumed New Mexico or Arizona by the terrain. He described going from rushing cold water to climbing rocky cliffs. He could have been on the Coast of Maine or in Morocco for all anyone of us knows. He traveled by magic.

"The Shaman there, who Tristan refers to as 'Ancient One,' allowed him to spend time reading the scrolls. And then he was instructed to bring the mock-up of the invention and the blue prints back with him."

Mariah interrupted, "That is an amazing story. I guess he had a chance to share a lot with you on your long hike."

"That's true." Rob assumed his teaching tone. "I'm quoting here *'will the beautiful people that have incarnated on the planet manage to destroy the place before they have a chance to evolve to the next level'*? Straight from the Ancient One."

What a natural he is, thought Mariah.

"The thinking regarding Atlantis is, that when the continent blew up and sank into the sea, many people were destroyed. But the priests who had foretold the destruction were able to escape in boats. They landed on shores of many different continents. Some went to Greece and others landed in South America, settling in the Andes and Peru. That is why you see similar symbols and structures like pyramids in these far-apart places. Even the native tribes, the Maori in New Zealand, use the spiral as a sacred symbol. This is also prevalent in Egypt and Greece."

Mariah knew this, but it was nice to hear such a concise description.

"Some people think that mankind has always needed a boost from friendly Angelic beings that periodically provide help, or clues, or nudges."

"Or a huge shove," she interrupted.

"I was going to say 'push', to help direct our evolution."

"You know, blowing up a whole continent, like you are suggesting, is more like a shove."

"I'm not suggesting this is accepted by many as fact."

"I get it, please continue."

"I think the pattern is to step in when we're eroding into oblivion or are about to self-destruct. Which is the case here. And also we are on time with the Mayan calendar, and the forefathers of the Maya most likely originated in Atlantis."

"How did Atlantis come to such a horrific demise?"

"It was the scientists. Their inventions and technology were moving fast in the wrong direction. They were beginning to clone humanoid bodies. They thought of them as human; they were trying to create a slave class. But of course, they were man-made, therefore soul-less, not

463

to be confused with humans, who are created by God complete with souls."

"I agree, there are a lot of parallels with our culture today. Mega -biological research, and stem cell research, and cloning body parts. Who knows how far they have gotten in secret laboratories?"

"It seems that God gets upset when certain lines are crossed. And then environmentally speaking, progress runs fast down the wrong path. We miss something, and have to be redirected."

"Redirected and preserved. Sometimes, I think that our group's being here is much like the boarding of the Ark before the lands were flooded. We have gathered a diverse bit of the human race into this safe haven or Ark, if you will, to protect us, while the storms outside rage. The battles and the wars go on, yet our men, women, and children will be safe."

"Complete with some from Atlantis who know how to survive through this next shift," Rob finished for her.

"You're right. You mean the Law of One. That is what this is all about. Remember, they say that Geronimo has been consciously reincarnating to see this through. To make sure his people join with our culture so we can survive."

"They know a lot. Way more than they tell us. I think they have legends that explain what is about to occur. They spend generations preparing their own people with stories."

"Much like when the Essenes were preparing for the coming of the Messiah. They were not sure when he would arrive. But they could read the signs, and they readied their people to birth him into their community," Mariah said.

"Psychic awareness has been increasing rapidly in the last eighty years. Children are born remembering their past lives. Ancient secrets from mystery schools are being made clear so everyone can learn and study to become enlightened. Knowledge of the numinous for those who will hear. But that is what Jesus said, '*Those who have eyes let them see, and for those with ears let them hear*'."

"I know, we look without seeing, and people speak, yet we're sometimes deaf to the full meaning. Yet all who are vibrating at this frequency are hearing the call. They come and join in the new way. I mean, look at all those who found us. It was random. And yet Cowboy tried to kill me, and he was bit by a snake," Mariah said. "He was eager to get out of here after that. No one wants us that bad. Not bad enough to die for. There's a vibrational safety net over us now. We've been guiding others to raise their vibration to create this higher frequency within. It's working. I noticed that the larger the group who gather, the magnetic pull intensifies. This magnetic power draws others to this place."

"Tonight is our first joint feast. I wonder what things will be like this time next year?" Rob said. "The Law of One is happening now, and we are right here in it."

Tristan and Jack Java, joined Rob and Mariah.

"True." Tristan came and sat cross-legged on the soft fern rock beside his Mom. Removing his moccasins, he placed his tired feet in the warm pool. "But how and to whom? How do we give it? If Hunter gives it to Scofield or Gilbert."

"What?"

"That's what he wants to do. Can't beat 'em join 'em logic. It's a great invention."

Mariah was incredulous. "I thought he wanted to join us out here."

Jack Java explained, "Hunter found us before we broke camp. He seemed to have lots of ideas about the invention, although he had no clue about what it was or how we came to have it. His advice was 'Scofield has the financial power to mass-produce it. And distribute it. Sell it to Scofield.'" He then made the point, 'If we put it in the hands of the people, what will the people do with it?'

"He doesn't realize we've pegged Sharky and his cronies as the Evil Elite," Mariah said.

"We have to give it away. It's not ours to sell." Tristan's voice was tired. "It was given as a gift from the Indians, in the past or future, I can't tell anymore, but in order to save the planet. It has to get into the right hands. I've been struggling with the best way to do that."

Indians began to gather. A large group of Indian council soon surrounded them. They were all milling around with their dark faces turned toward Tristan. He had unveiled the gift, and now stood holding the small crystalline object in his hand. They all stared at him and the box. They were curious as they approached to see what it did.

"I think I can help you." Sunowa, who had been listening intently spoke up. "More information is needed for you to understand. Tonight at the feast, our Storyteller, Gabriel, will tell you our story. Tonight we can assemble with the stars around the Big Fire. This story will blow your minds open to new perception. I advise you all to be there." With that admonition, Sunowa' looked hard at each one of them.

* * *

After a quiet late lunch with her family, Mariah strolled through the impromptu camp. She spotted her sister.

"Max, it's good to see you all settled in with your beautiful daughters. Hi girls." Mariah waved as she joined Max.

"They have learned exponentially. Grown in a lot of ways. I'm stunned and proud,"Max said.

The two found a boulder by the river. "I'm sorry about Hunter. I just thought, you know, that he would join us."

"Me to. More for his sake than mine, though. You know we just got along because we were quite alike. Mentally, I thought. But ultimately, not really."

"I agree. You seemed to have so much in common."

Max shrugged. "You mean like a baby?" They both watched a deer drink from the stream. Then it turned its doe eyes to look at them. They both watched in stunned silence. Mariah turned to Max, not breathing, as though not to startle the doe. Paul sidled up and took Max's hand.

"It really is going to be OK," Max said, and exchanged a look with Mariah. "Paul and I led together, or rather took over your group on the Exodus."

"I've got that double hammock all set up as promised. If you are still interested," Paul said. He turned to Mariah. "Max and I had some tenacious debates during our long hours and days of hiking."

Mariah's eyes popped out of her head and back in. "Sure Max, you go on. We can catch up later."

"You sure?" With that look that said it all. 'I love you Sis, but this is a guy.'

Mariah started to say something—sorry about Hunter or... no. She wasn't going to put her foot in it. She stumbled backwards as she tried to mask her shock.

"Uhh...Nikki needed to show me something. I had almost forgotten." She turned to hide her embarrassment. Wow Paul and Max. Opposites attract I guess. Dark curly hair, just like Nikki's dad. Greek. Tall and handsome. Max's type totally. A bit older, but that's what she likes. She turned to sneak a peek without staring. The two were climbing swiftly towards a tree up a bit higher with a hammock balanced in the shady part. Perfect. What a perfect couple, she thought. And I thought I was such a matchmaker.

"So Nikki, what do you have there?" She called to her niece. Anya and Nikki were busy at their camp. They called her over with a friendly wave.

* * *

While they were dressing for the evening meal, Isabella found her mom was distracted. "Mom, can I talk to you a bit?"

"Sure hon. What's up?" Mariah asked.

"I think you had your heart set on Hunter joining us out here. I suspect you think he may still come."

"Yes, you're right. I thought he would decide to at the last minute."

"You know the Anointing Ceremony? How it changes us when we do it? It transforms us and rids us of our demons. In that process we learn to see better, more clearly. I can see like that. I mean I always could, more than most. I think I was scared of my abilities and didn't want to acknowledge them or use them. Tristan seemed to go on faster than anyone, so no one noticed he was tapped in. I'm used to being thoughtful and super-analytical—I often got stuck in my head. But now that I have been Anointed, I have the courage it takes to develop my abilities through use. I even see in hindsight with new depth.

"For me, the demons or worldly ties we had to abandon were a bit superficial, and they hadn't taken a firm hold. But Hunter is immersed in his demons." Isabella said.

"Whew, that's insightful. Yet, he helped us. He told me about the Oil men," Mariah said.

467

"You mean the Evil Elite. So you explained in detail. I also witnessed his talk with Tristan, where he suggested stealing his invention. Like he could. Bottom line is, he distracted you. He told you a lot of stuff you mostly already knew." Her brown eyes were kind. "It's tricky."

"You're right." Mariah said slowly. She hadn't quite pieced the events together yet.

"See? You trust too much. We were worried, if he had his way, you wouldn't make it back at all. I was so glad to see you! Back to Hunter, the demons are woven into him like threads in a tightly knotted weave, not like a thread one can pull and it just flies out. It's different for him. I mean it's like the good in him, lies down next to the evil worms in him. You didn't see him when he came to talk to Tristan that day. He was so close to betraying us and all we stood for. He didn't even know it was wrong. He has a completely dislodged moral compass. I don't know how to explain it.

"I just think you should be happy that *we* are here. If he tries and he can pass the Anointing Ceremony, well, that will be like a kind of miracle in itself. But if he can't..." She shrugged. "What I'm trying to say to you is, well you remember Thomas? He became crippled. Completely crippled, after his anointing. He can't even walk. He says he would rather have his soul intact than be able to walk. But still."

"I know he's so strong. He says his soul can soar. His body is tied to the earth but his mind and soul are free."

"That's why it's such a fully personal commitment," Isabella said. "You know, free choice?"

"I just can't believe it. I don't want to believe it. I mean about Hunter," Mariah said.

"I know. It's hard to think about."

"You are so right, my sweet girl, I will rejoice for all of us," Mariah laughed with happiness. She pulled her very grown up daughter into a hug. "Thank you," she said muffled into her hair.

CHAPTER 40 *Celebration*

"For centuries, we the Apache, have held in secret how to access the hidden mysteries of Earth." He looked around, but his eyes were half shut, slit with age.

Chief Nuage's older brother, Gabriel, thin of stature, frail and ancient, spoke. Mariah suspected he saw more with his eyes closed than they all did with their eyes open. As tribe storyteller, his role was to remember the stories, and retell them often—to the youths as they came of age, or to sharpen the memory of all the tribe. The hushed audience was in rapt attention.

"I'm speaking of the ancient mysteries of Earth, and her forgotten sciences that have been lost to other tribes, but not to the Apache. We remember still. We know our Mother. We know her secrets: her underground rivers, pure and clean; her hidden canyons, caves, and archways, that lead to the last sacred groves and meadows, tended like a prayer.

"There are a few places, like the hidden cave where Tristan studied, that must be entered through water. This limits its access. However, when you know the water tunnels, and are skilled in the art of transformation, you can travel to many hidden places around the world. Thus Tristan traveled with Daniel, and visited the Ancient One in the Hall of Records. He preserves all the scrolls. Here is a narrow archway access through a crystal cave behind this waterfall. One can walk in with food and belongings with ease.

"For centuries, we the Apache, kept this archway concealed, for through it one can enter our tribe's home; a secluded, sacred place filled with rolling hills, meadows, forests, and clean water. All is kept hidden by high, sheer cliffs. It's the *heart* of what Peter's ancestors call, The Ranch. This heart of the land is kept clean, by living crystals and the pure waters surrounding us.

"Our ancient stories speak of a time when our mother tribe, the Atlanteans, took refuge through the crystal cave in a time of great turmoil. Many thousands of years passed before our ancestors deemed it safe to return. A group of our people, now known as the Apache, came back through the hidden arch and found our Mother Earth healed and welcoming to our people. We spread out, and for several thousand years, our people roamed and flourished on the wide-open spaces.

"Our tribe grew large. We branched out into many tribes; all taking great care for Mother Earth and her bounty. When the Washichu came, they did not remember the ancient ways, nor did they know our Mother. They knew not the language of Mother Earth. They had forgotten the knowledge of the Sacred and Holy Tree of Life: the Purifier of Demons, Healer of Nations, and Barer of All Manner of Fruits. We desired to share our stories with them, but their spirits were young and unable to hear. The Great War waged, and the tribes grew small and were hunted to extinction. Many of the tribes lost the hidden access points to our ancestors. But we, the lost tribe of the Apache, held close these sacred ways. We held the Tree of Life in our hearts, preserved her wisdom, and her multitude of uses.

"The other tribes were lost to the darkness brought with the Washichu. Our tribe was hunted almost to extinction. Geronimo saved us. He led our people to this land. We once again entered the arch to our ancients' home, and we reunited with our Atlantean brothers. We, *The Forgotten Tribe*, disappeared from your world. We once again grew strong. But we did not wish to abandon the Earth again. We cared for the Mother's creatures here. It's essential that the land here remains pristine. The crystals must be left to grow; the water to run pure and clean, the animals to live unmolested, and the trees to breathe and grow tall.

"Over the last one hundred and thirty years, while our tribe once again grew powerful, we endeavored to speak with the young souls of the Washichu. Pathfinders came through to see that the land remained connected to the hidden, sacred groves and meadows. Long ago settlers came but they were unable to grow their water-hungry crops. Then Peter's great-grandfather came, with his great-grandmother, Helen. Helen loved to gallop her horse on the Texas wilderness territory and took the family on trips here.

"From her influence, through the generations, her son felt this land, and knew its soul. With the fortunes he amassed on the East Coast, he bought out the remaining settlers. He created a trust to protect The Ranch. When Peter's grandparents died, the trust fell to their only daughter, Peter's mother, Louise. She too, knew the land was sacred. She left the Ranch to her two daughters, and the controlling shares to Peter.

"Peter decided to live here. He accepted his role as steward, and labored to build natural water cisterns for the animals, preserve the caves and crystals, and protect the land. Peter thrived on the land. We made ourselves known to him. Through him, the tribe met Mariah.

"Long ago, when Mariah slept in the tepee, our elders perceived an ancient soul that remembered our ways. We had finally grasped a link to the young souls of the Washichu. As she grew and came back with David and their children, we realized that young Tristan and Isabella could assimilate and understand the ancient wisdom. Several years ago, Joseph met the little ones. He wanted to instill a desire to return to us."

The sun-weathered man grew in stature, his voice melodious in its warm tones of burnished amber. Mariah realized she could listen to this rhythmic, calming, almost hypnotic, speech, with its slight touch of accent, forever. It was a bit foreign in a way she couldn't place.

"Everything altered when Peter was murdered. This land was again at risk. We danced and prayed for the ones who would return. Then, in early spring, this sun cycle, Mariah brought all of you to us. Mariah could feel the call of our prayers and dancing. Thank the Great Spirit, she answered.

"We welcome you, David. We welcome you, Tristan. We welcome you, Wind Angel." Mariah nudged and squeezed David's hand at the use of her new name. Gabriel nodded to each in turn. "We welcome you, Isabella. We welcome you, Rob. We welcome you, Jack. We welcome you, Paul. We welcome you, Pat. We welcome you, Jody. We welcome you, Max." Each came forward and took the Chief's hands. He bent and lightly kissed each on the top of the head. One by one, he welcomed each new member into the tribe.

"Through this archway lives our tribe. Our homes are strong and comfortable. We live in peace and abundance with our Mother. From the Tree of Life, and her many manner of fruits, we grow everything we need, living rich, creative, lives. Many families have opened their homes to each of you and will teach you. While you study and build your own family dwellings, you will learn the ways of our crystal power. You are now *one* with our united tribe. As you join in dancing, singing, and creating, you will flourish and grow in your connection with the Mother.

"You have been tested. You have endured. You have been cleansed by the Sacred and Holy Anointing Oil. You have examined your souls, and found them light as a feather. Tonight we will feast and dance together, and at the break of dawn we will travel into a new way of life in accord with our Mother Earth."

Enraptured by Gabriel's discourse, few noticed, as the afternoon waned and turned into evening. Heavy cloud cover had blocked the sun all day, making everything somber. Now as it grew dark, Mariah assumed it was later than it was. The air grew chilly without the sun's warmth. Folks huddled close to one another for body heat and better hearing.

Gabriel had barely uttered the last sentence, when the clouds cracked open, and sun shot gold fingers into the crowds. All eyes looked toward the west. Amber light illuminated the crowd like a spotlight, etching the group, the meadow, and the rocks with a fiery orange glow like an aura. Rosy marshmallow clouds rolled like waves in a frothy sea, as the wind blew through the canyon and swirled in the valley. Clouds painted luscious pink, peach, coral, and amber had a fuchsia and gold edging. At the base of the tableau was the red-stained horizon, capping the scene with the indigo blue of the encroaching night sky. As Mariah watched the majestic scene unfold, she could almost hear a great, Angelic choir of voices.

Everyone shielded their eyes as they stared at the sky and into the sun. Blinded, they could not see this place to which Gabriel had so proudly referred. The timing was too perfect. It was as though orchestrated.

"For us," Mariah whispered, awestruck. From her view, standing near the front, listening to Gabriel's story, she was mesmerized.

Gabriel raised both of his arms to bestow blessing, his dark form now silhouetted by the sun. Gold glowing rays radiated behind him. Again she was reminded of the figure of Peter, as she had seen it in her dream so long ago, ascending into the clouds, arms outstretched. Like Christ, ascending into the heavens.

Tomorrow morning, she and David, along with the rest of the group, would offer their gift of the three best Tree of Life harvests to Chief Nuage. This was their gift, in pure thanksgiving, for being united forever with their Indian brothers.

CHAPTER 41 *Back to the Garden*

Sunday morning at dawn, they came, hands clasped, as they danced to their places in the circle. They came in two's and three's. already humming and chanting a joyful song as they moved into place with mats or scarves to sit upon. Once again they gathered in the new meadow, its grasses deep and gold. The wide semicircle held many rows of people. Was the mood predicated upon Gabriel's speech the night before? Pinon smoke still hung in the air. Probably few understood the precise meaning of what was happening. Or was it the dancing and drumming by the huge fire that had burned long into the night? All were smiling. Rob, Tristan, and David stood for a moment together on the jagged rock to begin the ceremony.

Rob laughed gently before he spoke. "Remember, the rules of Christ. Three guidelines you can say as a mantra: *Love God. Love one another. Say NO to false gods or demons.*"

Tristan held the precious oil up for all to see. "Our brothers have made this special oil for us with the flowers from the tree of life, olive oil, cinnamon, and very secret herbs. This will activate the three glands: the pituitary, the pineal, and the hypothalamus, at an even deeper level. Rejoice."

"Rejoice," David and Rob echoed.

Rob moved to sit among the crowd. Tristan and David followed suit. All began to meditate as the fiery orange sun rose splendid upon the horizon, with the jagged hewn rock a platform for its glory.

As before, they passed the bowl of oil and anointed one another. As each member of the crowd meditated, they focused on the line of connection between the three glands, the pineal, pituitary, and hypothalamus, activated by the oil. Together they formed a triangle of invisible force, like a force field that encases the heart. The heart chakra pulsates with love, while each person felt consumed and encased by this love.

In this way, they meditated, all sitting cross-legged on their mats in the grass. Someone began a chant that evolved into waves of sound. The energy vibration grew, from low in the gut, like a rumble from below. Some high notes of song lay atop in waves of light. They sat this way four hours or more, each in his own trance of sound and harmony. Although they had begun at dawn, it took time for all to be anointed. Thus they sat, with focused faces raised towards heaven. The sun brightened as it rose. By ten a.m. it was burning the oil into their foreheads and chests.

Mariah sat, lost in the group, her eyes now closed, watching the movie in her mind. All she could see was the face of Jesus the Christ. Her eyes were closed. Her mind was filled with this singular image. Christ from Saint Faustina's vision of the Divine Mercy; Jesus, with his long hair shimmering in the sunlight. His face too, facing gently tilted toward the sun. The triangulated fire of the activated chakras, contained his head and sacred heart. Mariah knew this was the Cosmic Christ, reborn, and present in their midst. She sat still and rapt, as all around her voices were raised in song. She sang too. The haunting melody of the Gregorian chant went in rounds, erupting in harmony. Then there was a slight pause, and a low Aum began again. She was dimly aware of the hawk circling above all of their heads. The bird chatter was a syncopated backdrop.

In this position, the fire burned into her chest and third eye. She knew that she must listen, pay rapt attention to hear a message, just a small insight—about The Way or The Work. The present, the Future? But His face remained clear before her, in her mind's eye. And then she perceived a smile as his lips turned up slightly. In the gleam of his eye she knew his humor. This is a way of worship she realized. Utter concentration on the triangle of The Christo's, outside under the blue sky in the meadow. And that is *All*.

Her inner voice was an impassioned cry—*Let this fill me as I sit entranced.* She was unable to move a muscle, as she was utterly immobilized and captivated by this one vision. She now felt a deep happiness bloom in her heart, like pure water bubbles up from deep within the earth. Her own smile matched His. And then all things, past and present, rushed back and forth, and in together at once. She listened as the others chanted. She connected to the divine, and she knew all, and that is all she need know.

Here in this meadow, not in a church, surrounded by all those she had come to know and love, Mariah sat in complete adoration of the living Risen Christ. She sat clothed in sunlight, covered in this burning oil. The sounds of the chiming, babbling, whispering water over stones became a background chant. The wind kissed her hair as the sun bathed her cheek. She knew, she was certain, "He *is* present among us."

Mariah opened her eyes and all at once began to search the crowd. She searched the faces looking for His face.

As she sat in this large semi-circle of people, she recalled the Dream of long ago, before any of this—before Peter died. She turned to Rob who was now beside her and said, "I just remembered my old dream, *I was at The Ranch in a circle of Indian elders, around a fire. It was a group of only seven or eight and me. And they said Peter had died. And I mourned. Then they pointed and I saw him, arms outstretched, ascending to the sky. With a beatific look, he rose into the clouds. Then they turned to me and explained, he's leaving, but we have a Gift to give you. We must prepare you for the Gift.*" Rob nodded, but didn't speak. Mariah's face was aglow with the memory. Her eyes still darted all around to find His face.

She had thought she had come to avenge Peter's death, and now she realized, she had come to find the truth of it. The meaning:

And Heaven is upon the Earth.

At long last,

We have found the Garden.

CHAPTER 42 *The Gift*

Tristan had the blueprints for the perpetual motion machine, that the Ancient One had termed, the Dynamo-eterna. The crystal scale model was a jewel in elegance and design. He studied the writings and the diagrams. First he had to believe that perpetual motion was possible, and second, figure out how to build the apparatus. It reminded him of when he was young and had built his first battery using wires and magnets. It had been rudimentary, but had still felt like magic once it was working.

In the solitude of his small dwelling, Tristan meticulously stacked the pile of blue prints. He aligned the thick parchment edges and rolled them together. He tied the gut string securely, knowing what he held in his possession was ancient. He had studied the diagrams and writings, taking notes as he did so. He needed to contemplate what he'd read, to best understand how to create the first prototype.

Outside the air had turned icy. The dew floated in the air and caught the sunlight. Crystalline air, he breathed it in. He watched the first freezes of the growing cold weather. The ice crystals on the top of puddles sat in bowl-forms in the rocks. The gold fall leaves trapped below the ice, glinted up. Water bubbles were trapped below the thin shell of ice. In his heightened state of awareness, he studied winter moving in around them. He had been entrusted with this gift. He knew he had the solution within, and around him, yet he would have to be the one to move all the elements in place to make it work. It was now all up to him. He must have complete comprehension. All at once he remembered his Mom saying she got glimpses. She would then take action, allowing herself to be led, or invited—almost seduced—

into the next step. Once she was fully engaged, things always tumbled into place. She was never in charge. She let herself be led, as her heart's desire was always true. She cultivated an open attitude. Always willing to try. The gears in his brain began clicking into place. Air -fire -water –earth; air, fire, water, earth. He repeated them like a mantra. It was simple. The solution must be simple. He was sure of that. It would be as simple as the cosmos and how it worked. Awareness dawned in his consciousness as slow and steady as the sunrise.

As he meditated on the cliff top, he faced the vast expanse of the now desert ocean. He watched waves of atmosphere reflect the glowing red of the dawn as it spread its vermillion hue across the sky. In solitude he would find his answer. The principles were simple. Macrocosm is like the microcosm. *As above so below.* The planets were held in motion by a gravitational pull from the sun-center of their solar system. People and the moon were held on the earth by the gravitational pull from the Earth Mother's central core.

He abruptly realized that the mineral makeup of the earth's core, was actually significant to the strength of the magnetic pull upon all the bodies on earth. If earth were a hollow ball, it would lack the magnetic strength to maintain its position in the solar system. The magnetic energy of negative and positive poles on either end of the earth resulted in rotation. The earth was spinning in space in the comforting endless rotational orbit around the sun. God, the Great Creator God of the universe, had designed it, and made it perfect. Then He had set it all in motion. How much power; energy-force; spark—did that take to set it all in motion?

Everything is always moving in nature. We are not responsible for making it move. In or out, up or down. We're not in charge, it's always in motion. Like rivers running to the sea, or apples falling from the tree. Or even answers blowing in the wind. People with magnetic personalities hold others in their orbit. Perhaps our very heart within our bodies exerts a magnetic pull on all the molecules that compose our bodies and pull us into Form. Perhaps death is the evaporation of the soul, and all is inert once it ceases motion.

This principle is at work all the time in our universe. Laws of attraction, laws of magnetism. Simple principles create order in the whole universe. Wait a minute, he thought. If we can understand where order lies, then we can understand chaos as well. But first!

He must build this, and set Dynamo-eterna, a new organizing principle upon the planet.

He visited Joseph in his dwelling. The heat and cooling system in his house worked this way. Sun heated air would rise naturally, creating a vacuum that would be filed with the cooler air from the earth. In the summer, the hot air would be allowed to escape creating a continuous pull up through the rooms of cool air. In the winter the hot air would be blown down the walls creating a continuous flow of moving warmer air. The fifty-five-degree earth air was much easier to heat with the sun to a comfortable temperature than the outside thirty degree air would be. The rise and fall of the air happened naturally. This is how the pyramids in Egypt were kept acclimatized. The climate system was built into the stone design of the chambers and passageways. The interior of the Great Pyramid at Giza was continuously cooled from the hot desert sun, and fresh air was let in through air lock systems.

Joseph's dwelling also had air locks to prevent outside air from dropping the internal temperature. Tristan imagined the negative and positively charged particles would work in tandem, similarly to the hot and cold air. Tristan knew, in order to build the Dynamo-eterna, he must focus on these principles until he fully understood the diagrams before him.

He knew he must arrange all the elements for the Dynamo-eterna in a vacuum. This would be similar to outer space where planetary bodies exert magnetic pull within a vacuum. That way there would be no particles to exert friction on the device. Once he could enact the positive and negatively charged particles within the vacuum chamber, the chamber would also need room to turn. He spent time trying to diagram how this would work.

He could see the outer glass cylinder could be filled with water, and the inner chamber within would be a vacuum. That was easy. If he dyed the water blue, it would be easier to see the cylindrical glass vacuum within it. The metal pronged central spine needed to rotate, and this would generate the power necessary to run things. He imagined the central spine could be a hollow metal pipe with sleeves containing the metal prongs fitted around it. This way, they would turn and spin around the pipe; much like the human spine, running through the central nervous system in the body. The spiny core should be hollow, he realized, just like the human core is hollow, allowing energy to run straight through. When all the chakras are spinning correctly, the energy is not impeded. The energy runs through the hollow core, and out the feet, around the body, and back through the head and the crown chakra. The human body is an energy machine, he realized. In the Dynamo-eterna apparatus, negative pressure was needed in the hollow core. Therefore, the negative pressurized core would be within the positive vacuum. Ideally, this enclosure should be composed of a thick glass. This could be suspended in the stainless steel cylinder filled with blue water. They could use old diving tanks for the mock-up. If they had a clear glass plate at the top, they could assemble the parts prior to submerging them in water. This would also provide a window to observe the motion. The blue water allowed the clear vacuum to be discerned. The heat from the sun was magnified on the metal pole by the layers of thick glass lenses and a mirror to bounce the magnified light into the tank. This solar heat thus magnified, might create enough heat to ignite the rotation.

As he studied the diagrams he could see the possibilities in his mind's eye. Tristan was convinced, that if he could construct a crude example with the materials at hand, it would be enough to prove it worked—beyond theory, and into manifestation. Next to the diagram, there was an image of a person seated in a yoga position with his hand up, palm showing. It was much like those from India.

They all worked together to build the perpetual motion machine with materials at hand. Once it was complete, they had to set it in motion. To create enough spark to ignite the internal metal core, they used other powerful lenses outside the Dynamo. Once started, the tube began somersaulting, top over bottom, the entire length of the tank. As it somersaulted its way to the top, it would reverse directions and keep on spinning. He was awed by the force of the spin. His heart thudded in his chest, as he realized it was not only spinning, it was not slowing down.

He would make adjustments, of course. He realized the shape had to be altered. He wasn't prepared for the speed of the dynamic movement. The metal prongs were spinning in the spiral pattern of the DNA molecule. He didn't know why it reversed, it just did. As the team watched and studied the motion, Tristan realized that was what the water was for. The motion was creating waves in the tube that eventually had enough momentum to flip the whole tube. The glass window allowed them to observe the action. It was like capturing waves in a bottle.

It was the world in reverse; space within air, within water. All this needed to be held in balance in some bed of something. The chemical translation of this was O2 in H2O in what? What was needed now? It was beautiful to watch. He looked at the crude materials they had used to construct this first prototype. The group of members working on the experiment took turns watching it around the clock. They wanted to document how long it would stay running from the initial push into action. Friction would cause it to stop eventually. The base must be something without friction. Oil. It dawned on him, oil.

Oil had the same viscosity as human blood. Perhaps oil is the earth's blood? Not a good idea to remove it from the core. The oil worked well. It wasn't being burned so it would last a long while. They used the olive oil they had on hand in their first experiments. Over time, the movement would slow due to friction and evaporation.

Tristan thought about Hunter's offer. Hunter had offered friends with money—funding, factories, mass production—all for a good cause. He was tempted, not by the thought of the money and wealth the invention would bring, but just to see it built with state of the art materials in a pristine factory. He could envision the elegant manufactured steel sphere with the spinning molecules of power inside.

He had proved it worked. It was working. They would be able to generate power. That was a certainty. He would have to find someone he could trust. Really trust, to build this.

The Dynamo-eterna was like a wave enclosed within a sphere. The magnetic pull of the tide ebbed and flowed as the metal tube spun within the glass vacuum. Tristan contemplated the simplicity of it—

space, in air, in water. It was an inverse microcosm of energy. An energy machine that could propel vehicles, and run generators. This could truly be used to change the balance of power on the world stage, if not the whole planet.

CHAPTER 43 *Alone*

Hunter's legs burned as he climbed the hills. It had been years since he'd had a good long ride. These roads were barren and glared with heat from the noon sun. He felt exhilarated as he thought of The Ranch ahead of him. As he burned the miles, each one brought him closer to his destination, as the unused muscles sprang into action.

Mariah and her family would welcome him back. They were good people, easy to forgive past transgressions, he was sure. Almost. His mind continued to replay the disaster the past year had been. The chaos and turmoil still wrapped around the country like a mean snake, shooting poisonous venom out in spurts, shattering everyone's hopes and dreams.

It had begun with the blackouts. Mariah had been at his house for the first one. Then the blackouts had become more frequent. They became commonplace in cities all over the US., as people couldn't pay the enormous power bills. People on autopilot plugged along thinking each blackout would pass, and they could go to work as usual. Then there would be another blackout, until it seemed it was dark more often than light. People had exited office towers through ten-story stairways. The fixed window systems made the buildings become like sealed tombs, with no fresh air.

And then the shortages. Stores emptied out and no new supplies arrived. He tried to think about all that had gone wrong. First it was the weather. Unprecedented snowstorms, icy winter zero degree-days, even snow in Texas. He had felt sorry for Mariah and David then, poor guys toughing it out with scarce shelter, he'd assumed. But it hadn't let up. It went from icy arctic blasts, to a spring filled with torrential down-pours and monsoon like rains. A series of earthquakes killed the pipeline that was trying to bring oil from the Ship channel to Canada. Everyone was glad that happened before it was complete. That disaster would have been monumental had the pipeline been full of oil, thus contaminating the aquifer.

Rainfall soon buried massive Texas oil refineries under water. Office towers and residential towers now sat vacant without electricity. Buildings became tombs. The victims sealed alive. People in cities could no longer survive. Everyone strove to get out and get to the country. Tent cities sprang up.

By the time folks figured it out, they were on freeways trying to exit the cities they had become trapped in. People just walked out of the cities once the mass transit systems shut down. Cars on freeways ran out of gas. Stations were out of gas and there was no way trucks could get through to refuel. Gas stations were dry and abandoned. Abandoned cars littered the roads.

All his clients owed him big time but they were all bankrupt. They were aging diplomats. Politicians sick and disfigured with diseases beyond any normal aging he had seen before.

The TVs crashed, leaving only radio communication. The statement, *'The country is in a state of emergency,'* became cliché. He had a trip to Washington a few weeks before he had given up. The rapid aging apparent on the faces of the power brokers was astounding. Skin white as parchment, crinkled like prunes and brittle. Ghosts had been running the country he realized. These men, these Trilateral and Bilderberg Group guys were old. A fragile spectral of men. They had been pulling strings like OZ behind a curtain, until there was nothing attached to the strings any more. Bankruptcy was rampant, especially among the elite who tried frantically to work the system.

The floods stopped and created massive growth. Plants grew in a frenzy. The nuclear reactor in Tennessee was covered in kudzu. Texas refineries and factories were strangled in vines, briers, and bamboo. Freeways in Georgia had become like strange giant topiaries. Plants were marching on the city. Plants pushed up through concrete. Four-story brick box-buildings once eyesores were now unrecognizable. Birds were bigger for some reason, Hunter thought as he watched crows and ravens picking their way through debris and trash left abandoned.

The food shortages had begun when Taglot industries had tried to put all there mega-farming operations into biodiesel corn production. This was to be the new oil. First that meant food shortages. This made food prices escalate. Then the cornfields crashed in the extreme weather conditions that seemed like an attack on the world.

He thanked God he had somewhere to go. That desperation and need for help was an unaccustomed feeling as well. Of all those scrambling around like a stepped on ant pile back in the city, he alone knew where to go. He didn't tell anyone. He just got in his Toyota with great gas mileage and drove out of town as far as he could get. He had his bike strapped to the back and his backpack stuffed with his old camping gear. When he was one hundred miles out, he ran out of gas and used the bike.

His heart soared in anticipation as he flew downhill before the next hard pedal back up again. His mind played the disasters over and over again like a record on repeat. His thoughts spinning. These desolate miles were a relief compared to the chaos he'd left behind.

The crash had come in waves. Still some people trudged on. One pull of the thread and all was unraveling so fast it was head spinning. The media had tried to spin the truth until they were all tangled in an uncompromising web. Everything everyone had predicted was happening now. He had to get to The Ranch and find Mariah and Max. Mariah had spotted disaster lurking just beneath the surface when she had visited him in San Antonio. It had been so clear to her. She was desperate to get away from him that last week. She and Tristan had seen it coming. They had rejected it on moral grounds, because all was false and motivated only by the dollar.

He knew where to go. He'd seen enough. He'd gotten out of town. Now he looked forward to the good food and friendly faces that would greet him. As he neared the place he passed through Lakeville. It stood like a ghost town, one door to the real-estate office swinging on its hinges in the breeze. He speculated the folks seeking shelter may find these old towns and fill them up again.

Hunter congratulated himself. Somehow he had managed to get back to The Ranch despite the complete breakdown of the fragile system everything was built upon. It had been a year of disasters. He had his head buried in work, billing at a furious rate. He had logged a mad amount of hours. Then it had all crumbled. Humpty Dumpty had a great fall. History was repeating itself. These high-powered types had gone bankrupt. They couldn't pay him. He pulled his head out of the sand and looked up. It was already too late. It had suddenly clicked.

Too late though. He was too late.

EPILOGUE *Alone*

It was deadly quiet now, as if the water had stopped flowing and the wind stopped whispering. Hunter sat on Big Rock, alone in deafening silence. Last time he had meant to be alone, he had run into a whole world of people. Now his ears strained to hear voices, or laughter. It seemed like he did, just below the whish of water over rock. He picked up a rock, he weighed it as he closed his hand around it and felt warmth from the stone. When he finally tossed it into the water below, the splash sounded hollow in the stillness. He wished for the friends he had found last time. Just a few years ago he had found a tribe of people here. He had come to be alone with his grief and instead his sorrow had turned into a strange joy—feasting; family; friends—just as it had been in the old days. Peter had inspired such gatherings. Everyone had come and carried on in his absence. It had been as though he were still here. That is how it had seemed to him.

Now everyone was gone. The trees still arched beside the water. The new spring buds on the trees shone in the sunlight. He knew Mariah, David, Max, and the others would have to leave, sooner or later. Someone would happen upon them, as he had. Or the cold of winter would have driven them from their sunny tents and casual outdoor sleeping arrangements. Not very practical. It had looked like such fun. Feasting in community, and enjoying one another. He missed them. He stared at the fresh tendrils of spring grasses, lime green by the banks of the smooth water. It was still as clear as drinking water. He was confused. Mariah had kept talking about disappearing. And she spoke of the interior. Had she invited him? Had she been trying to tell him something?

He'd found the stone ranch house empty and forgotten. He broke in and found some canned food. He had no appetite. He'd wait until he was desperate.

The only trace that he had even known them, had been the occasional postcard from Roxi. Seems she had been working her way around the country, traveling, and waitressing in turns. Yet Mariah and Max. Where had they gone?

He'd hiked to Indian Point many times. But nothing. It was all receding in his memory as if he'd imagined it. The dust swirled around in a mini tornado, as though mocking him. He was beginning to doubt his sanity. This place was even worse now. He realized this was what he had avoided by never coming back. In his 'real Life' he thought he was about to amass a real fortune with all the cases he had been handling—money worth nothing now. He was utterly alone.

The thrill of the hunt had gone out of him. He sat, glued to his spot as the sun turned blood orange and began slipping down at the edge of the canyon hill.

In the semi-darkness he made his way back to the bike he had dropped by the stone house in his eagerness to find everyone. He pulled his sleeping bag out of his pack, still perched by his bike.

He unrolled it, and lay upon his back. He stared up at the sky. As he lay listening to the night noise he felt the chill stillness surround him. Why hadn't he joined them? Why had he insisted on staying in the city? Yet he knew why. The noise and the busy-ness had kept him from thinking about anything clearly—buffered and isolated from the truth.

Where had they gone? How could they really have returned to their own lives after all the progress they'd made? There was a niggling in his brain. Mariah had kept hinting at things she thought he had been privy to because he had been so close to Peter. Peter had spoken to him. Peter had been paranoid about some suspicious behavior. Before. Before. Yes that was before Peter had died. It might even have been their last conversation. He had seemed like he was losing it a little. Talking weird, as though a bit delusional. About something odd. Ah, Native Americans. That was it.

This was now a mystery greater than all the complicated cases he had ever tried to solve. The sound of the wind in the trees, and the screech of an owl, just mocked him. He felt drawn here, pulled here through the long ride that took days. Now that he was here, he couldn't pull himself away. He unpacked his mini-camp stove and brewed some coffee.

He didn't want them to be gone. All through the past years he had imagined them still out here. He held hope in his heart through the long ride. And then the silence. The damned silence when he finally arrived.

He had that last memory of Tristan's hand upon his shoulder. Huh. Some invention or other. Free energy? Really?

At the time he had an important client, one he had inherited from his dad. He had to keep him happy. He'd been given a direction. Watch those French girls. Detain Mariah. Scott Scofield was sure he would be elected to the State Senate. In the end...what a disaster. Hunter shuddered involuntarily, as he told himself he hadn't done anything terrible. He'd just been aloof and noncommittal to Mariah, been the skeptic he was. It's a good thing that invention wasn't real. It had almost been like taking candy from a baby. Huh.

But if Peter was murdered, as Mariah suspected, and it wasn't just a random thrill kill...he shuddered. He couldn't go there. No way. He pinched himself and poured more coffee. He sat down on the yoga mat he carried with him. It had been Mariah's, he realized. She had forgotten it at his house. He wasn't hungry. He'd go ahead and stay outside tonight.

How could that many people just disappear?

Where had they gone?

As Hunter lay on his sleeping bag contemplating the sky, he felt the night welcome him home. All the disasters nature had raged on the planet were forgotten as he watched the comforting blanket of the star-filled sky. He could go in the house, he knew, but the thought seemed strange now. He felt closer to Mariah and her clan if he lived as they did.

TRISTAN *Dynamo-eterna*

Tristan had the machine. He was testing the mock-ups but he knew it couldn't be released until the time was right. He would be given a sign. Until then they didn't need it. They knew how to live by the old ways. Up with the sun; star watching at night beside a comforting fire, and telling stories, just as they had always done. They were beyond content, they were happy. As the years passed their numbers would surely grow as the Indian tribes had. They had steadily, generation by generation quadrupled their numbers with each new babe in arms learning the way. In time perhaps his children would be the ones to venture out and heal the earth. For now, his job was to perfect this machine.

After much discussion, the brothers decided to send an early prototype of the Dynamo-eterna to India on a trial run. Tristan suspected the guru's would have the key to operating the device hidden in their sacred texts. Theirs was a culture that would understand how it worked.

The Dynamo-eterna was powered not by the suns energy, or oil or fire. It was powered by *human energy*. The sacred powers all humans had been born with, had been lying dormant within each soul on earth all along. When a person sat in meditation with all his chakras open and aligned in a perfectly aligned spine, the spinning would create energy. This posture had to be held for twenty minutes. Then with another loved one, the two joining hands would produce the spark.

"Where two or more are gathered in my name I am present," Jesus had said.

The spark ignited the Torus–Dynamo-eterna. These instructions had been described in Sanskrit. They had been encrypted in the form of poetry in many of the sacred texts throughout history. The ancient texts had truly predicted the future. There was no record of the physical existence of such a machine. Yet it had been mentioned in the Rig Vedas—the name literally meaning *'Praise Knowledge'*— over six thousand years ago. Similar descriptions were recalled in the Upanishads from 400 BC. and again in works by the guru Isha in 300 BC. Ancient Hindu texts held secrets that had been kept safe for centuries. In 48 BC the destruction of the Ancient Library of Alexandria had resulted in huge losses in terms of much Egyptian and ancient wisdom. Still today, no one has been able to duplicate the secrets contained in these precious texts and scrolls.

Once they received the Dynamo-eterna, a whole cardboard city in Bombay got up and began to march into the countryside near the river. Soon, working together they were able to create a new village with lights and cooking stoves. It seemed, when they hooked the small electric generators together they had plenty of power. This was the only place on the planet with power. Free Power. That was the key. It was *free* power.

In fact, in order to use the machine, a person had to be pure of heart. Those who were not, had immediate adverse effects—nausea, heart palpitations, and emotional outbursts that betrayed their dark intentions.

The Indians, Mariah, David, Tristan, Isabella, and all the others, knew this field of energy for what it was. A physical, perceivable, electromagnetic field, created by the motion of the gift that produced usable electrical energy, while creating an invisible force field of sanity. It was truly an amazing gift. Perhaps—no, definitely, miraculous.

As the newly powered village near Bombay soon found out, they had electricity for running water, lights, irrigation, refrigeration, and the like. As people discovered this, they not only came to help rebuild a new society, but to escape the madness of the evildoers that were no longer capable of dwelling amongst them in secret.

As long as this remained in the right hands, growth and rebuilding may begin from the bottom up. Only those with the Dynamo-eterna had enough power to run the Internet. The group in Texas could communicate with India, half a world away.

The Light, and Purifying Power of God, had descended upon mankind once again.
12.22.2026

The rain falls, on Mothers and Daughters, Fathers and Sons— God and Man. The rain is unifying. A cleansing water that washes all equally. With smiles and hugs, and the rain falling, all are laughing.

The colors are blurred by the rain as it washes each child of God. Big white-teeth smiles are visible as faces shine with a happy glow, and the sun-bright rain sparkles like diamonds. The man made construct of fear has fled. The playing field is leveled, and all are human upon the earth, with water, and rivers, and dirt. All things can heal when the energy is reversed. The cleansing cycles are still there.

The meek shall reclaim the earth.
The humble shall heal the earth
The gentle shall be healed by the earth.
The double rainbow comes again.

The End